HETTIE OF HOPE STREET

Annie Groves lives in the North West and has done so all of her life. Like her first two sagas, *Ellie Pride* and *Connie's Courage, Hettie of Hope Street* takes place in the tumultuous years leading up to, during, and after the First World War. Annie has drawn upon her own family's history, picked up from listening to her grandmother's stories when she was a child, for inspiration.

Also by Annie Groves:

Ellie Pride
Connie's Courage

ANNIE GROVES

Hettie of Hope Street

HarperCollins*Publishers*

HarperCollins*Publishers*
77–85 Fulham Palace Road,
Hammersmith, London W6 8JB

www.harpercollins.co.uk

Published by HarperCollins*Publishers* 2005
1

A catalogue record for this book
is available from the British Library

ISBN 978 0 00 780515 0

Set in Sabon by
Palimpsest Book Production Limited,
Polmont, Stirlingshire

Printed and bound in Great Britain by
Clays Ltd, St Ives plc

Acknowledgements

I would like to thank the following for their invaluable help:

Lynne Drew, who has supported and encouraged me so marvellously.

Maxine Hitchcock, my truly wonderful editor who has the patience of a hundred saints, and who has held my hand through the births of Ellie, Connie and now Hettie.

Samantha Bell for her skilled copy-editing.

Everyone at HarperCollins who has made it possible for Hettie to reach publication safely.

Tony, who does so much of my research for me.

My writing friends, whose support and kindness means so very much to me.

But most of all my thanks to my readers. Author, editor, publishers, researchers – we are all part of a team that creates a book, but you, the reader, via your enjoyment of it are the one who breathes life into it.

To my father who we all loved and miss so much.

Thank you for being you, Dad.

PART ONE

ONE

'Mam, Mam, just wait until you see this.' Excitement sparkled in Hettie's dark eyes as she thrust the open page of the *Liverpool Post* underneath her mother's nose. 'They're advertising for a "young lady" to sing to people during afternoon tea at the Adelphi hotel in Liverpool. It says you have to write to this address here. Oh, Mam, I'm so excited. It would be the perfect job for me. Just imagine – I could sing every day and get paid for it!'

Ellie Walker looked at the advertisement her step-daughter had shoved in front of her, her face clouding slightly. 'Oh Hettie, love.' Ellie said uncertainly. 'I don't think . . .'

Immediately Hettie's excitement gave way to anxiety. 'But Mam, you know how much I love to sing and everyone said how good I was when I sang in *The Mikado*. Miss Brown said I had the best voice of any girl she had ever taught.'

Ellie sighed. 'Yes, Hettie I know that, but singing

in a small private theatre to help raise money for charity is a very different thing to singing in public and,' she hesitated, 'and for money.'

Ellie hated to see the excitement dying in Hettie's eyes and being replaced by mutinous disappointment. But Ellie was very protective of all her children and even though Hettie was eighteen, she was still a child in so many ways. In so many ways, but not in all. Ellie glanced discreetly at her step-daughter's body. Although slim and delicately boned, Hettie nevertheless had a very well-developed bosom. And then, of course, there was her unusual, sultry beauty – that mingling of the delicate bone structure Hettie had inherited from her Japanese mother together with some features from the Englishman who had been her father and Ellie's first husband.

Ellie had waited until she had felt Hettie was old enough to understand properly before explaining to her step-daughter the troubled circumstances surrounding her own birth and her parents' deaths.

Hettie had never known her father, having been born after he had left Japan to return to Liverpool. Her Japanese mother, as Ellie had explained to her, had pined so much for the English lover who had sworn undying love to her, and promised he would return to her, that she had set sail for Liverpool with her baby to find him. To arrive there and discover that her beloved Henry-san had taken his own life had broken her heart, Ellie had told Hettie gently, adding that two such sensitive people as her parents had suffered dreadfully because of the separation imposed on them.

'But my father was married to you,' Hettie had pointed out unhappily.

'Indeed, Hettie,' Ellie had concurred. 'Unfortunately, as sometimes happens within families, both your father and I were pushed into marriage with one another even though our hearts lay with other people. Naturally, as Henry's widow, I felt responsible for your mother and for you . . .'

'You were kind to us,' Hettie had interrupted her, remembering the comforting warmth of Ellie's voice and arms.

'Your poor mother had no wish to live with your father gone. She went out one cold winter night and accidentally fell into the dock and drowned there, poor lady.'

'And then you married Gideon and he adopted me and I had a new mother and father,' Hettie had stated matter of factly.

'Indeed you did,' Ellie had agreed tenderly. 'And you must never forget how much we love you, Hettie.'

And Ellie did love Hettie, even though she sometimes feared for her a little, as all mothers must for a pretty, sometimes wilful daughter. With those flashing, faintly almond-shaped eyes, the rosebud fullness of her mouth, the thick poker-straightness of her long black hair in striking contrast to her pale, almost sweetly doll-like round face, it was no wonder the people of Preston turned their heads to look at her beloved Hettie.

Stubbornness now flashed in Hettie's eyes, causing Ellie's maternal heart to suffer fresh misgivings. She could well remember the turbulence of the early years of her own young womanhood, and the pain they could bring. The love of her own life at Ellie's age had been her beloved Gideon, now her husband, but at that time he was the young man her mother had forbidden her to see.

'But I want to do it so much. I have to do it. I *need* to sing.' Tears glistened in Hettie's eyes. 'It's all I want to do,' she continued passionately to Ellie. 'It's all I've ever wanted to do, you know that.'

Ellie sighed. Hettie was such a fiercely intense girl, her emotions like quicksilver, changing from laughter one minute to tears the next. Ellie couldn't help but worry for her. She seemed to feel things so much more than other people, especially when it came to music, and her singing. Ellie had seen her reduced to anguished tears when listening to a particularly sad song and then the next minute dancing around happily when she heard a more gay one.

'Hettie, I do understand.'

'How can you say that? You don't understand.' Red spots of emotion burned in her pale face. Even when Hettie was angry she still looked so very pretty, Ellie acknowledged; coupled with her beautiful voice, it was little surprise that those who had bought tickets for the little show put on by Miss Brown, Preston's foremost music and singing teacher, had given her a standing ovation.

'To you singing is just . . . just a . . . a pretty accomplishment, something to pass a few pleasant hours,' she told Ellie almost scornfully. 'But to me it is so much more than that. To me it is everything, and if I cannot sing as I want to sing then I think a part of me will die!' she finished dramatically before rushing out of the room.

Why couldn't Ellie understand how she felt? Hettie wondered miserably half an hour later as she stood in front of her bedroom window, the view of Preston's fashionable Winckley Square, which lay beyond it, blurred by the tears filling her eyes.

She loved her step-mother, of course she did. Ellie and Gideon were in reality the only parents and the only family she had ever known. And Ellie loved *her*, she knew that too, even if certain members of Ellie's family – like Ellie's starchy aunt, Amelia Barclay, who lived almost opposite them on the other side of the square – had made it plain that they did not approve of Ellie having brought up Hettie, the illegitimate child of her first husband's Japanese mistress, as her own daughter.

Hettie could actually remember overhearing Amelia say to Ellie that Hettie's birth was a scandal that could give the whole family a bad name. But Ellie had replied firmly and calmly that her aunt was mistaken and that, in Hettie's mother's land, it was perfectly respectable for a man to take a 'pillow friend' and for this lady to be treated with respect and included within the family, along with her children, and that only the ignorant and narrow minded would not be aware of this.

It had seemed to Hettie that, after this exchange, Amelia Barclay had ceased to make references to Hettie's parentage and background.

But even though Ellie had treated her just as she did her own children, Hettie knew she was different to them. And not just because she *looked* different.

Music and singing were important to her in a way that was not shared by the rest of her adopted family. Not even Ellie's younger sister, Connie, who was so much fun and who loved nothing better than a music hall show.

Hettie loved being asked to stand up and sing for people. It gave her such a wonderful rush of exhilaration and happiness and for as long as she could remember it had been her dream to become a singer. She could recall how much she had loved it as a young girl when Ellie's younger brother, John, had called to see them, and Ellie had urged him to accompany her on the piano whilst she sang. There had been a special rapport between her and John in those days, but he no longer visited them as frequently, mainly because he was busy with the flying school he and two friends had set up. John, she knew, felt as passionately about his flying machines as she did about her singing.

John had been her best and most special friend for what seemed like for ever. She had always felt she could talk to him about anything and everything, and had spent many happy hours as a child strolling with John along Preston's fine walks and the banks of the River Ribble whilst he photographed the countryside and taught her to appreciate its beauty. John had teased her and protected her. And she in turn had given him her heart and her trust.

'What do you think, Gideon?' Ellie asked her husband later that evening when they were alone in the comfort of their bedroom. They had been married for fourteen years now and, thanks to his inheritance from his mother, and his own hard work, Gideon had risen from being a mere drover – living virtually hand to mouth and nowhere near good enough to marry Ellie, the daughter of the butcher whose brother he had once worked for – to being a person respected and admired within the town. Ellie knew how much this meant to him, especially after his struggles; and she too, if she was honest, welcomed the manner in which she and her family were treated, especially when she remembered the hardship and poverty of the years following her own mother's death when she and her siblings were separated and life seemed something to be endured not enjoyed.

'No respectable family would allow their

daughter to go on the stage,' she continued without waiting for him to answer her, 'and I can just imagine what my Aunt Amelia would have to say about it.'

'Aye, she'd blame what she chooses to call Hettie's "bad blood", no doubt,' Gideon agreed.

Ellie shook her head. 'Hettie is so spirited, Gideon, and so very, very pretty. She looks so . . .'

'Beautiful?' Gideon supplied.

'Vulnerable, I was going to say,' Ellie told him. Silently they looked at one another.

'I worry for her, Gideon. She is reaching that age where a young girl's thoughts and feelings can so easily lead her astray. Perhaps if her own mother had lived . . .' Ellie sighed, remembering the tragic circumstances surrounding the death of Hettie's real mother. 'I love Hettie so much but sometimes I fear she may feel that she is less loved than our own two boys, even though, if anything, I tend to favour her above our Richard and David.'

'Ellie, my dearest love.' Gideon took hold of his wife's hands and looked at her tenderly. 'I know you are only concerned for Hettie, and you want to protect her. But you and I know that, much as we love Hettie, we must be careful that in protecting we are not trying to re-create her as we wish her to be rather than as she actually is. Hettie is very gifted, we both know that, and her singing teacher has told us herself how very special Hettie's voice is – that, after all, is why we agreed that she could have these extra lessons with her.

Who knows what trouble we might cause by not allowing her to use that gift?'

'What are you trying to say to me, Gideon?'

'I think that first of all we should check with Miss Brown to see what she thinks, and then, if and only if she thinks it right, we should allow Hettie to apply for this position she has seen advertised – the Adelphi hotel is, after all, a highly respectable establishment. Hettie would only be singing during the afternoon and, I dare say, in front of a mainly female audience, for I cannot imagine that many men, never mind the unsavoury sort you fear her being exposed to, would be taking tea at the Adelphi hotel in the middle of the afternoon. Apart from anything else, such types would not be allowed in.'

Gideon watched as Ellie struggled to accept what he had said. He hated the thought of anything upsetting or hurting her – especially now – and he knew how much she loved and worried about Hettie. 'Ellie, neither of us would want to see Hettie take the same path as Connie,' he added quietly.

'No,' Ellie agreed, 'although Connie is very happy and settled now with Harry and their children.'

'Yes indeed. But both she and you had to suffer a great deal of pain before she found that happiness. Remember how she got herself involved with some awful types and we didn't hear hide nor hair from her for years when she took off like that?

Hettie, like Connie, possesses a certain stubbornness and a very strong will.'

'She can be the sweetest girl, though, Gideon.'

'You need not defend her to me,' he assured her. 'I love her as much as you do, and it is because I love her that I am saying these things to you, Ellie. She is very young. Who knows, she may very well find that she does not like singing and the stage as much as she now believes she does. And if that is the case, I know we would both want her to know that she will always have a home here with us.'

'Yes, you are right. I suppose I am being selfish in wanting to keep her here by me. They are all growing up so quickly, though, Gideon. Richard is already talking about wanting to learn to fly, even though he is still at school, and . . .' She placed a protective hand over her stomach.

'Have you told Iris yet?' he asked her, concerned.

Iris, in addition to being one of Ellie's closest friends, was also a qualified doctor.

Ellie shook her head. 'It is too soon, and after all it is not as though I have not had a child before,' she reminded him with a small smile.

In the early days of their marriage they had both hoped there would be the proverbial quiverful of children, but there had only been the two, so to discover now that she had conceived again so many years later had been rather a shock.

'Gideon, please don't look like that. I want you

to be happy about this new baby we are to have,' she told him when she saw the anxiety he couldn't hide. 'I know why you are worrying.'

'I am worrying because I think you worry too much about everyone else.' Gideon stopped her with false heartiness, but both of them knew the real reason behind his anxiety.

Ellie had been just sixteen when her own mother had died in childbed, having been warned not to have any more children. Gideon knew how dreadfully the little family she had left behind her had suffered. But he was not Ellie's father, and she was not her own mother. Ellie had not been warned, as her mother had, that she must not conceive more children because of the risk to her health. But the length of time since the birth of their last child had, Gideon admitted, brought home to him how relieved he had been to think there would not be any more, and that Ellie therefore wasn't going to be exposed to even the slightest risk. He had said as much to Ellie only weeks before they had discovered that there was, after all, to be another child.

'You really mean it. You really mean that I can audition? Oh Mam, thank you, thank you, *thank you*. Oh, I love you so much.'

Giddy with excitement and happiness, Hettie ran to her step-mother, hugging her fiercely and kissing her, before turning to dance round the sitting room, singing as she did so.

'Hettie, dearest, do calm down a little and listen to me,' Ellie protested lovingly.

Gideon told her a little more firmly, 'Hettie, that is enough. Come and sit down, please.'

Hettie sat down next to Ellie, taking a tight hold of her hand, her whole body almost quivering with excited impatience as Gideon explained: 'I have spoken with Miss Brown and she has assured me that she knows of no reason why we should feel concern. She knows the pianist at the Adelphi, and his wife, who are both fellow music teachers. Miss Brown has asked us to warn you, though, that even if the Adelphi Hotel does grant you an audition, such a position is bound to attract many applicants.'

Gideon glanced at Ellie, well aware that she was half hoping Hettie would not be accepted and would remain at home with them in Preston where Ellie could keep her under her motherly eye.

'Oh yes, I know that.' Hettie was all impatience and excitement. 'But did Miss Brown say whether or not she thought I might get the job?'

'She said you are an accomplished pupil, but that you have a tendency to consider – what were her exact words? – "little acorns to be fully grown trees".' Gideon answered her with restraint, mindful of the music teacher's additional comment to him that Hettie was extremely talented but not wishing his adopted daughter to spoil herself by becoming swollen headed. 'But Miss Brown has suggested she should write in response to the advertisement, recommending you as a possible candidate,' he continued, unable at last to conceal his pride.

Hettie glowed with fresh excitement. 'You mean that Miss Brown is willing to recommend me?' Immediately she was off again, springing up from the sofa, trying to drag Ellie with her and, when Ellie resisted, whirling into a dizzy polka, her cheeks flushed with happiness.

'My goodness, what's this?'

'John!' Hettie exclaimed in delight at the sight of her old partner-in-crime, laughing herself as she heard the amusement in his voice and saw the teasing look in his eyes, and abandoning her impromptu dance to run to his side.

'Where have you been?' she demanded. 'It seems an age since we last saw you. I suppose you've been too busy taking photographs from your flying machine and teaching other young men to be as besotted with them as you are to think about coming to see us.'

'Oh, besotted is it? Well, that's rich coming from you.' John grinned. 'Does she still terrify the neighbours practising her scales before cockcrow, Ellie?'

Ellie's heart warmed at the sight of John and Hettie slipping instantly into their old banter and routine, and she acknowledged that her younger brother and her adopted daughter, with no blood tie and only a mere eleven years between them, were the closest thing she had even witnessed to a true friendship between the opposite sexes.

Right from the start John and Hettie had formed

a close bond. There had never been a time when Hettie had not been able to wind John around her little finger, but Ellie knew that Hettie was equally fond of John and would do anything for him.

Pouting flirtatiously and tossing her head, Hettie informed him pertly, 'Well, for your information, soon I shall be singing a lot more than just scales!'

'Oh?' John cocked an enquiring eyebrow in Ellie's direction. 'Is Miss Brown to put on another charity piece? I was – ahem – disappointed to have missed the last one.'

'No, you weren't,' Hettie told him forthrightly. 'Why don't you admit it, John? You have no ear for music, unless it's the horrid whine of your flying machine engines.'

'I'll have you know that requires a very finely tuned ear indeed. In fact, a flyer's good ear for the healthy sound of his engine can make the difference between life and death.'

'Oh John, I wish you wouldn't remind me of just how dangerously you live,' Ellie protested.

'Flying is not dangerous at all if you obey the rules, Ellie.'

Behind Ellie's back Hettie shot John a look of pure enchanting mischief and challenge. 'You are such a fibber, John,' she accused him. 'I haven't forgotten you telling me that the reason you love flying is because it is so thrilling and exciting.'

John shook his head. 'Indeed it is, but that doesn't mean it's dangerous.'

'So, what brings you to Winckley Square,'

Gideon asked him cheerfully, desperate to change the subject and stop Ellie worrying even more about her impetuous younger brother.

John gave him a sheepish look. 'I have a favour to ask you, Gideon.'

Gideon frowned slightly. Of all of Ellie's family, John was his favourite, and he had happy memories of the friendship John had shown him years before when he had been Ellie's poor and, in her mother's eyes at least, unwanted suitor.

'If you're going to try to persuade me to take on another of your lame dogs, John, let me tell you that the last ruffian you persuaded me to hire turned up for work so drunk that it took three days for him to sober up.'

The whole family knew that John had a soft heart and was inclined to take up the cause of anyone he thought was hard done to.

A faint tinge of guilty colour crept over John's handsome face. Like his father, John was an extremely handsome man, tall and broad shouldered with bright blue eyes, strong white teeth, and thick dark curly hair.

'Well, she is neither a ruffian, nor lame . . .' John began awkwardly.

'*She*?' Gideon and Ellie demanded in unison.

A big grin split John's face. 'Yes "she",' he replied. 'Just wait until you see her. I've left her in the kitchen with Mrs Jennings. Gideon, she is just the prettiest thing and so affectionate, you will have her eating out of your hand in no time at all. She's only young, not fully grown, and with no bad habits. I'd keep her with me but I'm away such a lot that it just doesn't seem fair. I confess I had no intention of having her, but when I saw the way she was being abused. The poor little thing was cowering and shaking . . .'

Ellie was looking unhappier with every word her brother uttered, but Gideon had begun to relax. It was Hettie, though, who burst out laughing and exclaimed, 'Mam, don't look so worried. John is talking about a dog, aren't you, John?'

'What? Oh yes, of course. She is the prettiest little collie bitch, Gideon, and the chap I bought her off was treating her dreadfully.'

'Oh John!' Ellie scolded him, shaking her head.

'I must leave soon,' John told them. I have some new pupils to collect from the station and take back to the airfield.'

'How is business?' Gideon asked him.

'We are not yet making a profit, and I doubt I shall ever be able to match your success.' John smiled. 'But we are just about managing to make ends meet, thanks to you. Without your help I'd never have been able to set up the school in the first place.'

'Think nothing of it,' Gideon assured him clapping him on the shoulder. 'I suspect Ellie thinks I've done you more of a bad turn than a good one by helping you. She worries that living in a wretchedly ill-equipped and damp farm worker's cottage will ruin your health.'

John laughed. 'The cottage may not be Winckley Square but it suits me.'

It was now three years since, with Gideon's help, he had bought the large area of flat farmland with its worker's cottage. The flatness of the land meant it was perfect as an airfield, and, whilst neither the cottage nor the barracks-like building which housed the pupils could be described as anything other than extremely basic, John had lavished as much money as he could spare on the hangars for his two aeroplanes.

'So, minx,' John teased Hettie expansively. 'What charity is Miss Brown supporting this time? I dare say I shall have to buy tickets for it, even if I don't get to come along and hear you cater-wauling.'

'It isn't for charity and it isn't for Miss Brown,' Hettie answered him indignantly. 'It's a proper singing job, and in public, so there!'

'Singing in public? What do you mean?'

The good humour vanished from John's expression. Sensing her brother's disapproval, and seeing Hettie begin to pout, Ellie was about to explain but Hettie spoke first.

'I shall sing for the ladies of Liverpool whilst they take tea, and they will love me and I shall become famous,' Hettie trilled giddily, oblivious to the shadow that had crossed John's face.

'What Hettie means, John,' Gideon explained hurriedly, 'is that Miss Brown is recommending her for a recently advertised position as a soloist to be accompanied by the pianist at the Adelphi Hotel.'

'Oh John, just imagine.' Hettie clasped her hands together and stood in front of him, her whole face alive with happiness, her eyes full of dreams. 'It will be just as though I were on a stage. Only, of course, I shall not be because it is only a hotel, but who knows what it may lead to?'

'I can't see that any good will come of it, Hettie, other than filling your head with even more nonsense,' John told her so sharply that her face flushed.

'What are you saying?' she demanded hotly, but Ellie hurriedly intervened before John could answer her.

'Hettie, love, I was looking at your blue dress this morning and I thought we might re-trim it.'

'Thanks for agreeing to home this little lass for me, Gideon,' John said gruffly a few moments later, bending to rub the collie bitch's ears. They had moved down to the kitchen so that John could introduce Gideon to his new charge before leaving, Ellie and Hettie having remained upstairs.

'I'm sure both Philip and Richard will enjoy keeping her company when they're at home,' Gideon replied with a chuckle.

John smiled. Philip was the youngest of the Pride children, the baby whose birth had resulted in his mother's death, and who Gideon had firmly insisted Ellie's aunt hand over into Ellie's care to be brought up alongside their own children.

'Gideon, are you sure it's wise for Hettie to go to this audition?' John asked abruptly. 'After all, she's still so very young. Hardly more than a child.'

Gideon shook his head. 'You may not be aware that she has become a young woman, John, but I can assure you that she believes she has, and so too do the young men who hang around after church on Sunday hoping to be introduced to her. She's eighteen now, you know.'

'Even so, she has led a very sheltered life, and for all that she claims to want to sing on the stage, I believe she has no real idea of what such a life entails.'

'Maybe not, but I would far rather she discovers that in the safe environment of the Adelphi hotel, where she has Connie close at hand should she need her, than risk having her do as Connie herself did and run away from home.'

'Connie left our aunt's because she was ill-treated there, and fancied herself in love,' John protested.

'Well, whilst I hope Hettie will never feel that she has been ill-treated, she too is passionately in love, you know.'

'What? She might fancy herself in love with some lad, but she's too young even to know what love is.'

John's voice was grim. 'What I meant was that she feels very passionately about her music, just as you do about your flying machines. Besides, it may be that she is not called to audition for the post. Miss Brown, her singing teacher, believes there will be many applicants.'

Gideon was wrong in thinking he was not aware of how much Hettie had grown up, John reflected sombrely as he left the house. He was only too aware of it, and had been for some time. But it had been most obvious to him that, whilst his feelings for her had undergone a change, the old companionable affection he had always felt for her replaced by a man's longing and love, Hettie's feelings for him had remained as they always were. And nothing could have proved that more than her behaviour today, he admitted bleakly.

TWO

The much longed for and awaited letter from the Adelphi hotel had finally arrived, and as she watched Gideon opening it Hettie hardly dared to breathe, her breakfast left untouched as she waited in almost unbearable anxiety.

Whilst Gideon silently and slowly read the letter, Hettie looked appealingly at Ellie.

Loathe as she was to lose Hettie's company, Ellie couldn't help but feel for her. 'Gideon, please tell us what it says,' she begged her husband.

'It says,' Gideon answered her, 'that Miss Henrietta Walker is to present herself at the rooms of Mrs May Buchanan on Thursday of this week in order that Mrs Buchanan may assess her suitability to sing for the Adelphi's guests.'

'Oh!' Such was the intensity of her emotions that Hettie was completely unable to speak. Instead tears poured from her eyes and, with a small choked sob, she got up from her chair and ran to Ellie's side to bury her head against her shoulder, her whole body shaking.

'I still can't believe that I am actually to be auditioned,' she confided to Miss Brown two hours later, having begged Ellie's permission to visit her teacher to give her the good news. 'And it is all down to you,' Hettie told her teacher earnestly. 'Mrs Buchanan must have taken note of your recommendation.'

'I wrote no less than the truth, Hettie,' Miss Brown assured her. 'Nature has granted you a very special gift and given you a truly excellent voice.'

'But it is because of you that I have learned how to use it,' Hettie replied earnestly.

'When is your audition?' Miss Brown asked her excitedly.

'It is this Thursday. I'm already feeling nervous. My mother has a sister who lives in Liverpool and so we are to take the train Wednesday to be there in plenty of time and stay with my Aunt Connie. What do you think Mrs Buchanan will ask me to sing?'

'I am sure that she will expect you to have a piece ready prepared,' Miss Brown answered her. 'So we must choose something that both shows off the range of your voice and which will fall pleasantly on the ears of ladies taking afternoon tea. This is not a situation where I would recommend the singing of a complicated aria.' Miss Brown pursed her lips thoughtfully and then said shrewdly, 'Perhaps something pretty and sentimental would be best.

'Oh, and I would advise you to wear something smart but loose, so that your voice is not constricted in any way. You will be apprehensive, of course, and anxious, that is to be expected. It is Monday already so we must decide quickly what you will sing so that you can practise it. What about "Auf Wiedersehen"?' she suggested. 'After all, Vivienne Segal was just your age when it made *her* a star.'

Hettie nodded in agreement. She was far too excited to be able to speak. She could hardly believe that in three days time should would be singing at the Adelphi!

The bus had set them down at the corner of the road, and Hettie moved closer to Ellie's side as her apprehension grew. She had felt more and more nauseous and tearful with every minute that had passed since leaving her Aunt Connie's.

The rooms where Hettie was to have her audition were in a street off Lime Street, not very far from the Adelphi. The house itself was halfway down the street, and like all its neighbours it had a clean if somewhat austere appearance, its front step donkey-stoned and the doorknocker well polished.

'Oh, Mam . . .' Hettie whispered shakily.

'What is it, Hettie?' Ellie asked her gently. 'Have you changed your mind?'

Immediately Hettie shook her head, missing the faint sigh Ellie gave and the look of anxiety in her eyes.

A small, neatly dressed maid in a crisply immaculate apron and cap opened the front door to them and directed them to a dark back parlour, its furniture heavily festooned in dark brown material. Ellie and Hettie perched awkwardly on a bulging sofa.

The faintly worn areas in the turkey carpet made Hettie wonder just how many anxious feet had paced across it whilst their owners waited in the room's sombre silence. Thick net curtains obscured what light could have entered the room, making it seem even more gloomily oppressive.

She reached out and placed her hand in Ellie's. She wanted this more than she had ever wanted anything in the whole of her life, more than she would ever want anything ever again. She wanted it so much that it physically hurt, she told herself dramatically.

The door opened, making Hettie jump. The parlour maid announced, 'You're both to go in now, if you please.'

'Good luck, my love,' Ellie whispered to her as they both got up, kissing her lovingly whilst Hettie gripped her hand.

Hettie had never felt so clumsy, nor so awkward. Her face was burning, and her throat had gone so dry she was afraid she would not be able to sing at all.

The maid escorted them to the door of the front parlour and then whispered, 'Knock on the door and then wait until she says to go in.'

When her step-mother's knock went unacknowledged, Hettie cast her an anguished look. 'Perhaps she didn't hear,' she began and then stopped as a firm contralto voice from the other side of the door called out commandingly.

'Come.'

With Ellie pushing her firmly ahead, Hettie stepped in to the room. Here there was no over-stuffed sofa but instead a row of uncomfortable looking hard-backed chairs. But it was the piano and, more dramatically, the woman seated at it, that commanded Hettie's attention.

Mrs May Buchanan was almost the complete opposite of Miss Brown, being tall and stately where Miss Brown was small and thin; and her jet-black hair, unlike Miss Brown's untidy grey bun, was drawn back into a formidably elegant chignon. Miss Brown's manner was fussy yet gentle, whilst Hettie could tell, even on this first meeting, that Mrs Buchanan was chillingly distant.

Hettie could feel herself tremble as Mrs Buchanan's merciless gaze focused sharply on her.

'Your teacher has some very complimentary things to say about you, Miss Walker. She seems to think that you have a soprano voice of surpassing excellence.'

Hettie looked towards Ellie for reassurance, not sure how she was meant to respond.

'Do you have the same high opinion of your voice as your teacher, Miss Walker?'

'I know that I love to sing,' was all Hettie could find to say. Mrs Buchanan was making her feel very small and unimportant; she was even beginning to wish that she had not put herself forward for her criticism.

'Very well then. Please stand up.'

Obediently Hettie got to her feet. She felt sick with nervousness, and she just knew that she was going to do everything wrong.

As she sang the opening bars of the song, she could hear the uncertainty affecting her voice and her heart sank with distress and panic. The song was so familiar to her that she knew it by heart, and yet in her agitation she almost missed a note. But then, as always when she got into the song itself, the music began to take her over and she became lost in its enchantment and the role it had cast for her.

As she sang the last few notes she saw the emotional tears in Ellie's eyes, and her spirits soared upwards in triumph and pleasure. But she was brought quickly back to earth when Mrs Buchanan commented coldly, 'You were off key in the first bar.'

'I was nervous.'

'If you are nervous about singing in front of me then how do you think you will be able to sing in front of an audience of a hundred?'

Hettie did not dare look at her mother. She knew if she did she would burst into tears of shame and disappointment.

THREE

'You have been gone such an age. What happened?'

'Poor Hettie was very nervous,' Hettie heard Ellie answering as Connie ushered them both into her cosy parlour.

'I was off key in the opening bars,' Hettie added, watching as Connie's expression grew grave and sympathetic, and then laughing and saying, 'But I am to have the job because Mrs Buchanan says that I am the best of all the applicants.'

'Oh, you terror, letting me think that you hadn't got it!' Connie chided her, laughing back.

'And I am going to board with Mrs Buchanan's sister, aren't I, Mam? She lives in the same street and only takes in female lodgers. I will have lessons with Mrs Buchanan every morning for a month and then I shall sing at the Adelphi hotel every afternoon. Except, of course, for Sunday, which will be my day off. Then after that I will have two days together off each month, which means I can go home to Preston.'

'Well, in between times you must come here to us, then. You will enjoy listening to our school choir, and it will be so lovely to have you. Dr Kenton, the school's music teacher, is very proud of them, and says they are far superior to the Bluecoat School boys.'

Connie's husband Harry was the headmaster of a private boys' school and he, Connie and their children lived in the headmaster's house right next to the school. In addition to her responsibilities as a headmaster's wife, Connie was also still very involved in the nursery for children whose parents were out at work or who, in some cases, had no parents to care for them at all. She had set up this nursery prior to her marriage to Harry.

'So, when do you start your new job, Hettie?'

'Next week, but I shall need to have a new dress first, shan't I, Mam?'

'Yes, my love, you will. Mrs Buchanan has told us that Hettie will need a proper tea dress to wear when she sings,' Ellie explained to her sister.

'Well, you will be certain to find something here in Liverpool. We shall go out together tomorrow and look.'

'Connie, I wonder, would you mind taking Hettie to get a dress without me? Only I have already arranged to see Iris tomorrow.'

Hettie stared at her step-mother in consternation. 'But you must come with me,' she protested. 'Please, Mam, I want you to,' she pleaded desperately. For although she wanted her new life and its independence, inwardly Hettie felt vulnerable and uncertain, and very much in need of Ellie's love and support. How could she think of putting seeing Iris before something so important as helping her to find the right dress for her new job? Even Connie was frowning at her.

'Hettie, I am sorry,' Ellie said, seeing the disappointed look on Hettie's face. 'But Iris is only in Liverpool for tomorrow, and it is important that I see her . . .'

'But I need you to help me choose my dress.' Hettie was ready to burst into tears.

After one look at her pale face and tear-filled eyes, Connie attempted to placate her by saying calmly, 'Of course you are disappointed that your mother can't go shopping with you, Hettie. But I can come with you and I'm sure between us we shall be able to find the right thing.'

Somehow Hettie managed to swallow back her tears and nod her head, but it just wouldn't be the same fun without her.

Even worse was to come!

At four o'clock, the whole family, including Connie's three young children and her husband, all sat down together to eat a traditional high tea as a treat. Afterwards, Hettie entertained the children by playing spillikins with them, and telling them jokes, until it was time for them to go to bed.

'You've made a rod for your own back now, Hettie,' Connie teased her when she returned to the parlour having tucked her children up in their beds.

'They are already demanding to know when they will see you again, and I can see that from now on Sunday will definitely be their favourite day of the week.'

Hettie smiled. It was a comfort to know that Connie, Harry and the children were just around the corner. It made the whole move to Liverpool a little less daunting.

'Connie, I've been thinking.' Ellie broke in to her sister's conversation. 'It seems foolish for Hettie to return home to Preston with me, only to have to travel all the way back to Liverpool again within a matter of days. Could she possibly stay here with you until she moves into the lodging house next week?'

'But Mam, I will need to go home with you to pack my things,' Hettie protested anxiously. Her pride wouldn't let her behave like a baby and say that she had just discovered she wasn't quite ready to leave home so very quickly and that she wanted to say goodbye 'properly' to all her favourite things and, more importantly, her favourite people. An uncomfortable, unhappy feeling was lying like cold stone in her chest. For virtually all her life she had taken Ellie's presence and love for granted. Now she was both hurt and shocked that Ellie should talk about parting with her so easily and casually.

'It is just as easy for me to pack them for you,

Hettie, and have your trunk sent direct to Mrs Foster's,' Ellie told her.

'Of course Hettie is welcome to stay here,' Connie said, smiling.

But Hettie couldn't smile. A huge lump of misery was blocking her throat. At first, Mam hadn't wanted her to leave home at all, but now it seemed as though she couldn't wait to be rid of her. Hettie had to concentrate very hard to squeeze back the tears threatening to fill her eyes again. The dizzyingly intense feeling of happiness that had filled her when Mrs Buchanan had told her that she had got the job had been replaced by a forlorn sense of loss.

'Ellie, you aren't asleep yet, are you?' Connie whispered, opening Ellie's bedroom door and stepping inside. She looked questioningly at her sister as she lay in bed, propped up against the pillows. 'Only it's been such a busy day we haven't had time to talk to each other properly.'

Ellie smiled as Connie sat down on the side of her bed, and put down the book she had been reading.

'Hettie is very disappointed that you aren't going to be able to go with her to choose her dress,' Connie began, watching as a small shadow darkened Ellie's eyes. She sighed. She too, in truth, had been surprised. She knew how much Ellie loved Hettie, the only girl in her family, whom she had brought up as her own from a very young age.

'I know. I'd love to be able to go with her, Connie, but I have to see Iris.'

The shadow was there again and Connie's heart missed a beat.

'Ellie, something's wrong. I can tell, what is it?'

'I'm going to have another child.'

Connie frowned. 'But, Ellie, surely that's good news?'

Ellie gave her a wan smile. 'Connie, I'm thirty-five, and my youngest child is ten. Gideon and I wanted there to be more children, but after so long without there being one . . .' Ellie paused and looked at her sister. I can't say any of this to Gideon because he is already worrying enough . . . because of our mother.'

'Our mother? But she was older than you and had been warned not to have any more children,' Connie protested, and then looked anxiously at her. 'Ellie, tell me you have not been given the same warning?'

'No, no. Nothing like that. But . . . This time somehow it feels different – not right in some way. I can't explain it properly, Connie, but I just feel so worried, and I thought if I could see Iris and talk to her about it . . . The problem is that she's been away, and she's only going to be in Liverpool for a few hours in between journeys. I'm to see her at her father's Rodney Street Chambers. Naturally, I don't want to say anything to Hettie about my reasons for wanting to see Iris. She would worry and feel that she had to stay at home with me and the last thing I want is for her to have to carry the same burden of guilt our mother's death left to me.'

'But Ellie, you are not our mother, and you must not think such dreadful things. There is no reason for you to fear there is anything amiss,' Connie told her bracingly, causing a small smile to flicker across Ellie's face. How very typical it was of Connie's training as a nurse that she should adopt such a stalwart and reassuring manner! 'You are right, though, to see Iris. She is a wonderful doctor and very highly thought of. I do think, though, that it might be better if you explained to Hettie why you want to see Iris. She's feeling very hurt.'

'It isn't as straightforward as that, Connie. At first when Hettie said that she wanted to apply for this audition I was against it. And I admit that a large part of me would still prefer her to remain at home. I had looked forward to having her at home with us until she marries, to be my friend as well as my daughter. But Gideon is concerned that if we refuse she might . . .'

'Run away as I did?' Connie suggested before shaking her head. 'Hettie loves you and Gideon, Ellie, and is loved by you – you needn't worry that she is going to flee the nest and cut her ties.'

'I know that, and I know too that if she felt I needed her she would stay, but it would be wrong of me to allow her to do that when I know how much her singing means to her. And it is because of that I cannot tell her why I need to see Iris.

Please don't tell her, I beg of you,' Ellie beseeched her younger sister.

'Very well, Ellie, if that is what you wish,' Connie agreed, unwilling to add to her sister's distress by telling her of her own belief that nothing good could come of keeping something so important a secret from Hettie. With reluctance, Connie agreed she would remain silent.

Alone and unable to sleep in the pretty guest bedroom her new grown-up status had entitled her to occupy, instead of sharing the nursery with Connie's children like she normally did, Hettie sat up in bed, wrapping her arms around her knees. A tear trickled down her cheek followed by another. She had been so happy hours before but now she was so *un*happy, and all because Mam had told her that she wouldn't be going back to Preston.

Didn't Mam care about her any more? Didn't she love her any more? Suddenly Hettie longed to be a little girl once again, able to pad barefoot from her narrow bed in the nursery downstairs to the big bedroom Mam and Dad shared, and then to find her way through the darkness to Mam's side of the bed where somehow she was always awake and waiting for her, ready to lift her up and tuck her against her side. There, secure in Ellie's arms and Ellie's love, Hettie had easily forgotten whatever it was that had woken her and gone contently back to sleep.

Hettie looked hesitantly towards the door, wondering if she should go and find Ellie now. But she was not a little girl any more, was she? It was time to stand on her own two feet.

FOUR

'We'll go straight to Bon Marche, I think, Hettie,' Connie decided vigorously as the three of them sat around the breakfast table. Harry had already left for work, whilst the children had been despatched to the nearby park for some fresh air in the charge of the young orphan girl Connie had taken in who helped her with them.

Hettie forced herself to smile and nod her head, knowing that normally she would have enjoyed the thought of a shopping trip with Connie, and not wanting to be thought rude. But both Connie and Ellie noticed how strained she looked and how her mouth trembled as she tried to smile.

'We don't want to lose any time so if you've finished your breakfast I think we should make an early start. If we do, we will have time to go into Bon Marche. They have all the very latest fashions in that department-store,' she added importantly. 'Not that I am suggesting you should have anything from there, Hettie, it would be far too expensive, but there would be no harm in just looking round to get some ideas.'

Obediently Hettie pushed back her chair and stood up.

'What time are you meeting Iris, Ellie?' Connie asked her sister.

Ellie put down her teacup and said lightly, 'Actually, Connie, I've changed my mind about that, and decided to come along with you and Hettie instead. Your shopping trips sounds too much fun for me to miss and I know that Iris will understand. I'll telephone her, though, if I may. She's staying with her parents, and I was going to see her there.'

The two sisters exchanged silent looks whilst Hettie, oblivious to their exchange, rushed towards her step-mother, her face breaking into a wide smile as she exclaimed, 'Oh Mam, I'm so happy that you're going to come with us.'

'So am I, my love,' Ellie responded gently. 'Now go upstairs and make yourself tidy, we don't want the posh sales ladies in Bon Marche to think we've taken you to the wrong department and that you're a schoolgirl still and not a young lady!'

Humming happily under her breath Hettie almost danced from the room, the sound of her happiness as she sang to herself all the way up the stairs drifting down to Ellie and Connie as they stood together in the parlour.

'Ellie . . .' Connie began, but Ellie shook her head.

'Connie, I could hear Hettie crying in her sleep last night, just like she used to do when she was little. I forget sometimes just how sensitive she is, one minute up in the heights of happiness, the next in the depths of despair, but always no matter what her mood so very loving. Besides, as you pointed out to me yourself, there is no real reason for me to worry, and I am sure Iris would say as much herself.'

'Well, if you are sure.'

'I am,' Ellie answered her firmly. 'Now, I'd better go upstairs and make myself tidy as well. But first I'll telephone Iris.'

'Oh, how lovely it smells in here,' Hettie exclaimed as she took a deep breath of Bon Marche's perfumed air, one arm tucked into her step-mother's and the other into her aunt's, her face alight with happy anticipation.

'All the wealthy ladies of Liverpool come here to buy their clothes,' Connie told her importantly. 'Why, one can even buy gowns here that have come all the way from Paris, made by by Mr Worth himself.'

'Connie, don't put ideas into Hettie's head, please.' Ellie laughed. 'Gideon is a generous husband and father, but even his generosity does not stretch as far as a couture gown. This is a special treat to celebrate Hettie's new job but we must still be sensible.'

'Mm. Remember that dress you made for me

before you were married, Ellie? It was so very pretty. The fabric was cream with small bunches of cherry coloured flowers, and you'd trimmed it with cherry red ribbons.'

In the years when she had had to struggle to support herself and her brothers and sister, Ellie had managed by sewing things for other people, at first by hand and then later with the sewing machine she had bought by selling off locks of her long hair.

'Ooh, look at that!' Hettie exclaimed, looking round-eyed at a display of rouges and other cosmetics.

'You are pretty enough without needing to use any of that, Hettie,' Ellie warned firmly, determinedly drawing her away.

It took them over an hour to make their way through the exclusive department store as Hettie was constantly distracted and delighted by the luxurious goods on sale. She had never seen clothes such as these. Gowns in rich jewel-coloured delicate fabrics. Silks and satin, and all in the very latest bias-cut style. So very different from the far more sturdy garments in stout, sensible worsted woollens and brightly printed cottons that Hettie was used to.

These fabrics shimmered and danced beneath the chandeliers with every passing movement. Hettie longed to reach out and touch them but did not dare to do so. These were clothes for women who lived a life very different from the one her family led, Hettie acknowledged. These were clothes for rich 'ladies' not working class women like themselves. And the styles! Dropped waists, short skirts, huge bowed sashes – dresses for every imaginable occasion.

Under the eagle eyes of the hovering sales assistant, she gazed in awe at the evening gowns and luxurious furs on display, for once lost for words.

'That would suit you, Hettie,' Ellie murmured, pointing out to her a red silk tea dress displayed on a mannequin, the fabric overprinted with orange poppies and the hem of the dress fashionably short to display not just the mannequin's ankles, but also her calves. Hettie reached out and touched the silk gently, and then looked uncertainly up at her step-mother.

'But you said we would buy my dress from George Henry Lee's and that we were only coming in here to look,' she reminded her.

'I've changed my mind.' Ellie smiled. 'This dress would be perfect for you, wouldn't it, Connie?'

Hettie could not believe she was serious. The ravishingly pretty dress was beyond anything she had ever even dared to dream of possessing.

'It's beautiful,' Connie agreed immediately. 'And the colour would be perfect for Hettie with her dark hair and lovely pale skin.'

Hettie looked from one smiling face to the other. Her da was always teasing her mother that the women of the Pride family were strong and determined to get their own way, and now Hettie could see how right he was.

An assistant was sailing majestically towards them, sniffing out a potential sale. 'Mam, I think we should go,' Hettie hissed.

But Ellie ignored her and turned instead towards the assistant, saying firmly, 'My daughter needs a tea dress. I would like her to try on this one.' She indicated the red silk.

Immediately the assistant's smile widened and her voice when she spoke was warm. 'An excellent choice, if I may say so, madam, especially for your daughter's colouring. The dress is French, and its designer was apprenticed to Monsieur Worth himself, as I am sure you will already have guessed. And red is very modern this season, although of course not all young ladies can carry it as well as your daughter will. Is it to be for a special occasion?' she asked.

'A very special occasion,' Ellie confirmed, giving Hettie a tender look.

Ten minutes later, standing before her mother and aunt, her cheeks almost as poppy red as the dress, Hettie waited anxiously for their opinion. When neither of them spoke, her heart thudded to the bottom of her chest. As she had looked at herself in the mirror after the assistant had arranged the deceptively simple straight lines of the dress to her satisfaction, and tied the wide sash around Hettie's slender hips, Hettie had hardly been able to believe that the reflection staring back at her was her own. Were her throat and arms really so slender and white, her wrists so ethereally fragile? And were those shapely calves and fine-boned ankles really hers? Surely even her lips looked a deeper colour than before. But now the silence from both Connie and, more significantly, Ellie made her wonder what she really looked like.

'Oh, Connie!'

To Hettie's consternation, Ellie's eyes had filled with tears.

'Mam,' she protested quickly. 'It's all right. If you don't like it I don't mind. I'm sure we shall find something else.'

'Not like it? Oh, Hettie, Hettie. Of course I like it.'

'Then why are you crying?'

Dabbing her eyes with her lace-edged handkerchief, Ellie laughed. 'I'm crying, my love, because you look so beautiful.'

'Indeed she does, madam,' the sales assistant agreed eagerly. 'And if I may suggest, a nice pair of the new shoes we've just had in will set off the dress a treat – silver, with the new heel. Oh, and perhaps just a small bow for her hair?'

'We'll just take the dress for now,' Hettie heard Ellie break into the sales assistant's suggestions. 'And we shall think about the shoes. Hettie, my love, go and get changed back into your own clothes.'

Later, with the dress paid for and swathed in layers of tissue paper, the three women left the shop and Connie announced, 'Well, I don't know about you two but I am parched.'

They found a small tea shop a short distance away from Bon Marche where Hettie, despite claiming she was far too excited to eat, managed to speedily dispose of several delicate sandwiches, a piece of slab cake and two fancies. Ellie, on the other hand, merely sipped at her tea, smiling at Hettie who thanked her over and over again for her dress.

'When you look back on this time of your life, Hettie, I want all of your memories to be happy ones.'

'Oh they will be, Mam. In fact, I am so happy right now I could burst.'

'That isn't happiness, Hettie, it's too much cake!' Connie teased her, and although Ellie joined in their laughter she had to place her hand against the side of her stomach to quell the discomfort nagging at her.

She was just tired, she assured herself, that was all. Connie had been right to say that she was worrying unnecessarily, and even if she had seen Iris what more could her friend have done than echo Connie's reassurance? Besides, she wouldn't have wanted to have missed this special time with Hettie. She had no regrets on that score. No, not even about the shocking expense of Hettie's dress. For all that she could be wilful and tempestuous at times, Hettie had never been greedy or asked for anything.

When they had finished their tea, she would take Hettie back to Bon Marche and get her those shoes the sales assistant had suggested, Ellie decided, and perhaps she might even be able to buy some pretty little surprises to hide in Hettie's trunk as well.

To Hettie's delight, instead of returning to Preston when she had originally planned, Ellie decided she would spend a couple more days in Liverpool. It was arranged that Gideon would drive over to pick her up on Saturday, so that she would have time to pack Hettie's trunk and have it despatched to her.

'P'raps now that you are staying longer you will be able to see Iris after all, Ellie,' Connie suggested as they were clearing the breakfast things one morning.

Ellie dipped her head so that Connie wouldn't see her face. She didn't want her sister to guess how much her own forebodings still troubled her, and how much she wished she had been able to see Iris. The last thing she wanted was to be reminded of her own fears. Trying to ignore them she said as lightly as she could, 'No, she will already have left Liverpool by now, but it doesn't matter. I have been feeling much better.'

Much better but still not entirely 'well'.

FIVE

'These young buggers come here and think they know everything. They don't know how to treat a flying machine with proper respect, that they don't.'

John smiled as he listened to Jim Ryley, his mechanic, grumbling about their latest intake of pupils. 'They're eager and enthusiastic, Jim.'

'Aye, and some of them are downright reckless. That lanky red-headed lad for one. You want to watch him, John. He's a right wild 'un, and a troublemaker.'

John's smile turned into a frown. It was true that Alan Simms was inclined to be reckless and overconfident. When John had taken him up for a lesson earlier in the week he had tried to ignore John's instructions and wanted to loop the loop. As John had pointed out to him then, the skies were not a forgiving place in which to make an error of judgement or skill.

'Still, he'll be on his way soon and we'll have

the next lot coming in. How many will there be this time?'

'Not as many as I'd like,' John admitted.

It was a perfect day for flying, with a light wind and a clear sky, and if it wasn't for the fact that the small problem which had caused the prop to stutter so badly yesterday meant he was grounded until he could fix it, John would have been up there enjoying it. Not that, for once, his thoughts were entirely on flying.

He picked up the letter he had received earlier in the week and re-read it. It was from a friend, a fellow flyer he had met during the war, their mutual love of flying machines giving them a shared passion which had transcended their social differences and given rise to an unlikely friendship between John, with his working class background, and Alfred, who was a member of the aristocracy. It was Alfred and not John who had initiated the friendship, brushing aside John's awkward protests and objections about their social differences.

Alfred had written that he intended to escort his sister to Liverpool where she was boarding a liner to travel to New York this coming weekend, and they would be staying at the Adelphi hotel for a few days prior to her departure.

'Thing is, old chap, I thought that maybe we could get together. Fact is, there's a small business matter I'd like to discus with you. Must say I envy you – your flying, I mean. Unfortunately, I'm grounded now. Responsibilities and all that. Still, mustn't grumble, I suppose.'

Alfred always looked on the bright side of life – it was one of the things John admired about him – but maybe it was easy to be optimistic when you didn't have to worry constantly about making ends meet. Alfred was, after all, an earl, whilst *he* was merely an ordinary working man. No, he was even less than that, John acknowledged as he looked round the rundown and shabby cottage that was his home. No self-respecting working man would live somewhere like this.

The cottage had an earth floor over which stone slabs had been laid, the result being that, when it rained, water seeped up over them and even froze when the temperature dropped sharply.

But he had slowly improved the conditions. When he had bought the property a standpipe outside had provided water for both the cottage and the livestock, but John now had water piped into the cottage itself. The outside lavvy had been little better than a latrine and a health hazard until he had built his own cess pit to accommodate not just his own needs but those of the men who came to him to learn how to fly. Indeed, their quarters were equipped with modern if basic bathrooms and sanitaryware, thanks to the generosity of his brother-in-law, Gideon. Since the cottage did not have its own bathroom it was simpler for him to use the pupils' facilities rather than to struggle with the tin bath that hung in the washhouse.

One day, of course, he would find the time and money to install that range Ellie was always cajoling him to buy, and then he would be able to have the luxury of hot water, as well as hot food. One day . . . Maybe . . . If the business ever made him any profit.

'Put up your fees, John,' Gideon had advised him. But he knew if did that then those young men who, like him, were captivated and driven by the lure of flight, would not be able to afford them. The truth was that at the moment he earned more by taking aerial photographs for those government bodies that required them than he did from giving flying lessons.

Travelling to Liverpool would mean leaving Jim on his own to sort out the problem with the prop and cancelling some of the lessons. It would also mean struggling to wash and iron one of his few remaining decent shirts, because Jenny Black, the kind-hearted soul from the village who had taken it upon herself to 'look after him', couldn't be trusted not to scorch them, as he already knew to his cost. And then he would have to dig deep into his pockets to find the means to travel to Liverpool at all.

But Hettie was in Liverpool, and if he were to agree to meet up with Alfred then he would have a cast iron excuse for calling on Connie and seeing Hettie again.

'What time will Da be here?' Hettie asked her stepmother anxiously. They had just finished breakfast and were in Ellie's room where Hettie was helping her pack ready for her return to Preston.

'He said he would be leaving early.'

'He won't forget about my things, will he?'

'No, of course not. I posted him a list to give to Mrs Jennings. Oh, and guess what? He is to bring John with him.'

Hettie beamed at this unexpected news. 'Oh! May I put on my new dress for him and Da to see?'

'If there is time. Now, where did I put those new handkerchiefs I bought, Hettie?'

Obligingly, Hettie searched for the missing items, finding them on top of a chest of drawers. Sunshine splashed through the windows and across the floor, matching her own happiness. She was going to miss home and her family, of course she was, but the fear and misery that had beset her earlier in the week had now gone and she was beginning to look forward to her new life.

'You will make sure that Miss Brown gets the "Parma Violets" scent I bought for her to say thank you, won't you?' she asked Ellie anxiously.

'I shall take it to her myself,' Ellie assured her.

Should she tell Mam about the small vial of 'Attar of Roses' bought with the precious store money she had saved and carefully hidden in Ellie's valise? Hettie wondered, Or should she do as she had originally planned and leave it as a surprise for Ellie once she reached home? She imagined

Ellie's pleasure on finding it when she unpacked and decided to keep quiet.

Hettie hoped she would like the card she had chosen to go with it, bearing the words, 'thinking of you always, dearest mother'. And it was true that she would be thinking of her and of home every day.

'Oh Da.'

'There, there, Hettie lass, there's no need to tek on so!' Gideon soothed, patting her on the back as she clung to him and wept, overwhelmed by her own emotions now that the final moment of parting was so close.

'I'll bet you'll be to-ing and fro-ing that often from Liverpool to Preston and back again that the railways will give you your own special seat,' he teased her when Hettie had finally been persuaded to release him.

'We left her trunk at the lodging house like you asked us to, Ellie.'

'And what did you think of the place, Gideon? Did you see the landlady?' Ellie asked fretfully.

'We did and she was very pleasant. The house looked clean and tidy. You should be comfortable and well looked after there, Hettie, shouldn't she, John?'

John! Hettie dimpled a smile at him, but did not run to him like she used to, self-consciously aware of the fact that she was now a young woman and no longer a mere girl. Instead she said importantly, 'Just wait until you see the dress Mam has bought for me to wear – I am going to put it on after tea to show you.'

'Oh John, it is so lovely to see you. You don't come to Liverpool often enough,' Connie reproached her brother as she bustled into the parlour.

'That is because there is nowhere for him to land his flying machine, Connie,' Harry joked.

Soon their chatter and laughter filled the small room, but Hettie's was the voice John could hear most clearly, and her pretty, excited face the one he looked to most frequently, John admitted reluctantly, torn between conflicting feelings as he saw how the girl who had doted on him was turning into a beautiful young woman.

Gideon had confided to him as they drove over to Liverpool that Ellie was to have another child and that news too had added to the sombreness of John's mood. The death of their mother after giving birth to Philip had left its mark on all of them. Certainly he knew that for him there was always that feeling of anxiety when he knew one of his sisters was with child. But Ellie was strong, in body and spirit, and he hoped that she would come through this unexpected pregnancy without any problems.

As soon as tea was over, Hettie ran upstairs to change into her new dress, having first begged her mother's services as a lady's maid.

When the dress was safely on and the sash tied,

Ellie smoothed Hettie's thick dark hair and smiled at her reflection in the mirror.

'You are smiling but you look sad, why?' Hettie asked her.

'I was just thinking of your mother,' Ellie explained. She had always felt it important that Hettie know about her birth mother and so had never shied away from mentioning her.

'I can hardly remember her. Only that she cried a lot and was sick on the ship,' Hettie told her pragmatically. So far as she was concerned, Ellie was her mother, and her memories of warm loving arms holding her as child were always of Ellie's arms.

For all that, physically, she looked so unique, with the compelling blend of her English and Japanese features, Hettie's nature was entirely English, Ellie acknowledged. She certainly could not imagine Hettie with her determination and high spirits ever behaving towards a husband in the subservient manner that Ellie's own first husband, Hettie's father, had told her was traditional amongst Japanese women.

When Hettie had been growing up, Ellie had dutifully bought her books to read about her mother's homeland, but for Hettie's own sake she had not wanted her to be singled out as 'foreign' or 'different'. If Minaco were able to see her daughter, would she feel as proud of her as Ellie herself did right now? Or would Minaco resent her and think that she had usurped her role from her? What would a mother want for the child she had to leave behind?

'Come on, Mam,' Hettie urged, disrupting Ellie's thoughts. 'Let's go downstairs so that I can show Da and John my dress.'

Connie had cleared a space for her right inside the door so that she could make a grand entrance and that she did, pirouetting in front of her audience with flushed cheeks and shining eyes.

Hettie could see Gideon frowning slightly as he looked at her exposed arms and calves, but it was towards John she turned in happy anticipation, awaiting his awed recognition of her metamorphosis. However, the look of grim anger on his face was such a shock that it caused her to teeter in mid pirouette and almost stumble, her face paling as John got up to leave the room.

'John!' She caught the door as it slammed behind him, and pulled it back, following him into the hallway. 'What is it?' she begged him. 'Why did you look at me so? Don't you like my dress?' Her eyes were more sparkling than ever with her shocked bewilderment and confusion, the small hand she extended towards him in desperate appeal trembling.

'How can you even think of parading yourself in public in such a garment? Where is your modesty?' John could see that his harsh words had shocked her, but she had shocked him. How could he explain to her that seeing her like that had suddenly reminded him of the poor, too young

55

girls he had seen during the war around the camps, selling themselves for the price of a loaf of bread? How could he explain to her that his reaction was caused by his own contradictory feelings – part male arousal and part fierce desire to protect her from that arousal?

Hettie snatched back the hand she had extended to him and tucked it behind her back as a child would have done. 'What do you mean? It is the fashion . . . modern . . . everyone is wearing shorter skirts now.'

'Maybe so but they are not wearing them to expose themselves for the pleasure of every man who cares to walk in off the street to ogle them, are they?' John couldn't help saying jealously.

Hettie could see that John wasn't convinced but rather than argue with him she tossed her head and said determinedly, 'Well, Mam chose this dress for me, so there! Thank you very much! Besides, it is only ladies taking their afternoon tea who will see me.'

'Aye, and their husbands, sons, and fathers, when they come to join them, which they will do, especially when they learn that there is a singer to be found all tricked out in a costume designed to entice them,' John muttered unkindly.

'Oh! Why are you being so horrible to me? I am grown up now, John, and not a child any more, and I won't be treated as one,' Hettie burst out defiantly, unaware of the fact that John had only wanted to protect her.

Unable to understand what was happening – why John, who was supposed to care about and be happy for her, was being so mean – Hettie declared crossly, 'I hate you, John Pride, and I shall hate you for ever!' before turning round and running up the stairs to throw herself full length on her bed and sob out her hurt feelings.

He shouldn't have walked out of Connie's parlour like that, John acknowledged bleakly, and nor should he have spoken so unkindly to Hettie, but the sight of her tricked out in her fancy frock and looking like a stranger had done something to him he couldn't understand himself. He felt ashamed of himself for the way he had behaved. His sisters sometimes scolded him that, whilst he had generally inherited their father's amiable and kind nature, sometimes he could be as they put it 'as stubborn as a mule'.

Somewhere in amongst his anger there had also been pain. But although John could understand the reason for his fierce anger, he could not understand why he also felt such a sharp sense of loss and despair.

Couldn't Gideon and Ellie see the danger of allowing Hettie to parade herself around as though she were a grown woman and not still in reality a girl? Couldn't they see, as he so plainly could, that Hettie would lure men to her with her beauty and innocence and that for her own sake she needed to be protected?

His angry thoughts had taken him past the Bluecoat School, Connie's husband Harry's 'rivals', without him noticing. Rather than wait for a bus, he decided he might as well walk the whole way to the Adelphi – it might help him clear his head of the mass of confusing and unhappy thoughts which besieged it.

The hotel had been rebuilt in 1912 to the designs of Frank Atkinson, and was still considered by Liverpudlians to be, as Charles Dickens had once written, 'the best hotel in the world'. The turtles for its famous turtle soup were, so it was said, kept in a tank in the basement.

As he reached the hotel, the liveried doormen were busy opening hackney cab doors and assisting elegantly dressed guests to alight whilst another doorman whistled up porters to take charge of the luggage. Skirting past them John walked into the marble foyer and glanced absently at the listing of transatlantic crossings prominently displayed.

Beyond the entrance hall, thronged with a confusion of arriving and departing travellers, a flight of steps led up to the large top-lit Central Court with its pink pilasters.

Ignoring the glazed screens with their French doors that filled the arches and opened up into the large restaurants on either side of the Central Court, John made his way to the Hypostyle Hall, which was where Alfred had suggested they meet.

Several of the tables in the large square empire-style hall were already filled with people taking afternoon tea, and as John surveyed them he was approached by an imposing flunkey who demanded condescendingly, 'H'excuse me, sir, but h'if you was wanting to take . . .'

'I'm here to meet a friend,' John stopped him calmly.

'Oh, and 'oo would that be, sir?'

'The Earl of Camberley,' John told him.

The immediate change in the flunkey's attitude towards him would normally have made John chuckle, but on this occasion he was still too heart sore from his earlier outburst to do more than ignore the man's pleasantries as he led him to a table.

'Shall you be wishing me to 'ave His Lordship called, Sir, or . . .'

'No, that won't be necessary. I'm a few minutes early.' He looked past the flunkey to the area just in front of the entrance to the open-air courtyard where a large grand piano stood on the shiny marble floor.

Was this where Hettie was going to be singing?

Refusing the waiter's offer of tea, John studied the occupants of the other tables. They were in the main family groups, passengers, he guessed, for tomorrow's Atlantic crossing, although there were some tables filled exclusively by ladies sipping tea and busily talking to one another.

'John, old chap.'

He had been so engrossed that he hadn't seen Alfred, and as he stood up to shake his hand his friend drew the young woman at his side forward and announced, 'Polly, allow me to introduce to you my very good friend, John Pride. Pride, this is my sister, Lady Polly Howard.'

'Pooh, Alfie, you have scared poor Mr Pride half to death by being so formal! Since I am going to be living in America for a while, Mr Pride, where everyone is of equal status and there are thank goodness no archaic stuffy titles, I intend to be known simply as Polly Howard, and that is what you shall call me.'

John smiled as she shook his hand but knew he would do no such thing.

He had thought Hettie's dress was shockingly short, but Lady Polly's was even shorter, a narrow tube of emerald green satin, sashed in black, which showed off her narrow boyish figure.

'Polly, I know you have some letters to write so we will not keep you.'

'Oh pooh, I know you are just saying that because you want to be rid of me, Alfie. Well, you shall not be. I intend to sit here and order a delicious afternoon tea and enjoy myself. But you need not worry I shall eavesdrop on your conversation with Mr Pride.'

'My sister is one of these very stubborn and modern young women, I'm afraid, John.'

She laughed as she opened her bag and removed a long cigarette holder into which she fitted a cigarette whilst John tried not to look shocked. 'Alfie, do be a dear and light this for me. Do you think I am very fast and shocking for smoking, Mr Pride? I assure you that my dear darling brother does. He thinks it dreadful that his sister is so modern and daring. Do you have a sister, Mr Pride?'

'I have two.'

'Oh, what fun! And are they modern?'

'Polly, you ask far too many questions. I apologise for her, John. I am afraid she has been dreadfully spoiled.'

'And whose fault is that? If I had been allowed to go up to Girton as I wished, instead of being forced to stay at home, then I would not have nanny to pet me, would I, and then I would have become a bluestocking. Do you dance, Mr Pride?'

She was like quicksilver, John thought, mercurial and dizzying, not to mention droll, with her carmined lips and short bobbed hair.

'John is far too busy to waste time on dancing.'

'Alfie, how can you say such a thing? No one should be too busy to dance. What do you do then, Mr Pride, that makes you too busy to dance?'

'He teaches fortunate fellows to fly,' Alfie said before John could even open his mouth to answer.

'You do? Oh how whizzy . . . Could you teach me? I would love to fly. It must be so much fun. Wait! I have the most terrific idea. Why don't you teach me to fly and I shall teach you to dance?'

'You are leaving for New York tomorrow,' Alfred reminded her.

Immediately she pouted. 'Oh, but maybe not. Maybe I shall change my mind.'

'I apologise for my sister, John,' Alfred said later when Polly had finally been persuaded to leave them alone.

'There's no need.' John couldn't help smiling. Lady Polly had been fun and he had enjoyed her company.

'Now tell me more about this flying school of yours. You will have more eager pupils than you can take, no doubt.'

John shook his head. 'Not at the moment. Business is slow and with the Depression . . .'

'Indeed, a nasty business and not likely to get much better very quickly, I'm afraid. So, if you are not getting as many pupils as you would like, maybe you would care to think about joining my own little venture?'

John frowned. 'I thought you weren't flying any more?'

'I'm not, but I've been asked to take over a local flying club. It's on our land, after all, and we need a new instructor, someone modern who knows what's what. I thought immediately of you.'

'I don't know what to say,' John told him truthfully.

'Then don't say anything right now, but promise me you will think about it. We've got a good bunch of chaps at the club, and plenty of young blood coming in eager to learn. I'm going to look at a new flying machine next week. She's a beauty. Tiger Moth.'

John listened enviously as Alfred extolled the

virtues of the new machine, and then frowned as he suddenly broke off and exclaimed admiringly, 'Oh I say!'

Whilst they had been talking a short, over-weight, middle-aged man dressed formally in tails had seated himself at the piano, with a stunningly pretty blonde-haired young woman standing next to it, obviously about to sing.

Alfred raised his monocle in order to study her more closely.

John felt the return of his earlier anger and misery. The girl wasn't Hettie but she might just as well have been. Her dress was even shorter than the one Hettie had been wearing, showing a provocative amount of slender calf, and even from this distance John could see that she was heavily made-up, whilst her short hair was crimped into head hugging waves.

'What a corking looking girl. And a bit of a goer by the looks of it. Pity I've got Polly on my hands otherwise I might have been tempted to ask her to join me for dinner, although I dare say a girl like that has plenty of admirers already.'

The young woman was looking towards them and when, a few seconds later, she started to sing, she made sure that it was in the direction of their table that she turned the most.

When she had finished, Alfred clapped enthu-siastically and the singer smiled and inclined her head, and John knew that he was witnessing a transaction as old as Eve herself.

And this was the life Hettie had chosen for herself. He had thought he knew her but now, John decided bitterly, he realised he had never known her properly at all.

SIX

Hettie stared uneasily around the room to which she had just been shown. A long, narrow attic room with a row of equally narrow beds, each separated by a small cupboard. There were threadbare rag rugs on the dusty wooden floor, and equally threadbare covers on the beds. Her trunk, which had been carried up the stairs by two disgruntled and sweating men with dirty hands and clothes, called in from the street by her landlady, was on the floor at the bottom of the bed furthest from both the door and the window and thus from any fresh air. Already the heat of the autumn sun and the low ceiling had made the room uncomfortably warm, its air clogging the back of Hettie's throat. Or was that her tears?

This was not the pretty, well-furnished room she and Mam had been shown when they had visited before, but when she had tried to say as much to Mrs Buchanan's sister, the landlady had simply told her sharply, 'Them rooms are three times what you are paying, miss, so if you've any complaints to make then make them to yer ma.'

Hettie had tried to stand her ground, remembering that Mrs Buchanan had told her mother that her 'keep' would be deducted from her wage and that what was left would be handed over to her in spending money. But when she had mentioned this, the landlady had given her a contemptuous look and announced, 'Your mother must have misunderstood. Only those who can afford it get to sleep in my best rooms and they are always top artists, not little nobodies like you.'

Hettie's stubborn streak had reared itself and she had wanted to stand her ground, but the landlady had simply not given her the opportunity to do so and now she was up here in this dreadful, dingy dormitory of an attic room.

The sound of several sets of footsteps on the stairs and female voices made her turn round and face the door as it was thrust open and half a dozen or more laughing, chattering young women came rushing in, only to stop and stare in silence at Hettie.

'So 'oo might you be, then?' the tallest and, Hettie guessed, the oldest of them demanded, her hands on her hips as she surveyed Hettie.

'Hettie Walker,' Hettie introduced herself hesitantly.

'Leave off, Lizzie,' one of the other girls

protested. 'You're half scaring the poor little thing to death. Tek no notice of Lizzie, Hettie, she's allus like this when she starts on her monthlies.'

'Oh, and you ain't, I suppose, Sukey Simmons?' Lizzie turned away from Hettie to demand sarcastically, before adding, 'Lor, but I 'ate bloody Monday matinees. Why the hell does management do them, it's not as though anyone comes in, especially now there's a Depression going on.'

'P'raps you should tell 'em that they don't know how to run their own business, Lizzie,' another girl called out, laughing.

'Oh aye, and lose me job. No thanks,' Lizzie retorted, but she was smiling, Hettie noticed, and she relaxed slightly.

'So what show are you in then, 'Ettie?' Lizzie asked. 'I know they were looking for a couple more chorus girls for the show at the Empire, and no wonder, since 'e pays even less than that bloody so and so we work for. But you don't look tall enough for a chorus girl.'

'I'm going to be singing at the Adelphi,' Hettie explained shyly, trying not to look shocked by the girl's coarse language. 'During the afternoon, accompanied by Mr Buchanan.'

'Wot, that old . . .' Lizzie began scornfully, only to stop when Sukey gave her a quick dig with her elbow.

'So you're a singer, then?' Sukey asked.

'Yes.'

'Where have you appeared before?' another one

of the girls asked as they all began to move around the room, some of them going over to fling themselves on their beds, others sitting down on them and bending to massage their weary feet.

'Nowhere,' Hettie admitted.

'First time away from home, is it?' Sukey asked her sympathetically.

Hettie nodded, relieved to see that it was Sukey who had the bed next to her own and not Lizzie.

'Well, mind you don't let Ma Buchanan cheat you,' Sukey warned. 'If she's anything like 'er sister, she'all be as tight as a duck's arse. What's Ma Marshall charging you here for your bed, by the way?'

Hettie shook her head. 'I don't now. Mrs Buchanan said that she would deduct all my expenses from my wage and that I could have the rest. I think there's been a bit of a misunderstanding, though, because I thought I was going to have a room to myself.'

A couple of the girls started to laugh, although not unkindly.

'Pulled that old one on yer, did she kid?' Lizzie chuckled. 'I suppose old misery guts Marshall showed yer ma one of her best rooms and let 'er think you'd be 'aving one o' them instead of kipping in here with us?'

Hettie nodded, embarrassed.

'Yer should have asked to have all yer wages handed over to yer and then divvied them out to pay for yer room. And mind that yer don't leave nothing valuable lying around in here, or she'll have that off yer as well.'

'But surely if you complained . . .' Hettie began, shocked.

'Complain? To her? She'd have anyone who tried out on the street, and bad mouth them as well so as they'd never get digs anywhere else in town, and then what'ud happen – they'd be out of work, that's wot!'

As Hettie listened to this impassioned speech she acknowledged that, appalled as she was by her landlady's deceit, if she were to inform her parents of it they would insist on her returning home immediately. Upset and intimidated though she had felt by the landlady's manner towards her, and the other revelations from the other girls, she couldn't bear to lose the job she had wanted so badly for years.

'There's a lad down at the ironmongers who's a bit sweet on Aggie, he'll put yer a padlock on yer trunk for yer if she asks him nice enough.'

A tall, blonde-haired girl who had been examining her feet straightened up and screwed up her face. 'Well, you'll have to come with me, I ain't going to be left on me own with 'im. Nasty clammy hands he's got!'

'Aw, listen to it. Bet they ain't anywhere near as clammy as old Basher's. Calls himself an impressario. A dirty old man, more like. You should 'ave seen them costumes he wanted us to wear for that bloody revue in Blackpool, d'yer remember, Lizzie?' another girl chipped in.

''Ow could I forget, Babs, mine felt like it were cutting me in two,' Lizzie answered whilst Hettie looked on perplexed when they all burst out laughing.

'Gawd, my feet,' Babs complained. 'But that's what you get for being a chorus girl – corns and blisters.'

'Are you all in the same chorus?' Hettie asked her a little timidly. These girls were nothing like any of the girls she knew back in Preston. Their language, for one thing, and their loud confidence. But nevertheless, she liked them, she decided.

'At the moment there's a big panto coming off at the Royal Court Palace, and there's two hundred girls in the chorus, plus the understudies. We've bin rehearsing for the last six weeks, plus doing our ordinary shows as well – six nights and six matinees. It's damn near killin' me. So what do yer sing, then, Hettie?' Babs asked.

'Soprano,' Hettie replied automatically.

'Oh, soprano is it,' Lizzie mocked, putting on an exaggeratedly posh accent.

'Oh leave off, Lizzie, give the poor kid a break,' Babs told her, giving Hettie a friendly smile.

'Don't mind Lizzie. Her tongue's sharper than her wit sometimes. No, I meant what sort of songs do you sing. You know, what's your repertoire?'

'I don't know. I haven't got one,' Hettie admitted.

'Well, you should have,' Babs reproved her. 'And with them dark looks of yours being all the rage right now, you want to cash in on them and get yourself a repertoire that will get you some decent parts. Lor, but I'm hungry,' she moaned, changing the subject and taking the spotlight off Hettie, for which she was very grateful. 'Anyone else want to go out and get some supper?' she called out.

'Go out for supper?' Hettie repeated, concerned. 'But I thought that all our meals were included in the rent?'

'Did you hear that, girls?' Lizzie called out, shaking her head and laughing mirthlessly. 'The only supper you'll get here is a bit o' mouldy bread and some soup wot looks as though Misery Guts peed in it.'

Hettie made sure she joined in the others' laughter as though such coarse talk was as familiar to her as it obviously was to them.

'You don't 'ave to come with us if you don't want,' Babs told her. 'I'll bring you back a nice bit o'sommat if you want – not fish, though, cos if Misery Guts smells it she'll be wanting more rent off all of us – it's extra if you bring in your own grub. Still, at least 'ere's clean, not like some of the digs you can get. Lor, but I were scratching for months after one place where I stayed, covered in bites I were and me hair full o'nits.'

When Hettie shuddered, Babs laughed and

shook her head. 'My, but you're a green un, aren't you? Never mind, we'll tek care of you and you'll soon find yer feet. Just don't let Ma Buchanan boss yer around. Dance do yer as well as sing?'

'A little,' Hettie agreed.

'That's good,' she approved, getting up off her bed.

Lizzie called out impatiently, "Ere Babs, are you coming wi' us or what?'

'Give us a minute,' she called back before coaxing Hettie, 'Go on, come wi' us. A bit o' fresh air will do you good.'

Uncomfortably aware that both her parents and John would have been shocked by and disapproving of Babs and the others, Hettie gave in to the hunger in her stomach. Besides, if this was to be her home for the foreseeable future, she would have to try and fit in.

The street might have been quiet when they all spilled out on to it, but its silence was quickly shattered by the laughter and chatter of the girls. Despite their aching feet, two of them suddenly took hold of one another and danced along, performing a high-stepping routine that caused two men on the opposite side of the street to stop and stare.

'Ere, Lizzie, go over and tell those two gawpers over there that that's two shilling and sixpence worth they've just had.'

'Mary, you're out of time and you missed a

step,' another criticised, causing the dancing pair to stop as one of them – Mary, Hettie assumed – turned on her critic.

'Sez who?' she demanded. 'You couldn't keep time even if it was beaten into yer. That's why yer at the back of the line and I'm at the front!'

'Who does she think she's kidding?' Hettie heard someone else mutter. 'The only reason she's still in the bloody chorus at all is because she's been keeping old Charlie sweet.'

Fifteen minutes later, squashed up on the narrow wooden bench seats in the snug between Babs and Lizzie, a plate of appetising beef and dumpling stew on the table in front of her, Hettie felt a world away from the person she had been this morning. Her eyes widened as she saw the relish with which the other girls were drinking the port wine they had also ordered.

'Try it,' Babs urged her.

Unwilling to be mocked yet again by sharp-eyed Lizzie, Hettie dutifully sipped at the liquid Babs had poured into her empty glass, and then fought not to show how sour and unpleasant she found it, valiantly emptying her glass.

It was shortly after that she became aware of how very tired she was, and now her eyes were starting to close as her head dropped toward Babs's shoulder.

'Look at 'er, Babs,' whispered one of the others. 'Poor little kid. What a bloody shame.'

After studying Hettie's sleeping profile Babs

sighed and said determinedly, 'Come on, we'd better get her back.'

'Lor, Babs, we ain't bloody nursemaids,' Lizzie protested, but even her expression softened a little as she looked down at Hettie, sleeping peacefully as if she didn't have a care in the world.

SEVEN

It was almost two weeks since Hettie had moved into the boarding house, and in that time she had learned that, behind her sharp manner, Lizzie hid the kindest of hearts, and that she had not just herself to support but her mother and a sick sister as well; that Babs with her easy going nature was the one who always calmed the others if trouble threatened to erupt; that quiet, blonde Aggie was nursing a broken heart having fallen in love with a theatre manager who was married; that shrewd Mary wasn't averse to leading on any man if she thought it would benefit her; and that the twins Jenny and Jess were the naughty girls of the troup, continually playing practical jokes on everyone and getting up to all manner of japes.

She was now as familiar with the girls' dance routine and songs as they were themselves, and Babs had taught her all the steps of the modern new dances, including the tango, claiming that she would need to know them just in case, as she had put it, 'some young spark teks it into 'is head to dance with yer one afternoon. I mean, yer wouldn't want ter make a fool of yerself by not knowing all the newest steps, would yer?'

'No one would do that,' she had protested, half shocked, half giggling at the thought of whirling around the Adelphi.

'You'ud be surprised what these young blades will do,' Babs had warned her darkly.

But she had not mentioned any of this either on her visit to Connie or in her letters home. Neither had she mentioned the lack of her own bedroom, or the poor food, or the fact that Mrs Buchanan was nowhere near as good or thorough a teacher as Miss Brown, for all the airs she had put on for Ellie's benefit, and moreover that she frequently cut Hettie's lessons short so that she could fit in another pupil.

It was not that she wanted to deceive her family, she assured herself; it was simply that she didn't want to worry them. Nor had she spoken of the camaraderie that existed between the girls, or what fun they were to be with. Mam and Da were a bit old-fashioned about some things and Hettie thought they might not see beneath the girls' stage paint and ripe language to the good-heartedness that lay beneath them.

''Ow did the lesson go today?' Babs asked her over an illicit cup of tea made in their attic room, dunking a Rich Tea biscuit into the hot liquid before demanding, 'is she still making yer do them scales?'

'She didn't today. She said that I'm to go to the Adelphi tomorrow morning and practise there with Mr Buchanan, because the singer I'm to replace has decided to leave sooner than she originally said. Next week I am to make my debut.' She gave a small shiver of nervous excitement. 'I do hope that Mam and Da will be able to come over from Preston to hear me.'

'And 'ow are they goin' to do that, then?' Lizzie demanded. 'Cos them bloody waiters turn their noses up at the likes o' us.'

'My parents are very respectable,' Hettie protested, pink cheeked, wanting to defend them without offending Lizzie.

'I ain't saying they ain't, but there's a difference between being respectable and being a toff,' Lizzie pointed out. 'And yer ma and pa will need pretty deep pockets if'n they're to sit at one o' them tea tables.'

'Stop upsettin' her, Lizzie,' Babs ordered. 'Don't you worry, 'Ettie, if your folks can't make it then 'appen some of us u'll manage to be there. Even if we 'ave to find some way to persuad one o' them snotty waiters, eh Mary?'

Hettie smiled, but inwardly she wasn't sure it would be a good idea for her new friends to be there at her debut. However, since she didn't want to hurt their feelings, she enquired instead, 'What about your corn, Babs, is it any better?'

'No, it's them damned shoes, but if I tell old Basher I need a bigger pair, he'll give me the 'eave.'

'What? Surely not?' Hettie protested, indignant on her friend's behalf.

''E gets a good deal because he buys all the same size shoes for us,' Babs told her matter of factly. 'If'n they don't fit, you're out, so we have to pretend they do even if they don't.'

'But anyway, if yer at a loose end, why don't you come down to the theatre with us and watch us rehearsin'? It'ud be a sight more fun for you than sitting here on yer own.'

'Could I?' Hettie asked her enthusiastically.

'Of course, we can allus smuggle yer in, like, if we have to.'

Hettie could hardly wait to see the girls at work, and a proper stage show being rehearsed. Maybe she would even be able to sing on a stage one day!

EIGHT

'I am to have my first proper rehearsal at the Adelphi tomorrow and I am to sing there on Thursday afternoon,' Hettie told Connie excitedly after church on Sunday, as she helped her with the little ones whilst they walked back to the house.

'It all sounds very exciting,' Connie agreed.

'I have written home to tell Mam. Oh, I do hope they will be able to be there.' Hettie's face clouded slightly. She bet someone wouldn't be coming, and that someone was John. She hadn't heard from him since their argument and she wondered if they would ever go back to being the close friends they had always been.

'I am sure they will be. I am certainly looking forward to it. I think the last time I went to the Adelphi was when cousin Cecily took us there. You can be sure she will want to come and hear you as well, Hettie, and I dare say she will bring her mama-in-law along too, so you will have some sturdy support from your family for your debut.'

'I think that will make me even more nervous.' Hettie laughed, and then said uncertainly, unable to shake him from her thoughts, 'Is John still angry with me, do you know? I know that he doesn't approve of what I'm doing, but I would so much like him to be there.'

Connie gave her a swift hug. 'And so he shall be. I shall be with him myself. And as for him not approving, I dare say it just gave him a bit of a shock to see you looking so grown up. Men can be the oddest of creatures at times.'

Connie herself had enjoyed the fun she had had as a girl training to be a nurse, and she could see how much Hettie was enjoying her new independent life and the different friends she had made. She had blossomed in less than a month and had a new kind of worldliness about her.

'I just hope that Mam will be well enough to come,' Hettie continued. 'When I telephoned yesterday, Mrs Jennings said that she was in bed and feeling sickly.'

'Yes, the unseasonable heat has been pulling her down a little,' Connie replied hastily. Ellie had said specifically that she did not wish to make it widely known yet that there was to be a new baby. Thankfully, though, she was no longer worrying so much about her own health or that of the coming baby.

Later in the day Connie watched indulgently whilst Hettie tucked hungrily into her dinner. All this singing was obviously giving her a good appetite. She was happily unaware that her Sunday dinners were the culinary highlight of Hettie's week because the meagre amount of 'pocket money' she received from Mrs Buchanan was barely enough to buy her one decent meal a day.

'You are enjoying that Madeira cake, Hettie, would you care to take a couple of slices with you to share with your friends?' Connie invited her.

'Oh yes, please,' Hettie accepted, unblushingly allowing Connie to parcel up the whole lot for her, knowing that she herself would be the one to eat the lion's share of it. Then she felt guilty at not sharing with Connie what life was really like at Ma Marshall's. But as Babs had told her wryly, 'sometimes it's best not to let folks at 'ome know just how things are, 'Ettie. Saves 'em worrying then, like.'

'My husband will be waiting for you at the Adelphi, Miss Walker. You will enter the hotel via the staff entrance at the rear of the hotel and not the main entrance – that is reserved for hotel guests. Once you are inside you will ask for the housekeeper and she will see to it that you are escorted to the room Mr Buchanan uses for practice. It would not do at all for the Adelphi's guests have their ears subjected to the noise of scales in the main salons.

'You will present yourself at the hotel every morning this week at 10.00 a.m. and you will remain there until Mr Buchanan says that you may leave. Then, provided that he is satisfied with you, on Thursday you will bring with you your stage dress ready for the afternoon's musical entertainment. Do you understand all of that?'

'Yes, Mrs Buchanan,' Hettie confirmed obediently. She could hardly believe the wait was nearly over!

'Gideon – we don't often see you up here,' John greeted his brother-in-law warmly as Gideon stepped out of his car.

'Aye, well if you will choose to make a living in such an outlandish way,' Gideon joked, automatically ducking as one of John's students took off, the wings of his flying machine wiggling alarmingly.

'Ellie sent me up with a message for you.'

'Ellie? Is she . . .' John began anxiously.

'She's fine,' Gideon assured him immediately. 'It's Hettie I'm here about. She's to have her debut performance at the Adelphi this Thursday and she's said special like that she wants you to be there. Seems she took what you said to her about her frock to heart.'

'I can't pretend I'm happy about what she's doing,' John replied. 'Or the kind of life she'll be exposing herself to . . .'

'Aye, well you'd best blame me for that, John. My thinking is that the lass will soon tire of it and want to come home. Having Connie run off like she did was that upsetting for Ellie I didn't want to risk it happening again. And Hettie can be head-strong just like all the other Pride women.'

Reluctantly John allowed himself to smile. Both his sisters *were* headstrong in their own individual way, and perhaps it was unfair of him to expect Hettie to be any less determined than her adopted mother and aunt.

'Well, that's as mebbe, Gideon, but it's my belief that the stage is no place for a decent woman.'

'Aye, but the difference is that Hettie is a singer not an actress. The lass has to have her chance, John. That's only fair. I've seen what happens when a person is denied the right to make their own free choice,' he added heavily, and John knew he was thinking of the way their own mother had forced Ellie to part from Gideon so many years ago and the unhappiness that had caused them both.

'How's business?' Gideon asked him, changing the subject.

'Not as good as I'd like.'

'Having so many men out of work is hurting us all. I'm getting closer to having to lay men off meself, but Ellie is adamant that we'll cut back at home before she'll see a working man laid off and his wife and children going hungry. Fortunately, I've got a bit put by and even if I have to cut the rents on the properties we should be able to pull through. There's many a business as won't, though. They're saying already that Liverpool has been hit very badly. There's no shipping to speak of, the docks are lying empty and there's not much of any other kind of work either. It's a bad business and no mistake, and the politicians don't seem to be doing anything about it.'

'There's a lot of men asking if they survived the war only to be left to starve to death,' John agreed sombrely.

'Anyway, lad.' Gideon returned swiftly to his real reason for being there. 'You'll be there for Hettie's debut, won't you? Only your Ellie will give me a real telling off if you aren't.'

John laughed. 'Yes I'll be there,' he promised, even if the thought of seeing Hettie again, and in such a way, caused his heart to skip a beat.

It was hard for Hettie not to feel both nervous and excited as she hurried across Lime Street towards the Adelphi hotel, skirting the imposing main entrance and going instead to the staff entrance, where she found a group of chambermaids complaining about the meanness of the guests whose rooms they had just been cleaning.

'Not so much as a farthing, they give us, and 'er dripping in diamonds and furs.'

'Just as well then that you helped yourself to her fancy perfume, eh Nancy?' Hettie heard one of them joke as she squeezed past them.

''Ere, where do you think you're going?' A fat bald uniformed doorman stopped her.

'I'm here to see the housekeeper, Mrs Nevis. I'm the new singer for afternoon tea,' Hettie explained.

'Well, next time make sure you have a number so as we can sign yer in,' he warned her before giving her directions for the housekeeper's room.

Mrs Nevis told her that she was far too busy to bother herself with her and gave Hettie directions for the room where she would find Mr Buchanan.

These proved to be so complicated that Hettie had begun to fear she must have misunderstood them as she trudged up endless flights of stairs and along equally endless corridors before finally coming to an open door through which she could hear music being played.

Having knocked and received no response, she walked hesitantly through the door and into the room. Immediately, the pianist stopped playing and looked at her.

'Mr Buchanan?' Hettie asked him shyly.

'Yes indeed, and you must be the delightful new protégée whose company I am to have the pleasure of.'

He was nothing like she had imagined, being small and rotund with black hair as shiny as patent leather pulled in strands across his bald head. But at least he was much jollier and kinder than his wife, Hettie acknowledged with relief.

'Well, my dear wife has excelled herself – you are indeed a pretty child. The ladies will all envy you and their husbands will insist that their wives are to take tea here every day so they can join them and secretly admire you. I hope, my dear, that you have a gown that will do more for that pretty face than the clothes you are currently wearing, eh?' he asked jovially, pinching Hettie's cheek. 'A gentleman likes nothing more than to be able to admire a neat ankle and a delicate shoulder.

'And a word to the wise. When you sing, it is towards the ladies you must look, but making sure when you do that the gentlemen can also see you at your best advantage. Maisie knew to a nicety how it should be done, but unfortunately she has grown above herself and must go. So, my beloved helpmate has been making you practise your scales, I hope, and now today you will sing them for me.'

Obediently Hettie took off her jacket and turned to face him.

'No, no.' Immediately, and to Hettie's shock, he placed his hands on her body, one on her arm and the other on her waist, holding her so tightly she could feel their hot clamminess through her clothes.

'You must stand by the piano like so,' he told her, manipulating her so that she was turned away from the instrument and with her back to it. 'You are to sing to the ladies, and not to me. However, if you were to be asked to sing in the *evening* then you would stand close to my shoulder and perhaps even lean forwards to turn my music for me. But then an evening audience is a very different thing and mostly for the gentlemen guests. Now, shall we try again?'

*   *   *

It was four o'clock before Mr Buchanan declared himself satisfied enough with her progress to dismiss her for the day, by which time Hettie was starving, since they had not stopped for any lunch.

Rather than go back to the boarding house she decided that, since it was virtually only across the road, she might as well go to the Royal Court and walk back with the other girls as their matinee performance would now have finished.

Frankie the doorman knew her by now and grinned as he let her in through the stage door. 'They've just come orf,' he told her.

Squeezing past him, Hettie made her way back stage to the large communal dressing room shared by the chorus.

''Ere 'Ettie, come over 'ere and tell us 'ow you've gorn on,' Lizzie called out when she saw her.

Eagerly Hettie made her way through the busy room filled with chorus girls, no longer embarrassed as she would once have been by their various states of undress.

A mirror ran the length of one whole wall of the long rectangular room, with an equally long 'dressing table' top beneath it. Each girl was supposed to have her own small section of this table and her own chair, just as each girl was also supposed to have to herself one of the lockers on the opposite wall, and a coat hook. But as Babs had explained to Hettie, since there was never enough dressing table and mirror space or lockers, it was a case of first come first served, and frequent arguments and fights broke out amongst the girls over who owned what.

From one of the shorter walls, a door opened into the domain of the wardrobe mistress, and what space there was left was filled with racks of costumes all jumbled together.

The air in the room smelled stalely of cheap scent and sweat, but despite that Hettie loved the atmosphere of the dressing room with its frantic bustle and sense of excitement and urgency.

''Ere, help me get out of these bloody feathers, will yer?' Lizzie puffed, tugging at her headdress and heaving a sigh of relief when it was finally removed.

'So what was 'e like then, 'Ettie?' Babs asked her.

'Well, he was . . .'

Suddenly the dressing room door burst open and a woman rushed in still in full costume and make-up.

'Oh gawd,' Sukey muttered. 'Now we're in for it.'

'Who is she?' Hettie whispered curiously, as immediately all the girls seemed to be very busy ignoring the newcomer.

'She's the bloomin' star, that's wot, and she's 'ere to mek trouble,' Sukey told her.

'Where is she, then?' The imperious contralto voice rang theatrically round the now silent room.

'Come on, you little sluts, no way are yer all deaf, even if yer dance like yer've never heard a tune in yer lives. Where's the little slut wot's bin making sheep's eyes at my man?'

'Just as well Maureen's already left otherwise Gertie'd rip her to pieces,' Babs muttered to Hettie.

'Gertie, my darling, what on earth are you doing in here?'

Hettie goggled as a tall, handsome, blond-haired man walked into the room, ignoring the chorus girls and approaching the infuriated contralto.

'You know bloody well what I'm doing,' the contralto howled. 'I'm looking for that little whore you've been seeing behind me back, that's what. Well, you won't be doing it no more, matey.'

Before he could move, she had picked up one of the heavy hand mirrors the girls used to check the back of their costumes and brought it down hard on a place no lady ever looked at on a gentleman. As he doubled up in pain Babs whispered, 'Gawd, she's cracked 'im one right in the Kaisers,' sounding more impressed than shocked. 'Bloody 'ell that will put an end to his messing about.'

'If you touch that little tart again, I'm cutting it right . . .'

As they both left the dressing room still arguing, Hettie looked at Babs and asked her curiously, 'What was all that about?'

'Well, she's the star of the show, see, and 'e's one of the angels.'

'What's an angel?' Hettie interrupted.

Lizzie, who had been listening, sighed and

explained, 'An angel is wot we calls someone wot puts up the money to put on a show. Bertie has a bankful of money he got for marrying his wife.'

'He's married but . . .'

'Gawd, but you're a know-nothing, ain't yer, Miss Innocent. Of course he's married. They allus are. But that don't stop any of them messing about, like. Of course, the moment Gertie clapped eyes on him she'd got her mind set on 'im and 'oo can blame her? It's part of tradition, see, that the leading lady gets her choice of the men, and 'eaven help any hoofer wot steps out of line on to her territory. Mind you, it's past time Gertie retired, and if you want my opinion it's because she's so old that he's bin messin' around with Maureen behind Gertie's back.'

'She didn't look very old,' Hettie had to protest. She had looked very glamorous with her rouged cheeks, cherry red lips, and her short skirt revealing her legs.

'That's on account of all the greasepaint. You oughta see 'er close up. More lines on her face than a tram station, she's got. Anyway it was when we wus doing *Cinderella* a couple of seasons back that Bertie first come on the scene. Madam there was swarming all over 'im right from the start, and of course it weren't too long before 'e got the message and the two of 'em became an item, like. But now he's getting fed up wi' her and he's got a bit of an eye for our Maureen who better watch out because that thump she gave him in the balls is nothing to what Gertie's likely to do to her. Gawd, she left the girl who made eyes at her last fella wi' a right nasty scar on her face. Threw acid at her, so I 'eard.'

Hettie gasped with shock.

'There, don't look so scared, young un,' Lizzie comforted her. 'She won't do owt to 'arm you, why should she? So, what did you think of 'im, then, Ma Buchanan's 'usband?'

'He was kind and very jolly, not like I expected at all,' Hettie told her innocently.

'Was he now. Well, you just look out for men wot is kind to yer, cos like as not they'll want sommat from yer, if yer knows what I mean,' Lizzie warned her darkly.

Half an hour later, they all trooped out into the autumn sunshine, laughing and joking as they hurried to the chop house a short walk away from the theatre. The owner of the chop house gave them a good reduction off his normal prices on the understanding that they came in to eat earlier than the other customers, and brought their gentleman admirers in whenever they were asked out to dinner by them.

Hettie was hungry and she breathed in the warm, roasting-meat scented air appreciatively as she slid into one of the banquettes.

''Ere comes your admirer.' Sukey nudged her when the owner's young son suddenly appeared at their table.

He was still at school, and only just beginning

to shave, but he had still Brilliantined his hair and he blushed bright red as he looked at Hettie. ''Ave the steak pie,' he advised her in a mutter. 'Me Da has 'ad the chops in for so long they're about to get up and walk out of their own accord.'

'Yes, we'll all have a bit o' it, young Max, and make sure we gets plenty of gravy and 'taters wi' it,' Lizzie told him firmly. 'And yer can stop gawking at our 'Ettie as well, otherwise yer ears will be getting a rare boxing. Cheek of it!'

They all laughed, including Hettie, but the truth was that she was grateful to her new friends for their protection of her, not from Max, of course, but from everything that was so new and alien to her. She didn't know what she would have done without them.

'I'll be right glad when that red-headed lad is gone,' Jim told John grimly as they stood watching the group of young men sauntering across the airstrip in the direction of their accommodation. 'You can't tell him anything. He thinks he knows it all, and he's beginning to get the others thinking the same way. It's not even as though he's going to make a good flyer. Too much of a risk taker by half, he is. I caught him trying to get into the hangar this morning when his lesson wasn't until after dinner.'

John frowned. 'Did he say what he was doing there?'

'Aye, sommat about having left his helmet in

there, but I'd been in there working meself and there was no helmet there.'

'Would you prefer me to take him up for the rest of his lessons?' John offered. Normally they split the students into two and then kept them in those groups so that they could monitor their progress individually.

'Nah. I've made sure he knows I'm on to him, and I gave him a bit of dressing down in front of the others this afternoon, told him that the only way he'd ever be good enough to loop the loop would be with a toy flying machine. By the way, did you manage to get the photographs you wanted?'

John had spent most of the day photographing the North West coastline for a government department whilst one of his previous students had come over for the day to fly the machine for him. The Ministry paid well and promptly, and he certainly needed the money.

He had read in the papers that a certain type of wealthy young rip was now making flying lessons extremely fashionable, and that flying clubs were springing up all over the country to cater for their new passion. These wealthy young socialites apparently liked nothing better than to drive up to their flying club in their expensive motors, and then take to the skies to show off their skills to their admiring friends and 'popsies', as the article had referred to their lady friends. He suppose he shouldn't have been surprised after what Alfie had said about his new venture when they had met up at the Adelphi, the same weekend as his quarrel with Hettie. He may not have seen Hettie since, John admitted, but that did not mean he hadn't been thinking about her – and worrying about her, too.

Them as who had written that article ought to come up to Lancashire and see how real people lived. But of course the likes of the young toffs the article had referred to did not have to concern themselves with the problem of the country's two million unemployed, John acknowledged bitterly. He had never thought of himself as an activist of any kind, but he had seen at first hand what poverty did to people. As a lad growing up under the roof of a father who was a butcher, his belly had always been full; but after their mother's death, with the four of them – Ellie, Connie, baby Philip and himself – shared out amongst his mother's sisters to be brought up by them, he had come to discover what hardship was.

You only had to go to Liverpool's once proud docks and look into the pinched bitter faces of its working men to know the true state of the country, John reflected. The country was in a sorry way and his business with it. Tomorrow, instead of dressing himself up in the cast-off suit of Gideon's that Ellie had sent up for him and sitting watching Hettie sing, he should by rights have been working on his figures and thinking of ways to bring in some much needed extra money. His flying machines were sound enough but getting old. He thought enviously of the new machines Alfred had told him he was ordering for his own club. The science of building flying machines was changing almost by the day. Only weeks ago the Americans had stunned the world by announcing that they had used flying machines to drop bombs on a captured German boat.

If the unthinkable happened and there should be another war, would his beloved flying machines be used to rain death down out of the skies? If so, John prayed he would not be there to witness it.

NINE

Having refused Connie's suggestion that she come to her house to prepare for her debut, and that Connie and Harry escort her to the Adelphi, Hettie was now wishing she had agreed and was longing for the support of those closest to her as she stood in her shift and gazed anxiously at her red gown.

''Ee tha looks that pale, 'Ettie. Not getting nervous, are yer?' one of the girls asked her sympathetically.

'Only a little,' Hettie fibbed.

'Everyone gets stage-fright, Hettie,' Babs comforted her. 'But yer family are going to be there, didn't yer say?'

'Yes. Mam and Da, and Aunt Connie, and Mam's cousin Cecily. And John has promised to be there as well,' Hettie added.

'John? So 'oo's this John, then?' Babs teased.

'He's Mam's younger brother,' Hetie explained.

'So 'e's yer uncle, then?'

Hettie shook her head. 'No, because Mam is

my step-mother – I'm adopted, you see. John and I are the best of friends, thick as thieves – or we used to be anyway,' Hettie trailed off.

'Oh ho, I see now, and yer sweet on this 'ere John, are yer?'

'No,' Hettie denied, but she still couldn't help blushing as Babs laughed at her.

'Oh yes you are, I can tell. Tell us all about him then, 'Ettie. Good looking, is he?' Mary demanded.

'Yes,' Hettie admitted honestly. 'But it isn't like that, Mary.'

'No, of course it ain't, and I'm a monkey's uncle.' She laughed and winked. 'I wish we wasn't doing a matinee and then we could come along and get a look at this 'ere John of yours.'

Hettie bit her lip, uncomfortably aware that she was actually relieved the girls would not be there. She loved them dearly and they were terrific fun, but somehow she suspected Ellie would not see them in the same light as she did.

'Who are you kidding, Mary?' Lizzie challenged her. 'No way would they let the likes of us in the Adelphi for afternoon tea.'

'Why not? My money's as good as the next person's, I'll thank you to know,' Mary responded pertly in a mock posh voice, tossing her hair as she did so.

'Come on, let's get Hettie into her frock and get a bit of rouge on her face to liven her up a bit,' Babs broke in.

Hettie held her breath as Babs took control.

'Ooh. Yer look a real treat,' Babs breathed approvingly. 'Doesn't she, girls?'

'Aye, a real treat for some masher, who will want ter gobble her up whilst his wife's sipping her tea,' one wit chirped up, making the others laugh and Hettie blush nervously. She felt uncomfortable at the constant talk of men leering at women and especially at her. Maybe at the Royal Court but she couldn't imagine such a thing happening at the Adelphi.

'You watch out for them posh chaps, Hettie. They'll only be after one thing, mind, no matter what they tells yer. And then before yer know it you've got a swelling belly and no wedding ring.'

'Leave off, Mavis, that's enough of that vulgar talk,' Lizzie scolded. 'Hettie isn't like that . . .'

'Mebbe *she* ain't, but show me a fella who ain't and I'll show yer an Ethel,' Mavis, one of the other girls Hettie hadn't spoken to much so far, chortled.

'What's an Ethel?' Hettie asked Lizzie in bewilderment.

'Oh now see what yer've done, Mavis,' Lizzie complained.

'It ain't my fault if the kid's too green to know what's what.' Mavis shrugged.

'Well, I suppose it u'll have to be me who has to tell her then.' Lizzie sighed. 'An Ethel, 'Ettie, is what we calls a man who isn't a proper man, like.'

'Not a proper man?' Hettie was still confused.

'What Lizzie means is that an Ethel is a chap wot only does it with other men,' Mavis clarified, adding bluntly in case Hettie still hadn't grasped what she was trying to say: 'Instead of shoving it up a woman like other men, he wants to shove it up another chap's arse.'

Hettie's face went brick red with embarrassment and shocked disbelief. She knew in a vague sort of way what happened between married couples, although it had never been fully explained to her, but now Mavis's brutally frank explanation had shocked her on two counts.

''Ere, that's enough, Mavis. The poor kid doesn't need to know about that,' Babs told her, adding, 'Come on, 'Ettie, let's brush yer hair for yer, and put this flower in it'.

She had to say one thing for her chorus line friends: they were expert ladies' maids, Hettie admitted, as her hair was brushed and then rolled into sleek elegance and a pretty red silk flower pinned into it.

'All yer needs now is a touch of carmine on yer lips – yer don't need no blackin' on yer eyelashes like blondes do.'

Hettie wasn't sure she should be wearing the carmine either but she didn't want to offend kind hearted Babs by saying so. She could always rub it off before her family saw her, she consoled herself as her helpers finally decided she was ready for her debut.

* * *

John stepped out of the tin bath and reached for one of the cans of water he had filled earlier, leaning over the bath to sluice his head and torso with it before repeating the exercise for the lower half of his body whilst standing in the now tepid bath water itself.

The sunlight coming in through the cottage's small windows gleamed on flesh pulled taut against firm muscles, his arms and chest tanned brown from the hours he spent shirtless, working to ensure that the grass his sheep didn't crop was kept short enough for the flying machines to land on.

John was not a vain man – he had more important things to worry about than silly lasses – but Ellie was for ever sighing over him and telling him he was the image of their good-looking father, and John had seen the looks young women gave him.

He reached for a towel and started to dry himself. There wasn't a cloud in the sky and the thought of spending such a perfect flying day sitting togged up in a straitjacket of a suit, sipping tea, was not one that appealed to him. But Connie had told him how Hettie had begged her to ask him to go.

Luckily there were no flying lessons on today's schedule, the students instead receiving instruction from Jim on the maintenance of flying machines.

John dressed quickly, smoothing his hair

straight, and wondering if he would have time for a bite to eat when he got to the station. He had decided to cycle there rather than walk which meant he would have to fold up his suit jacket instead of wearing it.

He looked at his watch. Jim would have started his lecture, and rather than go and interrupt him John decided he would leave without saying good-bye to him.

He was half a mile from the station when he heard the familiar sound of the flying machine's engine. Frowning, he stopped pedalling and got off his bike to look up. Suddenly, with an awkward movement, the pilot took the machine into an amateurish and unsafe loop.

'Christ, you fool, you're too low; you're too bloody low, climb. Get back up. Get back up!'

John was screaming the words into the sky as he got back on his bike and started to cycle as fast as he could back to the airfield. The flying machine was floating in the sky belly up, the engine stuttering as the machine lost height while it slowly rolled over.

John prayed as he had never prayed in his life, even though he knew it was futile. The machine was so low that he could see the four helmeted heads in the cockpit.

'Ease back, ease back, give her a chance to get some air and then take her up, take her up . . . Oh God, Oh God,' he heard himself cry.

The engine coughed, and then the machine

surged forward, before the engine coughed again and then died, the sounds of its struggle followed by an eerie silence, and then a mighty bang.

John could see the plume of black smoke rising like a pall, but then there was a second horrific explosion, with flames and smoke shooting up into the sky.

Ahead of him lay the airfield. Where the flying machine hangar had been there was now merely flames and smoke.

Leaving his bike he ran towards the inferno. Jim was in there somewhere. Jim, his friend and partner. Jim, who had warned him that he feared their rebellious student would do something reckless. Jim, who he hadn't listened to, because he had had more important things on his mind. Jim, who was now being burned alive because of him . . .

John could hear the clang of the fire engine bell, and people were coming running from all directions; farm workers out of the fields; villagers who had seen and heard the explosion. He could feel strong hands dragging him back from the fire, whilst tears ran down his face.

He would bear the burden of the guilt of this day for ever.

Why had she ever thought she wanted to sing at the Adelphi? Hettie wondered nervously as she stood, trembling from head to foot, behind the screen that shielded the doorway to the staff stairs from the guests.

This morning Mr Buchanan had taken her down to the Hypostyle Hall – where she had gazed up in awe to where the four massive Ionic columns supported the ceiling, hardly able to take in the grandeur of her surroundings – so that she could practise her songs there and familiarise herself with the hall. She knew that after he had played a few introductory notes she was to walk in and go to stand in front of the piano, but to one side of it so as not to obstruct anyone's view of Mr Buchanan, and that he would then play a piece of Bach during which she was to turn and gaze admiringly at him until he had finished.

Then he would play the first of her songs and she was to remember that if there were any gentlemen seated at the tables she was not to look towards them.

This, Mrs Buchanan had already given her to understand, had been the cause of her predecessor's downfall, and a shameful reflection on the moral laxity of modern young women.

Hettie wished she could see through the screen. Had her family arrived? Would John be with them? Connie had assured her he would but what if he changed his mind? His anger had hurt her and she very much wanted them to be good friends again.

Mr Buchanan came down the stairs, his 'patented' strands of hair gleaming in the light of the chandeliers, the tails of his morning coat almost sweeping the floor.

'My goodness, Hettie, I scarcely recognised you,' he told her with a smile, adding warmly, 'You look very pretty, my child.'

The way he was looking at her made Hettie feel slightly self-conscious, but she told herself she was being silly as he strode towards the screen and then walked beyond it.

Hettie could hear the polite applause of the guests. In another moment she would have to follow him past the screen. She couldn't do it. How on earth could she sing so much as a note feeling like this? She . . .

She froze as she heard the opening notes to the Bach and then, as though someone else were controlling her movements, she discovered she was walking past the piano, keeping her face towards the guests as Mr Buchanan and, more helpfully, the chorus girls had taught her to do, acknowledging the applause with a demure hint of recognition before taking her place to one side of the piano, her gaze fixed as she had been instructed on Mr Buchancan.

'Oh look at Hettie, doesn't she look beautiful?' Connie whispered emotionally to Ellie as she reached for her handkerchief.

Thanks to Cecily and her mother-in-law's intervention, they had all been accommodated at two tables right in front of the piano, and now Connie grasped Ellie's hand as she saw her sister bite her lip to stop it trembling, her gaze focused on Hettie.

'My goodness, I hadn't realised she would be wearing such a very modern frock', Cecily whispered half disapprovingly to Connie. 'I would never allow either of my two girls to show so much ankle.'

'Cecily, you get more like your mother every time I see you,' Connie told her forthrightly, ignoring the mantle of angry colour that stained her cousin's pretty face.

Cecily's mother was Connie's least favourite aunt and she had, until Ellie had moved into Gideon's mother's far grander house in Winckley Square, lorded over the rest of her family with her status as a doctor's wife, plus the fact that she lived in the most exclusive part of Preston.

The Pride siblings' mother had been one of Preston's famously beautiful Barclay sisters, but unfortunately Cecily's daughters, although good-hearted girls, had not inherited those good looks, Connie decided smugly. Unlike her own daughter, Lyddy, whose resemblance to her mother and her Aunt Ellie was always much commented on by people.

'I thought you said John was going to be here,' Cecily whispered to Connie.

'He should have been and in fact I cannot think why he isn't,' Connie replied.

'Hettie will be disappointed.'

'Ellie, my dear, what a lovely sprite of a child

your step-daughter is,' Cecily's mother-in-law commented warmly. 'I am so sorry that Iris could not be here to see her.'

'She wrote to me the other week to tell me she is very busy helping her friend, Dr Marie Stopes, with her newly opened clinic,' Ellie responded.

'Indeed. Iris has always been vigorous in her support of birth control,' the older woman agreed without any trace of embarrassment.

Ellie sighed. She herself had always followed the advice Iris had given to her as a new young wife, but obviously she had not been vigilant enough lately which was why she now had this new life growing under her heart. Unlike her other babes this one lay still and quiet, but somehow more heavily, causing her far more discomfort than she had with her others. The disquieting symptoms she had experienced earlier on had thankfully now ceased, although she did not feel quite as well as she tried to pretend.

'The hotel is very grand, isn't it?' she whispered to Gideon without taking her gaze off Hettie, who was standing perfectly still with her face turned towards the pianist.

'Aye, and very expensive, far too expensive for the ordinary folk of Liverpool.'

'You are still thinking of this dreadful Depression,' Ellie guessed. 'Do you think it will end soon, Gideon, and things will get better?'

'I wish that they might, Ellie, but I don't think we've seen the worst of it yet.' He patted her hand

and told her firmly, 'But we won't talk of such things today, eh, my love? Let's enjoy listening to our Hettie singing her heart out instead. After all, that's why you've forced me into wearing these damnably uncomfortable clothes.'

Ellie laughed softly 'Uncomfortable, are they? You looked as proud as a turkey cock when you wore them to the Lord Mayor's dinner,' she reminded him affectionately.

'Aye, well. That was in January, when it was cold.'

'Shush. I think Hettie is about to sing,' Ellie warned him as the pianist finished his piece and stood up to sweep a bow to the applauding audience.

Oh, but she was so nervous and she felt so sick. Hettie had seen her family and felt a momentary surge of pride in them, especially Ellie who looked so pretty. But then she had noticed that John wasn't there and immediately she had felt upset. Where was he? He had promised he would come and now he wasn't here, and she had so much wanted him to see her and hear her sing.

But Mr Buchanan was playing her introductory notes. Hettie turned away from him to face her audience, tentatively took a deep breath, and began.

'Oh, but when those ladies at the next table said that Hettie had the prettiest voice they had ever heard, I was so proud I wanted to burst,' Ellie exclaimed, dabbing at her eyes with her handkerchief.

'And then to give you an encore, Hettie. The waiter serving us told us he had never ever seen that happen before,' remarked Connie.

'Aye, lass, you've got a lovely voice,' Gideon said proudly.

'Well, Hettie, I must say I was concerned when Ellie first told me what you were to do and certainly I would never allow one of my daughters to sing in public, but having said that the Adelphi is a first class hotel and not some common playhouse,' even Cecily grudgingly admitted.

Her face flushed with happiness and excitement, Hettie listened to the praise of her family as she stood close to Ellie, her step-mother's arm around her waist as she held her close.

She had not, of course, been able to go to them afterwards in the Hall, but they had been waiting for her in the hotel lobby and now they were all on their way to Cecily's mother-in-law's for a special dinner.

'Mam, where is John?' Hettie demanded. 'He promised he would come to hear me sing.'

The first person she had looked for after Ellie had been John and she had been bitterly disappointed not to see his face amongst the others.

'Well, Hettie . . .' Ellie began gently, unsure of what to say.

'Hettie, you are too selfish. John is a very busy man,' Cecily interrupted Ellie. 'He cannot be expected to leave his business on the whim of a mere girl. Goodness me, imagine the state the country would be in if our men folk all behaved so foolishly.'

Anger flashed in Hettie's eyes as she listened to Cecily's disapproving words. 'It is John who is the selfish one and not me. He promised he would be here.'

Suddenly she was close to tears. Why hadn't John come as he had promised he would? He may not have approved of her dress, but surely he would have had to add his praise and applause to those of everyone else if he had been here to hear her sing?

'Hettie, you are becoming overwrought. This is your special day, don't upset yourself,' Ellie told her gently, looking anxiously at Gideon as she did so. He gave her a small negative shake of his head that Hettie was too distressed to notice.

'I wanted John to be here. I shall hate him for ever now that he has not come,' she announced pettishly, oblivious to Ellie's sigh and the despairing look she exchanged with Gideon.

Correctly interpreting his wife's glance, Gideon put his arm around Hettie and turned her to face him. 'There is obviously a very good reason why John could not be here, Hettie,' he told her sombrely.

He and Ellie had discussed at some length the shocking telephone call they had received from John telling them of the accident and insisting that they were not to say a word to Hettie about it so as to avoid spoiling her special day. Ellie typically had been torn between her love for Hettie and her anxiety for her young brother, but in the end she had agreed to abide by John's wishes.

TEN

'Mr Buchanan, may I ask you something, please?'

'Of course, Hettie my dear. Did I tell you how very pleased I am with you, by the way? Several of the ladies have commented most favourably on your choice of songs as well as your voice.'

Hettie gave him a small nervous smile.

It was over two weeks now since she had made her debut at the Adelphi, and two more frocks had been added to her wardrobe, via a shopping trip with Connie. Connie had wanted to treat her niece to something special after her successful debut and Hettie reluctantly agreed, but only after Connie said it would be an early Christmas gift from her.

They had gone to George Henry Lee's where Connie had bought her a modern sleeveless silky dress in green with white spots on it, its neckline dipping to a 'V' at both front and back, trimmed with white braid with its dropped waist also sashed in white. Plus a second dress – in deep cornflower blue, with a big white collar and pin tucking all down the front – which they found reduced in price because of a small mark on the back which Connie had said could easily be removed. The advantage of their choices was that Hettie was able to wear her white t-bar shoes, and her long white gloves, with both frocks.

She tried to tell herself that if John wanted to be nasty and not get in touch to explain why he had not come to her debut, then that was his affair, and she certainly wasn't going to waste her time worrying about it. But she had been upset and a part of her still was.

Mr Buchanan was patting her arm, and Hettie longed to move away from him.

'I have applauded Mrs Buchanan, my dear help-mate and wife, for her excellent choice. You are a pleasure to have around, my dear, unlike your ungrateful predecessor. Now, what is it you wish to ask me? If you wanted my opinion on whether or not you should add another song to your repetoire, then . . .'

'No, it isn't that.' Hettie stopped him hastily, taking a deep breath before plunging doggedly into the speech she had been rehearsing all week. 'When Mrs Buchanan spoke with my mother, she told us that once I was singing here at the Adelphi you would give me the whole of my wages, less my bed and board, and not just a small amount of spending money because then I would not have to pay for any lessons.'

'Yes?'

'Well, it has been two weeks now and I have not had any wages . . .'

Mr Buchanan had started to scowl at her and Hettie could feel her stomach churning nervously. 'I see. Well, yes of course you must have your wages, Hettie, since you have been promised them. But I am surprised that my good lady wife seems to have forgotten to have told you that there are certain expenses that have to be deducted from them first.'

'Expenses?' Hettie faltered.

'Indeed. There is the cost of your sheet music for one thing, and then the cost of the room we use to practise, plus the refreshments you have.'

Hettie could feel her spirits sinking lower with every word he spoke. Her spending money had not even covered the cost of her food and she knew that without the good-hearted generosity of the other girls many a night she could have gone to bed on an empty stomach. She had been looking forward not just to having a little bit more money in her pocket but also to repaying them for their generosity, but now, from what Mr Buchanan was saying to her, it looked as though she was not going to be any better off.

'There, Hettie, I can see how glum you are looking. You are a good girl and I don't want to see you upset. Let me have a little think and see if there isn't some way we can make things a bit better for you. It is a pleasure to have the company of such a pretty, biddable girl, and I dare say you know how to make a man appreciate your beauty to its full, my dear. But no saying anything to Mrs Buchanan, mind, she will chastise me if she thinks that I am being over generous to you.' Smiling genially at her, Mr Buchanan slid his hand down her back to her bottom and very determinedly squeezed one cheek, causing Hettie to cry out in protest and jump away from him.

'Now, Hettie, that wasn't very appreciative of you,' he chided her sharply. 'I had looked for a more grateful response to my generosity. We will say no more about it on this occasion but I hope you will remember in future that if I am to be generous to you, then you will have to be correspondingly generous to me. Ah, poor child, I can see that I have upset you. Come here and let me make you feel better.'

To Hettie's horror, he had grabbed hold of her before she could escape, forcing her back against the piano with the weight of his body. She could feel his moist, panting breath against her neck, and as she tried to push past his restraining arm he put his free hand on her breast, and squeezed it.

No man had ever attempted such an intimacy with her and nor had she ever imagined that they might do so. Ellie had been a loving and very protective mother, anxious, although Hettie did not realise it, to safeguard her children from the unhappiness and danger she herself had experienced as a young girl, vulnerable and alone after her mother's death.

Hettie felt close to fainting. The sensation of Mr Buchanan's slack wet mouth pressing against her skin made her feel sick with loathing.

'I knew you would be a hot-blooded little thing. I've heard how you orientals know a thing or two about pleasing a man.' Mr Buchanan was panting. 'Come, my dear, and give me your hand and let me find pleasure in your hold . . .'

Mr Buchanan's voice had gone thick and both it and he were shaking with excitement as he pressed his body into hers, Hettie recognised in trembling fear. He was plucking, no *tearing* at the fabric of her blouse, and her breast hurt from his rough handling of it.

'Mr Buchanan. No . . . Please, let me go,' she begged him frantically, but instead of obeying her he simply grunted and pushed himself harder against her.

Her head had begun to swim with panic, a horrible cold, weakening feeling taking her strength, and Hettie was mortally afraid that she might actually faint and be left to his mercy. But then to her relief someone started to turn the door handle of the practice room and, with a speed that astonished her, Mr Buchanan not only released her but stepped away from her, smoothing the black strands of hair over his forehead and keeping his back to the door as he intoned, 'Yes. As I was saying, Hettie, about adding another song . . .'

When he broke off, feigning surprise at the entrance of the housekeeper, Hettie took advantage of her opportunity to escape, hurrying out of the room, not caring that her housekeeper might think her behaviour odd.

She was still trembling several minutes later when she had left the hotel and was standing on Lime Street, longing for the comfort of Ellie's arms around her and her soothing voice assuring her that what had happened would never happen to her again.

Mr Buchanan had mentioned her red dress, though, and she hadn't forgotten how angry John had been when he had seen her wearing it. Was it somehow her own fault that Mr Buchanan had behaved the way he had? He had certainly given her to understand that it was.

Her head ached and she felt sick. If she couldn't go home to Ellie then at least she could telephone her. There was a public telephone box in the station and she hurried over to it, pulling open the heavy door and stepping inside.

When the telephonist asked her what number she required, she was trembling so much she could hardly speak, but at last she managed to say the number. Gripping the receiver with one hand and her money ready in the other, Hettie waited for someone to answer.

When at last they did it wasn't, as she had hoped, Ellie's voice she heard but instead that of Mrs Jennings, her cook-come-housekeeper.

'Oh what a shame, Hettie, yer ma and pa have gorn up to the Lakes,' she told Hettie.

Tears filled Hettie's eyes. She replaced the receiver and walked back to Lime Street, feeling more alone than she ever had in her life.

John re-read the letter he had just written, and then got up to go and stand at the cottage door and look across the airfield. At the far end where the flying machine hangar had once stood, there was now a pile of twisted metal and charred rubble, all that remained of his hopes and dreams.

He had attended the funerals of each of the young men who had lost their lives, and suffered the accusatory looks of their families at every one. He could have defended himself from them by pointing out that the person responsible for their deaths was not him but one of their own friends, but what was the point now with them dead and their families already burdened with the pain of their grief? He had no wish to add to it by telling them that they had brought the deaths on themselves by breaking the rules.

Far worse, though, had been Jim's funeral. He and Jim had been friends for almost half of John's life. It had been Jim who had tolerated his questions and curiosity when, as a young boy, he had hung around him and the other men with their flying machines, coaxing Jim to tell him everything he knew about them. Jim had been the best of men and the best of friends, and John knew he would never forgive himself for what had happened to him.

As soon as Gideon and Ellie returned from the Lakes, John intended to tell them he was leaving the area. He knew Gideon and Ellie understood why he had insisted Hettie was not to be told about what had happened, and that he had not wanted to spoil her debut with his own dreadful news. She had probably not even missed him anyway, he decided bitterly, not with all the admirers she no doubt had now, paying her compliments and wanting to walk out with her. Hettie was young. She wanted fun and laughter, and they were the last things he felt like right now.

In fact, he felt as though he had the cares of the world on his shoulders. Even if he had had the money to do so, at this moment he had neither the heart nor the stomach for starting again and building another flying school here.

He couldn't stay here because if he did there would never be a day when he didn't look across to the charred ruin and know that, if he hadn't selfishly agreed to go and listen to Hettie singing, because he had been so desperate to see her, four foolish young men and his best friend would still be alive.

The blame wasn't Hettie's – how could it be? – but it was his for putting his desire to see her before his duty.

The letter he had just finished writing was a request to Alfred asking if the job he had mentioned to him was still open. The sooner he was away from this place and its painful memories the better.

'Gawd, 'Ettie, yer look like you've been bawling yer eyes out, what's up?'

Hettie had hoped that she would have the attic room to herself as she returned to the boarding house, but she had forgotten that Mavis had had a fall-out with the producer and was currently understudying, which meant she was refusing to go to the theatre for rehearsals.

'It's nothing,' she mumbled.

'Nothing? Giveover, come on, what's to do? Old man Buchanan hasn't been trying it on wiv yer, has he?'

Hettie promptly burst into tears and within less than five minutes Mavis had dragged the whole sorry story out of her.

'Ee, he's a right nasty piece of work, doing that to yer. Only that's the way it is in this business! But keeping yer wages back, so as to get yer to give 'im what he wants . . . That's right mean, that is. Ee 'Ettie, yer didn't let him have his way wiv yer, did yer?'

'No.' Hettie told her vehemently as she shuddered at the very thought of the man.

'Well that's all right then, lass. Now dry them tears and I'll tell yer what yer have to do.'

Obediently Hettie did as she was instructed whilst Mavis settled herself comfortably on her bed and lit up a cigarette, in flagrant breach of one of Mrs Marshall's most stringent rules.

'Now listen to me, the next time he tries anyfink like that on yer, yer 'as ter to tell him that you're going straight to Mrs B to tell 'er what he's doing.'

Hettie gazed at her in disbelief. 'Oh, I couldn't do that.'

'Yer won't have to,' Mavis assured her with a grin. 'All yer have to do is say it like yer mean it, that will put the s . . . the fear of God right up him,' she amended hastily.

'But what about my wages?' Hettie asked her miserably.

'Aye, well I fink yer can kiss goodbye to them, 'Ettie. His missus might call him ter order for messin' wiv yer, but she won't be willing to hand over yer money. Tight arsed old bat. Oh, and 'ere's another tip for yer. Allus carry an 'at pin wiv yer . . .'

Hettie's forehead crinkled in confusion.

'Yer sticks it into any fella who gets too frisky wiv yer,' Mavis explained patiently. 'Works every time, especially if yer sticks it into his best friend.'

Hettie's confusion deepened. 'But why would sticking it into his friend help if he's the one . . .'

When Mavis burst into raucous laughter, Hettie gave her a pink-cheeked look of enquiry.

'Oh, 'Ettie. Gawd but yer wet behind the ears, aren't yer. A man's best friend is his old man.'

When Hettie still looked confused, Mavis heaved a large sigh and said, ''Ettie, afore you came here how much exactly did yer ma tell yer about the birds and the bees?'

Hettie's face grew even hotter. 'I know where babies come from, if that's what you mean,' she said quellingly.

But if she had expected to stop Mavis from laughing she was disappointed because instead Mavis laughed even harder, pausing eventually to wipe the tears of mirth from her eyes and to splutter, 'Aye, but do yer know how they gets there in the first place?'

When Hettie continued to blush Mavis told her in a more kindly voice, 'Well, his best friend, or his old man, is what a chap puts into yer . . . well, yer privates. It's down there *his* privates are, like. He's got his old man and his balls, and we've got our privates and they fit together like they was made for one another. Which they was, of course,' she announced matter of factly.

'First time he does it, he teks yer virginity,' she continued, 'and that can 'urt a fair bit if he's a bit rough, like, but after that it can feel good like as well,' Mavis revealed fairly. 'Specially if yer sweet on him, like. Anyway, it's his old man that gives yer what babies come from. So that's why if yer lets one of 'em have his way with yer, yer have to be careful to mek sure he doesn't leave it inside yer.'

Hettie had been nodding her head vigorously throughout this explanation but the truth was that she wasn't very much the wiser. What she did know, however, was that the thought of any man, but most of all Mr Buchanan, attempting to put his 'best friend' into her 'privates' was one she found thoroughly disgusting.

Later on, when the other girls had returned, Mavis insisted on telling them all what had befallen Hettie.

'Poor little kid,' Lizzie sympathised with her. 'He wants it chopping off, he does. So what are yer going to do if they don't give yer yer wages, then, 'Ettie?'

'I don't know,' Hettie admitted.

She had had time now to rethink her first frightened impulse to tell her mother what had happened. She knew that Ellie's reaction would be to insist she came home, and that wasn't really what she wanted to do. Besides, the other girls had laughed her out of her fear now and made the whole situation somehow seem so much less frightening. And, of course, she felt so very grown up having been admitted to that world where she knew all about the kind of things that young girls did not know about.

'Well, if you do want to earn a bit extra money, Hettie, Jack at the chop house was saying that he was desperate for someone to help clear the tables and wash up,' Babs told her. 'I'all have a word with him for you, if you like. It won't be much money and it will be hard work, mind,' she cautioned as Hettie's face immediately lit up.

'I don't mind that,' Hettie assured her. In fact,

she wouldn't mind anything so long as it helped to made up her lost wages and meant that she didn't have to worry about the prospect of Mr Buchanan pushing his 'best friend' into her.

'I'll have a word with him for you, then,' Babs promised her, adding quietly so that only Hettie could hear, 'And as for what Mavis has been telling you, later on when it's a bit quieter, you and me are going to have a proper talk about that, Hettie.'

'So you're definitely going to take this job, then, John?' Gideon asked quietly as Ellie poured her younger brother a fresh cup of tea.

John had arrived unannounced at the house Gideon owned in the Lake District just over half an hour ago to tell them that he had been to see Alfred, and it had now been agreed that he would take over his new duties as the chief flying instructor at the club in just over a month's time.

'Yes,' John confirmed tersely before adding, 'I know you don't want to sell the land we bought, Gideon.'

'There's no need for you to worry about that, John. I dare say we can lease it to a farmer for the time being.'

'I'd like to have some kind of memorial plaque put on it once all the mess has been cleared away. It's the least I can do for Jim. He didn't deserve to die like that, and it's my fault that he did.'

Ellie made a small sound of distress and put

her hand on his arm. 'John, you must not say that. There was nothing you could have done. The other students all confirmed that Alan Simms was a very headstrong and reckless young man who had made it plain that nothing was going to stop him from taking up a flying machine and making good his boast that he already knew everything there was to know about flying and didn't need to listen to either you or Jim. Didn't they? You said so your-self.'

'But don't you see? If I'd been there, Alan wouldn't have been able to take the machine in the first place because I would have been using it for a lesson,' John protested in an anguished voice.

'On that occasion maybe,' Gideon intervened firmly. 'But by all accounts he was the kind of young fool who would have kept on until he got what he wanted. The pity of it is that he managed to persuade three other young idiots to go with him and, even worse, that the machine crashed onto the hangar and killed poor Jim. But none of that is your fault, John, and if you take my advice you must accept that.'

'Hettie was very distressed that you weren't there at her debut as she had hoped,' Ellie told him.

'You didn't tell her . . . what happened, or about Jim?' John immediately asked anxiously. 'I know how much this singing business means to her and I didn't want to spoil it for her with bad news.'

'No. We did as you had begged us to, John, and said nothing,' Gideon assured him.

'There is a letter here for you from Hettie,' Ellie told him quietly.

Reluctantly John took the envelope she was holding out to him, and then opened it. Although the notepaper wasn't scented it seemed to John that somehow it carried a soft sweet fragrance that was in some way the essence of Hettie herself.

'Dear John,' she had written. 'I was very sorry that you could not come to hear me sing at the Adelphi. Mam and Da and Connie had all said that you would be there but then you didn't come. I hope that you are not still cross with me because of my frock and because I want to sing. Most sincerely, Hettie.'

'She was very disappointed that you weren't there,' Ellie repeated as John folded up the letter and tucked it back in its envelope.

'She is so very young,' John answered her seriously. 'A child still in many ways, Ellie.' His own problems and feeling of guilt were weighing very heavily on his shoulders, and the laughter he had once shared with Hettie now seemed to belong to another life and another person.

'How are you feeling?' he asked Ellie meaningfully. He didn't want to cause his sister anxiety when she was in a delicate condition. That would be even more guilt than he could bear.

She gave him an affectionate smile and assured him, 'I am fine. Gideon fusses over me so much you'd think this was to be our first child and not our third. I am hoping that Iris will be able to attend me during the confinement. She has promised that she will, but I know how busy the clinic is keeping her. But tell us some more about your friend Alfred and his flying club, John. I feel I hardly know anything about it,' Ellie pressed him.

'The flying club does not belong to Alfred as such, but he has given the club the land. It is very well organised,' he explained 'and they are soon to take delivery of two new machines. I am to live in an apartment, as they call it, in a building adjoining the flying club. I have half of the whole of the upper floor, and down below me is an office and the clubroom, over the flying club. The chap who does most of the bookwork has the other half, whilst the engineers and maintenance crew work in shifts and do not live on site so that there is always a maintenance crew there. It has all been very well thought out and organised,' John reiterated.

'This is a new start for you, John,' Ellie told him lovingly. 'I pray that you will be happy.'

He smiled weakly at her but inside he felt despair. He had no right to look for happiness. Not when five men were dead because of him. He had no right to want happiness, and no right either to yearn for the sound of Hettie's laughter.

ELEVEN

Hettie hummed happily to herself as she washed the dishes piled up to one side of the sink.

Thanks to Babs she now not only properly understood the confusing facts Mavis had given her, she also had a job working in the kitchen of the chop house, where Sarah Baker, the wife of its owner, Jack, and mother of her youthful admirer, insisted on Hettie eating with them before the evening rush of customers began. She'd never devoured so much food in her life as these past few days!

'We're lucky to be so close to the theatre, otherwise we'd probably be suffering too, what with so many men being out of work,' Sarah confided to Hettie as they shared the unending task of washing up.

It was true that Liverpool was becoming an increasingly subdued city as the lack of work bit deeper into the soul of its menfolk. Connie and Harry talked worriedly about it whenever Hettie visited, fearing that the situation was going to grow even worse, and Sarah Baker kept a big basket into which she and Hettie put whatever leftovers could be salvaged, to be handed out to those poor souls who could not afford to buy food. It was her way of doing her bit, she explained to Hettie.

Hettie thought back to her enlightening talk with Babs. It was true that at first she had been shocked when Babs had matter of factly explained the mystery of the intimacies of married life to her, and the manner in which babies were conceived; and she had been very apprehensive going to her first practice after Mr Buchanan had tried to touch her. But as soon as he had put his hand on her arm she had done as the girls had told her and warned him that she would tell Mrs Buchanan of his behaviour.

Her threat had worked like a magic charm, and he had not tried to touch her since, much to her relief.

Of all the girls, Babs was her favourite and the one to whom she felt the closest, with Lizzie now a close second. Lizzie tended to mother her these days, and in return Hettie was happy to listen to Lizzie's anxieties about her own mother and the sister who would never, as Lizzie put it, 'grow up proper, like'.

'Ever so loving she is, Hettie, but she's that big now and she doesn't know her own strength. When she squeezes your hand it doesn't half hurt, but she doesn't mean any harm.'

Whenever she could, Lizzie went home, and when one day Hettie had returned from her singing practice to see Lizzie sitting on her bed, clutching a letter whilst tears rolled down her face, Hettie asked her immediately, 'Oh Lizzie, what's wrong? Is it your sister?'

'Yes, she's had a fall and she's been taken to hospital. She's been crying and asking for me. Mam wants to know if I can go and see her, but I haven't got any time off due to me. Three of the girls are off sick and we're that busy with rehearsals I daren't just go, even though it would only mean me missing the one day.'

'You could go if I stood in for you,' Hettie told her. 'It's my Saturday off this weekend, but I can't go home because my Mam and Da are up at the Lakes still, and that's too far to go.'

'What? No, you couldn't do that. You're not tall enough for one thing,' Lizzie protested, but Hettie could see that she was tempted by the idea.

Lizzie had been kind to her and, to Hettie, this was an opportunity to repay her kindness. When the others came in, she told them what had happened and what she had offered to do.

'You? Stand in for Lizzie?' Mavis laughed. 'You aren't tall enough!'

'That what I told her,' Lizzie agreed.

'Well, I reckon it's a good idea and that we could get away with it if one of us came forward and we put her at the back,' Babs argued. 'We could always do sommat to make her taller. Give her a headdress, put some blocks on her shoes or sommat.'

'Oh yes, and how the 'ell is she going to do her high kicks wearing shoes wiv blocks on them?' Mavis demanded.

'Course she can,' one of the twins joined in.

'Yes, but what about Lizzie's solo?'

'What about it? We can learn her the song easy enough, and if she gets it wrong then we'all just have to sing louder to drown her out. She'll be okay with the dancing, she knows most of the routines already from watching us. 'Ere, Hettie, come over here and watch this,' Sukey ordered, immediately striking a pose before launching into a song that had Hettie's toes tapping, even if some of the words seemed a little risqué.

'Well, it's easy enough to see why you'll never make it out of the chorus, Sukey,' Mavis commented witheringly. 'Call that singing? Sounds more like two tom cats having a fight.'

'That's cos I'm a bleeding contralto and not a ruddy soprano like Lizzie here,' Sukey defended herself, clearly miffed.

Hettie could see that Lizzie's resolve was weakening.

'I won't let you down,' she promised her fervently.

Lizzie shook her head. 'I shouldn't be agreeing to this and I wouldn't be if it weren't for the fact that Mam says our Rosie's that desperate to see me.'

'Don't worry, Lizzie, we'll look after her,' Babs chipped in.

'Never mind looking after her, we'd best start getting her trained up,' Mavis warned. 'Come on, 'Ettie. Let's see how many of the words you can remember.'

Willingly, Hettie started to sing, prompted by Babs whenever she stumbled over one of the words, whilst the others clapped in tune and cheered her on.

To Hettie's relief, Connie made no objection when Hettie telephoned her to say she was not having a Saturday off now but would be working instead. It was, after all, the truth, even if was not quite the truth that Connie would assume it to be.

The other girls had rehearsed her rigorously, coaching her both in the chorus line dance steps and the solo song she would have to sing. Doing Lizzie's solo would be much easier than taking her place in the chorus line, Hettie suspected, as her 'helpers' made her stand still in the middle of the attic floor whilst they bustled about fitting her into her costume.

Trying to walk with the headdress, with its towering pink feathers, balanced on her head was difficult enough without having to actually dance with it on, she decided.

'Gawd, look at 'er,' one of the twins giggled. ''Er headdress is nearly as big as she is.'

'Come on, Hettie, let's see yer walk in them

shoes. Hold yer head up, mind, and keep yer back straight.'

It was just as well that Lizzie had left early to catch her train, Hettie acknowledged as she struggled to obey the instructions she was being given.

'Right, you two, Jenny and Jess, you'll have to stand either side of 'Ettie and support her. Ready? One, two three . . .'

'Higher, Hettie, you've got to kick higher than that. And don't bend your head. Gawd, if Mary Jane catches sight of yer we'll all be out of a job.'

'Who's Mary Jane?' Hettie whispered to Jenny.

'He's the one who does the dance routines,' Jenny explained. 'We call him Mary Jane because he's a right old Ethel and no mistake.'

''Ere, let's'ave a look at yer then, 'Ettie?'

Obediently Hettie stood still whilst the formidable girl who she had been told was the most senior of all the chorus line dancers pursed her lips and warned Jenny, 'One step out of line for her and there'll be trouble for all you lot.' Helen glared at her.

''Ere, Babs, put bit more rouge on her, she looks as white as a piece of steamed cod,' Jenny demanded.

Then Babs told her, 'Now remember, Hettie. For the first half you're in the chorus, and then when we come off you change into your solo outfit, and at the beginning of the second half you do your solo.'

If John had thought the dress she wore to sing at the Adelphi was shocking she didn't want to think what he would have said if he could see her now, Hettie admitted as she tried not to feel self-conscious about her chorus line outfit with its miniscule skirt and spangles.

'Come on, you lot, curtain's going up.'

A buzz of anticipation seemed to seethe through the grouped dancers, and then suddenly they were moving and Hettie was moving with them, her anxiety giving way to excitement as they stepped out on to the stage in perfect time, to a roar of applause from the waiting crowd.

To the right, to the left, back kick, forward kick, then double kick. Hettie felt herself being swept along in the exhilaration of actually being able to keep time with the others. But that exhilaration was almost her downfall because suddenly she realised she had missed a step . . . She faltered and if it hadn't been for the quick thinking of Jenny and Jess on either side of her, who virtually picked her up and carried her with them, she suspected she would have fallen over her own feet.

'Kick now, Hettie,' Jess muttered out of the side of her mouth. 'Now this way again,' whispered Jenny at her other side, and somehow she managed to pick up the rhythm again and get back in time. Her earlier panic now over, Hettie could clearly see the allure of the chorus line.

*   *   *

It seemed a lifetime before the first half was finally over, and Hettie was all too conscious of the chorus line leader's grim gaze on her as they danced off into the wings.

'You were out of time in the first routine,' she told Hettie sharply.

'Ah, come on, she only missed one step,' Jess defended her.

'What's going on here?'

The whole troupe froze as a very dapper looking middle-aged man suddenly appeared.

'The comedian's really going to love you lot squawking like parrots and ruining his act.'

Hettie had never seen a man with dyed blond hair before and she couldn't take her eyes off him.

'Helen, someone was out in the first routine.'

Horrified, Hettie tensed, waiting for Helen to denounce her but instead, to her astonishment, the other girl simply shrugged and said calmly, 'You try keeping in step wearing these bloody head-dresses.' At the same time she managed to move so that she was standing between Hettie and the choreographer.

'Well, it better not happen again otherwise I'll be looking for new heads to fit them.'

'She'd better not miss a step tonight,' Helen warned Jess and Jenny as soon as they were all in the dressing room. 'Cos if she does, the whole lot of yer will be looking for work.'

'Come on, 'Ettie, let's get you into this costume,' Babs was demanding, pulling a face at Helen's back.

For Lizzie's song in the second half Hettie had to go on stage wearing a milk maid's outfit, complete with a yoke and milk pails. Her song was a cheeky complaint about her work and her envy of the heroine of the piece with her rich father and handsome sweetheart.

Fortunately, the mob cap she had to wear came complete with its own improbably coloured blonde ringlets, and by the time Babs had finished making her up Hettie doubted that her own mother would have recognised her.

'Remember, we go on, do our routine, and then you come on and go stand in front of Helen and –'

'– and then I put the pails down and start to sing,' Hettie concluded.

There wasn't much room in the wings and Hettie had to stand sideways in order to watch for her cue. But when it eventually came she was ready, and to her own astonishment the moment she stepped out on to the stage, half dancing, half skipping as she had been instructed to do, it was as though somehow she really was Bo the Buxom Beauty who yearned to exchange her milk pails for the arms of a handsome lover.

With an extravagant sigh, Hettie put down her pails, bending from the waist as she did so and flouncing her full skirts so that the audience got a glimpse of her frilled undergarments. When her action earned a roar of male approval, she turned round and put her hands on her hips and shook her head before launching into her saucy solo.

When she had finished, she went to pick up her pails and then almost froze with shock as suddenly the whole theatre seemed to be yelling and cheering.

'Give 'em a curtsey, Hettie,' the nearest chorus girl muttered. 'And smile at them, for gawd's sake . . .'

Obediently Hettie sank into a curtsey and then stood up.

'Now get orf before the leading lady comes out and drags yer orf. Gawd, this is goin' ter make her as mad as fire.'

'But what did I do wrong?' Hettie asked in bewilderment an hour later when she had been advised not to so much as put her nose outside of the dressing room.

'What yer did wrong, 'Ettie, was ter sing better than Amy, the lead,' Babs explained patiently. 'Gawd, I knew yer could sing, but I never realised yer could make such a noise . . .'

Hettie didn't understand. She had, of course, made sure her voice could be heard right at the back of the theatre because she had assumed this was what she was supposed to do, but now it seemed that she had been wrong.

'Watch out, here comes Mary Jane,' one of the girls warned as the dressing room door was suddenly thrust open to reveal the choreographer.

Hettie could vaguely remember being told what it meant to call a man an 'Ethel' but she was too nervous to dwell on it right now as she tucked herself out of sight behind two of the taller girls.

'Pray enlighten me, ladies. It seems a song thrush has flown into our little nest. A song thrush, moreover, who dances like a cart horse, and who appears to think she is a comedienne.'

Someone tittered nervously.

'I trust this rare species will not be making a long stay with us, otherwise our own dear sweet lark may not be very happy. Indeed, I insist that our visiting song thrush takes flight herself, and by tomorrow. Do I make myself clear?'

He was gone before anyone could reply, leaving Hettie with a burning red face and anxiously churning stomach.

'He don't miss much, our Mary Jane. Sharp as box of knives, he is,' Mavis muttered.

'And now we've got ter keep yer out of her ladyship's way otherwise she'll have yer guts for garters,' she warned Hettie. 'We should have warned yer not to let her see that yer can sing better than wot she can. She's a jealous cat and no mistake. Course, she was only the understudy, but then the lead got sick – some say because Amy slipped her sommat – and Amy had to take over. 'Ere, when you bent down like that and showed the audience yer bum, I nearly bust out laughing meself. What made yer do it?'

'I don't know,' Hettie admitted. 'It just felt right.'

A serious look crossed Jenny's face. 'Did it an' all. Well, that's what we call having greasepaint in yer blood, 'Ettie, when yer just know how to play to an audience . . .'

Greasepaint in her blood. Hettie exhaled happily as she sat on the banquette almost half asleep. The sound of the applause she had received for her evening's and final performance was still ringing blissfully in her ears.

'Mary Jane' had made another visit to the dressing room after the second show, his pale blue gaze raking down the line of undressing girls until, or so it seemed to Hettie, it came to rest on the girl behind whom she had concealed herself. He hadn't said a word, simply standing there before turning on his heel and going back to the door where he had paused to turn round and say coldly, 'I meant what I said earlier.'

'Thank 'eavens Lizzie's coming back tomorrow,' Jess had muttered as she wiped off her stage make-up, 'otherwise he'd sack the bloody lot of us.'

'Well, I don't see why he should, just because Hettie sings better than lardy face Amy.'

'Much you know, then, because she's our Mary Jane's cousin, that's wot!'

'Come on, sleepy head, let's get you back and into yer bed,' Hettie heard Babs saying affectionately.

Of course, when Lizzie returned she had to be told the whole story, including Hettie's triumph and Mary Jane's dictat.

'Oh, Hettie, I am so grateful to you,' she exclaimed as she laughed and hugged Hettie and told them all how her sister was.

'Well, 'Ettie does have a lovely voice, Lizzie, and no mistake, but she's never going to make a proper hoofer,' Jenny opined.

'Mebbe not, but it's a shame with a voice like that, Hettie, that you aren't on the stage yourself instead of just singing at the Adelphi,' Lizzie, who was now far more kind and friendly towards Hettie, announced.

The same thought had crossed Hettie's own mind. She had got such a buzz from performing on stage, which was nothing like how she felt singing at the Adelphi. The thought of returning to sing in front of the genteel ladies there filled her with an unexpected gloom.

She craved the attention, the excitement of the stage again. But she knew that she had had a hard enough time convincing Ellie and Gideon to let her sing at the hotel and they would never give their approval for her to join the chorus line. Aunt Amelia would never let them live it down!

'The fancy pants at the third table on the right just asked me to give you this.'

Hettie blushed as the waiter handed her the small, carefully folded note. It was a month now since she had first started to sing at the Adelphi and in that time she had already received several notes from gentlemen who had heard her sing and then requested the pleasure of being allowed to offer her some refreshment.

Hettie had, of course, always refused these approaches, having been warned by the other girls that her admirers had a more devious purpose in mind than sharing a mere cup of china tea. But this particular gentleman had sat at the same table every afternoon for the past week, his gaze fixed on her and never moving from her whilst she sang.

Naturally, she had pretended not to be aware of his attention on her, and also naturally she had been. Who would not? For one thing he was exceptionally handsome, with his slightly olive toned skin, thick black hair, and oddly piercing dark eyes. And rich, too, by all accounts. Certainly the head waiter seemed to think so.

'An American gentleman he is, and he's got the best suite in the hotel. Says he's here on business but he ain't said what manner of business he's in.'

All in all there seemed to be an exciting air of mystery surrounding Mr Jay Dalhousic.

Hettie read his note as she hurried upstairs to change out of her dress and into her street clothes, wondering what on earth he could mean by the words, 'There is a business proposition I would like to put before you.'

Whatever it was, she could not possibly accept his invitation to have dinner with him.

The room the housekeeper had allocated to Hettie to change in was up several flights of stairs and next to the maids' quarters. She hurried into it, closing the door which did not possess a lock behind her.

She had just removed her dress when she heard the door opening. Clutching her dress to her body, she turned round expecting the intruder to be one of the maids, but to her horror instead it was Mr Buchanan, his face red and shiny, and his breathing laboured.

'Getting ready to meet your lover, are you, you little jade. Well, he shall not have you until I have had my fill of you. Did you think I couldn't see what was going on? How he looked at you . . .' As he spoke he was coming toward her, *launching* himself at her, Hettie recognised, as she made a panic stricken attempt to evade him and get to the door.

For a short, overweight man he was surprisingly light on his feet and as he guessed what Hettie was trying to do he hurried to place himself between her and the door.

'You have enflamed me beyond all endurance with your mock modest looks and your wanton body. I must have you. I shall have you . . .'

He was mad, Hettie decided, terrified as he lunged towards her and his fingers clawed into the silk of her dress as she held it in front of her. She screamed as she heard the fabric rip, but her terror only seemed to increase his ardour. Words she had never heard before but whose meaning was shockingly plain fell from his lips along with his spittle. His face was so red and shinily tight that Hettie thought his skin might actually split.

'See what you have done to me,' he told her thickly, his hand going to his own body as he tore at his trouser buttons.

Panic filled Hettie. Instinctively she turned her head so that she wouldn't have to see what he was doing.

'Look at it. Look at it, you little whore. Look! You will look at it, and you will feel it mastering you and teaching you a well-deserved lesson.'

If only she could get to the door. Hettie started to inch towards it, shaking with relief as her fingers found the edge of it. If she could just pull it open and then slip through it . . .

'Whore. Whore . . . Why do you give yourself to him and not to me?'

Hettie screamed as he saw what she was doing and tried to slam the door shut on her hand with the weight of his body whilst his other hand tore at the fragile strap of her petticoat, his nails leaving raised marks on the white skin of her breast.

'Please, Mr Buchanan, you must not do this,' she begged him in terror. 'I have not given myself to anyone.'

'Liar! I saw the way he looked at you today. I saw the note he passed to you. A note that no doubt contained all manner of lewd thoughts and suggestions . . .'

'No. No, you are wrong.'

Hettie could feel his hot sour breath on her face and then on her throat. Something that looked like a fat white grub was dangling from the opening in his trousers.

Hettie's stomach heaved.

'You must go away and let me get dressed,' she told him. 'Otherwise I shall tell Mrs Buchanan.'

'Tell her, then, for I have to have you, Hettie. I cannot sleep for my need of you.'

He was gabbling now, a wild look in his eyes. Hettie panicked. She had thought the mention of his wife would stop him in his tracks but he was evidently beyond that. Hettie could hear footsteps on the stairs outside the door, and two girls talking. She could see Mr Buchanan looking warily towards the door, and she took advantage of his momentary lapse in concentration to pull it open and slip through it.

The housemaids on their way down the stairs stared open mouthed at her dishevelment, but Hettie didn't care. There was no way she would risk going back for her day clothes, Hettie decided shakily as she pulled on her dress and hurried down the steps, far too terrified to look back in case she should see Mr Buchanan coming after her.

'It has been the loveliest time here, Gideon dearest.'

'Aye, I own I shall be sorry to leave and go back to Winckley Square.'

Ellie and Gideon were seated in the garden of their Lake District house, enjoying the view out over the lake itself.

'By, Ellie, I never thought when I used to work as a drover for your uncle that one day I would have me own place up here.'

Ellie smiled lovingly as he took her hand in his.

'We have been so blessed, my love,' she told him gently. 'Connie and I have been lucky enough to find happiness and love. I wish that John might do the same. He has taken this tragedy very hard, Gideon.'

'Aye, he blames himself for what happened.'

'But why should he blame himself? It was not his fault.'

Gideon sighed. 'It's part of what comes with being a man, Ellie my love. The responsibility, the duty. And John *is* now a man.'

'He is also my brother and I wish he was not going to live and work in Oxfordshire. It's so very far away.'

'Always the little mother, eh Ellie.'

She laughed. 'I cannot forget that they suffered so cruelly when our mother died. Oh . . .' She gasped as suddenly a spasm of pain seized her.

Gideon demanded sharply, 'Ellie, what is it?'

Her face had gone pale and beads of sweat were forming on her forehead. 'I – I don't know.'

Another pain seized her and she cried out and tried to stand up. As Gideon rushed to help her, she gasped, 'Gideon, I think it's the baby, but it is much too soon.'

Beneath her loose thin summer dress Gideon could see the gentle swelling of her belly suddenly contort and fear filled him. Ellie was gasping and moaning, leaning heavily on him as the pain seized her.

'Ellie. We must get you back to the house . . .'

The pain came in black waves edged with jagged red teeth that tore into her body, savaging it in surge after surge of red-hot agony. She cried out against it and tried to escape from it, but there was no escape. She could smell blood and the visceral scent stirred memories that knifed her with fear. She cried out for Iris and then for her mother as nature tore the life from within her womb and destroyed it.

'Oh Hettie, you poor little love. Don't worry about your frock, Cissy in wardrobe will be able to mend it for you so as you'd never know it had been torn. But from now on you'll have to go to the hotel wearing your singing dress.'

Hettie gulped and sniffed, the near hysterical state of distress in which she had arrived back at the lodging house calmed by the practical concern of the other girls as she sobbed out her story to them.

'But what about when I have to go to practice, and it's just the two of us in the room?' Hettie whispered shakily as she kept the cotton pad soaked in witchhazel one of the girls had made for her pressed to her scratches.

'If I was you I'd go and have a quiet word with

the housekeeper. Tell her that yer can't abide closed doors and that yer come over all faint because of them. Ask her if yer can have one of them pieces of wood wot yer slide under 'em to keep the door open – if she's got anything about 'er she'll know well enough why you want the door open.'

''Ere,' one of the girls suddenly called out urgently, 'looks like there's going to be a new lodger.'

All the girls including Hettie crowded round the small window to look down into the street at the woman who was about to mount the steps to the front door.

'That's Mrs Buchanan,' Hettie gasped.

'You mean that's his wife?'

Hettie nodded her head.

'Well, you said as how old Misery Guts is her sister, didn't you, Hettie, so like as not she's just come on a visit,' Babs said comfortingly. But Hettie couldn't help feeling apprehensive.

''E's the one who's done wrong, Hettie, not you,' Lizzie pointed out robustly.

They could all see how anxious Hettie looked.

Five minutes later, the door to their room opened and the grubby tweeny maid, whose adenoids gave her problems, snuffled thickly, 'Hettie Walker, you're to go downstairs this instant, on account of Mrs Buchanan is here to see you.'

Hettie gave her friends an anguished, imploring look and whispered shakily, 'I don't want to go.'

'You'd best go down and see what she wants, Hettie love,' Babs told her gruffly, adding more firmly, 'And mind you tell her what he did to you.'

Hettie was shaking from head to foot by the time she had followed the tweeny back down the stairs and along the hallway.

There was no need for her to knock on the parlour door because it was already open. Mrs Buchanan was standing there waiting for her, her face set in an expression of cold fury.

'So what have you to say for yourself about your disgraceful behaviour then, Miss Walker?' Mrs Buchanan demanded as she dragged Hettie into the room and closed the door behind her.

'I . . .'

'I could scarcely believe my ears when my dear husband informed me of his shocking discovery that you have been encouraging the attentions of a hotel guest. Indeed, more than encouraging them. Your mother assured me that you were a respectable young woman and now I find that you are anything but. How dare you behave in such a fashion and bring disrepute on respectable professional people? My husband could scarcely bring himself to tell me of the lewdness of the embrace in which he caught you – alone in an hotel room with a gentleman to whom, not a hour before, he had witnessed you secretly passing a note, no doubt to make the disgusting assignation.'

Mrs Buchanan's bosom heaved as she shuddered and then impaled Hettie with furious glare.

'That is not true!' Hettie burst out indignantly.

'What, you impudent hussy? You *dare* to deny my husband's accusation? When you were caught in the very act, *en déshabillé*, with a man holding you in his embrace? Mr Buchanan says that he had questioned one of the waiters who had confirmed that notes were passed between you.'

'No. I only received one note, and I . . .'

'That is enough! I will not tolerate any more lies from you. Mr Buchanan could hardly bring himself to sully my ears by describing to me the nature of your indelicate behaviour. Furthermore, for the sake of other vulnerable gentlemen and in order to protect our own good name Mr Buchanan wishes me to terminate your employment as of now. Indeed, he has confided to me that you have actually had the temerity to flaunt yourself before him and to suggest that your wages should be increased in return for certain unmentionable familiarities.'

Hettie gasped. 'No! That is not true.' She could feel her eyes filling with shocked, humiliated tears.

'Silence! You will not speak until I give you permission to do so. Your behaviour is an affront to all decent people. Were I to follow the inclinations of my own feelings you would, as Mr Buchanan has requested, be dismissed forthwith, and a letter sent to your family revealing exactly why your presence can no longer be tolerated in a respectable household.'

Hettie couldn't believe what was happening to

her. How could she ever convince her Mam and Da it was a pack of lies?

'However,' Mrs Buchanan continued grimly, 'as I have explained to my dear husband, we have a responsibility to the Adelphi hotel which means that until we can find someone to replace you we shall have to endure your unwholesome presence. As a punishment for your appalling behaviour, you will not receive any money from now on.'

'I have done nothing wrong,' Hettie blurted out passionately. 'It is Mr Buchanan who has lied. He is the one who . . . Oh!'

Hettie cried out in pain and lifted her hand to nurse her smarting cheek after Mrs Buchanan slapped her face with such force that Hettie staggered a little.

'Do you dare to impugn the reputation of my husband, you little harlot! Who would believe you? No one! Mr Buchanan is a respectable married man, an *Englishman*,' she emphasised, 'whilst you are nothing but the filthy product of fornication, the issue of a suicide, and a foreign whore, from what I've heard. Mrs Fazackerly, as is a personal friend of mine from when we was at school together, told me all about you.'

'Mrs Fazackerly?' Hettie protested. 'But I don't know any Mrs Fazackerly.'

'No, because she's far too respectable to have anything to do with the likes of you. Her husband was cousin to your father, he who brought disgrace on his family by what he did. By rights you should be living in a whorehouse by the docks like the rest of your kind,' she added malevolently.

Hettie cowered away from the flood of verbal venom being directed at her. Thanks to Ellie's protection and the sheltered life she had led, Hettie had never previously been exposed to hostility because of her parentage, or been told that she should be ashamed because of it.

Now suddenly she was filled with bewilderment and shocked confusion, with a small cold kernel of unwanted knowledge. She was different. She had always known that. She had, of course, heard her mother explaining her circumstances to Mrs Buchanan during her initial interview in answer to the music teacher's request to know more about Hettie's background. But she also knew that all Ellie had said was that she was her step-daughter, and the child of her first husband.

Did other people secretly think the same as Mrs Buchanan? Was she an outcast, a misfit? Doubts and uncertainties swarmed over her, and misery gripped her stomach.

'You will never, never repeat the vile insinuations you have just attempted to make,' Mrs Buchanan told her coldly. 'Otherwise it will be the worse for you!'

Hettie stared back at her numbly. She knew the story of how her Japanese mother had come to England with her looking for the man she loved, and how out of unhappiness and despair her father had taken his own life before they got there. But when Ellie had related this story to her she had done so with kindness and respect for Hettie's mother, and had said that Hettie should always remember that her parents had loved one another and that she, Hettie, was the child of that love. But the circumstances surrounding her birth lay in the past now, Ellie had said firmly, and it was best that they were left there and not spoken of in public.

TWELVE

''Ere, 'Ettie, you've been ever so quiet these last few days, not sickening for something, are you?' Babs asked her.

Hettie shook her head. She had not told the other girls the full story of what Mrs Buchanan had said to her, only that Mr Buchanan was blaming her for what had happened and that Mrs Buchanan was refusing to hand over to her any of her wages.

'It's a pound to a penny she knows what he's up to right enough, otherwise she'd have had you turfed straight out onto the streret,' had been Babs's opinion, and the other girls had agreed.

Hettie had followed their advice and a piece of wood had duly been provided in order that the door to the practice room could be wedged open. Hettie had not spoken one single word to Mr Buchanan since his wife's visit to deliver her ultimatum, simply practising her songs and then singing them for her audience, steadfastly ignoring the pianist.

But worst of all, somehow she could not bring herself to write home about what had happened. Suddenly it was as though there was a barrier between her and the family she had innocently always thought of as her own, but which she had now been forced to acknowledge was not.

'They're going to be auditioning for that new musical tomorrow, why don't you come along and try for it, Hettie?' Babs encouraged.

She was tempted; after all, nothing could be worse than her present situation.

'I'm too short for the chorus,' she reminded Babs uncertainly.

'There's other parts, and you've got a lovely singing voice. Me and the twins are going to get our hair cut in that new bob this afternoon, why don't you come along with us and do the same? It would fair suit you, and you'd look a lot more modern.'

Cut her hair? Hettie's eyes grew round.

'You'd be bound to get a part then. Bobbed hair's all the rage. Come on, give it a go,' Babs coaxed.

Hettie hesitated, but the other girls were urging her on, saying how much short hair would suit her, and somehow she heard herself saying breathlessly, 'Very well then, I shall!'

'Madame Francaise, that's that hairdresser on Lord Street, will do our hair cheap for us, Hettie, if we let her girls use us as models,' Babs explained an hour later as the four of them hurried across Lime Street. Then they cut down Roe Street, heading for Holy Corner, as the junction between Lord Street, Church Street, Whitechapel, and Paradise Street was known locally, the twins in front and Babs linking arms with Hettie behind them.

As the twins turned a sharp corner the wind blasted their thin summer frocks, lifting their skirts and causing both girls to shriek in mock dismay whilst passers-by turned to watch.

''Ee, let's give 'em something to look at, shall we?' Jenny urged, but when she and Jess started to fool around, aiming a few high kicks from their chorus routine, Babs hissed at them fiercely.

'That's enough, you two! Me and Hettie don't want to be made a show of, thank you very much.'

'Spoilsport.' Jess laughed as they were about to turn into Lord Street, breaking off to call out, 'Ooh, look, Bunney's!'

Immediately the twins rushed over to the famous shop.

'Look at them,' Babs sighed. 'They look more like kids than anything else with their noses pressed up against the window like that.'

Bunney's was famous throughout Liverpool for its exotic and oriental goods which it imported from all over the world.

A one-legged sailor was standing outside the store, a parrot on his shoulder. The bird was shrieking and whistling, in between calling out insults, much to the delight of the children who paused to stare at it. Further along the road was an organ grinder, his little monkey chattering and waiting, cap in hand.

Normally Hettie would have been only too happy to have pressed her own nose up against the window, but now suddenly she was acutely conscious of her own 'oriental' blood and she drew back into the shadows. Ever since she could remember, Ellie had told her she was pretty, but now she could see that her prettiness was not the same kind as that of other true English girls. She was smaller, her face was rounded, her hair darker and her eyes, despite their roundness, were still somehow slightly almond shaped.

'Come on, you two,' Babs called out. 'If we don't get there soon there'll be a queue and we won't get in.'

Madame Francaise's establishment was halfway down Lord Street, elegant gilt lettering in its window proclaiming the excellence of permanent waving and the very latest French hairstyles.

Inside, half a dozen girls wearing pink aprons were busy washing and snipping hair.

Hettie examined her surroundings uncertainly. Ellie and Connie both had long hair, which they wore up, and she did not know of anyone other than her mother's friend Iris who had had their hair bobbed.

A very tall, very thin woman with a long pointed nose and thin carmined lips was bearing down on them, her own short hair immaculately sculpted in waves to frame her face.

'Yes?' she demanded sharply.

'We've come about the advertisement in the paper,' Babs answered her. 'The one that said you could have your hair re-styled for half price.'

Madam Francaise gave Babs a cold look. 'You cannot have read the advertisement properly for if you had done so you would know that it said that those who wished to take advantage of my generous offer should present themselves for my inspection after hours.'

Babs flushed and looked uncomfortable. 'Oh. I'm sorry,' she began, turning towards the door, the others all following her.

'No, wait,' Madam Francaise commanded catching up with them and, to Hettie's discomposure, putting a hand on her shoulder. 'I will do *your* hair.'

'Hettie isn't staying without us,' Jenny announced quickly. 'Are you, Hettie?'

Hettie shook her head. The truth was she did not want to stay without them.

The thin carmined lips became even thinner. 'Very well then. All of you, wait here. Marie will take you upstairs and get you ready.'

As she swept away to summon one of the pink-uniformed young women Jenny dug Hettie in the ribs and grinned.

Ten minutes later they were all seated together upstairs in a drafty room nowhere near as elegant or glamorous as the downstairs salon, whilst Marie and two other girls began to take the grips out of their hair.

'Quick,' Marie urged. 'Madame will be up here in a minute and she won't half go mad if we're wasting time.'

Once the grips were moved and the girls' hair was loose, Marie, Josephine and Pauline, as the other girls had introduced themselves, began to tug it this way and that, causing Hettie to wince when her turn came.

There was a sudden increase in tugging activity from all three girls when Madame's head appeared at the top of the stairs, followed by her rail-thin body.

'You, come and sit down here,' she commanded Hettie. 'And you three as well,' she added. 'Pauline, Marie and Josephine, you will watch and then follow what I have done exactly.'

A little nervously Hettie sat down on the chair Madame pushed in front of her.

'You will remain perfectly still,' she warned Hettie before beginning to snip busily at her long hair.

Hardly daring to breathe never mind move Hettie watched out of the corner of her eye as long strands of her hair fell to the the floor, but it was not until she felt the coolness of air on the back of her neck that she began to wonder what on earth she had done.

'Now, you three, do exactly the same,' Madame

instructed, leaving Hettie to watch as the apprentices busied themselves copying their mistress.

'Oh my gawd,' Jenny cried at one point when the floor all around them was covered in hair.

'What 'ave you made us do, Babs?' She started to sob noisily, quickly joined by her twin.

'Go downstairs and get a jug of water, Josephine,' Madame ordered coldly. 'It is an excellent cure for hysteria.'

As though by magic both girls stopped crying, sitting nervously clenching the arms of their chairs whilst Madame slowly and silently inspected the work of her young trainees.

'Josephine, you have missed a bit there,' she pointed out, adding, 'And how many times must I tell you how important it is to keep your scissors sharp. This poor girl's hair looks as though it has been hacked with a blunt knife and fork.'

Babs, the 'poor girl', looked aghast but Madame ignored her, returning to Hettie and proceeding to push Hettie's head forward so that her chin was resting on her chest.

'Now for the second stage when we shape the hair into the new style,' she intoned. 'Watch me very carefully.'

Obediently the three girls clustered around Hettie, watching as Madame began to snip painstakingly into her hair.

If she carried on like this she was not going to have any hair left, Hettie decided, tensely listening to the busy snip of the scissors and the heavy breathing of the apprentices.

'In order for the hair to fall right it is most important that the back is cut like so. Now, let us see how well you have observed me and remembered.'

Hettie lifted her head cautiously and watched as the girls went to work on the backs of her friends' heads, snipping off the smallest amount of hair so that incredibly the ugly pudding bowl shape started to disappear and instead an elegant new style began to take its place.

Again Madame inspected what had been done and again she returned to Hettie, this time cutting and shaping the front and sides of her hair. When she had finished, she produced a comb from the pocket of her close-fitting cover-all and flicked it through Hettie's hair, finally stepping back and announcing almost theatrically, 'Voila, le style Francaise.'

'Oh Hettie . . .' Babs's voice trembled with emotion. 'Oh, but you look lovely.'

'Gawd, 'Ettie, I'd never 'ave known you if I didn't know it was you,' Jenny breathed in awe whilst her twin nodded her head in agreement.

Pauline brought over a mirror so that Hettie could see herself. A small, delicately shaped face stared back at her surrounded by a cap of silky feathered hair that clung to her cheeks and somehow made her eyes look huge.

'Oh my, Hettie. Yer look like a real flapper now,' Jess sighed approvingly.

'You three continue,' Madame instructed, heading for the stairs.

Unable to take in the difference her new hairstyle had made to the way she looked, Hettie sat in silence watching the apprentices work the same magic on her friends, until Madame reappeared to announce, 'You, Hettie, is it? In a few minutes a photographer will be here to take your picture, so that I can show my clients the elegance of my new hair style.'

Of course, the new hairstyles had to be shown off, first to the others and then, at Jenny's insistence, to the world at large via a visit to the Vines public house which was situated next door to the Adelphi on the corner of Lime Street and Copperas Hill.

Hettie was reluctant to go, but Babs soothed her fears, explaining that the Vines was a very respectable establishment and regularly frequented by theatre folk.

It was certainly noisy, Hettie decided as she followed the others inside the riotously Baroque building.

''Ere, look who it isn't,' Jenny whispered, nudging Babs. 'His nibs and our leading lady all coseyed-up together, talking sweet nothings.'

'Oh quick, Jenny, don't let them see us,' Jess begged anxiously, hurrying to skirt past the semi-private booth where the leading lady was sitting with the Royal Court's Manager.

'I thought Mr Johnson was married?' Hettie whispered.

'He is, but she likes 'em like that. It gives 'er a kick to take someone else's man, doesn't it, Babs?'

When a waiter appeared to take their order, Jenny made a point of preening and stroking her newly shorn hair as she ordered her porter. 'What's the betting we *all* get taken on for the new production now,' she gloated.

'Bang-up to the minute we are, and no mistake.'

'How is Ellie?' John asked Gideon anxiously after he had been admitted to the Winckley Square house and shown into Gideon's study.

'Very weak,' Gideon told him heavily. 'I would have preferred to stay up in the Lakes until she was stronger before travelling home, but she was insistent that she wanted to be here and getting herself in such an overwrought state that Iris feared she might suffer a relapse. Thank God Iris was able to come up to look after Ellie. Without her I dread to think about what could have happened.'

John could see how worn down his brother-in-law looked, and no wonder.

'Iris has given her a draught to keep her calm whilst she recovers her strength. At first she refused to accept that . . . that there was no longer a child, and then when she did she blamed herself for not consulting Iris earlier. Ellie wanted this child so much and now it is not to be she has sunk into a melancholy from which nothing seems to rouse her,' Gideon continued.

'What is to be done, then?' John asked him anxiously.

Gideon shook his head. 'Iris says we must let nature take its course and allow Ellie to grieve. Oh God, John, when I thought that I might lose her . . . She is everything to me, my whole life. Without her . . . And yet she refuses even to look at me and turns her head away when I enter her room.'

His grief seemed to fill the room with a leaden burden of dark despair.

'Perhaps if I were to speak to her,' John suggested awkwardly.

Immediately Gideon shook his head. 'No. Iris has advised me that for now it is best if Ellie does not see anyone. She says the balance of her mind is so affected by the loss of this child that anything, even the sight of a familiar face, could be enough to upset her.'

John didn't know what to say or do to comfort Gideon. 'I have to go to Oxford to take up my new post at the end of the month, but if you would like me to delay leaving?'

'No, John. It is kind of you to offer, but there is no point. Iris is insistent that the best thing we can do for Ellie right now is to allow her to recover at her own pace. She has said that she will remain here until Ellie is well enough to be left and I know that Ellie could not be in any safer hands. You must not delay starting your new life on our account. Will you see Connie before you leave?'

'Yes. I had planned to see her this weekend. I can then travel by train down to London and from there to Oxfordshire.'

Was there any chance he might see Hettie whilst he was in Liverpool? John wondered. And if he did see her, how was he going to feel? Would he still be torn between angry resentment of her singing, and the choice she had made – a choice which had excluded him from her life – and anxiety for her because he feared for her and wanted to protect her from all the dangers he suspected her new life could hold? Or would he find, perhaps, that he too had changed and she no longer meant to him what she once had?

THIRTEEN

'They *would* choose the Bank Holiday weekend to audition,' the girl next to Hettie in the queue sniffed crossly.

'I was supposed to be going to Blackpool with me fella and now I've had to come here instead.'

'Well, no one forced you to audition, Mary,' another girl chipped in.

It was hot and stuffy in the cramped area off the wings of the small theatre where the auditions were being held, and Hettie, who should have been at the Adelphi practising, prayed silently that she would get taken on. She didn't think she could bear much more of Mr Buchanan or the slyly triumphant looks he kept giving her.

'So what's it going to be, this musical then?' someone else asked.

''Oo knows,' the girl standing next to Hettie answered.

'It's some fancy pants composer from London wot 'as written the music.'

'I've heard they want three hundred for the chorus and that whoever gets the lead is bound to end up in films, it's that good a part . . .'

'Well, I wouldn't mind being another Gertie Lawrence,' someone else said enviously.

'Ooh, Hettie, I'm that nervous,' Babs whispered.

'Me too,' Hettie agreed.

They had all been told they would have two minutes to show off their skills, and, knowing she wasn't tall enough for the chorus, on Babs's advice Hettie had decided to do a bit of tap, and then sing.

'Cos if you was to get a part, Hettie, they'd want to know you can dance as well as sing.'

There was only Babs in front of her now and Hettie held her breath when a disembodied male voice called out, 'Next.' Babs hurried on to the stage. Hettie couldn't see her but she could imagine how her friend would look as the pianist struck up and Babs began to dance, and then stopped dancing to sing.

'Next.'

'Go on, it's your turn,' the girl behind Hettie told her impatiently. 'Unless you've changed your mind?'

It was impossible to see anyone in the seats from the stage because of the lights, but Hettie remembered what Babs had told her and focused on the darkness as though she could see someone she cared for there. She handed the pianist her music and waited for her to begin playing.

She had finished her tap and just sung the opening bars of her song when to her chagrin she heard an impatient voice call out, 'Thank you, that's sufficient. Next . . .'

'Oh Hettie, never mind,' Babs tried to console her as they left the theatre.

'He wouldn't even let me finish my song,' Hettie protested whilst Babs gave her hand a sympathetic squeeze.

Unlike Hettie, Babs had been told to go back for a second audition, and Hettie did her best to hide her own disappointment and to congratulate her friend instead.

'You going to your aunt's this Sunday?' Babs asked her.

Hettie nodded. She was badly in need of the caring, familiar face of Connie. It had been over two weeks now since she had last had a letter from Ellie. At first Hettie had been relieved that her parents were obviously too busy in the Lakes to write, because that meant Hettie would not have to lie to her about the Buchanans. But now, since Mrs Buchanan had forced her to recognise what she really was, Hettie had begun to wonder deep inside herself if Gideon and Ellie had thought of her more as a responsibility than a true part of their family, and were secretly glad she had gone.

Several of the girls from the boarding house had been told to attend second auditions for the new musical, and they were all talking excitedly about it.

'And I've heard this American is investing in it and is thinking of taking it to Broadway if it does well in London,' Hettie had heard one girl say.

'Oh Broadway,' another of them had sniffed. 'Paris. That's where I want to go. I've got a cousin who's got a friend in the Folies and she says nearly all the girls in the chorus there end up with rich fellas.'

It seemed that everyone but her had exciting plans, Hettie thought unhappily on Sunday morning as she walked past the Bluecoat School on her way to Connie's.

What would happen to her if the Buchanans dismissed her and Ellie and Gideon didn't want her back?

When she reached the school Connie greeted her quietly and seemed distracted. Her normal big smile was missing and she didn't make any comment about Hettie's hair other than to say it was very modern.

And then in the middle of the afternoon, when Hettie was entertaining the children by showing them a new dance routine, the parlour door opened and John walked in.

'John!' Immediately Hettie scrambled to her feet, her face flushed, a smile curving her mouth. 'Oh, I am *so* pleased to see you.'

'What have you done to your hair?' John demanded, unable to suppress his shock at seeing her lovely long hair gone, and a short bob in its place.

Self-consciously, Hettie touched her head. 'It is the new fashion. There is to be a new musical and I had it cut so that I could audition. By the way, why didn't you come to see me at the Adelphi? You said you would . . .' Her voice faltered as she saw the way he was looking her.

'Can you think of nothing else other than singing?' John demanded, knowing that he could not tell her the truth. He felt so worn down by the dreadful things happening. First Jim's death and now poor Ellie losing her baby . . . 'Ellie is desperately poorly and yet all you can speak of is some *musical*,' he burst out passionately, only recognising when it was too late, and the words already spoken, what he had done.

'Mam is poorly?' Hettie repeated, shocked. 'How . . . When? I – I didn't know . . .'

'How could you when all that concerns you is yourself.' He should be offering her comfort and not the anger he really felt for himself rather than for her, John recognised guiltily.

'No!' Hettie protested. '*No*, that is not true. What is wrong with Mam?'

'She has lost the child she was to have,' John told her bluntly. 'And has fallen into very low spirits because of it.'

Hettie couldn't take in what he was saying. Mam had been pregnant?

'John, love.' Connie came to an abrupt halt as

she walked into the parlour and looked from John's set face to Hettie's pale one.

'I'm going home to see Mam,' Hettie blurted out immediately.

'No, Hettie,' Connie told her firmly. 'The last thing Ellie needs right now is everyone making a fuss. Besides, Iris has said that she isn't to have any visitors.'

Hettie flinched. 'But I am not a visitor. I am . . .' She stopped and looked away, tears blurring her eyes. What exactly *was* she to Ellie? Nothing at all really. Not a blood relative, that was certain. 'Why did she not tell me there was to be a baby?' she whispered.

Connie sighed. 'Hettie, you cannot help Ellie by distressing yourself like this. She would have told you about the baby in due course, and as for you going to see her, Iris will not even allow *me* to visit her and I used to be a nurse. Now dry those tears and be sensible. I must go and tell Harry you are here, John.'

As soon as she had gone John went over to where Hettie was sitting, still trembling with shock. 'Hettie, I'm sorry. I should not have spoken to you the way I did,' he told her gruffly.

'I didn't know . . . Oh, I wish that I had never come here and that I had stayed with Mam, and then maybe . . .'

'Hush, you are not to say that.' John tried to comfort her, feeling ashamed now of his outburst which had been caused by his memories of how

169

his own mother had died in childbed, rather than because he genuinely felt Hettie was at fault.

But Hettie refused to be reassured, instead getting up and pacing the floor in agitation. 'Mam wanted to see Iris when we were staying here with Aunt Connie, but she came shopping with me instead,' she declared in an agonised voice, tears pouring down her face. 'She must have been concerned about her health and wanted to ask Iris's advice, but I acted like such a child and made her feel so bad she cancelled her visit.'

'Hettie, you must not torture yourself like this,' John protested, going to her and putting his arms around her, just as he had done so many times before when she had run to him with her troubles.

But she was not a little girl any more, and when she turned her face up to his, her lips parting slightly, John couldn't help himself. He bent his head and swiftly placed a kiss on her parted lips.

For a moment Hettie seemed to melt into him, and the scent of her intoxicated and dizzied him so much that he held her even tighter, but then suddenly she cried out and pulled back from him.

Immediately John released her, cursing himself for what he had done. How would she ever be able to trust him again?

John had kissed her! Hettie wanted to place her fingertips to her mouth to see if it was actually true, to see if she could feel the kiss, but she felt too confused to do so. She had known John for almost her entire life. She loved him, worshipped him, but lately he had seemed so angry with her. She had wondered if he would even speak with her again but now he had kissed her!

'John,' she began uncertainly.

But he shook his head, and told her stiffly, 'That should never have happened. I forgot that you are no longer a child.' He turned and walked out of the room, leaving Hettie to wonder what had just happened between them.

'Connie, I must leave you all now if I am to catch my train.'

Harry and John shook hands and then John kissed his sister and the children.

Hettie stood warily to one side. Why was John so angry with her every time they met? As a child she had loved him, and she had believed that he had loved her. But now he treated her with anger and contempt.

'John, since Hettie has to walk back past Lime Street station she may as well go with you,' Connie suggested.

Hettie waited for him to reject her suggestion but instead, after a small pause, he nodded his head and said brusquely, 'Very well then.'

They walked in silence past the Bluecoat School. But it was not the warm, companionable silence of two people at ease in one another's company. Instead it felt prickly and uncomfortable, and it was causing a hard lump to form in her throat, Hettie acknowledged miserably as she made herself keep pace with John's much longer stride.

'What is it like, the place you are going to, John?' she enquired, unable to endure the tension any longer. 'Will you send us some photographs so that we may see it?'

'I doubt I shall have time for taking photographs,' he replied curtly. 'And as for what it is like, it is like any other airfield.'

Hettie's face started to burn at his abrupt, dismissive manner. Tears filled her eyes and began to roll down her face.

Seeing her distress John stopped walking and challenged her sharply. 'I cannot see what cause you have for tears, Hettie. Think of someone other than yourself for once. You have given no thought at all to Ellie, or to what you owe her.'

'That is not true,' Hettie burst out fiercely. 'I am well aware of how much she has done for me. I have always thought of her as my mother and myself as her daughter, but I now know that it is only her kindness and charity that has allowed me to become a part of her family.'

John's frowned deepened. 'You misunderstand me,' he told her. 'I was referring to the fact that from what Connie has told me you seem to care more about having fun with your new friends than being with your family.'

'Connie said that?' Hettie demanded indignantly.

John looked away from her. In fact, what Connie had said to him was that she was pleased

Hettie was making new friends, that she had a new confidence and independence about her, that she seemed a million miles away from the frightened girl who had first arrived in Liverpool.

'It seems to me you prefer to ape the ways of theatre folk instead of modelling yourself on the example Ellie has set you. Look at your hair!'

John couldn't understand himself exactly why Hettie's new life should make him feel so angry, but rather than analyse his feelings it was easier for him to blame Hettie herself for them. He had too much to think of right now: his new job, his new life in Oxfordshire. Above all, how he was going to live with the guilt about what had happened at the airfield, nightmares about which plagued his every sleep.

'Your rightful place is at home with Ellie, especially now, not here in Liverpool singing.'

Without waiting for her response he turned away and started to stride out so fast that Hettie practically had to run to catch up with him.

They continued their walk to Lime Street Station in silence, only broken when they stood outside the station facing one another and Hettie begged passionately, 'John, please do not let us part bad friends.'

Something in the pleading way she was looking at him made his heart ache and then pound heavily against his chest wall. 'Hettie . . .' He reached out and touched her head, the shock of its silky shortness causing his fingers to tense.

He badly wanted to take the olive branch she was offering, but some stubbornness bound with pain wouldn't let him. He couldn't allow thoughts of Hettie to join the mass of confusing emotions vying for space in his head. And he could never be just friends with her now, not after that kiss, hard as he might try to forget it. It would be better for both of them if they had little to do with each other from this point onwards.

'I cannot see how it matters how we part,' he told her tersely. 'You have chosen your life, Hettie, and I have chosen mine, and it is obvious to me that we are destined to go in very different directions'.

He had gone before she could say anything, lost to her in the crowd of people disappearing inside the bowels of the station.

Later that night, lying in the darkness of the attic room, listening to the sound of the other girls breathing, Hettie relived that moment when John's lips had touched hers. It had felt so very different from the revolting sensation of Mr Buchanan's wet mouth on her skin.

But it was the manner of his parting from her that weighed most heavily on her thoughts, and the charges he had made against her. Unfair, untruthful charges, and so she intended to prove.

Her mind was made up, and nothing could change it. No matter what her Aunt Connie had said, she was going to tell Ellie that she intended to come home permanently to be with her. Singing might be in her blood, but some things were far more important.

FOURTEEN

'But what about the Adelphi and your morning practice?' Babs asked Hettie doubtfully as she watched Hettie count out the money for her train fare.

'I don't care about that,' Hettie told her fiercely. 'I'm going to tell Mam that I'm coming home.'

'But Hettie, you love singing so much!'

'I thought I did, but now I don't,' Hettie insisted stubbornly.

The truth was that John's disclosures and accusations about the loss of the baby Ellie had been carrying had left Hettie not just feeling guilty but determined to make amends, and to prove that she was not the naive foolish girl everyone seemed to think, but instead a responsible mature young woman.

'What time will you be back?' Babs asked her.

'I don't know. I may stay at home tonight and come back tomorrow.'

'Ma Buchanan will have forty fits if you do that,' Babs warned her.

Hettie gave a dismissive shrug. 'Then she'll just have to have forty fits. Why should I concern myself about them after the way they've treated me?'

'By, Hettie, that's the spirit, good for you,' Babs cheered.

Once the train had pulled into Preston station Hettie got off and walked along the platform before pausing to read the newspaper headlines telling of the fifty thousand strong crowd that had attended the funeral in Italy of the singer Enrico Caruso. What must it be like to be so famous and so adored? She would certainly never know. In future the only audience for her singing would be the occupants of the Winckley Square house. But she didn't care, Hettie assured herself firmly. In fact, she was glad!

She was wearing a pretty dress under a light-weight coat, her legs encased in a pair of the very latest Red Seal silk hose, which had cost her the last of her carefully saved 'emergency' money. Her bobbed hair was concealed beneath the neat cloche style hat she had had retrimmed with new ribbon to match the sash on her dress, but her stylish appearance was the last thing on her mind as she hurried towards Fishergate and then turned off to walk towards Winckley Square.

Preston seemed smaller than she remembered, its air different from Liverpool's slightly salty tang. Neither of her birth parents had originated from

Preston but to her it had always been home, just as to her Ellie and Gideon had always been her family.

As she turned into Winckley Square she looked automatically across to the large elegant house Gideon had inherited from his mother, frowning at the sight of an unfamiliar and very smart car parked outside it.

Traditionally the children of the family had always used the back door into the kitchen for their comings and goings, sure of a freshly baked ginger-bread man or some other treat along with a glass of fresh milk. But when Hettie turned the handle of the kitchen door and walked in the little tweeny maid stared at her as though she were a stranger, almost dropping the coal scuttle she was carrying.

'Oh, Miss Hettie, it's you. I didn't recognise you at first. My, what a shock you gave me!'

Miss Hettie? Since when had she been a *miss*? Hettie wondered.

'I've come to see Mam,' she explained.

'Oh, miss, she's been that poorly,' the tweeny said with a sigh. 'And the poor master . . . You'll find the master in his study,' she said hurriedly, aware she may have said too much. 'Dr Iris is upstairs with yer mam.'

'Oh, is that her car outside?'

'Yes, it is.'

Leaving the kitchen Hettie made her way through the hall and then pushed open the door to her father's study after a brief knock.

'Hettie! What on earth . . .'

'Da.' To her own chagrin Hettie burst into tears and flung herself into Gideon's arms. 'John and Aunt Connie told me about Mam and the baby,' she told him when she had calmed down.

Before he could respond the study door opened and Iris came in looking as surprised as Gideon had to see Hettie.

'I want to see Mam,' Hettie announced immediately.

'Hettie, she's sleeping at the moment, and it's best that she isn't disturbed,' Iris told her in a kind but firm voice.

'But I want to tell her that I'm going to stop singing and that I'm going to come home to be with her.'

'Oh, Hettie, no! You mustn't do that,' Iris objected. 'It won't help Ellie, and in fact it could even make her worse.'

Hettie looked at her in disbelief. 'But why? Why should me being here make her worse?'

There was just the smallest, telling pause during which Hettie saw Iris and Gideon exchange glances before Iris said calmly, 'Come and sit down, Hettie, and I'll try to explain.'

Anxiously, Hettie did so.

'Physically, Ellie is making an excellent recovery from losing her baby,' Iris explained carefully. 'That is to say her body is recovering well, but there is more to human beings than merely a body, as we doctors are beginning to recognise.

'Ellie blames herself for the fact that she lost her baby. She feels that if she had consulted me originally when she had wanted to, things might have been different. Of course, I have told her that she has nothing to blame herself for, and even if I had seen her it would not have made any difference, but she cannot let go of this belief that she is to blame. The fact that this baby would have been the daughter she longed so much to have has, I think, added to her suffering. We know that sometimes, even after a healthy baby has been delivered, a woman can suffer deep melancholy, and it is this melancholy that has taken a hold of Ellie.'

Hettie sat stiffly, feeling her heart pounding heavily and bitterly inside her chest. Why should her mother want another daughter when she already had her? Didn't she love her any more? Had she ever really loved her or had she just pretended to?

'What you want to do is very praiseworthy, Hettie. I know you want to help, but what Ellie needs is to be allowed to grieve for her lost child. At the moment she is all Ellie can think of or talk about. I know this is hard for you to hear, and I hope you will understand. I don't think that Ellie would want to see you – she has refused to see her aunt and her cousins, and has even requested that Connie does not come to visit.'

'They are not as close to her as me,' Hettie wanted to protest, but she knew she could not.

Gideon came over to her and took hold of her hand. 'Hettie, Ellie will not even share her grief with me.'

Hettie fought to control her desire to cry. 'But she will get better, won't she?' she appealed to Iris.

'I hope so, Hettie,' Iris told her quietly. 'But these things take time.' She looked across at Gideon. 'I have recommended to your father that, if things do not improve soon, he should take her away, perhaps to the Lakes again, for the air is very pure and strengthening there. Now I have to go back upstairs in a few minutes in case Ellie has woken up. She does not like me to leave her for very long, and she only sleeps fitfully, so I must say goodbye to you.'

'You will tell her . . .'

'I shall tell her that you are thinking of her and that you have sent your love,' Iris stopped her firmly. 'Please excuse me, I must go back to Ellie.'

'Iris has been wonderful. I don't know now how we would have managed without her,' Gideon declared as the door closed behind her.

'Da, please let me stay,' Hettie begged.

Sorrowfully, Gideon shook his head. 'You heard what Iris said, Hettie. Are you all right for money, by the way? I had intended to make arrangements for you to receive an allowance. I must speak to Harry about it.'

'I bought a return train ticket,' Hettie told him quietly.

Gideon smiled at her, 'You are a good child,

Hettie. Here is your five pounds now. If I am to take your mother to the Lakes there are arrangements I shall need to make . . .'

He could think of nothing and no one other than Ellie, Hettie recognised bleakly as he pressed five pounds on her as though already anxious for her to be gone.

'Thank goodness, that is the last one gone. I can't remember when we last had such a busy night,' Sarah puffed as she hurried into the chop house kitchen with more dirty plates and put them down beside the sink. 'Could you go and clear the rest of the plates for me please, Hettie, only I have to go upstairs and check on Granddad.'

Hettie nodded and then lifted a wet hand to push her hair out of her eyes before walking towards the dining room.

Tomorrow she would have to face the Buchanans who would want to know why she had not gone to the Adelphi this afternoon. She would lose her job there anyway just as soon as they found a replacement for her, which would only be a matter of time as they had already placed another advert, she reminded herself as she started to hum and then sing the first notes of a sad lament. Somehow it was easier for her to sing how she felt than to think about it.

The door to the street was still open and Hettie left it so, welcoming the cool evening air after the steamy heat of the kitchen. Still softly singing she cleared the plates and then began to wipe the tables. The song was one of her favourites, the lament of a young girl for the man she had loved and lost, from one of her favourite operettas.

'Bravo. You have a good voice.'

Hettie nearly dropped the plates she was carrying as a man rose from the dark shadows of one of the banquettes where he had obviously been sitting.

'Oh, I beg your pardon,' the stranger apologised. 'I didn't mean to scare you. I was just finishing my drink before leaving. You obviously sing professionally. Which show are you in?'

'I'm not. I mean, yes I do sing. At the Adelphi in the afternoon for the ladies who take tea. Or at least I did . . . But I am not in any show.'

'The Adelphi? The devil you do,' he said sharply coming towards her so that she could see him properly for the first time.

Hettie's eyes widened. 'You were at the Adelphi,' she told him.

'Yes. And you did not answer the note I sent you,' he agreed.

'I do not accept invitations from hotel guests,' Hettie told him primly.

He frowned, and Hettie guessed that she had annoyed him. To her relief Sarah came bustling down the stairs, obviously surprised to see a diner still in the restaurant. Leaving her to deal with him, Hettie whisked herself and her plates into the kitchen, firmly closing the door between the two rooms.

Was it a bad omen to see the handsome American again tonight – the one who had sent her the note that provoked Mr Buchancan into his attack on her? Did it spell further doom to come? She was not sure she could take much more at the moment. She'd never felt so alone, so unloved by those she thought her family. She couldn't even bring herself to go and see Connie now after what she had told John about her preferring new friends over her family.

Tiredly, she started to wash the last of the dishes. Somehow today her home had not felt like her home any longer. No matter how much she wished things were different, Iris's words had made it plain to her that Ellie did not think of her as her daughter. Because of that her pride had not allowed her to tell Gideon that she was likely to lose her job. She could not and would not go back to Winckley Square if she were not truly wanted there.

But what was she to do? The money she earned here at the chop house would not be enough for her to live on and pay rent to her landlady – if she even let her stay on after the business with the Buchanans, that was. She felt so very afraid of what the future held.

'Sommat wrong, 'Ettie?' Babs asked sympathetically when she saw Hettie sitting silently on her bed later that evening.

'Course there's sommat wrong,' Mary answered

for her scornfully. 'The poor kid's just lost her bleedin' job.'

'Never mind, Hettie, with those looks of yours you'll soon get work,' Sukey tried to comfort her. 'That Chinky look as you've got makes fellas think as how you'd be a real fast piece, even if we know you ain't,' she added giving Hettie a saucy wink.

'My mother was *Japanese*, not Chinese,' Hettie protested sharply, tears stinging her eyes as she saw the look the other girls exchanged and suddenly felt very alone and excluded. She *was* different, even if she herself did not want to admit it. And she had seen, too, the way that men looked at her in a different way than they looked at the other girls.

It was the same way the man at the restaurant had looked at her. What was she to do? What was to become of her?

PART TWO

FIFTEEN

''Ere, 'Ettie, there's going to be some new auditions for the musical. Seems like a couple o' the girls they took on 'aven't turned out to be right. Why don't you give it a go?'

Hettie heaved a small sigh and shook her head. 'They won't take me on now, not after they've already turned me down.'

''Oo says? By golly, 'Ettie Walker, I never thought you was the kind that was a quitter,' Babs told her sturdily.

A quitter? Angry colour burned in Hettie's pale face. 'I'll have you know, Babs Cheetham, that I am no such thing.'

'Good, cos I've already said as 'ow you'll be coming to the audition,' Babs announced smugly.

Hettie knew that her friends were trying to help her, but Ellie's rejection of her had left a deep and painful wound that was hurting very badly, and for once her singing was not providing her with any solace for her pain. It hurt so much that the two people dearest to her in the entire world, Ellie and John, should both have turned their backs on her.

She was feeling so low that she could not in all honesty see the point of even attending the audition, but Babs cajoled and bullied her into getting ready for it, insisting optimistically that Hettie had as much chance as anyone else of getting one of the three vacant parts. 'And more than most if'n you was to ask me to speak out honestly,' she assured Hettie. 'For none of 'em could sing as well as you do, 'Ettie.'

Hettie sighed. They had been through all this before. 'But I'm not tall enough for the chorus,' she reminded Babs again.

'You 'aven't bin listenin' to me proper, 'ave you? These parts aren't for the bleedin' chorus, 'Ettie. There's a trio of girls who 'ave to come on and sing a coupla songs, and one of them will 'ave to be the understudy for the second female lead, on account of one of the girls who left was the second female lead so her understudy has 'ad to take her place.'

Over thirty girls had been invited to auditions, and as she stood in the wings listening to them Hettie's heart sank lower and lower. Her voice might be as good if not better than theirs but they were all obviously well-seasoned performers, with most of them having chorus line experience.

At last, when there were only four girls left,

Hettie heard her name called out. But instead of walking calmly out on to the stage, she panicked and froze. She had to be pushed by the girl standing next to her, so that she half stumbled on to the bare boards.

They had all been told to hand in their music for their audition piece to the accompanist. But to Hettie's horror, as she tried to compose herself and ignore the blinding dazzle of the footlights, which were making it impossible for her to see the men she knew would be assessing and judging her, the notes the pianist was playing were not the opening notes for her own piece. Instead, she recognised a popular and cheeky vaudeville song that called for the singer to perform a series of naughty poses as she sang.

Hettie knew the song, but there was no way she could sing it. But the pianist was waiting for her. Tears burned the backs of her eyes. Helplessly, she looked at him and shook her head, explaining, 'That isn't my music . . .'

'Come along, what's the hold up?' a sharp male voice called out from the stalls.

The pianist shrugged his shoulders and looked bored.

Hettie bit her lip.

The safety of the wings was just feet away, but if she gave in and ran to them she would be the quitter she had so proudly told Babs she wasn't.

She took a deep breath and then announced into the darkness: 'The accompanist hasn't got my music, so I shall have to sing without it.' She could hear the impatient rustle and movement of her unseen audience.

Before she could lose her courage she inhaled sharply and began to sing. Perfect pitch, that was what Miss Brown had always praised her for . . . Perfect pitch. She sang at home on her own without music, so why should this be any different?

Determinedly, Hettie tried to ignore that she was singing for the unseen judges in the darkness beyond the footlights, and to pretend instead that she was singing at home in Winckley Square.

Her nervousness faded as her delight in singing took over. The pure true sound of her voice rose and fell in a cascade of liquid harmony, that had Babs, who had sneaked into the wings to listen, clasping her hands together and marvelling aloud.

Hettie had almost finished when she heard someone calling out from the stalls. 'That's enough, that's enough. Next.'

She had been so engrossed in making herself believe she was at home that for a few seconds Hettie couldn't register what was happening, and then suddenly and sickeningly she realised that her audition was over and she was being dismissed.

Hettie was vaguely aware of the sound of angry, raised male voices coming from the stalls, but the next girl was already coming out of the wings, giving a loud sniff of contempt as she hurried past her, and the pianist began to play her music.

She should never have allowed Babs to persuade

her to come here today, Hettie told herself miserably. She should have known she would be turned down. She *had* known all along that she wouldn't be good enough.

Babs was waiting for her in the wings, ready to give her hand a comforting squeeze and to whisper, 'Gawd, 'Ettie, just listen to 'er.' Grimacing and nodding her head in the direction of the stage, she added scornfully, 'What a screech she's making.'

'Huh, well it don't matter where she's concerned how badly she sings,' another girl commented overhearing Babs, ''cos 'er cousin knows someone 'oo knows the director, and I overheard her saying in the dressin' room as 'ow she's already been promised a part.'

'It's not your fault if you 'aven't been chosen, 'Ettie love,' Babs tried to comfort Hettie. 'That's the way it is sometimes in this business. It's a cryin' shame an all cos you have ever such a pretty voice, and I'm really going to miss you when we tek off for London, like. Oh 'eck, is that the time? I've got ter go. We're supposed to be rehearsing. We've got the bloody angel coming, and the director's acting as nervous as a virgin on her weddin' night. I suppose he's worryin' that this American chap is going to want to know what 'is money is being spent on.'

She'd gone before Hettie could say anything, leaving Hettie to make her way past the chattering groups of chorus girls hurrying from the dressing room, leaving the smell of chalk, scent and greasepaint hanging on the air. Dispiritedly Hettie watched the other girls. She couldn't help feeling envious of them and wishing that her own audition had been successful.

She had almost reached the stage door when a good-looking, fair-haired young man hurried up to her, exclaiming, 'Hey, you, Hettie Walker. You're to come with me immediately.'

'What? Why?' Hettie asked apprehensively. 'I . . .'

The young man shook his head and pulled a face. 'Come along, we've got to hurry. It took me ages to find you, and he isn't exactly in the best of moods, even if you have been lucky enough to catch his eye.'

'I'm sorry,' Hettie began uncertainly, 'but I don't think . . .'

'My dear, of course you don't think; none of us ever admit to thinking. How could we when we have to dedicate ourselves to the muse?'

His languid manner of speaking bemused Hettie. She wasn't sure if he was serious or trying to make fun of her. Whilst she was still debating what to do, he took hold of her hand and insisted, 'Come along. I've been told to get you up to his office immediately. Quick,' he instructed her, 'let's take these stairs here. They go right up to the office. Fair taken his nibs' fancy, you have, Hettie Walker,' he told her pointedly. 'And no two ways about it. Here we are.'

He was knocking on a door before opening it

and virtually pushing her inside the room before Hettie could even speak.

She could hear the door closing, shutting her inside the room with the man perched on the edge of the heavy mahogany partners desk that dominated the whole room.

'You,' she gasped, her eyes widening in recognition as she stared at the man who had sent her the note at the Adelphi and then commented on her singing at the chop house.

'They say third time lucky, don't they? I certainly hope they're right, and that this time you don't disappear on me.'

'Who are you? Why have you had me brought here?' Hettie demanded worriedly as she looked from his face to the closed door and then back again.

'My name is Jay Dalhousie,' he told her with a smile, 'and I can assure you that you have nothing to fear from me, Hettie Walker, and that there is no need for you to look so longingly at the door – you can go any time you please, although I sincerely hope you won't want to.'

'I wasn't . . .' Hettie fibbed, and then, feeling bolder despite herself, said, 'Your name is very unusual. I have never heard one like it before.' And then she blushed when he laughed.

'No? Well, it's the one my Daddy gave me, and what was good enough for him is good enough for me.'

'You're an American.' Hettie blushed again as

she realised that her comment sounded almost like an accusation.

'Creole,' he corrected her, watching her confused frown before explaining laconically, 'Way, way back when, my pa's folks came from France to settle in New Orleans, and we like to think of ourselves as Americans with a dash of something extra – something hot and spicy, a bit like our Cajun cooking.'

Something about the way he was looking at her whilst he talked was making Hettie feel both alarmed and excited. Instinctively, she knew that he was the kind of man who would entice a woman to make dangerous and reckless decisions. Her heart started to beat far too fast, and the colour burning her face now had nothing to do with any embarrassment.

'And your mother?' she asked him, trying to make polite conversation.

Instead of answering her immediately, he removed a cigar from the box on the desk, clipping it neatly and then striking and lighting a match against the leather sole of his shoe. 'These are the best cigars a man can buy. They say in Havana that their special richness comes from the fact that the women who make them roll the tobacco leaves between their thighs.'

The bright red burn across her cheekbones betrayed Hettie's shock.

'My mother's grandmother grew up in one of Mississippi's big plantation houses,' he continued, amused and touched by Hettie's sweet innocence. "Belle Visage" was what they named it. My mother used to tell me about how *her* mother had told her stories of my great-grandmamma wearing gowns that were made in France, and jewels worth a prince's ransom.'

'You mean she was the mistress of a slave plantation?' Hettie asked him, unable to conceal her disapproval. At school she had learned about William Wilberforce and his determination to put an end to the slave trade.

'No,' Jay told her laconically. 'What I mean is that she was the mistress of the plantation owner. My great-grandmamma was an octoroon; that is to say she had "slave" blood, and was one-eighth black. In New Orleans they have a name for every degree of "black blood" a person can have.'

Hettie looked at him a little uncertainly. His skin was very much the same shade of warm olive as Liverpool's Italian immigrants, rather than the shiny, almost blue black of the West Africans she had seen around the docks.

'*My* mother was Japanese,' she heard herself telling him without knowing why.

'So, already our mixed-blood heritage is something we have in common. In fact, I think that you and I could get along very well with one another, Hettie. Very well.'

He got off the desk and started to walk towards her, causing Hettie to back away from him in panic and anger.

'I'm not interested in that sort of thing,' she told him fiercely. She had backed up as far as the door now and had nowhere else to go. 'I'll have you know I'm not that sort of person. I'm a decent, respectable girl . . .'

Jay Dalhousie had folded his arms across his admirably broad chest and now he was actually laughing at her. She could see the white flash of his big strong teeth, his eyes crinkling up in amusement as the sound of his mirth filled the small room.

'I am sure you are, Hettie,' he told her more soberly when he had stopped laughing. 'But I think you may have misunderstood me. The role I wish you to take on is not that of my mistress, but that of the second lead in *Princess Geisha*. I thought when I heard you singing at the Adelphi that you would be perfect for the role, as much for your appearance as for your voice. However, when you did not respond to my note, I bowed to the wishes of our director and allowed him to choose his own artistes. I am, after all, merely the financial backer of the show and know very little of the intricacies of putting on a stage show, even if I do know what I like to look at and listen to.

'When I heard you singing in that restaurant, I thought again how perfect you would be for the part of Princess Mimi, the younger cousin of the female lead, and the go-between who helps her in her secret love affair with Prince Hoi-hand. But by then the part had been cast.

'However, since our second female lead has changed her mind and abandoned us, it seems almost a divine intervention that you should have attended today's audition.'

'But that was only for a very small minor part, and I didn't even get it,' Hettie protested. 'I was told that the understudy would be taking over the vacant role . . .'

'Certainly that was what Lucius Carlyle, our director, felt we should do, but having heard you singing again today I have insisted that the part should go to you,' he informed her.

Was she dreaming? Could this really be happening? Was she really being offered the *second female lead* in an operetta the other girls had already told her was to be one of the most expensive extravaganzas the London stage had ever seen?

'Well, Hettie, will you take the part?'

Eagerly, Hettie nodded her head, not daring to trust herself to be able to make any kind of lucid speech.

'Excellent. Since rehearsals have already started you will need to work especially hard, I'm afraid, to catch up. Your wages will seven shillings and sixpence per week.'

Hettie's eyes rounded. 'Are you sure that isn't too much?' she whispered anxiously.

Jay was laughing again. 'You are certainly a one-off, Hettie. I don't think I have ever been asked before if I am paying someone too much! Why don't you go back down to the theatre and watch what's left of the rehearsal? Eddie Ormond, who brought you up here to me, will be waiting for you. He will take you down to our director who will talk to you about your part and arrange for you to have any extra coaching he may think you need, so that you can catch up with the rest of the cast.'

She felt as though she were literally floating on air, and not walking on a piece of worn drugget, as Jay Dalhousie opened the door for her to leave.

How amusing that Hettie had suspected him of wanting to proposition her, Jay reflected after she had gone. Not that he didn't find her attractive – he did, and were she a little older and rather a lot more worldly he doubted he would have bothered trying to resist the temptation of taking her to bed and thus mixing business and pleasure.

But she wasn't and it was, after all, the fact that she was so perfect for the part of Princess Mimi that had first caught his attention, even before Lucius Carlyle – the stubborn and difficult but extremely experienced and highly recommended director they had taken on to bring this production to the stage – had refused to entertain the idea of anyone other than him deciding who would play each role.

There had been a terrible argument earlier when Jay had overruled Lucius and insisted that Hettie be offered not just a minor part, but the role of Princess Mimi. But Jay was a man who listened to and followed his instincts, and he was also a man who liked to take risks and to win.

'The girl's a nobody. We don't even know if she can act,' Lucius had protested, furious at having his decision questioned and then overruled.

'But we do know that she can sing,' Jay had told him firmly, ignoring the temper he could see burning in the other man's eyes.

Lucius did not approve of theatrical backers involving themselves in the productions they helped to finance, and he had said so very plainly. Equally plainly Jay had told him that his own situation was very different from that of a normal theatrical 'angel'.

And so it was.

Jay had first met Archie Leonard, the young composer and librettist who had created the operetta, in New York. The young Englishman had been working on Broadway, and he and Jay had attended the same party. They had fallen into conversation and when Archie had learned that Jay's family had widely extensive interests in New Orleans which included several steamboats, and that Jay, like his father before him, was a well-known and very successful gambler, Archie had proposed that Jay might like to gamble on him and provide the backing for the musical he had composed and written.

At first Jay had simply laughed, but he had been growing bored with his relationship with his mistress, and there was no way he had wanted to return to New Orleans and the sickly, complaining but very wealthy wife he had married to please his father – especially not now that he had done his duty and fathered two sons by her.

He had a yen to see Europe and what better place to start than England? And what better excuse than the kind of risky financially venture he most enjoyed? The financial rewards if he won – and he was determined that he would – would even bring a smile to his father's face. And then, of course, there were the 'extra benefits'.

Jay's whole body shook with laughter as he remembered Hettie's outrage. What a sweet pleasure it would be to teach her to beg him to want her instead of rejecting him! Was she still a virgin? A look of brooding sensuality darkened his eyes and stilled his body. Hettie aroused all those hot-blooded desires that the iciness of his wife's pallid body could only chill.

'Offered you the part, has he?'

Hettie gasped and put her hand to her chest, protesting, 'Oh! You scared me half to death,' as Eddie Ormond, the young man who had escorted her to Jay's office, suddenly appeared out of the shadows.

'Oh, poor little girl!' he mocked her. 'If *I* scare you, you aren't going to last a day once our director gets his teeth into you. He isn't at all pleased at the way our angel has stepped on his toes,' he warned Hettie.

'What do you mean?' she asked him nervously.

'Why, only that darling Lucius our director is none too pleased that our angel has insisted on you being offered the ingénue part, when he had already earmarked it for one of his own favourites. And as for the lady herself, she's spitting teeth and ready to scratch out your eyes. Anyway, Lucius wants to see you, and he hates being kept waiting.'

Hettie tried to ignore the anxiety gripping her tummy as she hurried to catch up with her guide, who had almost run down the stairs before disappearing into the darkness of the corridor.

She caught up with him just as he was about to knock on one of the several closed doors, her eyes widening questioningly at she looked at him.

'This is Lucius's lair,' he whispered to her. 'I'll wait outside for you because you're to go and see Madame Cecile the choreographer.'

'Come,' a sonorously elegant male voice commanded.

Eddie opened the door and Hettie stepped through it with trepidation.

The man frowning intently over what he was reading was as different from Jay Dalhousie as it was possible to be. Small and slight, with polished dark hair, deep set dark eyes, and a large beak of a nose, he exuded an air of authority and hauteur that immediately made Hettie feel even more apprehensive.

Whatever he was reading must be very important, Hettie decided, because so far he hadn't even looked up at her, never mind acknowledged her presence or asked her to sit down. Instead, he reached for a pen and proceeded to make notes on a piece of paper, whilst Hettie felt compelled to stand so ramrod still that she hardly dared to breathe.

Then he put down his pen, lifted his head and *smiled* at her.

Hettie exhaled gustily in relief, an answering smile lifting her own mouth.

'So, my dear, we are to welcome you to our little family. Your name is?'

'Hettie, Sir, Hettie Walker,' Hettie almost stammered, half inclined to bob a small curtsey as he stood up.

'Charmed, I am sure, Hettie. I, as I am sure you will know, am Lucius Carlyle, producer and director of our little show. To be sure, I am rather more familiar with the theatres of dear Shaftesbury Avenue and Drury Lane than those of the provinces, but . . .' His voice trailed away.

'You are to have the part of the second female lead, the Princess Mimi, the young female cousin of the heroine of our little operetta, I understand. At least your looks and lack of height will make you suited to the role, and I am sure we shall be able to persuade our composer to cut some of the songs from the part if you should find it too taxing. Unfortunately, you have missed our early rehearsals, so you will have to work hard to catch up. Tommy Harding our stage manager will provide you with a copy of your part, and everything else you will need, and he will also explain to you what will be required of you.'

Too over awed to say anything Hettie could only gulp and nod her head, relieved to discover that the director was not the dreadful, fearful person that Eddie Ormond had so meanly implied.

Perhaps this was going to work out all right after all, she reflected. Maybe Jay Dalhousie would prove to be an angel in every sense.

Naturally Hettie could hardy wait to tell her friends, and especially Babs, her good news. She was practically hanging out of the window waiting for their return, shaking her head impatiently when they came upstairs, Babs already starting to commiserate with her.

'Aw, 'Ettie, I am so sorry you did not get the part,' she said sympathetically.

'Don't be, because I'm not,' Hettie interrupted her.

'What?'

'No! I do not mind at all about not getting that chorus part – because I'm going to be Princess Mimi instead!'

'What?!' Babs exclaimed in patent disbelief.

Every one of the girls turned to stare at her.

''Ettie, that's impossible. Faye Wright 'as got that part now. And we all know know why,' she added darkly. 'It's all on account of 'er and Lucius Carlyle having worked together before. First he gets poor Flo Bardesly that upset that she teks up and leaves, and then sweet as apple pie our Faye steps into the part. No, 'Ettie, you won't be playing the second lead,' Babs told her shaking her head decisively.

'Well I am, so there,' Hettie told her, sticking out her chin crossly, upset that Babs didn't believe her. 'Mr Jay Dalhousie, who is backing the operetta, told me so himself.'

Six heads swivelled towards her, six pairs of eyes regarding her with similar expressions of disbelief.

'You've met the angel?' Mary demanded enviously. 'And just how in 'eck's name did you pull that one off, 'Ettie?'

'Ooh, Hettie, you've really put our Mary's nose out of joint now,' Jenny giggled. 'She's bin fancying her chances wi' him ever since she first eyes on him, 'aven't you, Mary?'

Mary tossed her head and flashed a murderous look at Jenny. 'Certainly not. Wot kind of a girl do you tek me for? Everyone knows as how he is married . . .'

'Well, that's never stopped you afore,' Hettie heard someone mutter, but fortunately Mary didn't seem to have heard.

'You want ter watch it, Hettie,' she warned sharply. 'If he has offered you the part it won't be the pleasure of listening to your voice he'll be after . . .'

Hettie's face had begun to burn with chagrin

and anger. She had been so looking forward to telling the girls her good news and now here was Mary spoiling it for her. 'Well, for your information, it's nothing of the kind,' she told Mary fiercely. 'Jay . . . Mr Dalhousie, wanted me for the part the very first time he heard me singing at the Adelphi. He says that I'd be perfect for it . . .'

'Perfect for his bed, you mean,' Mary muttered.

But Babs shook her head and told her firmly, 'Leave off upsetting 'Ettie, will you, Mary? I'm not a bit surprised that Mr Dalhousie wants her for the second female lead, she's perfect for it,' she defended Hettie loyally, adding, 'We all knows how well she can sing and just look at 'er . . .'

'Well, yes, I suppose she does 'ave a bit of a chinky look about her,' Mary agreed sulkily.

'I am not . . .' Hettie began angrily but Babs, who was standing next to her, jabbed her so hard in the ribs with her elbow that she broke off from what she had been about to say to give her an indignant look.

'But she can't dance, and we're halfway through rehearsals already, and if you was to ask me . . .' Mary continued, still glowering.

'But nobody is,' Babs interjected, and the matter, for the time being, was left to rest.

It wasn't until later when she and Babs were on their own that Hettie was able to tell her friend how disappointed and upset she'd had been by Mary's response to her news.

'Well, it's just a bit of jealousy, that's all, 'Ettie, and you mustn't tek it to heart. Mary's been trying to break out of the chorus for bloody years, but they keep telling 'er that her voice isn't strong enough, so you see for you to walk in and get the second lead just like that is bound to make her feel a bit sour. Don't worry about it, though, she's good-hearted enough and she'll soon come round.'

When Babs saw how upset Hettie still looked, she gave her a swift hug and coaxed her, 'Come on, cheer up. If you think that Mary 'aving a bit of a go at you is sommat to get upset about, how the 'ell you're going to manage when old Lucy starts on you, I don't know.'

'Lucy?' Hettie queried uncertainly.

'Lucius Carlyle, the director, remember? And then there's Madame Cecile, a right Tartar she is and no mistake. Gawd, but she makes you work until you thinks your bloody legs will drop orf and then all she can say is as how we ain't anything like as good as "Mr Cochran's young ladies."'

'That's the trouble when a backer knows nowt about the theatre and goes and hires London management and provincial artistes. Them in London think they knows it all and o' course they all 'ave their own favourites. If you ask me, it will be a bloody miracle if we even get to open here never mind get a full house and then move on to Drury Lane,' Babs opined with a world-weary air.

'I thought you'd all be pleased I'd got the part,' Hettie told her miserably.

Babs sighed heavily. 'There's a lot you're going to have to learn about the theatre, Hettie. And I don't just mean Madame Cecile's bloody dance routines. You see, no matter 'ow much another girl likes you, when you get a plum part and she doesn't it's bound to leave 'er feeling a bit sore, like. Any of us 'ud feel the same. Now come on, cheer up,' Babs commanded giving her another swift hug. 'Mary 'ull soon come round. Have you told your family yet? Your ma and pa are bound to be pleased for you.'

'No, not yet,' Hettie answered her. She was unwilling to discuss Ellie's condition, even with a friend as close as Babs. 'Babs, do you really think I am good enough for the part?' she asked anxiously.

Babs pursed her lips and tilted her head to one side as she studied her. 'Well, let's see. We all know as how you've got the voice; loud enough to drown out the whole bloody orchestra it is.' She chuckled. 'And you've certainly got the looks. But it isn't just about being good enough, 'Ettie,' she added seriously. 'Sometimes it's more about 'oo yer knows. Faye will kick up a right stink about you getting the part she wanted, yer can be sure of that. But don't you worry.' She gave Hettie's arm a comforting little squeeze. 'We'll all be watching out for your back. Now, come on, I 'ope you haven't forgotten that we're all going to the picture house tonight to see Rudolph Valentino?'

Immediately Hettie shook her head. Of course

she hadn't. Every woman in the country was in a fever of excitement about the risqué film which had just come to Britain and its handsome male lead.

'Thank 'eavens we're only rehearsing, otherwise we'd never have got to see the film,' Babs added.

Valentino's effect was such that some women were reported to be swooning just at the sight of his photograph, never mind his actual presence on the screen. The newspapers had reported disapprovingly on the frenzied behaviour of his female admirers, and it was said that no woman could remain immune to a look from his dark eyes.

And so it proved to be. In a cinema packed with women, every member of the audience gave an involuntary gasp of delicious shocked excitement when Rudolph turned to Agnes Ayres, his Arab robes lending an even more dangerous mystery to his already handsome features as he commanded, 'Fly with me – into another dawn.'

And one of the few male voices from the audience was heard to exclaim furiously, 'Maud, I demand that you cover your ears and your eyes immediately.' Much to the giggling delight of the girls, who nudged one another, their eyes shining with the heady pleasure of forbidden intimacy being offered to the film's swooning heroine.

''Ere, Aggie, what he just said, that means that . . .'

'Oh, put a sock in it will yer, Mavis,' Aggie

advised her impatiently. 'We all know what it means. Cor, what I wouldn't give ter have 'im say that ter me!' she added, returning her attention to the screen. 'I've never been so shocked in all me life.'

'Me neither,' Jenny agreed dreamily.

'No, nor me,' someone else agreed.

But Hettie didn't say anything. She couldn't. She was too caught up in the film to even move, never mind speak, and had to be nudged by Babs who hissed at her as the credits came up, 'Come on, we're going . . .'

Those thrilling words that Rudolf Valentino spoke had meant that he was going to make love to the heroine of the film. And they weren't even married. A funny little twisting sensation of excitement and something else was aching through Hettie's whole body. It made her feel rather like she had felt when John had kissed her.

John! Her heart gave a fierce jump and banged against her chest wall. What was he doing now? Did he ever think of her? Did any of them? Emotional tears started to sting her eyes.

It had been such as very exciting day and yet, somehow, deep down inside her there was a sharp ache of sadness, Hettie acknowledged, that would never go away.

'You aren't still reading them blessed lines, are you?' Babs demanded good-naturedly as she leaned over Hettie's shoulder to see what she was doing. 'I thought you said as how you was going to your aunt's for your Sunday dinner?'

'Yes I am, but I just wanted to read through my part again before I go,' Hettie told her importantly.

She had read through her lines so many times she almost knew them by heart already; and as for her songs, she loved them and couldn't wait to sing them for Lucius Carlyle. Already she was visualising the look of impressed delight in his eyes as he praised her singing voice and told her how pleased he was with her. The part could have been written just for her, Hettie admitted. It was perfect, even if Princess Mimi wasn't the female lead part, and there was no romantic interest for her. Her role was that of a mischievous and sometimes forgetful but always well-meaning young cousin who genuinely wanted to bring the two lovers together.

Her favourite song was her main solo when she had to sing about her frustration at the two lovers' inability to cut through the tangled knots of misunderstanding and protocol and tell one another how they felt. She especially loved the fact that there was a touch of comedy about her character.

'Oh Babs, it's so exciting,' Hettie told her, pink cheeked with delight. 'Just imagine, I'm going to be singing the second female lead, on a London stage!'

'Well, I wouldn't start getting your hopes up too high yet, if I was you,' Babs warned her.

'What do you mean?'

'We're still rehearsing and if the money runs out, as has been known to 'appen, we may not even get to open, and even if we do, if the critics don't like us we won't be going anywhere. It doesn't do to take anything for granted in this business, 'Ettie. Aw, come on, don't look so glum. You never know, this time next year it could be you wot is acting opposite Rudolph Valentino,' she teased. 'Oh, and watch out for that Faye as well,' Babs added. 'She'll be as mad as fire that you've got the part, and think on, 'Ettie, as how she's already got rid of one Princess Mimi. And there's no getting away from the fact that old Lucy favours her. Gawd knows why, she's as clumsy as an elephant and she can't sing.'

'I don't know why you're so unkind about poor Mr Carlyle,' Hettie defended the director primly. 'Eddie was really horrid about him, but Mr Carlyle was very kind when he spoke to me.'

'Eddie?' Babs queried. 'You mean Eddie Ormond, the set designer?'

'Is that what he does? He didn't say.'

'A youngish chap, tall and la de da with wavy hair and . . .'

'Yes, that's him', Hettie agreed. 'Mr Dalhousie sent him to find me, and then he waited with me before taking me to meet Mr Carlyle.'

'Well, 'e seems a nice enough young chap,' Babs admitted, 'although he's a bit too posh for my tastes. Oh 'eck, is that the time?' she exclaimed looking at her watch. 'I've got to go, I'm meeting someone at eleven.'

'Someone? You mean a man?' Hettie challenged her immediately.

Babs tossed her head, her face bright pink. 'So what if he is?' she said nonchalantly. 'It isn't against the law, is it?'

'Oh Babs, who is he, and why haven't you said anything about him?'

Babs gave her a coy look. 'There isn't anything too say. At least not yet. I met him last year when we were both working in the same panto. Stan Fisher his name is. He does a comedy turn with another chap. They've bin working in Blackpool all through the summer but now he's booked to do a panto here again this winter. Bumped into 'im the other day, I did, and 'e told me that 'e and some other lads are all boarding just round the corner from us. He asked me out straight off, like. Cheek! I wouldn't have accepted if he hadn't caught me in a weak moment, and I told him so an' all.'

'Where's he taking you?' Hettie asked her, both curious and slightly envious. She had heard the other girls talking about their various beaux and giggling over the kisses they tried to steal, but this was the first time she had known Babs go out with anyone.

'Oh, we're only going to 'ave a bit o' dinner somewhere and then go for a walk. He's rehearsing at four, and I told him there was no way I was risking meself staying out wi' the likes of him once it gets dark,' Babs announced meaningfully, causing Hettie to giggle.

The November day was cold and damp and had that kind of greyness that seemed to seep into everything. Hettie huddled deeper into her coat and started to walk a bit faster. Only another few minutes and she would be standing in Connie's warm parlour toasting her cold hands and feet, she promised herself. Her stomach was already grumbling hungrily at the thought of Connie's Sunday dinner. This would be the first time she had seen her since Connie had told her about Ellie, and Hettie was apprehensive, especially after what John had told her Connie had said to him. Would Connie be the same as Ellie, Gideon and John, and snub her?

The children saw her first, throwing themselves at her with shrieks of enthusiastic welcome that brought Connie out of the kitchen to exclaim, 'My, Hettie, but it seems an age since we last saw you. How are you, love?'

'I'm fine,' Hetie told her. She was dying to give Connie her wonderful good news but there was something more important she had to do first.

'How is Mam,' she asked urgently. 'Only whenever I telephone Da, he doesn't say very much except that she's resting and mustn't be disturbed.'

'Well, she's really taken the loss of this baby very hard, Hettie, and that's a fact. She still doesn't even want to see me and I'm her blood family – her *sister*,' Connie announced, oblivious that her throwaway comment cut through Hettie like a knife.

'According to Iris, Ellie is making some progress,' Connie continued. 'And now that Gideon has taken her to the Lakes for the winter, to try to raise her spirits, we must just hope that she continues to do so and that we shall soon have our old Ellie back with us.

'By coincidence I had a letter from John only yesterday morning asking very much the same question as you have just done.'

A sharp pain bit into Hettie's heart. John had written to his sister, but he had not written to her. And yet at one time, or so it seemed to Hettie now when she looked back, he had for ever been sending her silly jokey notes.

'He is happy, then, working for his friend?' Hettie forced herself to ask.

'It certainly seems so, although like everyone else in the family he is concerned about Ellie. I had written to him asking if he had made any plans for Christmas and if he would like to come and stay here with us, but he has written back that he has already accepted an invitation for a house party, if you please, from this posh friend of his. If you ask me, it sounds as though our John is going up in the world now he's mixing with all these posh folk,' Connie announced proudly.

'Anyway, what about you, Hettie?' she asked.

'Are you still enjoying singing at the Adelphi?'

'No, not any more. As it happens, Aunt Connie, I'm doing a bit of going up in the world of my own,' Hettie told her proudly.

'Oh?'

'Yes.' She wasn't going to let on to her aunt just how upset she was that she'd had to learn about John's new life from someone else. And she was also cruelly aware of the irony that John was putting his new friends above his family, just as he had falsely accused her of doing.

'I've been taken on to play the second female lead in a new musical . . .'

'A musical? You mean you are to on on the stage, like a music hall turn? Oh Hettie, I don't think . . .'

'It's all perfectly respectable,' Hettie stopped her quickly. 'And it's not music hall. It's an operetta . . .'

'An opera?' Connie breathed, obviously impressed.

Hettie knew that she should correct her aunt's misinterpretation of what she had said, but suddenly, before she could do so, a mental image of John all dressed up to the nines at his house party, dancing with pretty girls in their flapper dresses, slid into her head, and her pride stopped her. If John could attend a house party with his posh new friends then she could be in an 'opera', she decided fiercely.

'What a shame that Mr Caruso has just died,'

Connie mourned. 'Otherwise you could perhaps have sung with him.'

Hettie had to bite the inside of her mouth to silence her guilty laughter. It was sweet of Connie to rate her ability so highly. 'I start rehearsals on Monday and then in the spring, if we take well here, the whole production could be moving to London.'

'London! Oh, Hettie!'

Hettie was so pleased with the effect her words were having on her aunt that, over lunch, encouraged by Connie's eager questions, she started to tell her how impressed Jay Dalhousie had been with her voice.

'Oh Hettie,' Connie began, starting to look uncertain and anxious. 'This Mr Dalhousie, I don't know that . . .'

'There's nothing to worry about, Aunt Connie,' Hettie assured her. 'Mr Dalhousie is a gentleman and he is married. He told he that when he heard me singing at the Adelphi he knew right then that I would be a perfect Princess Mimi,' she added, mentally persuading herself that she was only *slightly* exaggerating what Jay Dalhousie had said to her.

She had no idea why it had suddenly become so important that when Connie wrote to John she was able to tell him how well she, Hettie, was doing and what a success she was becoming, any more than she had about why just thinking this could cause such a sharp angry pain so deep inside her heart.

The grey afternoon was just beginning to give way to an early dusk when Hettie finally got up to leave. 'You will tell Mam that I keep asking after her, won't you, Aunt Connie?' she begged.

'Of course I will, Hettie love,' Connie assured her.

Hettie had the dormitory to herself when she got back as the other girls were either at work or still out, and after having her regular weekly bath she curled up in her bed with her script, and tried not to think about John and the new life he was enjoying.

She wasn't left in peace for very long, though.

Within half an hour of her getting into bed, the attic door burst open and the twins came hurrying in followed by Mary and Babs, all four of them laughing and chattering.

'Well I never, what a piece of luck that was, Babs, us bumping into you and and Stan like that. I'all say one thing for them lads, they certainly know how to 'ave a bit of fun.'

'Ooh, me and Jenny were scared to death when that Billy Wainwright was driving. He went ever so fast. You missed out on a real treat, Hettie,' Jenny added. 'Didn't she, girls?'

'Huh, if you can call it a treat having your toes trod on by a clumsy great dolt of a chap who couldn't dance properly to save 'is life,' Mary complained.

'Oh ho, you didn't seem to be too concerned

about his dancin' when you was all cuddled up with him in the back of the motor on the way back,' Babs pointed out pithily.

Amidst renewed giggles, Hettie learned that a chance meeting between Babs and her new beau and the other three girls had led to Stan suggesting they call back at his boarding house to meet some of his friends, and that from there the whole party had set off for Blackpool in the two cars the boys had managed to borrow.

'And then when we hid from Billy and Ian . . . 'Oh, the look on their faces when they couldn't find us and then we jumped out at them . . .'

'It sounds as though you had fun,' Hettie said a little wistfully.

'Oh my, but we did. That Stan of yours is a real card, Babs.' Jenny laughed.

'Mebbe, but he could well be a real card without any lodgings tomorrow if his landlady finds out about him smuggling the lot of us into their digs, and all on account of you saying you fancied a cup of cocoa,' Babs retorted.

'It were Mary wot said that not me,' Jenny protested indignantly.

'Yes, but it was you who spilled the cocoa powder and then decided to paint the boys' faces with it,' Mary pointed out.

'Ooh but when Stan started crackin' them jokes, and doing them tricks, I laughed so hard I got a stitch,' Jess broke in.

The girls' day *did* sound as though it had been

fun, Hettie decided, feeling even more envious. Well, hopefully once the musical started there would be time for some of that for her, too.

'No! Stop!'

Hettie's stomach cramped sickly as she heard the anger in Madame Cecile's voice. She had spent all morning with the choreographer trying to learn the complicated steps for the solo dance. She hadn't realised the movements she would have to perform were more ballet than mere dance – there was no mention of it in her own script – but when she had tried to say so, Madame Cecile had flown into a furious rage and called Hettie an imbecile.

Hettie's whole body ached, especially her poor toes, and she felt like bursting into tears of misery and despair. She had no idea what most of the frightening sounding ballet terms Madame Cecile was shouting at her even meant. What she was being asked to do was completely outside her experience.

Madame's sharp voice called out coldly, 'Arabesque, avec attitude,' followed by the even colder and more contemptuous, 'Non, non, you do eet like zees . . . *en pointe*,' as she rose up on her toes and demonstrated an impossibly swift and complicated twirl.

Hettie had done her best to copy her, but she was not a ballet dancer and everything she did seemed to add to Madame's fury.

And then, to Hettie's humiliation, as she

wobbled uncomfortably on her toes the choreographer gave a hiss of disgust that caused Hettie to completely lose her balance.

'Oh, Babs, don't laugh,' Hettie begged miserably now as she told her friend what had happened.

'I'm sorry, 'Ettie,' Babs apologised, giving her a comforting hug. 'Madame Cecile has a real nasty temper on her and we've all 'ad a taste of it, I can tell you. I did hear as how it's on account of her wanting to be a ballet dancer, and then not being able to 'cos of having a fall and hurting her hip. That's why she 'as that limp, see.'

'But Babs, it doesn't say anything in the script about me having to do a solo ballet,' Hettie protested.

'Well, sometimes they change things, and o' course Faye does a bit o' ballet, like, and I suppose they was thinking that with Marilyn Miller doing so well on Broadway with *Sally*, and that 'aving a ballet solo, they would put one in. That's what 'appens sometimes. Maybe they'll take it out again now that you've got the part,' Babs added, but Hettie could hear the doubt in her friend's voice.

'Where are you going now?' Babs asked her. 'Only a few of us are going to meet up with the boys and go for a bit o' sommat to eat, and you'd be welcome to come with us.'

Hettie shook her head. 'I can't. I've got to go and see Mr Carlyle. He wants to hear me sing Princess Mimi's solo songs.'

'Well, at least you won't have any trouble with those,' Babs tried to comfort her.

'Oh dear . . .'

Hettie could hear the patient sympathy and commiseration in Lucius Carlyle's voice as he shook his head and got up from the piano stool to cross the stage and place a comforting hand on her shoulder.

'You have a very pretty voice, Hettie, and I am sure that, given the right setting, it will certainly show to its advantage. But I'm afraid that a stage and a theatre audience require something rather more. However, since our backer has insisted that you are to be our Princess Mimi, and we cannot afford to offend him, we must work together to find a way round the problems, mustn't we? Now, my dear. Let's try again. And perhaps this time if we try a different key? You are, we must remember, a young girl, with a young girl's trilling sweet voice.'

Hettie heard him exhaling tiredly and the weight of her burden of humiliation and despair grew even heavier. It had been bad enough that Madame Cecile had been so contemptuous of her inability to do ballet, but this was even worse. She had thought that she had sung well, but it seemed she was wrong.

'Of course, it does not help that our composer has written these songs for a soprano soubrette.'

'But it says in my script that the composer's

preferred voice for Princess Mimi is like mine, a soprano lyric,' Hettie told him in confusion.

'Let me see!' Almost snatching the script from her, he studied it frowningly before tearing it in half and saying dismissively, 'There has obviously been some error. Anyone who knows anything about opera can see that the part is designed for a soubrette.'

Hettie sighed. Her dreams of success seemed to be evaporating with every passing minute.

'Madame Cecile says that she can't dance a single step and Lucy says she can't even sing properly, so if you ask me if won't be two minutes before she's out on her ear, and good riddance, I say.'

'Well, I had heard as how she's never really done any stage work before, and that she only got the part on account of the backer tekkin' a fancy to her voice.'

'Are you sure it were just her voice he took a fancy to?'

Standing outside the half open dressing room door, Hettie felt her face burn as she overheard what was being said about her. Should she simply walk away and pretend she had not heard? She took a deep breath and pushed open the door. The immediate silence which descended on the room was more unnerving than the girls' criticism of her, Hettie decided shakily as she hurried to collect her coat.

A pair of shabby ballet shoes suddenly sailed

past Hettie's ear to land on the floor a few feet away. Hettie ignored them, the tips of her ears burning as someone gave a muffled giggle.

'Oh, sorree . . .' a mocking voice announced as a sharp-featured young woman came to retrieve them. 'You aren't a dancer, are you?'

'And she ain't much of singer, either,' another voice joined in unkindly.

Hettie's hands shook as she pulled on her coat, but she wasn't going to give her tormentors the satisfaction of seeing how much they had upset her.

'Seems to me like it won't be long before you've got your part back, Faye,' Hettie heard someone saying pointedly as she walked back to the door.

'And I should think so as well. We don't want upstarts like 'er pushing their way in where they aren't wanted. Blinking cheek of it.'

SIXTEEN

'I say, Pride, that was the most terrific lesson. First time I've managed to loop the loop, don't y'know. Good sport, eh? Can you fit me in again later this week?'

'I'll just have a look at the diary, Your Grace,' John answered him. At seventy-one, The Duke of Saltarn was his oldest pupil, and since as a hunting man the duke believed in throwing himself and his mount over whatever obstacle stood in their way, John always heaved a small sigh of relief once he had him safely back on terra firma.

'I could manage 2.00 p.m. on Friday, Your Grace,' he told him after he had studied the leatherbound, gold-lettered diary Alfred had given to him the evening before his first day officially working at the flying club. The diary cover had John's initials stamped on one corner, and already its pages were filling up as word got around that the flying club had a talented new instructor.

The duke's batman and valet was waiting

patiently to guide his master to the waiting Rolls Royce.

John's next appointment was for the first of a dozen lessons with a young man – a novice – who had apparently been recommended to the club by a friend.

The short grey November days might not appeal to him as a flyer, but they certainly appealed to the searing bleakness inside him, John acknowledged as he left his office to walk across to the hangar where the small sturdy flying machine he used to teach beginners was being made ready for him by the team of highly trained mechanics the flying school employed.

The morning's post had brought a letter from Connie letting him know that Gideon and Ellie had left for the Lakes a week earlier than planned. Would the change of scene help his sister to overcome her grief at the loss of her unborn child, as Gideon so desperately hoped it might? John certainly shared his brother-in-law's hopes, but he knew from his own experience that neither grief nor guilt were demons easily appeased.

Connie's letter has also contained news of Hettie and her forthcoming stage appearance. John frowned. Thinking about the last time he had seen Hettie gave him the same sort of sharp pain in his heart as probing an aching tooth with his tongue did to his face, only the pain in his heart was mixed with anger. He should not have kissed Hettie. He knew that. The old easy friendship he and Hettie had once shared had gone, and that was just as much Hettie's fault as his, John told himself stubbornly. *She* was the one who had changed, not he. *She* was the one who had not been content with her life but had instead plunged into this wild folly of singing in public.

And now John's own deepest fears had been confirmed. Hettie was, Connie had written, going to be touring in a show, albeit an opera, flaunting herself on a stage for men to ogle and admire. How little he had really known her, John acknowledged bitterly.

He sensed from the tone of Connie's letter that his sister did not understand that an operetta was a vastly different affair from an opera, as indeed he himself probably would not have done up until a week ago. Then, he had heard Alfred protesting to his sister that he was damned if he was going to be dragged to London to hear some ruddy opera, whereupon Lady Poppy had told him firmly, 'Don't be silly, Alfie dearest, we are not going to *listen* to an opera, but to *see* one of Gilbert and Sullivan's funny little operettas, and I promise you that you will enjoy it hugely.'

Alfred had told John afterwards that he would far rather have seen a decent revue, with 'lots of pretty girls', adding, 'But I daren't tell Polly that, for she would be sure to insist that she wanted to go as well, and it wouldn't be the thing. I keep telling Polly that she's shocking the old guard with these modern ideas of hers, but she won't listen,' Alfred had concluded gloomily.

Although Alfred had not said so directly, he had hinted to John that he was not too happy about his sister's unexpectedly early return from New York. And John could understand why.

Earlier in the week John had been summoned to Moreton Place by Alfred, who told him that he was at his wits' end with his sister, who was insisting that she wanted to learn to fly.

'Upon my word, John, I don't know what mad high jinks she will want to get up to next. I have, of course, told her that it is out of the question for her to have flying lessons.'

'And why should I not, brother dear?' Polly herself had demanded, bursting into the room to interrupt their conversation. 'John, tell my brother please that he is an old-fashioned fuddy duddy and that there is no reason why a woman should not learn to fly. After all, Daddy had no objection to my learning to drive.'

'Polly, this is ridiculous,' Alfred had spluttered.

'You will give me flying lessons, won't you, John?' Polly had wheedled, ignoring her brother.

'I'm sorry, Lady Polly, but since it is your brother who employs me . . .'

'Oh stuff,' Polly had stopped him, stamping her foot.

'Polly, that is enough,' Alfred had told her sharply. 'I forbid you to continue.'

'You are my brother, Alfred, and not my keeper,'

Polly had retorted, flying into a furious passion, 'and I *shall* learn to fly, just see if I don't.'

She had whirled out of the room before Alfred could say anything further.

The mechanics had brought the small, special modified teaching flying machine out of the hangar. Immediately John started to walk a little faster, his spirits lifting. Nothing had ever changed or diminished the sense of excitement and delight flying brought him, or his sense of wonder, not even the tragedy months before. Even though he understood every single principle that made man's flight possible, a tiny part of him still felt there was something almost magical about it.

As he reached the machine he lifted his hand to stroke the sturdy lines of its body. The flying machines commissioned by Alfred's flying school were a miracle of modern science, and could in John's opinion almost fly themselves.

He looked up as he heard the sound of a car engine and saw a gleaming roadster racing towards him, its driver barely visible. The car came to a halt, and his pupil got out, small and slender and already togged up in the necessary protective flying clothes, pulling on goggles to protect his eyes as he hurried to John's side.

'Po . . . Paul Mainwaring. Sorry I'm late. Better get going, what ho?' he introduced himself gruffly, extending a gauntleted hand for John to shake before turning towards the flying machine, leaving John to follow him.

Since it was to be Paul Mainwaring's first lesson, John would be flying the machine. He began explaining carefully to his pupil what he was doing and why, as the mechanics stepped back and the stout little craft raced down the runway and lifted obediently into the greyness, her engine humming as busily and happily as a little bee as she chugged importantly over the late autumn browns and tans of the newly turned fallow fields below them.

Suddenly a gautletted hand clutched at John's arm and a shockingly familiar *female* voice exclaimed excitedly, 'Oh John, this is just too, too spiffing!'

'Polly! I mean, *Lady* Polly,' John corrected himself as he battled against his shocked disbelief.

'John, you should see your face.' Polly giggled. 'I told you and Alfie that he wouldn't be able to stop me from learning to fly. I really fooled you, didn't I? Oh this is the most wonderful feeling. Even better than driving. Can we go faster? I do so adore speed, don't you? It is just the best feeling, even better than falling in love, and so much safer.'

Even over the sound of the engine he could hear the emotion in her voice as it trembled at those last betraying words.

'Have you ever been in love, John?' she called out to him. 'Oh, you are pretending not to have heard me because you do not want to answer me.

I am being too forward, aren't I? It isn't the done thing for a girl to ask a man such questions.'

He could just about see the face she was pulling beneath her cap and goggles.

'I hate *the done thing*, John, do you know that?' she continued. 'And sometimes I hate being a girl as well. I was in love – but it hurts so dreadfully that I never want to be again,' she yelled at him wildly.

She shouldn't be up here with him, and she shouldn't be telling him such things, but John didn't have the heart to tell her so.

'I wish we could stay up here for ever and never, ever have to go back down.'

'Well, we cannot,' John told her sternly. 'I am turning round and taking you right back to the airfield.'

'Why? I have paid for my lessons! Why shouldn't I learn to fly, just because I'm a girl?' Polly demanded passionately. 'Please don't take me back yet, John. I've been longing to fly so much. Oh, look down there, at the river. How pretty it looks. You know, when I was a little girl I used to try to imagine how it would feel to be a bird and to be free like this, and now I am. I never, ever want to go down . . .'

It was impossible for him not to be infected by her enthusiasm, John admitted, as she rattled off question after question, pausing only to draw breath and to say over and over again how much she was enjoying herself.

In the end, John kept the little aircraft up for almost a full hour, telling himself that, since she had paid for his time, he owed her something. It would have been fun teaching her, he acknowledged reluctantly, if only because her enthusiasm and excitement so exactly mirrored his own. But of course he could do no such thing, since Alfred had expressly forbidden it.

'Oh, we can't be going down so soon,' he heard her objecting as she realised what he was doing.

'We've been flying for over an hour,' he pointed out before warning her: 'And remember when we do land that you are supposed to be a young man.'

'Of course I will,' she assured him.

But ten minutes later after they had landed and were out of the plane it seemed she had completely forgotten his warning. She rushed up to him and, in full view of the mechanics, hugged him fiercely and kissed him on the cheek, exclaiming giddily, 'I am so very, very happy. When can we go up again, John? And this time, you must really teach me something . . .'

'I can't do that,' John began firmly as he removed her arms from round his neck.

'Why not?'

'You know why, Lady Polly. Your brother has already said that he does not wish you to have lessons.'

'Oh stuff! And don't call me Lady Polly,' she corrected him with a small pout. 'I will not be called Lady Polly by you, John. It is far too formal when you are such a close family friend.'

John could feel his face starting to burn. 'I am working for your brother,' he pointed out stiffly, 'and not . . .'

'Well, Alfie says you are the best flyer he has ever known. But you are his friend as well, John, and you must not think otherwise. He is always saying how much he respects you and what a grand fellow he thinks you . . . Oh, why must there still be this wretched ridiculous class thing, when it must be obvious to anyone with any sense that the war has changed *everything*. I had thought you a *modern* man, John, and above all that silly mediaeval forelock-tugging, I-knows-me-place nonsense.'

'If I didn't know my place, Lady Polly, I can assure you that there are plenty of people who would very quickly show me what it is, aye, and tek pleasure in doing so an' all,' John returned curtly, deliberately emphasising his northern accent.

'Why do you say that?'

'No reason,' John told her quickly, mentally cursing himself for betraying how much he resented the arrogant and patronising manner of some of Alfred's friends and fellow club members.

'You won't snitch on me to Alfie, will you, John?' Polly wheedled at him.

'This mustn't happen again,' was all John felt he could say to her.

But it seemed it was enough because she smiled

happily at him and exclaimed, 'I am so pleased you have accepted Alfie's invitation to be our guest over Christmas. We are going to have such fun. Do you like charades, John? I do, and sardines, too, and we shall have dancing as well. And I warn you that next time I come for my lesson I shall expect you to teach me properly.'

Her moods were as mercurial as an April day, John acknowledged wryly as he watched her speed off to her car. But it was, of course, his duty to inform Alfred of what she had done, a duty he could not and would not seek to avoid. He couldn't help but feel a pang of disappointment at the prospect of not teaching Polly, though.

'Going home?'

'Eddie!' Hettie exclaimed wearily, nodding her head and pushing the heavy weight of her hair back off her face as she looked up at him.

'Fancy going for a cup of tea first?' he asked her.

Hettie hesitated and then nodded her head again.

And then Madame Cecile said that I was an imbecile.' Tears welled up in Hettie's eyes as she recalled her earlier humiliation. '*I* didn't know that Princess Mimi had a solo ballet spot. It wasn't marked on the script I was given . . .'

'Poor you,' Eddie sympathised. 'Of course, Faye is pretty hot on ballet.'

'Oh, please don't tell me that,' Hettie begged him wretchedly. She hardly knew Eddie really, but he was so easy to talk to and so understanding, and she was desperately in need of a sympathetic ear right now.

'Madame Cecile has said that I am to have two extra hours of ballet practice every day.' She gave a small shudder. 'And I am frightened that if she complains to Mr Dalhousie about me he will wish that he had not given me the part.'

'Well, she won't be able to complain to him at the moment,' Eddie assured her, 'because he has gone to London, supposedly to sort out some problem with the theatre he has hired for the show. But of course we all know that in reality he has gone to see his girlfriend.'

'His girlfriend? But I thought he was married?' Hettie said innocently.

Eddie gave a careless shrug. 'He is. Perhaps I should have said that he has gone to London to see the mistress he keeps there,' he corrected himself. When he saw Hettie's expression he shook his head. 'He's a very rich man, Hettie, and rich men live by different rules from the rest of us.'

'Well, if that's what being rich means, then I'm glad that I'm not,' Hettie told him robustly. She had grown up amongst ordinary decent working folk, and she couldn't help contrasting the happy loving marriages of Ellie and Gideon, and Connie and Harry, with the kind of marriage Jay

Dalhousie and his wife obviously had, which in her opinion was no kind of marriage at all.

'Rich men marry for sons to pass their riches on to,' Eddie told her bluntly. 'And then they look for their pleasure outside their marriages. You'll find *that* out soon enough for yourself,' he warned her. 'Once we get to London you'll be besieged by stage door Johnnies wanting to take you out to dinner.'

'I shan't go with them if they are married.' She frowned as she saw Eddie trying to smother a yawn. 'You look tired.'

'Yes, I am,' he agreed. 'Tommy Harding the stage manager told us this morning that he wanted a new set designing for the first act, so I've spent all day painting scenery.'

'Is it always like this?' Hettie asked him. 'Things going wrong, last-minute changes . . .'

Eddie laughed. '*This* is nothing,' he told her. 'I worked on a new opera in Paris last year. It had eight different scenes and the director changed his mind about the stage sets for four of them two days before we opened.'

'Paris,' Hettie exclaimed, impressed.

'Yes.'

'That must have been so exciting. When you were there did you . . .'

'I don't want to talk about it,' Eddie told her abruptly, signalling to the waitress to bring them the bill, his manner suddenly curt and cold.

* * *

"Ere, 'Ettie. It looks like you've got an admirer,' Sukey Simmonds told her as they all huddled over the cups of tea she had just made them. 'When we was out today, one of the boys said as how he'd noticed you at the theatre and was asking ever such a lot of questions about you, wasn't he, Mary?'

'I'll say,' Mary agreed readily.

Hettie blushed and they all laughed, Jenny telling her teasingly that her 'beau' was in the orchestra and played the trumpet.

'You should see the lips on 'im, 'Ettie. Bet he can give a girl a real smacker with lips like them.'

'Oh, give over, Jenny,' Babs protested amidst Hettie's fiery blushes and the other girls' gales of laughter.

'Tek no notice, 'Ettie,' Babs comforted her. 'Sukey is just teasing you. All the poor lad said was how he had noticed you, and thought as how pretty you are.'

'The boys was saying as how we should all go out for a bicycle ride on our next half day,' Jessie put in.

'A bicycle ride? Me legs ache enough with all them high kicks we're 'avin' to do, without doing any bicycle riding, ta ever so much,' Aggie protested.

'It's Jenny and Jessie's birthday soon, so I reckon we should 'ave a bit of a party and invite the boys to join in,' Mary announced.

'A party? And how are we going to do that,

Miss Clever Clogs?' Babs demanded. 'We can't invite them back here. The minute the old battleaxe got word of anything like that, she'd turf us out and no mistake. And if you think I'm going to go round to their lodgings, you can think again. I've got me reputation to think about.'

'Oh, hoighty toighty! It didn't look much like you was worrying about your reputation when you was sparkin' with that Stan this afternoon,' Mary sniffed.

'We could ask Jack and Sarah if we could use that room off the chop house dining room, perhaps,' Aggie suggested, stepping in adroitly to avert a quarrel. 'I remember as how Sarah was saying they was thinking of hiring it out for parties, like.'

''Ere, Aggie, that's a brilliant idea,' Sukey approved excitedly. 'We could put on a bit o' supper and mebbe we could 'ave some music so that we could dance. I could buy mesef a new frock, one of them flapper frocks that are all the rage . . . You know, I was feeling really miserable on account of us not being able to go home at Christmas because we're in the panto, but now that we've met the boys, I reckon we're going to have a really good time.'

'You speak for yourself, Sukey Simmmonds,' Lizzie told her sharply. 'But I'll thank you to remember that we aren't all boy mad.'

'What's up wi' her?' Sukey demanded, red faced, as Lizzie slammed down her cup and stalked off to the other side of the room to stand with her back to them as she stared out of the window.

'Lizzie's got her ma and her sister to think of, Sukey,' Babs reminded her.

'Oh aye, I were forgetting about them,' Sukey acknowledged immediately. ''Ere, Lizzie, don't go off in a sulk like that,' she called out. 'I'm sorry if I put me foot in it. Be a good sport and come back.'

SEVENTEEN

'I can't do it.'

'Come on, 'Ettie, don't let that old besom get you down,' Babs coaxed her.

'It's no good. I just can't do that solo dance,' Hettie repeated wretchedly.

They were in the dressing room getting ready for the first full dress rehearsal.

'Five minutes, chorus girls,' Tommy the stage manager called out, banging on the door.

'Don't think about it, just concentrate on your singing instead,' Babs advised her.

'I can't even get *that* right,' Hettie told her miserably. 'Not since Mr Carlyle changed my songs to another key.'

'Chorus on stage, please . . .'

'Oh, Hettie,' Babs sympathised, hugging her fiercely before turning to join the other girls as they hurried out of the room.

At least Faye wouldn't be here to witness her humiliation, Hettie reflected thankfully. The other girl had a streaming cold and had been instructed to stay away from the theatre for a few days, in case she passed it on to anyone else. There was another bang on the dressing room door.

'Princess Mimi, five minutes.'

This was it. Hettie felt sick with the knowledge that she was going to let everyone down. No matter how hard she tried to master the complicated ballet steps, every time she performed them for Madame Cecile it seemed she had forgotten something or done something wrong.

'Eet ees impossible to choreograph a ballet for someone with so little skill. Thees is not a ballet any more.'

'And I am not a ballerina,' Hettie had struck back, overwhelmed by exhaustion and despair.

'You theenk I do not know that?' Madame Cecile had snapped, her small black eyes sharp with contempt. 'You thump around like a sack of ze coals, ze audience will leave their seats in disgust when zey see you . . .'

'Princess Mimi.'

Hettie opened the door and hurried up the stairs towards the wings, to wait for her cue.

The male lead was a famous singer who, rumour had it, their backer was paying a fortune to take the part. He had not deigned to attend previous rehearsals, so his understudy had had to stand in for him instead.

When Hettie heard her cue, she had to hurry on to the stage where she had to make herself visible to the audience whilst the hero was not supposed to be aware of her presence as he sang of his desire to find true love with a girl who was not interested in his wealth or position. As soon as he had finished his solo, Hettie had to appear from the shadows so that he could see her, whereupon they were to share a duet.

Hurrying now across the stage, Hettie realised that the male lead was not standing where he was supposed to be, so she had to change direction in order that she could end up facing him, which almost caused her to trip up on the hem of her over-long skirt.

Their duet took the form of a question and answer dialogue, and Hettie's heart bumped against her ribs the moment she heard the opening bars of her own part.

She started to sing and then realised in shock that she was out of tune with the music, which suddenly seemed much faster than it should have been. She could see the male lead frowning at her as she hesitated and missed a note completely.

Somehow she managed to get through the duet, although her face was burning with shame by the time she reached its end. And then, as if that hadn't been bad enough, in her rush to leave the stage she caught her foot in the hem of her costume and almost stumbled.

As soon as they were in the wings, the male lead began demanding loudly to see the director, and Hettie knew that he must be complaining about her performance.

Her ballet solo was in the second half and, although she did her best to struggle through it, once again the music seemed different and she was out of time so badly that she could hear the whispers rustling from the wings where the chorus was watching her.

She was less than halfway through it when Madame Cecile herself burst onto the stage in a fury, sceaming at Hettie, 'You are useless, useless!'

'What the devil is going on?'

Everyone, including Madame Cecile, froze as Jay Dalhousie's voice rang out from the darkness of the stalls.

'Stay where you are all of you,' he commanded as he strode towards them, past the orchestra and then leaping nimbly on to the stage, followed by an awkward-looking young man whom Hettie didn't recognise.

Eddie had told Hettie that Jay wasn't expected to return to Liverpool until after Christmas and it was obvious that both the director and Madame were shocked by his presence.

'I'm afraid that Miss Walker is not quite perfect in her role as yet, Jay,' Hettie heard Mr Carlyle explaining unctuously. 'You see, she has no ballet training, unfortunately . . .'

'Why would she damn well need any?'

There was a sharp, expectant pause.

'The part she is playing includes a solo ballet spot,' the director said smoothly.

'Since when? I don't remember any solo ballet spot.'

Hettie watched as Madame and the director exchanged brief glances.

'Well, no, but we did agree that we wanted to emulate the success of Broadway, and . . .'

'My pupil Faye is an excellent ballet dancer,' Madame joined in fiercely. 'But zees . . . nothing . . . she cannot dance at all.'

'I want to see both of you in my office right now,' Jay told them curtly, pausing as the young man said something to him. 'Get the conductor up here,' he instructed Eddie who was standing a few feet away.

The orchestra conductor was a fierce-looking Italian with a fiery temper, and Hettie shrank back a little as he hurried on to the stage, baton in hand.

'Our composer wants to know how come you've messed up his score?' Jay asked him bluntly, indicating the young man at his side.

'I change the key and the pace of the music because I am told to do so, by the director,' the conductor explained immediately. 'I tell him that it will not work and that the girl has a perfect voice for the score as it is written, but he will not listen. He insists the composer has instructed him to change the tempo and the key.'

'Is that right, Archie?' Jay asked the composer.

Hettie could see the young man's Adam's apple bobbing up and down in his throat as he cleared it and said nervously, 'No, it is not.'

The whole theatre was agog with what had happened. No one had ever seen or heard of anything like it before.

'Never seen a dress rehearsal stopped right in the middle and the director hauled off to explain himself,' Eddie confirmed later, shaking his head.

The boys had urged Babs and the girls to join them for tea whilst they waited to see what was going to happen, and now they were all speculating excitedly about what had taken place.

'You know what I think, 'Ettie,' Lizzie declared importantly. 'I think that his nibs and Madame were trying to make you look bad so that they could get your part off you to give back to Faye.'

'Lizzie, you're right,' Aggie agreed, nodding her head vehemently.

'I don't know,' Hettie protested.

'Well I do. Mean conniving so and so's,' Babs declared forthrightly. 'I just hope they get a taste of their own medicine.'

'Aye, well if they do, we are going to be left without a choreographer and a director,' Mary pointed out.

'Which means that we could be left without a show,' Eddie added.

They all looked at one another worriedly.

'But we're supposed to be leaving for London after Christmas.'

The gossip and speculation of the previous half hour gave way to anxiety and gloom. Maybe they would all be out of a job in a few hours' time.

'I'm sorry to have to drag you out here and away from your work, John, but as what I wanted to talk to you about concerns Polly and is rather personal, I felt it would be more appropriate for us to discuss it here.'

As he listened to Alfred, John was guiltily aware that he had not said anything to his friend about Polly's illicit flying lesson. He had thought long and hard about how to break the news to Alfred but kept drawing a blank as to how to do so and avoid getting Polly – and himself – into hot water.

They were in the library at Moreton Place, a shabbily comfortable, book-filled room that smelled of old books, tweed and tobacco. In short, a man's room.

'Polly has owned up to me about the way she tricked you into giving her a flying lesson, and I apologise to you on her behalf for putting you in such a difficult position.'

'I had intended to tell you . . .' John admitted readily. 'But the opportunity hadn't arisen.'

'Polly is inclined to be recklessly headstrong, I'm afraid. My father doted on her and spoiled her dreadfully, and I dare say I have done the same. It is very hard not to do so,' Alfred confessed ruefully. 'She is inclined to be a trifle wild at times, but she has the warmest heart and she means no harm. I do confess, though, that I wish she would be little less modern and out-spoken in her views.'

He was beginning to look and sound awkward and John wondered what he was leading up to.

'Polly had also confessed to me that she conducted herself most improperly towards you,' Alfred told him uncomfortably.

It took several seconds for John to grasp what he was trying to say, and that he was referring to Polly's impulsive embrace. But why? Because he feared that he might have got the wrong impres-sion and be getting ideas above his station, and because of that felt he needed to warn him off? But John already knew the 'rules'. It might be perfectly permissible for Alfred to befriend him, despite John's much lower social status, but there could be no question of John befriending Alfred's sister.

'It was nothing,' John told Alfred immediately. 'Lady Polly has a natural warmth and spontane-ity, and I did not for one minute imagine . . .'

'You are a good chap, Pride,' Alfred stopped him gruffly. 'Must admit I felt a bit shocked when Polly admitted what she had done. Not the done thing at all, and I told her that. Thought I'd better have a word with you about it. Well, I know you understand the situation. Had hoped to have seen

Polly suitable settled by now, but she claims she won't marry anyone if she can't have Oliver. Damned shame him being killed like that, right at the end of the war. Don't think she's ever really got over it. Oh, she puts on a a good show most of the time, but . . . I dare say that's part of the reason I'm over-lenient with her. Anyway, no need to say any more about the matter, eh?'

John nodded wordlessly, relieved but not a little disappointed that a line had been drawn underneath the whole Polly matter.

'Bravo, Hettie. That was first rate!'

Hettie gave Archie, the composer, a relieved smile as she hurried into the wings, almost bumping into Jay as she did so.

'Everything all right now, Hettie?' he asked her in a kind voice as he caught hold of her to steady her.

Hettie nodded her head and tried not to look self-conscious. He was even more handsome than Rudolph Valentino, she thought dizzily.

'Is it true that we're to go to London straight after Christmas now instead of instead of later in January?' she burst out and then blushed as Jay looked quizzingly at her and started laughing.

'You've heard about that already, have you? Yes, we are.' He released her and reached into the inside pocket of his tweed jacket to withdraw a monogrammed silver cigarette case, opening it and offering her a cigarette.

A little awkwardly, she took one. She didn't smoke as a rule, although nearly all of the other girls did, but she had no wish to look gauche and immature.

Taking one himself, he produced his lighter, shielding the flame for Hettie as he leaned towards her, just like she had seen actors do in films. She could she smell the clean fresh scent of his cologne and suddenly her heart began to beat far too fast.

'The theatre has become available now so we might as well use it.'

Was he moving them down there so soon because he was missing his 'girlfriend'? Hettie wondered, and then chided herself guiltily for her thoughts.

'I've engaged a new director and a new choreographer to work with the cast once we get to London. I'm sorry you had such a rotten time of it, Hettie.'

Her heart was beating even faster. There was no one else in the corridor but that hadn't stopped Jay from moving closer to her. 'I was afraid that I would lose the part,' she admitted shyly.

'That's certainly what that Machiavellian pair were aiming for,' Jay told her. 'I've been asking a few questions about them and it seems this isn't the first time they've altered scores and scripts to suit their own ends. I guess they thought they'd got a real greenhorn in me, but any gambling man worth his salt knows how to recognise a sharp from a flat.'

Hettie could hear the clatter of feet on the staircase above them. As she looked upwards, Jay looked at his watch and told her, 'I must go but I want you to know that you're doing fine, Hettie, and that Archie agrees with me that your voice is perfect for Princess Mimi.'

He had gone before she could thank him, leaving her to be swallowed up in the gaggle of chorus girls hurrying towards the stage door.

This was far from the first time he had visited Moreton Place, John had reminded himself stalwartly as he'd parked the sturdy little Morris he had just bought for himself out of sight of the main entrance. Maybe not, his inner critic had conceded, but this was the first time his visit would be purely social; the first time be would be mingling with people he knew belonged to a social class far above his own; the first time he would be a 'house guest'.

He was desperately afraid that he wouldn't fit in, or that he would say or do something to show himself up. Not that he thought money and position made other people better than he was himself. He didn't, but if he had been able to get out of accepting the invitation he knew that he would have done so. But like any other man, he had his pride and he wasn't about to admit that he was afraid of being humiliated because he didn't talk 'posh' and had had to call upon the expertise of Messrs Moss Bros in order to equip himself with the right clothes.

He had spent enough time with toffs and nobs during the war to know how much store such people put on etiquette and doing things right.

He had opened the boot of the car and removed his battered leather case. It had started to snow, soft fat white flakes of it tumbling from a leaden grey sky.

'Good afternoon, Mr Pride.'

'Afternoon, Bates,' John had responded, giving the butler a warm smile. He had at one stage attempted to address Bates by his Christian name, feeling that it showed him proper respect, but Alfred had told him that it made the butler feel uncomfortable to be addressed by anything other than his surname.

Automatically John had allowed the butler to remove his coat and hand it to the waiting footman.

'James will show you to your room, and then when you are ready His Grace will be waiting for you in the library.'

The footman had already taken possession of his case, so John had dutifully followed him up the wide marble staircase and down a long corridor where he'd come to a halt outside one of the doors.

Opening it, he had stood back to allow John to precede him inside the room.

Ellie, whose husband had inherited from his long-lost birth mother a very handsome house in the best part of Preston, would no doubt have been shocked by the worn turkey carpets and old-fashioned furniture, John had suspected ruefully as James placed his well-worn case on a luggage rack as tenderly and reverently as though it were made of the finest quality materials.

'Mr Bates said as 'ow I was to tell you that His Grace's valet Peebles will be 'appy to attend to your needs, Sir, seeing as you 'aven't brought your own valet with you. And he said I was to mention to you that there would be no need for you to change your clothes before going down to the library.'

His own valet! John knew he should not have accepted Alfred's invitation. He was going to be utterly out of his depth. Unlocking his case, he had pushed back the lid and frowned over its contents; stiff starched collars, equally stiff shirts, a dinner jacket, and all the other accoutrements Messrs Moss Bros has insisted were essential.

John was not a man who enjoyed wearing formal clothes. He had looked down at the comfortable Harris tweed jacket he was wearing, which he had spotted on a market stall, its fabric well worn in by its previous owner. His brogues, although well polished, were far from new, as were his shirt and trousers. But he liked them, and he felt comfortable in them.

He had tensed as his bedroom door opened suddenly and Polly hurried into the room, closing the door behind her, exclaiming, 'John, I saw you arrive from my bedroom and . . . What are you doing? You don't need to unpack. One of the maids will do that for you.'

'Lady Polly, I don't really think you should be in here,' John had told her formally.

'Oh stuff! I just wanted to tell you that I've come clean to Alfie and told him how I tricked you into taking me flying. I do mean to learn to fly, you know, even if I have to buy my own flying machine in order to do so! Do you have a light?' she had asked him as she opened the bag she was carrying and removed a jewelled cigarette case.

John shook his head, and frowned. He didn't smoke. Cigarettes cost money and as a young man he had not been in a position to afford them.

'What's wrong?' Polly had demanded. 'Don't you approve of women smoking?'

She wasn't just smoking, she had obviously been drinking as well, John had realised as he caught the scent of gin on her breath. As she stepped closer to him he could see a wild glitter in her eyes that caused his frown to deepen.

'What is it about you men that makes you so unkind and disapproving?' Polly had asked huffily. 'You may do as you wish, and behave as you wish, but you deny us the same freedom!'

For some reason, she suddenly reminded John very much of Hettie.

'That was what I loved so much about my darling Oliver. He understood me so well.' Tears had welled up in her eyes. 'Alfie thinks I will forget Oliver and marry someone else, but I won't. I couldn't. His birthday was on Christmas Day. He would have been twenty-six this year.' Tears were running down her face and splashing on to the floor.

John's initial discomfort that she should have come into his room was swept aside by his compassion for her.

'Death is so final, isn't it, John? It doesn't allow us to go back and say or do those things we wish we had said and done. I cannot bear it that I will never again share the most intimate of all embraces with Oliver. God can be so cruel. Do you believe in God, John? Because I don't think that I do. Not any more.'

'You shouldn't be here,' he had told her gruffly. 'It isn't fitting.'

'What do you mean?'

'You knows what I mean, right enough, Lady Polly,' John had told her, once again emphasising his accent. 'You'm a Lady and I'm just a working man.'

Her eyes widened and she shook her head. 'John that is ridiculous, and you know it. You are Alfie's friend and I very much want you to be mine as well. Please say that you will?' she coaxed him, immediately crossing to the bed and sitting on it as she added emphatically, 'In fact, I am not going to leave until you do.'

John shook his head, but he couldn't help smiling at her. 'Your brother is expecting me to join him downstairs,' he had told her.

'Yes, and I should be serving tea in the drawing room to Great-Aunt Beatrice, who smells of cats and complains that she does not approve of modern young gals, and her poor daughter Florence, whom she bullies so dreadfully. And our cousin Thomasina will be there as well. She will want to know why I am not married yet, and she will tell me yet again how she could have married a royal duke had she so wished. It is the same every Christmas and I hate it. I hate everything, and everyone, but most of all I hate myself because I am alive and Oliver is dead . . .'

John hadn't known either what to say or do. Neither of his sisters ever drank spirits, and certainly neither of them would ever have behaved in the way Polly was doing; but then the aristocracy were a law unto themselves, everyone knew that.

'Have you ever loved anyone, John? Really loved them so much that you cannot bear the thought of life without them?' Polly demanded passionately.

John stiffened. He had once thought he loved Hettie, but she had changed from the sweet girl he had thought her into a young woman who had made it clear that he meant nothing to her. As to living without her . . . Well, he had proved well enough that he could do that, hadn't he?

'I must go, otherwise my aunts will be sending out a search party,' Polly had announced as though John and not she were responsible for her presence in his room.

'You had best dry your face first,' he'd told her automatically, handing her his handkerchief.

A small smile touched her mouth as she took it from him.

'Dear John. You are so kind.'

'And have you heard anything from John, Aunt Connie?' Hettie asked, trying to seem casual although her heart was beating wildy at the mere thought of John.

It was Christmas Day and, whilst the other girls who had not been able to return home to their families were having fun together at Jack and Sarah's chop house, with a party to enjoy afterwards, she was at her aunt's trying to make herself heard above the excited noise of the children.

'John. Yes, we had a card and a letter. Did I tell you that he has been invited to spend the whole of Christmas with that posh friend of his and his sister?'

'I can't remember,' Hettie fibbed, feigning indifference and bending down, pretending to examine one of the children's toys to hide the sudden burn of her hot face.

Why should she care who John spent Christmas with? she asked herself crossly. He could be with as many posh friends and their sisters as he chose, she had her own friends now, after all. And tomorrow night she would be joining them for a big farewell party before they all went their separate ways, some of them to London with the new musical whilst those who were in pantos would be staying here in Liverpool.

Lord, had she wanted to do so, she could have gone out with a different lad every day of the week, Hettie assured herself. Only the other day she had had two boys plead with her to let them take her to a tea dance, and two more had begged her to join them as their mascot when they took part in a car race to Blackpool. No, she had no need to envy John his life, not when she had such a happy, exciting life of her own to enjoy.

'And you're off to London the day after Boxing Day? Well, we shall all miss you, Hettie,' Connie told her. 'You must let me know your address as soon as you are settled there. And don't forget to write and let your mother know, will you?'

'Why should I? She doesn't care for me. She wouldn't even let me see her,' Hettie announced bitterly.

'Hettie! How can you be so ungrateful? You must not say such things,' Connie objected sharply. 'Ellie has loved you as dearly as if you were her own.'

White faced, Hettie dropped her eyelashes to conceal the sudden sharp spurt of her tears. Connie had been cross and not at all like herself all day, and had talked of nothing except how worried she was that the whole of the school would go down with the influenza that was already responsible for several of the boys having to be quarantined in the school sanatorium.

Hettie couldn't help contrasting this Christmas with those she had enjoyed at Winckley Square. How different everything was now. Then she had been so happy, believing that Ellie loved her. Whereas now . . .

She made her excuses and farewells far earlier than she had originally planned, choosing to walk back rather than wait for a bus. The city was unfamiliarly quiet and empty, and Hettie shivered in the cold. It was hard to imagine that this time next week she would actually be in London.

London! She would have a whole new life there. A life where she would be a proper stage singer. Her spirits started to lift. The other girls would still be partying at the chop house and she was wearing her new dress. She had bought it from a neighbour of one of the chorus girls' cousins, a machinist in a dress factory, who made copies of their posh frocks for special customers who got to know about her by word of mouth.

Hettie's was the very latest style with a short skirt and a dropped waist. It was perfect for all those exciting modern dances she and the other girls practised in their attic bedroom and then taught the boys amidst much joking and laughter.

She had reached Jack and Sarah's chop house and, as she pushed open the door, she was enveloped in warm goose-scented air, and above the noise of the party goers she heard Babs yelling her name.

She could feel the tightness of misery and anger

loosening its grip on her heart to be replaced by warmth and relief. She was home, because home was here now, with her friends, and not Winckley Square and the Pride family.

EIGHTEEN

'It seems so funny, Lizzie not being here.'

'Well, like she said, 'Ettie, it 'ud tek too long for her to get back to her mum and 'er sister from London, and that's why she auditioned for the panto instead of trying for the musical like us,' Babs pointed out cheerfully before adding, 'Isn't it time we 'ad our sandwiches? I'm fair famished. Sukey, go and find the lads and tell 'em that if they want anything to eat they'd better be quick.'

The chorus girls and the new friends they had made amongst the young men from the orchestra were all travelling down to London on the same train, and it had been in a mood of light-hearted excitement that they had boarded the train earlier in the day – even Babs, who had had to part from Stan as he was booked to appear in a pantomime.

'Did you see the look that old man at the ticket office gave us when we said we was all wanting to travel together?' Sukey laughed.

'He's so old he probably thinks women should

261

still travel in separate carriages, and not be allowed to do anything unless some fella says that we can,' she added, tossing her head. 'Catch me ever letting any fella tell me what to do.'

A new mood was sweeping the country and its young women; a desire and a determination to escape the dark shadows of the war and all its lost young men, and to be be independent and have fun.

Young women now went out to work; they smoked and talked openly about subjects that would have shocked previous generations. Shop girls and factory girls, as well as debs, made it plain that they wanted to have fun in return for their hard work. They laughed and danced and stayed out until the early hours of the morning. They filled the picture houses, and went to afternoon tea dances on their days off. They enjoyed the company of a variety of young men in a way that shocked their own mothers. But nothing seemed to deter these strong-willed, determined daughters they and the war had raised.

'They had Mary Pickford on a news-reel film at the cimema the other night, and her dress was so short you could nearly see her knees,' Jenny announced.

'So what? Everyone will be seeing ours once the show opens,' Mary told her. 'And I heard Jay Dalhousie telling that Archie that he wants our skirts to be even shorter, just like they have 'em on Broadway.'

'I'll bet old fuddy duddy Harris had something to say about that. Just because she once stood in as wardrobe mistress for a show with Mr Cochran's young ladies in it, she thinks she knows everything there is to know about what's right and proper. How about you, 'Ettie? I heard as 'ow Jay Dalhousie is so pleased with your singing that he's asked that Archie to put in another song for you.'

Hettie felt herself blushing as they all turned to look at her.

'You never said owt about that to me, 'Ettie,' Babs reproached her.

'Well, it isn't definite yet,' Hettie defended herself.

'Seems to me our Mr Dalhousie has a right old soft spot for you, 'Ettie,' one of the other girls called out meaningfully.

'You can stop that right now, Sally-Anne.' Babs leaped to Hettie's defence. ''Ettie isn't like that, especially not with a married man . . .'

'Are you all right, Babs?' Hettie asked her friend anxiously an hour later, noticing her unfamiliar silence.

'I've never been in a London play before,' Babs answered her. 'I just hopes it isn't true as some folk have been saying that we won't run for so much as a week.'

'Huh. Them as says that are just jealous cats, that's all,' Sukey declared, joining in the conversation. But Hettie knew that her normally optimistic friend's uncertainty was shared by them all, and her admission turned the earlier laughter and high spirits into a much more sombre mood.

'We don't even know who this new director we're going to be getting is yet,' Eddie compained moodily.

'Jay told me that he's someone really good but that he doesn't want to say too much until he's definitely agreed to take us on.'

'Seems like *you* know a good deal more about what's happening than we do, Hettie,' Sukey said to her semi-accusingly.

'He just mentioned it when he told me that he had asked the composer to put in another song for me,' Hettie defended herself. 'Mervyn was there as well.'

Mervyn Rodgers was the male lead singer, and he and the female lead were making their own way to London.

'What else did he say?' Eddie asked her.

'Nothing much, just that the new director was also a choreographer.'

'Well, I hope whoever he is he doesn't want to make any more bleedin' changes to the chorus line routines,' Sukey complained. 'I don't know about the rest of you but I'm beginning to think I'd have bin better off sticking with panto. What with new routines and then having to open a week earlier on account of having to change theatres at the last minute.'

The train had started slow down.

'It's London.' Jenny shrieked excitedly, pulling her twin to her feet. 'Look, everyone, we're here!'

'I thought the old battleaxe's house was bad enough, but this place . . . Cor, but it stinks of cabbage. And have you seen the bathroom?' Aggie grumbled.

'Couldn't we find somewhere else to lodge?' Hettie asked unhappily as she and Babs looked round the cramped room to which they had just been shown by their new landlady.

'I doubt as we'd be able to get anything much better,' Sukey told them. 'Sharp as knives these London landladies are. They all want as much as they can get out of yer, that's wot I've been told at any rate, and at least 'ere we can all be together.'

'But it's so dirty,' Hettie objected.

'It's noffink that a bit o' scrubbin' and some bleach won't put right,' Aggie chimed in hardily, adding, 'I don't know about the rest of you but I'm fair famished and I noticed there's a chop house right on the corner.'

'Well, we'll have to go to the laundry first, cos no way am I sleeping on sheets I haven't seen washed with me own eyes,' Babs insisted firmly.

Hettie hadn't imagined that her first night in London would be spent washing sheets, she had to admit. The glamour and excitement she had expected seemed to be a million miles away from the grubby place which would be home for she didn't know how long.

*   *   *

'I say, Polly, shouldn't you be in the drawing room?' Alfred objected as the doors to the billiards room were flung open and his sister came in.

'Doing what? Letting Great-Aunt Beatrice criticise everything I do?' Polly retorted, pulling a face. 'I'd much rather be in here with you boys. It's so much more fun. Why on earth did you invite such dreadful bores, Alfie?'

'Family. Had to . . . Hey, that was my shot,' he protested indignantly as Polly picked up a cue and skilfully potted a ball.

'You would never have potted it, you are useless at billiards, you know that. Come on, John,' she called across the table. 'I challenge you to beat me. Loser has to perform a forfeit of the winner's choosing . . .'

John hid a small smile as he saw the look of helpless acceptance on his friend's face.

'Alfie, why don't you ring for Bates and organise some drinks? Tell him I want a martini – a strong one, too. And don't look at me like that. Our horrid government may have only given the vote to women who are over thirty and married, but just because I can't vote that doesn't mean that I can't drink or smoke. Look at you both,' she burst out passionately, throwing aside her cue. 'Why should you be able to vote because you are men? Why should men tell women what they can and can't do? You don't understand, do you, either of you?' Tears filled her eyes. 'Oh, why, why did my darling Oliver have to die? He would have understood . . .'

As she ran out of the room, slamming the door behind her, Alfred gave John an apologetic look. 'Sorry about that. Difficult time for Polly right now. Thought that this dance tonight might help cheer her up, but it seems not.'

'Don't be cross with me, John. I know I shouldn't be here, but I had to apologise to you.'

After his conversation with Alfred, John had excused himself and returned to his room closing the door, desperate for some time to himself. To his shock, Polly was lying on his bed.

'What are you doing here?' John demanded.

Tears filled her eyes. 'I can't bear to think that I will never see Oliver again. It hurts so much, John.' She gave a small hiccup, and sat up. 'I'm a disgrace, aren't I? Aren't you glad I'm not your sister? It's so horrid being a woman, John. A woman is so dependent on a man for everything and I hate that.'

She stood up and started to pace the floor. 'Will you dance with me tonight? Please do? And then tomorrow I shall take you for a drive in my new roadster. We can go to Brighton, and I shall drive as fast as the wind.'

Her eyes were starting to glitter as her tears dried. There was a half full martini glass on John's bedside table, which she had obviously brought to his room, and she picked it up, quickly draining the contents. 'Have you ever done something that changed your whole life, John? Something that you wish more than anything else you had not done?' she asked him morosely.

He thought instantly of the accident, his muscles compressing. And then of Hettie, his heart filling with despair.

'I have, and I hate myself for it,' Polly was continuing. 'At first I blamed Oliver, but it wasn't his fault. I blamed him because I couldn't bear to blame myself . . .'

John couldn't speak. What she was saying reflected exactly how he felt about Hettie. He had blamed her for changing and pursuing a new life because he had not been man enough to accept the blame himself for not telling her how he truly felt about her – that his concerns for her were born out of love and tenderness not authority and harshness.

He had lost her for ever now. He was filled with an aching sense of loss and emptiness. Had he been guilty of treating her as though he had the right to dictate to her what she did?

''Ere, Sukey, where 'ave you been?'

'Mind your own business, Mary,' Sukey relied sharply as she hurried into the dressing room, pushing a small package into her coat pocket before starting to get changed into her practice clothes.

'This is the third time you've been late for rehearsals,' Mary persisted.

'So what's that to you?' Sukey snapped.

Hettie and Babs exchanged wary looks and Babs grimaced silently. Sukey had become increasingly on edge and secretive since they had come to London.

'It's on account of the new director telling her she has to lose some weight,' Jenny guessed. 'Got herself into a right state about it, she has. Hardly touches her food any more. Of course, them sort allus want to see women looking like lads,' she added knowingly.

The new director choreographer was a fiery tempered Russian who had worked with the Ballet Russe, and had escaped from his own country to live in France during the revolution.

With his slicked-back black hair and flashing eyes he looked like Valentino, but he was, as they had all quickly realised, far more interested in the chorus boys than the chorus girls.

Hettie gave Jay Dalhousie a grateful smile as she heard him clapping her from the wings. He had been so kind to her and she was extremely grateful to him.

'That was good, Hettie,' Jay praised her, giving her arm a small squeeze. 'I want you to have dinner with me soon,' he told her abruptly.

Hettie looked at him uncertainly. 'To talk about the operetta? I thought you were pleased that . . .'

'No, not to talk about the operetta,' he stopped her softly. 'I want to take you to dinner so that I can talk to you, Hettie . . .'

How could she feel so excited and elated but so scared at the same time, Hettie wondered. 'I . . .'

'What is it? Don't you trust me to behave like a gentleman?' he teased her.

'Of course I do.' Her voice was indignant and her face pink.

She was so naive, Jay reflected, and so innocent. His pulse leaped and he had trouble stopping himself from taking hold of her right there and then. She was the reason he had ended his relationship with his now ex-mistress, and he was in danger of becoming obsessed with her.

'So it's a date, then?' he demanded, reaching for her hand and keeping hold of it. 'Opening night, after the show, you and I are having dinner together?'

Speechlessly, Hettie nodded.

Fortunately she had the dressing room to herself since the others were still rehearsing their final number. Sinking down on to a stool she stared at her reflection in the mirror, a delicious shiver of excitement racing down her spine. Her hand still felt warm from Jay holding it. And *she* felt warm from the way he had looked at her.

Hettie might be inexperienced so far as men were concerned, but she knew right from wrong and she knew too that her feelings of excitement and anticipation were not the ones she should be feeling for a married man. Only if no one else but she knew about them, that was all right, surely, wasn't it? And Jay had probably not even been serious about taking her to dinner, anyway.

The dressing room door opened and Sukey peered anxiously round it, and then hurried towards the hooks where they hung their coats, coming to an abrupt halt when she saw Hettie.

'Oh, you made me jump.'

Sukey might be thinner now but she did not look very well, Hettie decided. Her face was too flushed and too thin, and its thinness making her eyes look somehow as though there were bulging out of their sockets.

'I thought you were still rehearsing,' Hettie commented as Sukey grabbed hold of her coat and put her hand into one of the pockets.

'We are, but I wasn't feeling too good, so I had to come and get one of me tablets,' Sukey explained, her body tensing as she began to tug feverishly at her pocket, exclaiming, 'Me tablets. Where are they . . . I need them.' She looked almost panic stricken and started tearing frantically at her coat, her face burning hotly.

Sympathetic, Hettie got off her stool and went to help her. 'I didn't realise you weren't well, Sukey,' she said.

'I didn't want to tell anyone, and you mustn't either,' Sukey informed Hettie fiercely. 'Promise me that you won't.'

Hettie nodded whilst Sukey muttered, 'Perhaps I put them in me bag. Yes, I must have done . . .' before darting over to her clothes and pushing

271

them out of the way until she had found her hand-bag. ''Ere, go and get us a cup of water, will you, 'Ettie' she begged.

Dutifully Hettie hurried to the small kitchen and filled a glass with water, carrying it carefully back to the dressing room.

'Quick, give it 'ere,' Sukey commanded. She was trembling violently as she swallowed several small white tablets, and even though she held the glass with both hands, water still splashed out of it.

Anxiously, Hettie watched her.

'I'd better get back before anyone misses me,' Sukey told her.

'But if you aren't well . . .'

'I've just told you, Hettie . . . I don't want no one to know about that,' Sukey repeated angrily. 'So don't you go mentioning it to no one, you hear?'

They were opening on New Year's Day and several members of the cast had complained that it was a bad date on which to open and that the only reason Jay had been given the theatre early was because no one else would take that week.

'He might have got every blasted critic in London coming, but that just means there'll be more of 'em to give us bad reviews,' the actor playing the comic role of household controller to the royal household had prophesied.

Since she had finished rehearsals for the day she might as well go, Hettie decided. She had almost reached the stage door when she heard the sound of two familiar and very angry male voices – Eddie and their new director – and they were plainly quarrelling. If she walked past the open door to the small room they were in, they were bound to see her. But if she didn't, she couldn't get to the stage door, and she certainly didn't want to eavesdrop on them.

As she hesitated, her dilemma was solved for her when Eddie strode out of the room, turning back to say bitterly, 'Do you really think I don't know why you're doing this? If you think I'm jealous of that poxy little faggot of a chorus boy . . .'

Hettie gasped as the door was slammed in his face with such force that, if he hadn't stepped back, it must have hit him.

He wheeled round and then stopped as he saw her.

'I'm sorry. I didn't mean to listen. It was just . . .'

'I need a drink. Come with me, Hettie . . . Please . . .'

He had grabbed hold of her arm and was practically dragging her out of the theatre and down Drury Lane before she could stop him. It was raining and the streets were wet and shiny, busy with shop girls and office workers as well as other theatre people. The cold air smelled of damp and wet wool tinged with bad drains, making Hettie wrinkle her nose.

Eddie hurried her into a small smoky public house where they managed to find a solitary table tucked away in a corner. When the waiter came,

Eddie told him shortly, 'Absinthe, and be quick about it. What will you have, Hettie?'

'Oh, coffee, please.'

As soon as the waiter had gone Eddie leaned his elbows on the table and placed his head in his hands.

'Eddie, what is it? What's wrong?' Hettie asked him anxiously.

'Isn't it obvious? Hell, the whole theatre's gossiping about it.' His voice was thick with emotion. 'It's bad enough that Ivan's *here* without him tormenting me by making cows' eyes at that smirking little toad. I thought he loved *me*. He told me he did.'

Hettie bit her lip. There had been gossip about the intensity of the animosity between Eddie and their new director, but it still shocked Hettie to hear Eddie speak so openly about the situation.

The waiter returned with Eddie's drink and Hettie's coffee. She pulled a face as she saw the murky greenish colour of Eddie's drink.

'What *is* that?' she asked him.

'Absinthe? It's the drink of the devil and the damned,' he told her bitterly. 'Everyone in Paris drinks it. They say it can send a man mad. Sometimes I think I already am. I must be to have let myself . . . And now he's here mocking me, tormenting me.'

Eddie gave a deep shudder and Hettie realised with shock that he was actually crying. 'I can't bear it, Hettie. I can't bear this torment. It's killing me. But Ivan doesn't care. All he thinks about is his own pleasure. When he begged me for my love he told me that we'd be together for always.'

Hettie's shock and discomfort increased. She had never witnessed a grown man cry before.

'Was it for this that I broke my mother's heart and brought such shame on my family that my father declared that he wanted nothing more to do with me, and that he would rather I had been dead?' Eddie demanded with despair.

The discomfort and shock Hettie had originally felt immediately turned to sincere pity and compassion as she heard the agony in Eddie's voice.

'I should not be speaking to you like this,' he admitted. 'Tomorrow you must forget what I have said and blame the absinth if you do remember, for that is what I shall do,' he told her morosely.

'Oh, Eddie . . .' Not knowing what to say, Hettie reached out and placed her hand on his.

'You are a kind child, Hettie, and you have not yet learned to scorn and deride me and those like me. You cannot know the despair a perversion such as mine brings to a man. I carried the burden of that shame alone until I went to Paris. To be there and to know, to *mix* with others like me, to find what I thought was the most elevated form of human love, to have raised that cup to my lips and then to have had it dashed away . . .' Eddie gave a deep shudder. 'That one sip has poisoned my soul for ever, and I shall never recover. Absinthe is its antidote, the only thing that keeps me alive now. But why should I want to live? I wish I had never been born. I wish I had the courage to end it all. That would show him.'

Hettie didn't know what to say or do. Eddie's reckless confidences *had* shocked her, and she knew enough about life now to understand how dangerous it was for him to talk openly about a relationship that the law forbade.

'Eddie, you must not say such things, or . . . or speak to me like this,' she told him in a low voice.

He picked up his glass and downed its contents in one go. 'Poor little Hetttie. You just don't understand, do you?' he declared wildly before summoning the waiter and ordering another drink. As soon as the waiter had gone he continued bitterly, 'How could you understand? We live in different worlds, you and I.'

'I know what it means to love someone, Eddie,' Hettie found the courage to tell him. It was true after all. She had loved Ellie and Gideon – and she had loved John as well.

Eddie's mouth twisted. 'So sweet . . . But the kind of love that torments me is not sweet, Hettie. It is bitter, and it is cruel, and most of all it is forbidden. And yet I would sell my very soul to the devil for just one taste of his lips, for just one touch of his hand.' He had started to cry again. 'I am a cursed and damned man, Hettie, and there is no help for me,' he sobbed.

Hettie didn't know how to console poor Eddie.

She only knew how much it hurt when someone didn't reciprocate your feelings for them.

'And wot the hell's up with Sukey? One minute she's acting like we was 'er worst enemies and then half an hour later she's laughing and joking as though she hadn't got a care in the world.'

'And talking ten to the dozen as well. You can't shut her up,' Jenny complained as she patted night cream into her face and demanded, 'Move up, 'Ettie, will yer? I can't see meself in the mirror.'

They were all getting ready for bed in Hettie and Babs's room, a nightly ritual they had started on their arrival in London, and Jenny was busily complaining about Sukey, who still hadn't come in.

'I don't think she's very well,' Hettie defended Sukey.

'We all know *that*,' Aggie replied with a grimace.

'No, I mean *really* poorly,' Hettie insisted. 'She came into the dressing room this afternoon and she was shaking and trembling so badly she couldn't even get the pills the doctor had given her out of her coat pocket.

'Pills? Doctor?' Aggie demanded suspiciously. 'She 'asn't said anything about needing to see any doctor to anyone else, so how come she's told you, Hettie?'

'I don't think she wanted to make a fuss. She made *me* promise not to say anything to anyone else,' Hettie admitted uncomfortably. 'But anyone can see she's not well. She's gone that thin an' all.'

''Ere, hang on a minute,' Mary interrupted Hettie. 'Do you know what I think? I think it's a pound to a penny that Sukey has gone and got some of them diet pills from that quack doctor.'

'Wot, you mean she's taking them pills that Marge told us about?' Babs demanded worriedly. 'Them wot she said 'ad tape worms in 'em?'

'Tapeworms? Don't be daft, Babs,' Aggie snorted. 'It's not tapeworms as is in 'em, it's that cocaine. And if that's what she's tekkin, no wonder she's bin acting a bit odd, like. Mad as a hatter they'll make her, that's what I've heard. She's gonna kill herself if she doesn't watch out.'

'They've certainly made her as thin as a rake,' Jenny joined in, adding with a small sigh, 'I could do with a few of them myself. I've heard as how all them posh society debutantes take them so as they can get into their Chanel frocks, and the chaps tek it, too. Sniff it up like it were snuff, they do. Mad, the lot of them, if you ask me.

'You're lucky, 'Ettie, you don't need to worry about your weight,' Jess told her enviously.

It was true that she was naturally slender, Hettie acknowledged, and with the opening night only a few days away her nervousness was making her even more so.

'Wot happened to you this afternoon, 'Ettie? When we got back to the dressing room you was gone,' Aggie asked curiously.

'Eddie asked me to go and have a drink with him,' she explained.

'I hope you ain't getting moony over that Eddie, Hettie,' Aggie cautioned her.

'Of course she ain't,' Mary cut in scornfully. 'Hettie knows a nance when she sees one, don't you, 'Ettie?'

Pink cheeked, Hettie nodded her head. 'I just feel sorry for him,' Hettie admitted.

Sorry for him and somehow sorry for herself as well, Hettie thought tiredly. She had not expected to find London's streets paved with gold, of course, but with the excitement of their arrival behind her and the anxiety of their opening night now so close, Hettie had become victim to an inner sadness she couldn't really explain. She knew it had something to do with the gulf that now existed between her and her parents, and she knew too that learning John had spent Christmas with his friend and his friend's sister had added to it. There was an emptiness in her life that had once been filled with the small day-to-day diversions that came from being part of a family, and the girls, good friends though they were, were not family.

London was just as cold and damp as Liverpool, its street-children every bit as ragged and wretched, the faces of its poor just as pinched and hungry. And here there was no kind-hearted Sarah Baker, with her big basket of bread and potatoes to hand out to those in need. She had no need to count every penny now, Hettie acknowledged, because her wages had been increased as she was playing the second female lead. So she saved her pennies and half-pennies to drop into the grubby eager hands of the children who begged in small groups in Piccadilly Circus, darting off the moment a policeman spotted them.

'Well, leaving yer supper isn't going to help him, is it?' Babs chided her prosaically. 'Eat it up, 'Ettie, you're going to need yer strength. It isn't that long now 'til New Year's Day and our opening night, you know.'

Hettie couldn't help but laugh. Babs sounded so like Ellie. Her laugher died, a sharp hurting pain digging into her heart. Did any of them think of her? Ellie? John? She had written to Gideon begging him to let her know how Ellie was, and telling him all her own news, but as yet she had not heard back from him. How long did it take for letters to get to the Lakes? she wondered bleakly.

NINETEEN

New Year's Eve, and here he was spending it so very far away from his family and those who meant most to him, John thought as he battled with the bow tie he was attempting to knot, having refused the assistance of Alfred's valet.

No, it still wasn't right. Impatiently he pulled the crumpled fabric from his neck and breathed out heavily. He wasn't looking forward to this evening, and to judge from her behaviour earlier in the day neither was Polly, although Alfred had complained that she had been the one who had insisted he must hold a New Year's Eve dance.

This Christmas had been so different from the others he had known; the Christmases of his childhood in the cosy parlour above his father's butcher's shop. Life had seemed so safe and happy then. But then there had been those frightening years after his mother's death, when he and his siblings had been parted from one another, followed by his reunion with Ellie, then a young widow who had voluntarily taken on the responsibility for Hettie.

John smiled to himself, remembering the sharp pang of emotion he had felt the very first time Hettie had imperiously held out her baby arms to him. She had been a child of three, and he had been a boy scarcely a decade older.

And she had continued to tug on his heart in the years that had followed. First as the little girl who followed him around adoringly, but more recently as a young woman who aroused within him the feelings of a man rather than those of a friend.

He could still remember how confused and shocked he had felt last Christmas when Hettie, newly grown up, had appeared at the Christmas morning church service dressed as a young woman and not a child.

How she had pouted and looked cross when he had refused to kiss her beneath the mistletoe, and his heart had ached with longing to sweep her into his arms somewhere private so that he could kiss those sweet cherry-red pouting lips. He had gone home that night to daydream about the future and his ring on Hettie's slender finger. But Hettie had had her own dreams and they had not included him.

The noise of the dinner bell broke into his thoughts. He looked at his reflection in the mirror. The tie still looked slightly lopsided, but he could not delay any longer. Putting on his jacket, he opened his bedroom door and stepped out on to the landing.

'Oh John, goodness, what has Bates done to your tie?' he heard Polly exclaiming as she hurried towards him. 'Alfie, really ought to retire him. His eyesight is terrible . . .'

'I fastened it myself,' John told her stiffly, but instead of looking embarrassed Polly laughed.

'Oh, did you? No wonder, then. Daddy always used to say that no gentleman should ever be able to make a decent bow tie because that was why one had a valet.'

'Well, the reason I can't tie one is because where I come from no one wears them,' John told her sharply.

He had already overheard Alfred's great-aunt commenting to her daughter that she could not understand why Alfred had befriended 'a person so obviously from the lower classes', and he was grimly conscious of his own flat working class northern accent – and equally grimly determined that nothing and no one was going to make him feel ashamed of either his background or his upbringing.

'Oh John, I'm sorry. Please don't be cross with me. You're the only person who makes being here bearable.' Polly had stepped up to him as she was speaking and before John could stop her she reached out and quickly unfastened his bow tie.

Automatically John pulled back from her, but she shook her head and told him firmly, 'Keep still, silly, otherwise I'll never be able to fasten it properly for you. Ollie taught me how,' she added softly.

*　　*　　*

'Alfie, why have you turned off the gramophone?' Polly protested breathlessly. 'I still want to dance.'

'It's almost midnight, Polly, and Bates will be waiting to First Foot us. Besides, I rather think that some of our guests have been shocked enough for one evening. Let's put on the wireless so that we can hear Big Ben chime in the new year.'

'Why are they shocked?' Polly demanded as she pouted at her brother. 'Because of the way I was dancing? Oh pooh! Old fuddy duddies. Who cares about them? John, I want you to promise me that you will be my first dancing partner of the new year,' she insisted, turning towards John and reaching for his hand.

Her face was over flushed and her eyes were over bright, and John could well understand why Alfred had felt compelled to warn her that she was shocking his elderly guests. But at the same time John could not help but feel sympathetic towards her. She was so plainly unhappy and so obviously still grieving for the man she had loved.

'And so as Big Ben begins to signal the arrival of the new year . . .'

The wireless crackled and then, as clearly as though they had actually been there, the room was filled by the sound of Big Ben striking the hour of midnight.

Everyone began to cheer, the ladies, led by Polly, taking the initiative and kissing the men.

'I've saved you until last, John,' Polly whispered

to him as she stretched up on her toes and boldly kissed his mouth.

To his shame, John felt his body respond to her closeness, and even more shamefully he knew from the look she gave him that Polly was equally aware of the effect she had had on him.

The guests, led by Alfred, streamed out into the hallway to welcome in Bates and the new year.

'A toast,' someone cried out as glasses were filled with foaming champagne and passed from hand to hand.

'A toast of the new year and to the future . . .'

'I want to make a toast.'

Everyone turned to look at Polly, who was standing on the larger hall table, swaying slightly, a glass of champagne in her hand, her short beaded frock revealing her slenderness.

'I say, Polly, come down off there, there's a good girl,' Alfie began worriedly, but Polly shook her head.

'No. Not yet. Come on, everyone. Lift your glasses with me so that we can toast those who are no longer with us to toast themselves. All those gallant, doomed, dead young men who will never taste champagne again, never dance again, never kiss again. They were the best of us all and now they're gone. We're a doomed generation, all of us. They were doomed to die and we are doomed to live on without them until . . .'

John could hear the shocked uneasy whispers of the other guests. A female guest sobbed and a man close to him muttered, 'Bad form, what?'

'Raise your glasses everyone!'

There was a swift indrawing of shocked breath as Polly lifted hers and then, instead of drinking from it, flung it at the fireplace before collapsing on to the table, sobbing wildly.

'Every seat in the house has been sold!'

'Don't tell me *that*, Babs, you're making me even more nervous than I was,' Hettie protested feverishly as she dabbed powder on her flushed cheeks.

'I'll lay odds that Jay Dalhousie has given away half of them seats just to get bums on 'em,' Mary pronounced wisely. Especially wi' every bloody critic in London already saying as how no American can possibly know how to put on a decent show in London.'

''Oo cares whose bums are in them seats,' Jenny broke in, 'just so long as they keep 'em there? Do you remember that panto we was in, our kid, when half the audience walked out before the end of the first act and than the rest followed them during the second?'

'Yes. All apart from that bloody kid who stood up and started pitching rotten tomatoes at us,' her sister recalled.

Antagonistic critics, audiences who walked out, people throwing rotten food at them . . . Hettie shuddered with dread. She couldn't remember a single word of any of her songs, never mind a full line, and she had had nightmares last night in which Madame had suddenly reappeared and insisted that she was going to have to dance a ballet.

'Five minutes,' a young runner announced, banging on the dressing room door.

'At least we've got decent costumes.'

'You may call 'em decent, Mary, but I calls them positively indecent,' Babs contradicted firmly. 'And I don't care if Mr Cochran does dress his bloody 'young ladies' in the same sort of style!'

'The reviewers should like them, then.' Jenny winked.

'Break a leg, 'Ettie,' Babs whispered as the chorus girls headed for the door in a flurry of sequins, high heels and feathers. 'You'll do all right, don't you worry about that.'

The chorus had reached the end of their first number, the male lead and the male comic were singing their opening songs, and soon it would be her turn.

Hettie took a deep breath. She wasn't Hettie any more, she was a young Japanese Princess . . .

'Go on, 'Ettie! It's you wot they're yelling for.'

Eager hands pushed her back on to the stage.

The audience was on its collective feeet, calling out for Princess Mimi. The noise was like no other Hettie had ever heard. It rolled round the theatre and bounced off its walls, making the whole stage shake. Or was she the one who was shaking as she listened to the whistles, the stamping of feet, the shouts of approval and excitement?

The cast had already taken more than a dozen curtain calls, and now the audience was calling for her. Somehow she managed to make a small formal Japanese bow, and then get back to the wings.

'Hettie, Hettie, you little wonder, you've stolen their hearts and the show. The critics are in raptures.' Jay was standing there waiting for her, grinning from ear to ear with delight.

Hettie gasped as he took hold of her and lifted her off her feet, whirling her around. Jay was holding her so tightly that she could smell the hot male scent of his triumphant excitement. He kissed her – on the cheek and then on her mouth. Dizzily, Hettie looked up at him. She heard him groan her name and then he was kissing her again, a shockingly fierce passionate kiss, she acknowledged giddily as her heart started to beat even faster and all she could do was gaze up into his eyes, as though she were spellbound to him.

'I've got to go,' he whispered to her. 'The press are waiting for me at the Ritz. But I haven't forgotten about our dinner . . .'

'Where's Mary?'

After Jay had left, the director announced that Jay had told him to take the whole cast to a famous local chop house for a late celebratory supper, at

Jay's expense. So as soon as they had changed out of their costumes and cleaned off their stage make-up, they headed there, ravenously hungry now the ordeal of the First Night was over. They were high on success, adrenalin and youthful excitement.

Talking and laughing, her friends swept Hettie along with them, insisting that, from now on, she was going to be their good luck mascot; and insisting, too, on telling the chop house owner and everyone else who would listen that Hettie was going to be London's new female star.

Then a group of diners who had seen the show got up and started to clap and cheer as word got round as to who they were. Drinks were sent to their table, and glasses raised to them, and it was only now as the initial euphoria started to wear off that Hettie realised that Mary wasn't with them.

'Mary? She's probably having dinner with that chap who sent a message from the stage door saying as how he wanted to tek her out,' Jenny announced.

'A right posh toff he is too, by the sound of it. Sent up his card, he did, and he's only a *lord*, if you please.'

'How come *she* gets to have dinner with a lord?' Sukey asked sulkily, suddenly pushing away her meal.

'Gawd, Sukey, what's up with you now?' Babs demanded.

Jenny nudged Babs and muttered, 'You know

what's up wi' her, Babs. It's them pills she's tekkin.'

Hettie let the excited chatter flow around her. She still could not believe that it had actually happened and that Princess Mimi had won the hearts of the audience, and, even more importantly, at least according to Babs, the much harder hearts of the critics as well.

Someone had ordered champagne and Hettie's face burned bright red when the director stood up and toasted her.

Not that everyone was as pleased about her success.

'She won't last, of course,' Hettie heard the female lead saying pointedly as she gave Hettie a cold look. 'Her kind never does. They get too type-cast. Of course, one only has to look at her to see why she got the part . . .'

'Tek no notice, 'Ettie,' Babs told her. 'she's just a spiteful old cat wot's jealous of you.'

''Ere, waiter, we needs another bottle of champagne,' Jenny declared grabbing hold of a passing waiter. 'Gawd, but this stuff gets up yer nose a bit. Can't say as ow I can see what posh folks see in it, meself.'

'I've heard as how it doesn't give yer a bad head in the morning,' Aggie informed her knowledgeably.

They were all in such high spirits that Hettie wasn't totally surprised when several of the chorus girls, egged on by the others, got up and did an impromptu can-can, much to the delight of the goggling waiters and the other male diners.

'Common. That's what they are,' Hettie heard the leading actress sniff disparagingly.

'Like she didn't come up from the chorus herself *and* on her back by all accounts,' Aggie said wickedly with a knowing wink.

Further up the table Hettie could see the director and the other actors, but although she looked for him Hettie couldn't see Eddie anywhere.

Everyone else at the table was enjoying themselves, and of course she was thrilled and excited that the play and she herself had been so well accepted. How could she not be? But there was still a place inside her that felt empty and cold, a place that yearned for the warmth of Ellie's voice and Ellie's love; a place that longed for her family to be here with her to share in her success. Sharp tears pricked at her eyeballs.

It had been a dank, damp day, too wet even to go out shooting, as Alfred had complained irritably over breakfast; a day that John was only too glad to see coming to an end. He had hinted to Alfred that maybe he should take his leave of the household and get back to work, but his patron had insisted that he wanted him to stay.

Polly had not come down for breakfast, which, to judge from the tight-mouthed expressions of her female relatives, John suspected had been a wise move on her part. Nothing had been said about the events of the previous evening, but a strong odour of disapproval emanated from the other ladies, whilst Alfred was still plainly embarrassed and put out of sorts by his sister's behaviour.

There had been plenty of people the previous evening willing to suggest that Polly had had too much to drink, and it had been with a sinking heart that John had been obliged to listen to Alfred confiding to him how concerned he was about his sister, knowing that he could not offer him any comfort.

He had not seen Polly at all during the day, but she had come down for dinner, albeit looking wan and vulnerable. During the meal she had been uncharacteristically quiet, contributing nothing to the dinner table conversation and barely touching her food. John had witnessed, though, how her hands had been shaking so much that she had needed both of them in order to hold the glass of water that was all that she had had to drink.

'I suppose you're all waiting for me to apologise for last night,' she had remarked at the end of the meal. 'Well, I shall not do so. I shall never apologise for believing that the best of all of us are gone, taken from us for ever. But I do apologise to you, dearest Alfie, if I embarrassed you, for you are the best of all brothers, and you do not deserve to have such a wretched burden of a sister.' She had smiled tearfully at him and then got up and left the room.

'Well!' her great-aunt had fumed. 'I had heard that modern young people were lacking in manners, but I had not expected to see evidence of it with my very own eyes and from a member of my own family. Alfred, your father would never have countenanced such behaviour. If you want my opinion, it is your mother who is to blame for your sister's shocking behaviour.'

'I say, Aunt,' Alfred had objected. 'Mother died when Polly was still in the nursery.'

'Exactly! Had she lived she would have seen to it that Polly was brought up under a far stricter regime. It is a mother's duty to prepare her daughters for their role in society, not a father's, and I shall not have a word said against my nephew, your dear father, on that head.'

The ladies had all retired to their beds over an hour ago and now, as he made his way upstairs to his, John acknowledged that he was looking forward to returning to his normal life.

He opened his bedroom door and stepped inside the room, closing the door behind him, and then froze in disbelief. There, in the middle of his bed, lying on her side with her head propped up by her arm – her *naked* arm, John couldn't help but notice – was Polly.

'John, at last! I've been waiting for you for ever,' she reproached him. 'And I've drunk all the gin,' she added sorrowfully.

'Polly, Lady Polly,' John corrected himself firmly. 'This is not . . .'

'John, please don't send me away. Please let me stay. I can't bear to be alone tonight.' Tears filled her eyes. 'It was New Year's night when Ollie proposed to me . . .'

John felt his heart contract in pain for her. 'I do understand, but you must know that you can't stay here,' he said to her gently. But as he approached the bed he could smell the gin. The bottle beside the bed was empty and he wondered how much she had actually drunk.

'All I want is to *be* with someone . . . To be held and kept safe from my own dark places. You have no idea how much they torment me, John.' She shivered and the bedclothes slid away from her body. John was relieved to see that she was actually wearing a pair of silk pyjamas.

'Is that really too much to ask?' she asked tearfully. 'You have no idea how much I hurt here inside, John. Please, please let me stay. Just for tonight, that's all.'

It was unthinkable that he should agree, but how could he make her leave?

As though she sensed his dilemma, Polly looked up at him pleadingly. 'Please don't deny me this, John. Please don't. I promise you that all I want from you is the comfort of a brother and a friend . . . You do believe me, don't you?' she demanded emotionally. 'Tell me that you do?'

'Yes. Of course I do.' John tried to calm her.

She was sitting up in his bed now, her knees drawn up under her chin and her arms wrapped around them. She looked as young and innocent as a child, but if she were to be discovered in his room no one would believe either of them to be innocent.

'I want so much to sleep' she told him pathetically. 'I wish I could go to sleep and never wake up again.' She laughed mirthlessly. 'But God will not be so kind to me. He has not punished me enough yet.'

Suddenly she started to cry, her whole body shaking with the force of her emotion. Automatically John went towards her.

'Lie down beside me, John,' she begged him. 'Please, just lie next to me and hold me. Please make the pain go away for me.' Her voice was thick with gin and sleep,

'I will sit here beside you,' he told her firmly.

'But you will hold my hand?'

'Very well then,' he agreed. 'But only if you lie down quietly.'

Obediently, she did as he had told her, her fingers clinging tightly to his hand. 'Have you ever been in love?' he heard her asking him, as she had once before.

Immediately he tensed.

'You have, haven't you?' she guessed. 'What happened to her?'

'She wanted to go on the stage and sing.'

'And you are angry with her because of that? No, don't deny it. I can hear it in your voice. You were angry with her and so you made her choose between you and her singing. That is how men are.'

She was almost asleep. John held his breath and then released it when her fingers slackened their hold on his hand and her breathing slowed.

He waited another few minutes until he was sure she was fully asleep and then he moved slowly and carefully to the other side of the room, and the chair where he would have to spend what was left of the night.

TWENTY

'Here they are, I bought as many as I could.'

The girls clustered around Hettie's bed as Aggie put down the newspapers she was carrying, then pounced on them and turned quickly to the theatre pages.

'Oh, listen to this one,' Jenny instructed.

'"Last night at the Lytton Theatre, I witnessed the spectacle of the entire audience rising to its feet to applaud the talent of a new young composer, and deservedly so. I went to the Lytton firmly believing that I had had my fill of Japanese fairy tales and costume drama, but I left it knowing that I had been wrong. The experience of such talented actors as Jerome Hardy and Cecily Flowers assured the audience of an excellent evening's entertainment, and special mention must be made of Miss Hettie Walker who played the part of the young ingénue Princess Mimi most delightfully." Ooh Hettie,' Jenny squealed excitedly. 'Miss Hettie Walker, that's you! Give us another paper, will you, Babs . . .'

'Not yet. I'm reading this one. You 'ave a look at *The Times*,' Babs answered her firmly.

'It says here that American money and European talent have combined to provide a rare feast of enjoyment to welcome the new year. You aren't mentioned by name, Hettie, but it does say that Princess Mimi has an excellent and very pretty voice, which he would be happy to hear again in a more challenging role. Oh, 'Ettie . . .' Babs gasped, round eyed. 'That's as good as saying you should 'ave had the lead!'

'Here's one as says he predicts that we're going to run right up until Easter,' Aggie told them. 'Gawd, I hope we do. 'Ere, Mary.' She looked up as the door opened and Mary came in. 'What time was it when you came in last night?'

'Never you mind,' Mary answered, tossing her head.

'So where'd he tek you, then, this lord?' Jess demanded to know.

'The Savoy. *And* he's asked to see me again tonight,' Mary answered her importantly.

'Ooh he is keen then, Mary.'

'Aye, keen to get into her drawers,' Sukey put in pithily.

'I'll thank you not to make that kind of crude talk, Sukey Simmonds.'

'Well, what else would he be after.' Sukey insisted sulkily.

''Appen he's fallen for me,' Mary told her. 'After

all, plenty of Gaiety girls ended up with a wedding ring on their finger and a title. On account of 'ow they'd married lords.'

'Aye, and plenty more of them didn't,' Aggie pointed out dampeningly.

'Wot, you ain't surely thinking that's wot's going to happen to you, are you, Mary?' Jess asked.

'Why shouldn't it? Oh, Aggie, he's so handsome,' she breathed ecstatically, her eyes shining. 'And to think I nearly sent back 'is card with a message to tek himself orf.' She pressed her hand to her heart. ''E made me feel like a real princess.'

'Well, you ain't and if you'll tek my advice you'll remember that,' Aggie told her smartly, causing Mary to pull a face whilst Aggie's back was turned.

'Give us a cigarette, will yer, Aggie?' Sukey begged whilst Hettie smothered a tired yawn. She had been too excited to sleep properly.

There was a bang on the bedroom door and the maid called out sharply, 'There's some flowers just been delivered for Hettie Walker.'

'Seems like you aren't the only one wiv an admirer, Mary.' Babs chuckled as Hettie got off the bed and hurried to the door. 'Who are they from, 'Ettie?' Babs asked when Hettie came back clutching a huge bouquet of blooms.

'I don't know. I haven't read the card yet. Oh. They are from Jay. Mr Dalhousie,' Hettie amended, her face turning pink. 'Oh, and there's something else . . .' Her colour deepened still more when she found the small gift-wrapped box tucked in with the flowers.

'Go on, 'Ettie, open it,' Mary urged her.

Her fingers trembling slightly, Hettie did so. Inside the box was a small diamond-studded brooch in the shape of a letter 'H'.

'That's very pretty,' Aggie approved. 'And quite right that he should treat yer too, if yer asks me!'

'And bloody expensive by the looks of it,' Mary added. 'Gawd knows what he must have given the leading lady if he's given you that.'

'It will be 'Ettie as the public comes to hear, and not 'er, you mark my words,' Babs put in loyally.

'Oh, I don't know about that. I was very lucky to get the part,' Hettie demurred. But the other girls were having none of her modesty and insisted determinedly that she had been the 'star' of their first night.

'Do you lot realise what time it is?' Jenny interrupted. 'Or have I missed sommat and there's no rehearsal today?'

Hyde Park was busy with children enjoying their school holidays and Hettie, who had recently discovered that the park, with its fresh air and open spaces, somehow eased the ache she often felt for Preston and the life she had known there, paused by the Serpentine, comparing it to its disadvantage with Preston's Aveham Park's fish pond with its large fat goldfish.

She had written both to Connie and to Gideon and Ellie, sending them copies of her reviews and telling them all about her first night. She had already read the Christmas card she had received from Ellie and Gideon a hundred times and more, wondering if the fact that it was Gideon who had written inside it 'from your loving parents' meant Ellie was still no better, or if she had simply not wanted to write to her.

A small tableau on the other side of the lake caught her eye. A young boy was playing with a model flying machine, reminding her painfully of John. How many times had he taken her to the park, mock-lecturing her on the principles of flight and then demonstrating them to her? Those had been such happy, carefree days.

But she was happy now too, wasn't she? *Princess Geisha* was playing to a packed theatre and people were having to be turned away. The operetta and her own part in it had received the most wonderful reviews. What more could she want?

'And I heard that we're fully booked for all of this week and next as well, and that the management is talking about extending our run right up until *after* Easter. 'Ere, Mary,' Aggie changed subject crossly. 'That's our new frock you're wearing, and it was my turn to have it tonight.'

The chorus girls regularly clubbed together to buy a much coveted item of clothing, especially going-out dresses, and then took it in turns to wear their group purchase. But Aggie continued to scowl when Mary tossed her head and explained, 'Well, you can wear it on Saturday, if you want, cos that's when I should 'ave had it.'

'You're quiet, Babs, are you all right?' Hettie asked her friend worriedly when they left the dressing room ten minutes later.

'I am feeling a bit low, like, 'Ettie. It's on account of me missing Stan, what wiv him staying in Liverpool with the panto and me being here in London. And now it looks like we're going to be 'ere even longer. We can't even walk out proper like together.'

They both came to an abrupt halt as Jay Dalhousie stepped in front them and said briskly, 'If you've got a moment, Hettie, I'd like to have a word with you in my office.'

Babs gave Hettie's arm a small squeeze and whispered to her, 'Don't look so worried, 'Ettie. 'E can't be going to give yer the sack, not wiv them reviews you've bit getting. I'll see yer later.'

Hettie waited until Babs had gone before hurrying through the labyrinth of back-stage corridors towards Jay's small office.

He opened the door for her as soon as she knocked on it, shutting it firmly to enclose them in the room's small dark space.

'Did you get my flowers?' he demanded.

'Hettie nodded. 'Yes, thank you, and the brooch . . .'

'Did you like that, Hettie? I chose it especially for you.'

'It was very generous of you.'

'*Me*, generous to *you*? Hettie, don't you realise how much you have done for me, and how grateful I am to you? And I haven't forgotten that we were to have dinner together. Unfortunately, my business affairs have kept me very busy over these last few days. It seems that everyone in London wants to shake my hand and compliment me on my theatrical savvy and the success of my *Princess Geisha*. And it is all because of you, my little song thrush. You have stolen away the critics' hearts with your sweetness, little Hettie, and this is just the beginning of what you and I can achieve together,' he told her excitedly.

Hettie listened to him, her heart pounding.

'Come, this is no place to talk about my plans for you, Hettie.' As he spoke he took hold of her hand in his own, its warmth sending shocking thrills of pleasure up her arm.

But when he hurried her towards the door, she drew back hesitantly. 'Where are we going? What . . .'

'I am taking you to the Ritz for that dinner I promised you,' he told her, adding carelessly, 'I have a suite there, and we can dine there in private without having to endure the world and its dog coming to our table to trouble us with its questions. Oh, Hettie, Hettie . . . You don't know how happy you have made me. All those doubters who claimed that *Princess Geisha* would dig a big hole in my pocket are now having to eat their words. All my life I have followed my hunches and all my life I have been rewarded for doing so, but never as magnificently as on this occasion. And it is all thanks to you and that voice of yours.'

He had opened the door and was hurrying Hettie through it and down an unfamiliar corridor. 'This will take us to my private exit from the theatre. I know you will not want your friends to see you leaving with me.' He squeezed her hand tenderly. 'See, Hettie, how well I know you already and how I think of you? The first thing we must do now is arrange for you to have proper singing lessons. I have been looking into it already.' He opened a small door that led on to the street where a large shiny motor car was waiting.

'The Ritz, please, Hudson,' Hettie heard him instruct the chauffeur, and then she was being handed into the vehicle.

'Singing lessons?' she asked Jay uncertainly. 'But . . .'

'Yes. Your voice needs no training for the part of Princess Mimi, Hettie, but you are capable of so much more. I have already spoken with Archie and I have commissioned him to compose an operetta especially for you. And it will open not here in London but on Broadway. What do you think of that, my little song thrush?'

Singing lessons. Broadway. Hettie could scarcely take it all in. They had reached the Ritz, but they were not to enter the famous hotel by the main door, Hettie noticed as the chauffeur opened the car door for her.

'I told Hudson to drive us round to the side entrance.'

A side entrance it may well be, but there was still a uniformed doorman to open the door for them and someone to escort them along the elegantly decorated corridor with its gilt mirrors and wall lights to the waiting lift.

Carpets so thick that she felt as though she were sinking into them muffled the sound of Hettie's heels as they were escorted to a pair of double doors, and Hettie's eyes widened to see Jay yet again slip some money into the palm of the man waiting to be dismissed, as he had done to all the others.

Once she was inside the suite, though, all she could do was stare at her surroundings. 'I have never seen anything like this before,' she whispered to Jay.

'The hotel was designed to look like a French country house, in the style of Louis XVI,' Jay explained, smiling at her. 'Let me show you the whole suite, starting with the main salon.'

From the small ante room they were in, with its eau-de-Nil painted wooden panels into which were set heavily gilded mirrors, a pair of double doors opened into the room Jay had referred to as the 'main salon'. Almost timidly Hettie stepped into it, whirling round as she tried to take in every aspect of its wonderful décor. On the ceiling there was a painting showing all manner of smiling cherubs holding garlands of roses, its design echoed in the carpet beneath her feet. Swags of gilded plasterwork ornamented the delicately coloured panelled walls, and the chairs and sofa were covered in such a fine fabric that Hettie wondered that anyone would dare to sit on them.

Above the elegant marble fireplace there was a heavy gilt mirror, and a fire burned in the hearth filling the room with delicious warmth. Heavy velvet curtains covered the pair of high windows, in front of which stood a mahogany desk.

'Oh, it is all so very pretty,' Hettie exclaimed in awe.

Jay laughed. 'Ah, but you are far prettier, little Hettie.'

Blushing, Hettie dipped her head, hoping he would put the heat in her face down to the warmth of the fire.

'And see, here is a dining room,' he told her, throwing open yet another pair of double doors which led into a smaller oval room decorated in the same style as the salon but containing a mahogany dining table. 'And beyond this is a small corridor which leads to the bedroom and bathroom.'

'Oh.' Instinctively Hettie drew back and turned around to face the salon.

She was definitely still a virgin, Jay decided, and his body tightened in eager male anticipation of its future pleasure.

Princess Geisha's success had exceeded his own wildest gambler's dreams and Jay truly believed that by combining Archie and Hettie, his own discoveries, he could create a theatrical success like no other Broadway had ever known. The purity of Hettie's voice – like the purity of her virtue – could not be denied. But with the right teacher her voice, and Hettie herself, could and would bloom into true magnificence – her voice for the delight of audiences, and Hettie herself for the far more private delight of one man alone: her lover. And Jay fully intended that he would be her lover. But not yet.

'So many rooms for just one man,' Hettie commented brightly as she tried to cover the confusion of her own feelings. 'But then perhaps you are waiting for your wife to join you here in London.'

Immediately Jay's whole face tightened, and then darkened with anger. 'My wife does not, and will not, leave New Orleans,' he stated in a clipped, harsh voice.

The very thought of his petulant, demanding wife bringing her unwanted presence to London and his life away from her was enough to remind him of all the reasons he had wanted to escape from her in the first place. Not that he needed reminding.

Veronique was the spoiled and petted daughter of elderly parents, who had devoted themselves to her, unable to believe their good fortune in her birth when they had given up all hope of having a child. She had therefore grown up in a household where she was not just waited on hand and foot but worshipped and adored as well, and she had made it plain that she expected her husband to do the same.

But Jay had never had any intentions of doing any such thing. When she had insisted on taking to her bed and remaining there after the birth of their second child, Jay had shrugged his shoulders and left her to her day-bed in an over-heated room that stank of stale air, over-perfumed female flesh and pug dog. He had no desire to listen to her unending complaints about her poor health and his own unkindness towards her.

As a Catholic, it was impossible for him to divorce her even if he had wanted to; but her existence provided him with a useful barrier against any demands from his lovers to divorce her and marry them.

The truth was that Jay thought of himself and behaved as though he were, in actual fact, a single man, and thus Hettie's reference to his wife was not one he welcomed. Now, seeing from Hettie's expression that his anger had distressed her, he shook his head and affected an expression of sorrow, as he told her, 'My wife suffers from poor health and is confined to her bed, unable to travel.'

Hettie felt mortified. 'Oh I am so sorry,' she apologised, immediately feeling guilty. She could understand now how much her comment must have distressed him.

'There is nothing for you to apologise for,' Jay assured her warmly, concealing how very pleased he was by the result of his small ploy. 'You were not to know. I do not speak of it – or . . . her – very much . . . because . . .'

'Because it is too painful for you?' Hettie whispered sympathetically. 'Oh, poor lady. How she must long to be restored to full health so that she might be with you.'

Just in time Jay recognised that it might not be a good idea to awaken in Hettie too much sympathy for his wife. 'You are kind, Hettie, but tragically your sympathy would be wasted on my poor Veronique. She barely recognises me any more, never mind remembers that I am her husband. In fact,' he allowed his voice to drop to a confessional murmur, 'she cannot . . . we do not live . . . there is no longer that intimacy between us that should be shared by man and wife.'

Jay's mouth twisted sardonically. Well, that much was true. Veronique certainly did not recognise her duty to him as his wife, when it came to his husbandly rights, and had screamed at him that she never wanted him to touch her again after the birth of their second son.

'Naturally I have made sure that she has the best of care, but her doctors say that it is best that she is allowed to have peace and quiet.'

Jay had drawn a most affecting and distressing

picture of his wife for her, and Hettie felt her eyes sting with compassionate tears. What a truly dreadful thing it must be for both of them that this poor wife could not be a true wife to him, and how noble of Jay to speak so caringly of her. Hettie's heart swelled with emotion for him.

There was a rap on the outer door to the suite.

'Ah, that will be our dinner,' Jay predicted.

'I am afraid I am not really dressed for dining at the Ritz,' Hettie admitted, as the doors opened to reveal a huge dinner wagon and several waiters.

'Since we are dining here in my suite, it does not matter,' Jay assured her jovially. 'But don't worry, Hettie, we shall make sure you have something pretty to wear before too long.'

Now he was on familiar ground, Jay acknowledged. He had never yet had a mistress who had not been delighted to receive pretty pieces of jewellery and couture gowns. He was looking forward to taking Hettie to Paris and buying her gowns from Worth and Chanel, almost as much as he was looking forward to taking her to his bed and initiating her into all the arts of love-making.

By the time she stepped on to a Broadway stage as the leading lady in his new musical, he wanted her to be ready for that role, and not an ingénue any longer.

The hotel staff had lit the candles in the suite's dining room and the waiters were standing ready to serve dinner.

Extending his arm for Hettie to place her hand on, Jay smiled at her and invited, 'May I escort you in to dinner, Miss Walker?'

Jay made her feel as though she were gowned and jewelled like a duchess, Hettie marvelled gratefully as he led her into the dining room.

As soon as they were seated he turned to the waiters and told them coolly, 'Thank you, that is all. We shall serve ourselves.'

When they had gone, Jay explained, 'I don't want our private conversation being gossiped about through every kitchen in London. I have already drawn up a shortlist of possible singing teachers for you, Hettie. There is one in particular who has taught at La Scala who I think will be perfect.'

'La Scala? But that is an opera house,' Hettie whispered. 'And my voice is . . .'

'Your voice is soprano lyric,' Jay stopped her as he stood up and walked to the buffet table. 'Will you have some of the beef, Hettie?'

'Yes. Yes, please . . .'

Just watching him carve the meat reminded her poignantly of Winckley Square and those happy Sundays at home when she had been a child.

'I have checked with your old teacher,' Jay continued as he handed her a plate heaped high with mouth watering slices of meat. 'And she confirms what I believe myself, which is that with the right teacher you can look to take on leading female roles instead of merely second female leads.

311

'Think of it, Hettie,' he urged, coming to her side and catching hold of her hands in his own, his whole face taut and bright with the golden glitter of his dream. 'You will have the whole of Broadway at your feet, perhaps even be the must famous female singer Broadway has ever known.'

'But why should you do any of this for me?' Hettie asked him shyly later when they had finished eating. 'There are any number of singers who . . .'

'Any number of *singers*, perhaps, but only one you.'

He paused as someone started banging loudly on the outer suite door, and a male voice called out, 'Jay, it's me, Harvey. Let me in, will ya? Come on, Jay, I know damned well you're in there, and I'm not about to go away.'

'I'm sorry about this,' Jay apologised to Hettie as he stood up.

As Jay opened the main suite doors, a short burly man thrust his way in, laughing loudly and triumphantly as he did so. 'I knew it! I knew you were here even though those stuffed shirt jerks downstairs told me you weren't. Who've you got here then, Jay? Some little sweetie, no doubt.'

As he turned round and spied Hettie, he laughed again. 'Say, she *is* a sweetie. Where have you been hiding her, Jay?'

'Hettie and I were just discussing a private business matter, Harvey,' Hettie heard Jay telling him.

'Private business, eh? I'll bet it was. Aren't you going to introduce us?'

A little grimly Jay did so, announcing curtly, 'Hettie, allow me to introduce to you Mr Harvey Meyerbrock. Harvey, Miss Hettie Walker.'

'Charmed, I'm sure.' Harvey Meyerbrock began walking towards Hettie.

Immediately, Hettie stepped back from him, unable to stop herself. Something about him repulsed and frightened her, though she could not explain even to herself just what it was. It was true that he wasn't a handsome man like Jay, but it wasn't his lack of good looks that made her recoil from him so much as the lascivious way in which he was looking at her, his shiny, too red lips parting as he slipped a wet tongue tip over them in a way that made Hettie shudder.

'That's enough, Harvey,' Hettie heard Jay saying curtly. 'Hettie is the seond lead singer in the operetta I'm backing, and I wanted to talk to her about the singing lessons I am arranging for her in order to improve her voice.'

'Yeah, yeah,' he smirked. 'I get the picture, Jay. I know you, remember? Well, she is a dainty little morsel and no mistake. And when you've finished with her . . .'

He hadn't taken his eyes off her the whole time he had been speaking to Jay, and somehow he made Hettie feel that if she herself looked away he might actually physically pounce on her. The thought horrified her. 'I must go,' she told Jay unsteadily, her face still burning from being subjected to Jay's friend's uncouth remarks and his predatory scrutiny.

'I'll ring for someone to escort you down to the lobby and call you a cab,' Jay told her.

Inwardly Jay was cursing Harvey's untimely arrival, but he knew from past experience that there was no point hinting to the other man that this presence was *de trop* because then he would only delight in remaining. Like Jay himself, Harvey was a gambler and an American, and he was also, or so he had claimed to Jay, involved in the making of silent movies. Harvey had struck up a friendship with Jay when they had sailed across the Atlantic together en route for England.

Hettie could feel Harvey Meyerbrock's hot greedy gaze on her body as Jay took hold of her arm and escorted her towards the door. Something about the way Harvey watched her reminded her of Mr Buchanan, only with Harvey Meyerbrock her awareness of being in danger was a hundred times stronger.

'I'm sorry about this, Hettie,' Jay whispered to her as they stood in the corridor. He had pulled the door to, so that Harvey could neither see nor hear them.

'It was time for me to leave anyway,' Hettie told him. 'I don't want to be late for rehearsal in the morning.'

The lift had arrived and Jay watched as the bell-boy helped her into it.

* * *

'Cute little tootsie, Jay.' Harvey grinned when Jay walked back into the room. 'Wanna go shares?'

'Miss Walker is a professional singer, Harvey,' Jay told him coolly, ignoring the other man's grinning mouth and knowing wink and continuing, 'And, as I have already told you, our relationship is strictly business.'

'Don't give me that! There ain't no way you would be wining and dining her up here if *that* were true.' He laughed coarsely, and then shrgged. 'Fine, keep her to yourself if you want.'

'What are you doing here, Harvey?' Jay asked him sharply. 'What do you want?'

Harvey gave another shrug. 'I'd heard as how there was a big game coming off and I wanted to know if you knew about it.'

Jay sighed. As he had quickly discovered, the really big money gambling in London took place in private, in the kind of gentlemen's clubs where you needed blue blood and a pedigree longer than a prize bull to get so much as your nose through the door.

'Right now the theatre is about as much gambling as I want to do,' Jay told him firmly.

''Ettie, *at last*. I've bin worrying meself sick about you. Where the 'ell have you bin?' Babs asked crossly when Hettie let herself into their shared room.

'Jay Dalhousie wanted to see me,' Hettie explained.

315

'So I 'eard. But that were hours ago. Don't tell me you've bin with him all this time,' Babs demanded suspiciously. 'It's gone midnight.'

'Jay . . . Mr Dalhousie . . . wanted to talk to me and, and so he invited me to have dinner with him.' Hettie was almost stumbling over the words, her face a guilty red.

'What? Where did he tek you?'

This was something she hadn't been prepared for, Hettie admitted as she struggled to be discreet whilst at the same time trying to calm Babs. 'We had dinner at the Ritz hotel.' 'What? 'Ettie, for gawd's sake, you didn't let 'im persuade you to go back to 'is room with 'im, did you?' Babs asked as sharply as a mother hen.

Hettie's expression gave her away.

'Gawd, 'Ettie, 'ave you no sense?'

'It wasn't a room. He has a suite,' Hettie defended herself swiftly.

Babs looked at her in despair. 'Haven't you 'eard a word of what we've bin saying to Mary? What did he say to you?' she demanded before asking anxiously, ''Ere, you haven't let him have his way with you already, have you?'

'No!' Hettie told her, her face burning. 'And it wasn't like that anyway.'

'Come off of it, 'Ettie,' Babs told her scornfully. 'It's allus like that with men like 'im and girls like us.'

'He wanted to talk to me about business. About my singing,' Hettie insisted stubbornly, trying not

316

to show how much Babs's comments were upsetting her. 'He says he wants me to have a singing teacher.'

'And you believed 'im? Why the 'ell would *you* need a singing teacher anyway? I'm surprised at you, 'Ettie. I didn't think you was that sort of girl,' Babs told her loftily. 'I thought you was a proper decent sort.'

'I am,' Hettie insisted, but Babs had already turned over in her bed, and pulled the bedclothes up over her ears.

TWENTY-ONE

''Ettie, the postman's just been and there's a letter 'ere for you . . .'

Hurrying down the stairs, Hettie picked up the envelope Aggie was waving in the air, her heart thudding against her chest wall as she recognised Gideon's writing. 'It's from me Da,' she told Aggie as she hurried to open it.

'Well, you'd better read it quick, like, otherwise we'll be late for rehearsals.'

'Oh, it's all right, I've been excused this morning,' Hettie told her absently as she pulled the sheets of paper out of the envelope. 'Jay wants me to meet this new singing teacher he's found for me.'

She was too anxious to read her letter to notice the exaggerated eye-rolling look Aggie gave Babs before saying sharply to Hettie, 'Oh ho, it's all right for some, isn't it? Private singing lessons. Next thing we know you'll be going to rehearsals in a chaffeur driven car, wiv your nose stuck up in the air. Well, seein' as how as we ain't considered good enough to have private lessons, we'd better be on our way,' Aggie said sharply. 'Come on, Babs.'

'Give us a minute,' Babs begged her. ''Ettie, you won't forget that we're all going to Sam's Chop House tonight on account of it being Sukey's birthday, will you?' she asked, opening the front door to their lodgings and letting in a gust of raw February air that made Hettie shiver.

'Of course I won't forget,' Hettie assured her as she closed the door after her friends.

As she climbed the stairs, Hettie admitted to herself a little guiltily that she was quite pleased that she would have their room to herself so that she could read her letter in private.

Gideon started off by saying how pleased he and Ellie both had been to read the reviews Hettie had sent them, and how proud of her they were.

'You will be pleased to know, Hettie, that your Mam is much recovered, both in spirits and in body, and that we intend to make our way home to Preston.'

There was a second page to the letter and when Hettie turned to it, she gasped, quick tears filling her eyes as she recognised Ellie's writing.

Her hands trembling she spread out the single sheet and read it eagerly.

'Hettie, love,' Ellie had written. 'I am sorry to have caused you all so much anxiety and worry, but as Gideon has written I am now much more my old self. Hettie, I so much want to see you, my dearest. Could you, *would you* come home to us at Easter? I shall understand if it is not possible for I have read your reviews and know what a famous person you are become. We are both so proud of you, Hettie, and so excited for you.'

Ellie had signed the letter, 'Your loving Mam.'

Laughing and crying at the same time Hettie read it again and then a third time. Just as she had previously been glad to have their room to herself, now she wished equally intensely that Babs were here so that she could share her happiness with her. Only now reading the words Ellie had written to her, could Hettie admit how much she had feared that Ellie was lost to her for ever and that she would never recover from her grief.

Hurriedly she searched for her writing paper. They would not have returned to Preston yet, of course, but she wanted her letter to be there waiting for them when they did so that they could know how happy she was and how much she was looking forward to seeing them.

Half an hour later, on her way to the theatre to meet the singing teacher Jay had chosen for her, Hettie stopped off to post her letter.

The match sellers were already standing in a huddled row outside the theatre itself, waiting for the matinee audience. The sight of them, once brave fighting men but now reduced to poverty, tore at Hettie's heart and she remembered how both Ellie and Gideon had always shown generosity to those poorer than themselves.

Opening her purse she hurried up to the first of the men and gave him several pennies, hurrying down the whole line of men to do the same thing until her purse was empty.

'Bless you for that, Miss, and for your kind heart,' the last one told her hoarsely, tears shining in his eyes.

Jay had told her that she was to go straight to his office, and when she got there she found that he was already inside, speaking with a woman so large that there was scarcely any room for Hettie herself to squeeze in to the room with them.

'Oh Hettie. Good, you are here. Madame Bertrice, please allow me to introduce to you my protégée, Miss Hettie Walker.'

The large body somehow swivelled in Hettie's direction, a sharp glance from two small dark eyes, the colour of raisins, raking her from head to foot.

'She does not have the bosom for a powerful voice,' Madame Bertrice announced dismissively.

'Nor has she had the benefit of your famed teaching skills,' Hettie heard Jay saying smoothly. 'Unfortunately, the bosom we cannot do anything about, but as for your teaching . . .'

'Ah, you hope to persuade me to take your protégée as a pupil by flattering me, Monsieur. Well, I will tell you that I am not easily flattered, not even by a man as handsome as you.'

Not easily flattered and not easily bought,

either, Jay decided cynically, reflecting wryly on the amount Madame was demanding as her fee.

'You, girl.'

Hettie tried not to react when the Madame Bertrice woman jabbed a finger into her ribs.

'Let me hear your scales.'

Uncertainly, Hettie looked at Jay, who gave a small nod of his head.

Taking a deep breath, Hettie began.

'I thought you told me the girl could sing?' Madame told Jay derisively when she had waved Hettie into silence. 'That is not singing.'

'Maybe not, but you will acknowledge that she does have a remarkably clear, if untrained, soprano lyric voice,' Jay said coolly.

Madame Bertrice shrugged dismissively. 'Oui, she does have a soprano voice, but what of that? Pfff, it is nothing. To be a truly great diva one needs to possess a truly magnificent voice.'

'But I do not want to be a diva,' Hettie said fiercely.

The sharp gaze raked her again. 'No? Then why do you waste my time?'

'What Hettie means is that she does not want to be an operatic diva,' Jay explained, giving Hettie a quelling look.

They both looked at Hettie, making her feel both self-conscious and angry.

'I do not know what I can do with her,' Madame Bertrice declared disparagingly.

'Thank you, Hettie, you may go now,' Jay told

her abruptly, opening the door for her to leave.

Madame Bertrice was not leaving, though, Hettie saw crossly. No doubt the moment she had gone Madame would start telling Jay that he was wasting his time even thinking about lessons for her.

It was over an hour before Hettie was summoned back to Jay's office.

'I do not want you to waste your money on singing lessons for me, Jay,' she told him fiercely. 'Madame Bertrice made it plain that she does not think my voice is good enough.'

'We can discuss this better tonight – over dinner.' Jay smiled at her. 'Hudson will be waiting for you in the car after the show, and I shall instruct him to take you to the Ritz.'

'Oh Jay, I'm sorry but I can't.'

His smile gave way to a frown. 'Why not?' he asked her sharply.

'It's Sukey's birthday and we're all going out to Sam's Chop House,' Hettie explained uncomfortably as Jay continued to frown, very obviously displeased.

'Surely your career is more important to you than this Sukey, whoever she might be,' he remarked irritably.

'Sukey is one of the chorus girls,' Hettie explained earnestly.

'Oh, a chorus girl.' Jay shrugged dismissively. 'Why should she be of any concern to you, Hettie?'

'She's one of my friends,' Hettie told him, shocked by his attitude and his casual dismissal of Sukey. 'And if I don't go . . .'

'What do you mean, *if* you don't go?' Jay challenged her curtly. 'I thought we understood one another, Hettie, and that we were agreed that nothing should come in the way of our shared ambition to see you succeed on Broadway. That is, after all, why I am paying for you to have singing lessons as well as commissioning Archie to write a musical that will showcase you.'

Guiltily, Hettie realised how ungrateful she must seem.

'And besides,' Jay continued. 'If this Sukey is so much of a friend to you as you say, she is bound to understand.' He gave a small shrug. 'You can have supper with her another night, after all.'

John reached inside his jacket and removed Gideon's letter from his pocket as he opened the door to his private quarters. The letter had been there since the post had arrived much earlier in the day, but he had had a busy morning with two flying lessons booked, and this was his first opportunity to have some time to himself.

He made his way into his neat kitchen, where he filled the kettle and lit the gas stove. Whilst he waited for the kettle to boil he opened the envelope and removed the letter. Several newspaper cuttings fell out. Frowning slightly, John leaned over to pick them up, studying them curiously.

'Miss Hettie Walker *is* Princess Mimi.'

His heart struck a sledgehammer blow against his chest wall, almost depriving him of breath.

Still frowning he put the cuttings down on the table, carefully smoothing them out, and then began to read them, Gideon's letter forgotten until the shrill whistle of the boiling kettle jerked him out of his concentration.

Almost absently he reached for the kettle, then switched off the gas before pouring the boiling water into the teapot, still reading and re-reading the critics' praise for Hettie. He replaced the kettle on the stove and searched through the cuttings, and then the letter itself and the envelope, wondering if there might be a cutting which contained a photograph of Hettie. He felt both disappointed and relieved once he had assured himself that there wasn't.

He poured himself a cup of tea, stirred it, then took his drink and went to sit down at the small kitchen table so that he could read Gideon's letter. The news it contained about Ellie eased some of his tension. He was relieved to read about her recovery, both for her sake and for Gideon's.

He frowned suddenly as he heard someone knocking on the door to his private quarters. No one normally disturbed him when he was here unless it was urgent. He got up and pushed back the chair before striding through the kitchen and past the small, almost Spartan parlour into the narrow hallway, dodging the mounted stag's head, complete with antlers, that the previous occupant of the flat had left on the wall.

'John. At last. I was beginning to think you weren't going to let me in.'

'Lady Polly!'

Polly shook her head vigorously. 'How many times must I beg you not to call me "Lady" Polly, John?' she appealed to him, pulling off her driving gloves as she hurried in, leaving John with no option other than to close the door behind her and then take the fur-lined coat she was holding out to him.

'I do so hate February. It is the very worst kind of month, at least here in England. I have tried to persuade Alfie to take me ski-ing, but he says he is too busy. Do you ski, John? Winter sports are frightfully jolly.'

'No, I don't,' John told her, a mental image of the snow covered slope in Preston's park flashing inside his head, along with an image of himself sitting on the sledge he had made for Hettie, with her sitting in front of him, clinging to him as they sped downhill, her small rosy face alight with pleasure.

'John, come back, you aren't listening to me,' he heard Polly complaining.

'I'm sorry.'

Polly laughed and put her hand on his arm. 'Oh John, you are such a darling. It would be so very easy for me to fall in love with you, if only things were different and I wasn't still so very much in love with my dearest Ollie. I suppose you are going to tell me that I am interrupting your work, and that you are very busy.'

She was all bright chatter but John was still uneasily aware of the stark despair he could see in her eyes. She was lonely, and she wanted to fill the empty place in her heart and her life. John knew exactly how that felt. But there was a huge social gulf between them and he was also aware that her frequent visits to the flying school were beginning to make her the subject of innuendo and gossip.

'We are busy,' he agreed, 'and in fact I was just about to go back to the office.'

'You just want to get rid of me, don't you?' Polly remarked as John started to walk towards the kitchen intending to get his jacket. 'You don't want me here.'

'What I don't want is for anyone to accuse me of behaving improperly towards you,' John corrected her quietly.

'Oh, for heavens sake, why should it be improper for us to be friends?'

They had reached the kitchen. John removed his jacket from the back of the chair and started to put it on. 'You know why.'

'Because you are a man and I am a woman? Or because I am a Lady and you are not a Lord?' Polly demanded emotionally.

'Both,' John replied equably.

'Oh!' Polly exclaimed, suddenly distracted as

she looked down at the table. 'I didn't know you were interested in the theatre?'

'I'm not,' John responded shortly.

'But you are obviously interested in Miss Hettie Walker?' Polly quizzed him archly.

'Hettie is my sister Ellie's step-daughter.'

'Oh. Oh, I'm sorry, John. You must be very proud of her.' What is it, John? What's wrong?' Polly asked him when he made no response.

'I've got someone coming for a lesson in fifteen minutes.'

'You don't want to talk about her, do you? Why not? Is it because she is more to you than merely your sister's step-daughter? Oh John, she is, isn't she?' Polly guessed when he didn't respond. 'You love her, don't you, and you can never love anyone else, just as I can never love anyone other than my Ollie . . .'

'You not ready yet, 'Ettie? The others have already gone on to the chop house with Sukey. Not that she's likely to eat anything,' Babs announced as she watched Hettie removing the last of her stage make-up.

'Babs, I can't come with you.'

'What? Why not?'

'Well . . . It's all very difficult,' Hettie began awkwardly. 'You see, Jay . . .'

Immediately Babs's smile disappeared. 'Oh, I might have guessed,' she said angrily. 'You don't want to know us any more now that 'e's tekking a bit of interest in you. Well, mark my words, 'Ettie Walker, you're a fool if you let 'im turn your head, cos like I've told you before, he's a married man when all's said and done and even if he weren't there's only one thing 'is sort want from our sort.'

'Babs, it isn't like that,' Hettie protested, red faced. 'It's like I've already told you, Jay just wants to see me to talk about work.'

'Give over. I weren't born yesterday.' Babs snorted. 'If it were work he wanted to talk to you about what's to stop him doing it when you're here at work? No.' She shook her head forcefully. 'It's yer drawers he's wanting to get into, 'Ettie. Just like Mary's posh toff is after wanting to get into 'ers. 'Ettie, love.' She reached out and took hold of Hettie's hands. 'Don't go letting him turn your head.'

'Babs, he isn't doing. It isn't like that. It really is about work. And I've got to think about my future, Babs, and . . .'

'Oh I see, and this future of yours is more important than Sukey's birthday, is it?' Babs challenged her, her concern turning to a hostility that made Hettie's face burn with discomfort.

'It isn't like that,' she protested again miserably. First Jay had been angry with her when she had told him about Sukey's birthday, and now Babs was equally angry with her because she had told her about Jay.

'Well, it sounds to me like we just aren't good

enough for you any more,' Babs continued accusingly before heading for the door and then slamming it behind her as she left.

There was a painful lump in Hettie's throat and tears weren't very far away. Babs was the first real friend she had made at the boarding house in Liverpool, and Hettie felt as close to her as though she were an older cousin. It had never occurred to her that Babs would react the way she just had, and Hettie longed to be able to run after her and tell her that she had changed her mind. But how could she when she knew how angry Jay would be? He had gone to such a lot of trouble and expense on her behalf. So much so, in fact, that she felt duty bound to do as he wished and give up the pleasure of her evening out with her friends so that Jay could talk to her about his plans.

The dressing room door opened and Hettie spun round, her face breaking into a relieved smile. Babs had come back! Only it wasn't Babs who came hurrying into the room, but Mary.

'T'others have gone, have they, only I don't want another lecture from Aggie.' Mary pulled a face. 'Course, it's just on account of 'er being jealous, I know *that*. But wot you doing here, 'Ettie?'

'I'm having dinner with Jay,' Hettie felt obliged to tell her. 'He wants to talk to me about my singing.'

'It seems to me that you and me has sommat in common, now, 'Ettie,' Mary declared. 'We'd better stick together you and me, so as we can stick up for each other when one of the others has a go at us. You 'aven't got a spare pair of stockings handy, 'ave you?' she asked. 'Only I've laddered one of mine.'

'Yes. Here you are,' Hettie told her, proffering her spare pair.

'Oh, ta ever so,' Mary thanked her. 'And can I pinch a bit of yer scent as well?'

'Help yourself,' Hettie offered, changing into her street clothes whilst Mary sat down, lit a Craven and then proceeded to inspect her reflection in the mirror.

The rain they had been having earlier in the day had turned to sleet, and the wind whipping round the corner of the theatre was so bitterly cold Hettie felt as though it were stripping her skin from her bones as she hurried along the pavement towards the waiting car.

As Hudson opened the door for her she heard Jay's voice saying welcomingly from its dark leather scented interior, 'Hettie, poor girl, you must be frozen. Hudson, the Ritz and as fast as you like. I had another talk with Madame after you had gone, Hettie, but . . .'

'Oh please, don't worry about that. I truly don't mind that she doesn't think I'm good enough and doesn't want to teach me. To tell the truth,' she admitted, 'I would far rather have a different teacher. She scared me so much I'm sure even if she had wanted to teach me I would have been too nervous to learn anything.'

'I hope that isn't true, Hettie,' Jay told her lightly. 'Because Madame Bertrice has changed her mind and is now willing to take you on as a pupil. And there I was imagining how pleased you would be with my good news,' Jay continued nonchalantly.

Guiltily, Hettie looked at him. 'Well, I am sure that if she has changed her mind about me, I shall be able to change mine about her,' she told Jay valiantly.

It was wonderful to hear the approval in his voice as he reached out in the darkness and took hold of her hand, giving it a little squeeze as he said warmly, 'That's my girl, Hettie.'

His girl. She gave a small excited shiver and immediately his hand tightened on hers. Jay had such nice hands, Hettie decided. They were large and manly, his grip comforting and warm in a way that reminded her of how she had felt as a little girl with her hand held tightly in John's.

'You will have to work hard, of course,' Jay continued. 'But I know that you can and will do so, Hettie.'

They had reached the Ritz and, just like before, a uniformed doorman was waiting to hand Hettie out of the car whilst another held one the doors for them.

'We really must see about getting you some new clothes,' Jay mused aloud as he guided her towards the lift.

'For my lessons?' she enquired innocently. 'Oh

no, that won't be necessary, Jay, I have plenty of things.'

'Really? So then why are you wearing the same frock this evening as you were the last time we had dinner together?' Jay asked her gently.

They had reached the lift and, since they would be overheard by the lift attendant, Hettie had to wait to answer him until they were inside his suite.

'This is my best frock,' she told him with great dignity. 'I won't be wearing it for my lessons and, anyway, why should it matter if it do wear it more than once?'

'Why should it indeed?' Jay agreed. 'But has it not occurred to you, Hettie, that you are being a mite selfish?'

'Selfish?' Hettie felt confused.

'Very selfish,' Jay continued. 'Firstly in denying pretty clothes the pleasure of being worn by you.' Jay paused as Hettie started both to laugh and blush. 'And secondly in denying me the pleasure of buying them for you,' he concluded softly.

Immediately Hettie stopped laughing. She might be naive, but she was not *that* naive.

'I would not want you to do that,' she told him quietly, very much on her dignity.

'Ah. I see that I have offended you. Forgive me, Hettie, that was the last thing I intended. You will think me a very poor shallow fellow I know, but I confess that I do think it is essential that you dress appropriately for the new role you are about to embark on. For instance, it may very well be that when she was merely a second lead Cecile Courtly only had one best frock to her name. But I think you will agree that she would not be the Cecile Courtly the audience reveres were she still to dress in that fashion.'

Cecile Courtly was one of the London stage's most famous actresses and singers, and Hettie could not help but be entranced that Jay should suggest that, one day, she herself might be equally famous. Neither could she help but see the practicality of what Jay was saying. But she still had to point out. 'Only *she* will buy her own clothes, and not have them bought for her, and if you . . .'

'I see what you are trying to say, Hettie,' Jay acknowledged. 'You fear that were it to become known that I had bought your clothes, people might assume that I had also bought you.'

Hettie went bright red.

'Now I have upset you,' Jay said ruefully. 'And that is the last thing I want to do. In fact, what I want to do more than anything else,' he continued softly, reaching for her hands and taking hold of them in his own before Hettie could stop him, 'is make you happy. Do you think I could do that, pretty little Hettie? Do you think I could make you smile for me and look upon me and my foolishness with compassion?'

The sleet had turned to snow when Hettie finally let herself into her lodgings, but, late though it was, the others had still not returned and the room she shared with Babs felt cold and empty. After quickly washing her hands and face, Hettie undressed and got into bed. Was she right in thinking that Jay had actually been flirting a little with her tonight? If only Babs were here so that she could confide in her and ask her opinion. But would Babs give it? Or did the angry way Babs had spoken to her earlier mean their friendship was damaged for ever?

TWENTY-TWO

Her lesson had finished over an hour ago, but Hettie was still sitting spellbound in the small but warm room where Madame Bertrice's pupils waited for their lessons, listening to the last notes of the beautiful aria being practised by Madame's current pupil fade into silence. Lifting her hand to wipe away the tears the powerful emotions of the aria had brought her, she breathed out slowly and stood up.

Listening to Madame's opera singer pupils had become Hettie's special and unexpected treat since she had started coming to Madame's lodgings for her singing lessons. She had no idea what the words meant, but she did know that something within her reacted to them and to the music.

She was just about to leave when Madame herself came into the room, her full skirts giving her the appearance of one of Liverpool's majestic liners triumphantly coming home. Madame Bertrice had not embraced the modern fashion for narrower, shorter skirts, and preferred to dress very much as though they were still living in a more old-fashioned era.

'Hettie,' she exclaimed when she saw her. 'Why are you still here? Is something wrong?'

Feeling embarrassed, Hettie shook her head. 'No. It was just the music,' she explained simply. 'And . . . and the voice.'

Immediately Madame smiled at her and nodded her head, for, as Hettie had quickly discovered, whilst she insisted on her pupils working hard, Madame was not the ogre Hettie had initially feared.

'Ah yes. Who could not be moved by such an aria? It is a great pity, Hettie, that your own voice did not receive proper training when you were younger. Had you done so . . . But there is no point in us repining, for you did not. Besides,' she added, 'the life of an opera singer is not for everyone. It is very demanding and has broken more singers than it has lauded. It is a life that is especially hard for a woman. You are a good pupil, Hettie,' she told her kindly, 'and you will do very well in Mr Dalhousie's musical operettas.'

Hettie hugged those words of praise and encouragement to herself all the way to the theatre.

She had been excused rehearsals on those days when she had a singing lesson. But because she was growing increasingly and uncomfortably conscious of the rift that seemed to be developing between herself and her friends, and their growing resentment that she seemed to be getting what they had crossly described as 'special favours', she was determined to prove that she was not, as she had heard them whispering, growing too big for her boots or thinking herself above them.

At least she and Babs had made up their small quarrel, she comforted herself as she shielded her eyes from the brightness of the March sunshine whilst she waited to cross Piccadilly Circus before hurrying down Shaftesbury Avenue.

She had expected to find the dressing room empty because she knew rehearsals would already have started, but to her surprise it was full and the chorus girls were standing around in their practice clothes, smoking and chattering, so that Hettie could hardly see a familiar face for the smoke or hear a familiar voice for the noise. But then she spotted Mary and Sukey, and managed to wriggle her way through the tight knots of girls towards them.

'What's happened?' she asked when she reached them. 'I thought you'd all be in rehearsal.'

'So we should have been, but there's been a problem with one of the sets and we can't practise until it's sorted. Seems like the set designer hasn't turned in this morning, and he's gonna find himself in a right load of trouble if he doesn't get here soon,' Mary prophesied darkly.

'You mean Eddie?' Hettie asked her, her heart bumping heavily in her chest.

'Yes. He needs to lay off of the bottle, 'e does,

leastways if he 'e wants to keep his job,' Mary added.

Not even someone as innocent as Hettie could have remained unaware that Eddie was drinking too much. He had frequently turned up at the theatre over the past few weeks the worse for drink, and there had already been a good deal of gossip about his drunken rantings in which he talked wildly about his despair and the cruelty with which he had been treated, fortunately without mentioning any names.

''Ere, where are you going?' Mary demanded when Hettie turned to hurry back to the door.

'I'm going round to Eddie's lodgings to tell him that he needs to be here,' Hettie called back to her over her shoulder.

She knew where Eddie was lodging because he had happened to mention it to her, and for once as she plunged into the busy London streets Hettie's attention was not drawn towards the poor injured ex-soldiers patiently begging for pennies; or the raggedly dressed children with their thin weasely faces and too knowing eyes, their intent gazes assessing passers by for potential victims of their pick-pocketing skills. Even though she knew she should not do so, Hettie often gave them a few pennies, so that now when they saw her they followed her and begged her for more.

Eddie's lodgings were in a tangle of streets off the Haymarket, in a down-at-heel and so very disreputable looking building that Hettie hesitated before stepping through the open front door into a shabby hallway.

Unlike the lodgings she shared with the other girls, this boarding house did not seem to have a stout, stern landlady. An elderly man shuffling along the hallway stopped to stare at Hettie, the sunlight falling unkindly on his sunken over-rouged cheeks and carmined mouth.

'You won't find anything to your taste here, dearie,' he called out in a shrill, falsetto, over-refined voice, tittering as he did so and tossing his head, his sharp glance assessing her unkindly.

'I'm looking for Eddie Ormond,' Hettie told him, ignoring his rudeness. 'He's needed at the theatre.'

Immediately his expression changed. 'Second floor, third door on the left,' revealed. 'You'll have to knock loudly, though, if you're going to wake him.'

Thanking him, Hettie made her way up the stairs and along the corridor, pausing outside Eddie's door and knocking firmly on it.

When there was no immediate response she knocked again, and then leaned her head against the door, hoping to hear sounds of movement from inside the room.

'Cheer up, ducks, it ain't that bad,' a sharp male voice mocked her.

Straightening up, Hettie turned round to find that she was being watched by a very dapper look-ing middle-aged man, his clothes smart and his shoes polished.

'She's from the theatre, Charlie,' the old man she had seen downstairs called up shrilly.

'Oh, you are, are you?'

'I'm a friend of Eddie's as well,' Hettie informed both men firmly. 'There's a problem with one of the sets and he's needed.'

'Well, you'll be lucky to wake him. Poor bugger 'as half drunk himself to death already,' the second man announced dryly, much to Hettie's alarm.

'Surely someone has a key to his room?' she asked. 'He's going to be in some kind of dreadful trouble if he doesn't come to work.'

'Nellie, where's the spare key to his room?' the middle-aged man called downstairs to the older one. 'And don't you go pretending you don't have one.'

Hettie tried not to reveal her angry impatience when the older man suddenly produced a large bunch of keys and started to puff his way up the stairs. Why on earth couldn't he have told her that they had a spare key to Eddie's room in the first place?

'Nellie here likes to pretend that there aren't any spare keys. That's because he likes going through our things when we aren't here, isn't it, Nellie dear?'

'You shut your mouth, you poxy Martha,' 'Nellie' responded as he breathed heavily over the keys, finally and to Hettie painfully slowly selecting one which he inserted into Eddie's locked door.

The smell of alcohol from inside the room as

the door swung open gripped Hettie's throat, but she forced herself to ignore it as she hurried inside.

The room itself was surprisingly neat and tidy – far more so that those of her chorus girl friends, she admitted. The girls were inclined to leave stockings and other items of apparel strewn over doors and chairs, whilst hairbrushes and the like cluttered up dressing table tops.

Eddie himself was still in bed, and obviously asleep.

Hettie hesitated. She had never been in a man's bedroom before, never mind one where its occupant was actually in the bed. But she had matured a lot from the girl she had been, and so she took a deep breath and walked determinedly towards the bed.

Once there, she called Eddie's name loudly and, when this got no response, she cleared her throat and forced herself to place her hand on his bare shoulder. His skin felt warm and soft. Her courage returning, she gave him a firm shake, just as though he had been one of the girls.

He moved reluctantly and so Hettie shook him again. This time he opened his eyes and looked at her. 'Hettie.'

'You've got to get up and come to the theatre,' she told him quickly. 'There's something wrong with one of the sets.'

'What?'

He looked dazed, and very unwell, Hettie acknowledged. His eyes were bloodshot and his skin had an unhealthy yellowish cast to it.

'You must come to the theatre, Eddie,' she repeated firmly.

He was properly awake now, a dark-red surge of angry colour suddenly flooding his face. 'Why?' he demanded bitterly. 'So that *he* can mock me and humiliate me? So that he can torture me and tear my heart out of my body? So that he can eviscerate me and . . . Do you know what he did yesterday?' he demanded wildly, ignoring Hettie's attempts to calm him. 'He called me into his office and, when I got there, he had *him*, *it* . . . there with him, that little piece of shit he's bedding.'

'Eddie, please don't distress yourself like this,' Hettie begged him worriedly. She could see how upset he was and her heart felt heavy with sadness for him. 'You must get dressed and come to the theatre,' she repeated anxiously. 'Otherwise . . .'

'Otherwise what?'

'Otherwise, duckie, you will lose your job, won't he, Charlie? And we don't none of us want that, do we?'

Hettie had forgotten about the other two men, and had not realised that they had been listening. However, it was plain to her that, rather than being embarrassed by their presence, Eddie was actually calmed by it.

'You can leave him with us now, missie,' Charlie told her. 'Now that he's awake we'all make sure he gets himself dressed and off to work.'

Hettie hesitated.

'Yes, you go back, Hettie,' Eddie muttered.

'You will get up and come to work, won't you?' she begged him.

'Course he will, missie,' Charlie told her. 'We'll mek sure of that, never fear. He's the only one 'ere who's working and earning, ain't you, Eddie? And if 'e don't work, we don't eat.'

'Where are they? One of you 'as taken them, I know that you have. Well, you can just give them back to me.'

''Ere, Sukey, for gawd's sake calm downl No one has taken your blinkin' pills,' Aggie protested.

'Yes they have. I counted them last week and I had enough for this week and now I aven'. And I can't afford to buy any more until next week!'

'Well, you might have had enough when you counted them, but I've seen you taking them two at a time, and they get you in such a state I reckon you'd be hard put to remember your own name, never mind if'n you'd taken more than one.'

'That's a lie! You've never seen me taking two at a time. You're making it up!' Sukey was screaming at Aggie now, her face bright red, and her whole body trembling.

'Gawd, Sukey, tek a look at yourself, you looks like yer about to 'ave a fit or sommat,' Jenny told her unkindly.

Mary then protested grumpily, 'Sukey, stop that noise, will yer? I'm trying to get some sleep, if'n you don't mind!'

Suddenly, to everyone's shock, Sukey flew across

344

room and flung herself at Mary, pulling her hair and screaming at her. 'It were you, weren't it? Don't you go lyin' to me, neither. I know now it were you as took them.'

Mary herself had also started screaming, whilst Sukey pulled so viciously at her hair that Hettie was afraid she would actually tear it from Mary's scalp, her nails clawing the side of Mary's face.

'Bloody 'ell, Sukey,' Aggie objected. 'Give over, will you?' She hurried across the room obviously planning to try to help Mary, but before she got there Sukey's whole body suddenly contorted in a fierce convulsion, immediately followed by several more.

'Oh my God, she's dying,' Jenny wailed as Mary managed to step back from Sukey.

'No she ain't, she's 'avin' a fit, just like you said she would,' one of the other girls contradicted.

There was a sudden thud as Sukey collapsed on to the floor, her body continuing to twitch violently.

'Gawd, what the 'ell are we going to do now?' Babs asked anxiously.

The twitching stopped and Sukey went completely still.

'She's dead,' Jenny wailed.'

'No, she aint,' Aggie insisted stalwartly. 'Come on, let's get her off the floor and into her bed.'

'It's them bloody pills,' Mary concluded ten minutes later when Sukey, who had now come round and was moaning and weeping, had been carried over to her bed and placed on it. 'We've all bin telling 'er she's daft for taking them.'

'Don't you think we should get a doctor?' Hettie suggested uncertainly.

'What for?' Aggie challenged her grimly. She shook her head. 'No, Sukey won't thank us for doing that. We'll leave her to get some sleep and see 'ow she is in the morning. Let's just 'ope she'll see sense from now on and stop taking them bloody pills,' Aggie added, stepping back from Sukey's bed.

John was frowning as he closed the account book he had been studying and replaced it in his desk, carefully locking the drawer.

By rights he should have been smiling not frowning. Only three days ago Alfred had told everyone that, thanks to John, they now had so many new members joining the flying club that they had decided to employ another teacher – and that, from now on, John was not just to be their senior pilot but also the overall manager of the club itself. Alfred had added that John was to receive an increase in pay, and that he would be provided with an assistant to take over the more mundane clerical duties for which he was currently responsible.

'We can't praise you enough, John, for all that you have done here,' Alfred had told him enthusiastically. 'Fact is, old chap, that I've even had someone from the Air Force itself ask me if we could train up some of their young pilots for them. Seems like they do not have enough instructors themselves, and of course we're pretty close to their base here.'

Oh yes, he had every reason not to be frowing, John admitted. But it wasn't his work that was causing him angst.

Polly had arrived at the airfield earlier in the day, as usual driving in far too fast, leaving her roadster carelessly parked outside the clubhouse whilst she rushed into John's office, insisting that she had to see him.

All too aware of exactly what the smirks the group of young men who had witnessed her arrival and her demand to see him meant, John had determinedly escorted her back outside, saying clearly as he did so, 'Lady Polly, how kind of you. His Grace said he would ask you to drop those papers off for him.'

'What on earth are you talking about, John?' Polly had asked as soon as they were outside. 'And why are you calling Alfred His Grace?'

'It isn't fitting that you behave so informally towards me,' he told her quietly. 'It's bound to cause gossip.'

He didn't want to put his concern to her any more bluntly, because he did not want to upset her.

'Gossip?' Polly had shrugged indifferently. 'Pooh, who cares about that! John, I've had the most wonderful idea,' she told him, her eyes sparkling. 'I want you to fly me to the South of France for Easter. There's this wonderful hotel there, you will love it, and . . .'

John had felt his heart sink as he listened to her. She was constantly coming up with madcap schemes and ideas, but none of them had been as impractical and impossible as this. He had started to shake his head but she immediately stopped him, telling him determinedly, 'You can't say no John, because I have already booked the hotel!'

'What you're suggesting is impossible,' John had told her quietly.

The excitement in her eyes had been replaced by the sheen of tears. '*Why* is it impossible? And if you say it's because of some silly social . . .'

'It's impossible because I have already arranged to spend Easter with my sister,' John had cut in firmly.

'Your sister . . . But . . .'

'She hasn't been well, and I am very anxious to see her,' John had continued, steeling himself against the disappointment and despair he knew he would see in Polly's eyes.

'But John, I've got it all planned and . . . and I need you.'

'Your brother has already agreed that I may take several days off over Easter,' John had added, as though he hadn't heard her plea and as though too he considered her emotional request nothing more than her desire to make use of him as an employee of her brother. 'I shall ask around, if you wish, and see if there is a qualified pilot available who could . . .'

'Don't bother,' Polly had shouted fiercely to him before turning and running to her car.

The truth was that Polly was making it increasingly plain that she wanted to be close to him. She didn't love him, John suspected, but she did desperately need a confidant and a companion. And if things had been different, if there were not such a huge social gulf between them, he knew that he would have wanted to help her. And been tempted to turn their friendship into something more intimate?

It was not proper that he should have such thoughts, John told himself robustly as he left his office and closed the door.

Everyone else had gone home for the day now. It was gone six o'clock and growing dark. He had some letters he wanted to write and some articles on photography he wanted to read. They had been sent to him by his old employer and friend, and, although he did not have as much time for it as he would have liked, John still had a keen interest in photography.

The clubhouse was empty. One of the other things Alfred had mentioned to him was a request from certain club members that the clubhouse be opened in the evening, a bar installed, and a bar steward employed, in order that those members who wished to do so could meet together socially.

'That might lead to some of them drinking

before they fly,' John had warned him. 'And that is something I will not countenance.'

He could see a motor coming towards the club-house and his heart lurched as he recognised Polly's roadster for the second time that day.

She was again driving far too fast, and he had to step back to avoid the pall of dust thrown up by the wheels as she brought the roadster to a halt. The light from the building revealed that the motor's normally shiny red bodywork was filmed with dust. When Polly got out of the car he could see that she had been crying. She ran straight to him, flinging herself against him so that he had no option other than to take her in his arms.

'Oh John, I am so glad that you are still here. I am sorry I was horrid before. Will you forgive me?'

'There isn't anything to forgive,' he assured her.

'Oh John.' Her voice was muffled and he could feel the warmth of her breath seeping through his shirt to his flesh. 'I had to come back. I have to talk to you . . . Can we go to your quarters?'

He should really send her away. He knew that. But as she lifted her head to look at him he could smell the gin on her breath and feel the anxious tremble of her body. She lived too recklessly for someone so desperately fragile.

'We can talk, Polly, but I warn you I cannot and will not change my my mind about Easter. My sister has been very ill.' He didn't want her to think he was simply making excuses. He paused and then said quietly, 'There was to have been a child, but unfortunately it was not to be and she took it very hard . . . Polly, what is it?' he begged her as she lifted her hand to her mouth and began to sob uncontrollably.

'John, John, have you ever done something that you hate yourself for? Something so dreadful and so wrong that you can hardly bear to live with yourself?'

John guided her into the building and towards the door to his private quarters, remembering as he did so the last time Polly had asked him this question, at Moreton Place, at the New Year's party. 'Let's go upstairs and I'll make you a cup of tea,' he told her comfortingly.

'Tea? Don't you have any gin?' she asked him. 'When I feel like this, when I feel so cold inside that nothing can take the away the dreadful icy burn of that coldness, gin is the only thing that can warm me.'

'I'm sorry, I don't have any,' John told her as he ushered her up the stairs.

'This room looks like a monk's cell, John,' she complained as he took her into the small parlour. 'Do you wish you had been a monk? Is that why you live like one, without a woman in your life and your bed?'

It was the gin making her talk so wildly, and so improperly, John recognised as she dropped into one of the chairs and lay back, her face so pale it looked almost blue white.

As he kneeled down to light the gas fire, John thought that Polly looked thinner and more fine boned every time he saw her, as though something inside her was burning her away.

'I'll go and make that tea.'

'No!' She reached out and grasped his hand with her own. 'No, John, stay here with me, please. There's something I want to tell you. I have to tell *someone* before I go mad, because the pain of it *is* driving me mad. It never lets go of me; it's there all the time, night and day, and I can't escape from it no matter how hard I try. It was my fault that Ollie died. God took him away from me to punish me because of the dreadful thing I did . . .'

The wildness of her words was beginning to alarm him, John admitted to himself as he sat down in the chair next to her own.

'Promise me you won't hate me because of what I'm going to tell you? she begged him.

'I promise you,' John assured her quietly, holding both her hands in his own.

Without looking at him, she began, 'You know how much I loved Ollie and he loved me too?'

She was going to tell him that she felt she had betrayed Oliver because she wanted to love again, John decided.

'We were so young and so very happy, and we thought . . .' Polly plunged on. 'Please don't be shocked, John, but . . .' She raised her head and looked at him. 'I . . . I gave myself to Ollie. It was my idea. I wanted to do it. He tried to dissuade me.' There was laughter in her eyes as well as tears. 'But I was very determined and he loved me very much. You know, when you're a girl and you don't know anything, other girls tell you that your first time will hurt, but it wasn't like that with us. It was wonderful, and perfect, and I thought I had found heaven.'

Her voice trembled. 'I wanted us to be married straight away, but then Ollie told me that he had volunteered. I was so upset, so angry with him, and so afraid for him. But he said it was his duty and he had to do it. There was not going to be time to arrange a wedding, but he said that the war would soon be over and that we would be married then.

'They sent him to a training camp and it was whilst he was there that it . . .' She hesitated and then started to tremble, and a dreadful certainty seized John.

'I realised that I was to have a child. I could not believe it at first. I did not want to believe it. All the men were given a twenty-four-hour pass at the end of their training. I told Ollie straight away. He was as shocked as I was. He told me, he wanted me . . . His family were so very strict and old-fashioned, and my own circumstances . . .

'We did not know how how long the war would last. It was unthinkable that I should have a child outside marriage, we both knew that. I was dreadfully upset but Ollie told me that there would be other children. I knew . . . there was a woman I had met socially . . . There had been, talk. We both agreed that it had to be and that it was for the best. Ollie gave me the money and I went to see her.

'At first she pretended she didn't know what I wanted, but in the end she gave me his name. The doctor, I mean. I went to see him.

'It was horrid, John. Dreadful. This cold, cruel room, and this man with his icy eyes and cold hands. He gave me chloroform and it made me feel so dreadfully sick. I can still remember . . .' Her voice tailed away and she started to tremble violently.

'When I came round it was all over. I went home. The doctor had told me that I must stay in bed for three days. It was on the third day that the telegram came saying that Ollie had been killed. I had killed our baby and God had killed Ollie to punish me for my sin. I'd lost them both. My dearest love and the child that could have been my solace.'

She was sobbing wildly now and John managed to master his own shocked disbelief to try to comfort her.

He knew such things happened – but not to girls like Polly. Poor, down-trodden women with too many children visited back-street abortionists, as they were called, seeking illegal terminations of their unwanted pregnancies. And sometimes, too, frightened unmarried girls. But to deliberately end a pregnancy was against the law. Both in man's eyes as well as God's. And both the woman and her abortionist ran the risk of being prosecuted for manslaughter. It had never occurred to John that a decent young woman, never mind one of Polly's elevated social position, would seek such a remedy.

Was this the reason for her drinking and her wild behaviour? It made sense to him that it must be, especially with such a terrible secret haunting her. He tried to put himself in her lover's position and to imagine himself asking the woman he loved to take the life of his child, but his imagination simply could not take him that far. And yet he could well understand the circumstances which had driven them both to seek such a drastic remedy.

'I am cursed, John. I am cursed for ever. I am haunted by the cries of my lost child and by my own longing to have that child back. But it is too late. Too late.'

'Ivan said you wanted to see me?'

Although she herself wasn't aware of it, the fact that Hettie now felt so comfortable using their director's first name revealed the speed with which she had matured since she had come to London.

'Yes.' Jay agreed, getting up from his desk and smiling at her. 'I've heard from Archie, and he says that he already has several ideas for a new musical.'

Jay had sent Archie to New York with the

instruction that he wanted the composer to study what was happening on Broadway and to incorporate the best and biggest box-office draws in the musical he wanted him to write.

'My prediction is that by this time next year you will be starring in your own musical, Hettie. Now what do you think of that?' Jay enquired jovially.

Hettie gasped and coloured up, her eyes shining as she shook her head and protested, 'So soon? I know you did say, but I hadn't expected anything like this yet.'

'I'm not a man to let the grass grow under my feet, Hettie,' Jay told her.

Nor was he one to risk another man snatching so tempting a morsel as Hettie from out of his hand, Jay acknowledged inwardly. And Hettie *was* tempting. Deliciously and delightfully so.

'So I can take it that the thought of us continuing our partnership pleases you then, can I?' Jay teased her, walking up to her and sliding one arm round her waist, and then, before she could move, bending his head to kiss her very firmly and deliberately on the mouth.

It wasn't the first time Jay had kissed her, and it wasn't the first time either that the intimacy of his behaviour towards her had left her feeling both dizzily happy and at the same time horribly guilty. Jay was a married man after all. But whenever, in the aftermath of such intimacy, she resolved to reprove him for his familiarity towards her the next time she saw him, he always behaved in such a professional manner that she could not legitimately do so. In fact, she was often left thinking that maybe she had been overreacting.

And then, of course, there was the added problem that, shockingly, she was by no means averse to Jay's kisses.

'The thought of us continuing our *business* partnership *does* please me,' Hettie told him primly now.

Jay gave a great shout of laughter, his eyes crinkling in that way that quite made Hettie's heart somersault inside her chest. 'Ah, but what if the partnership I want to pursue with you, pretty little Hettie, is not of a "business" nature?' he challenged her softly.

'I know very well that you are teasing me,' Hettie responded.

'And if I wasn't just teasing?' Jay pressed fiercely. 'If I were instead very close to falling in love with you, Hettie. Then what?'

Hettie tensed and looked up at him. There was no amusement in the dark eyes now.

'But that can't be,' she told him shakily. 'It must not be. You are married. You have a wife . . .'

'A wife, yes, but I do not have love, Hettie. I have a millstone around my neck that I cannot cast off, but I do not have a woman to love, a woman who loves me. I do not have all those things I know that you and I could have together.'

'You must not say such things to me,' Hettie protested. 'It isn't . . .'

'It isn't what? It isn't proper?' Jay mocked her.

'It isn't fair,' Hettie corrected him bluntly. Something about the way Jay was looking at her made her heart hurt.

'You are so honest, and so unflinching in that honesty,' he told her ruefully. 'Is it any wonder that I am falling in love with you? And is it fair that I should be forced to live my life without you by my side? Is it fair that we should both deny ourselves the pleasure, the happiness, I know we would share?'

Jay's voice had thickened with emotion. Now, with his normal light-hearted teasing manner put to one side, with his allowing her to see his deeper emotions, Hettie knew that she had never been in more danger of falling in love with him in return. But she was still the product of a working class home where duty and decency and certain very strong moral values had been impressed upon her throughout her growing years.

'Hettie, Hettie, why deny us both?' Jay pleaded with her, reaching for her before she could move away.

She tried to stand stiffly and unyieldingly in his arms, but her tender heart couldn't remain unmoved by the extent of his passionate despair as he whispered her name into her hair. Helplessly Hettie looked up at him, and just as helplessly she succumbed to the fierce passion of his kiss as he drew her to him.

'You see, sweet Hettie,' he whispered to her as

he released her. 'You see how wonderful it will be for us, and how foolish it would be to deny ourselves the gift fate has given us? I do not want to escape our fate, Hettie, and I promise you that I shall ensure that you do not want to escape either it or me.

'Now, let me tell you about the surprise I have planned for you. You have worked so very hard and Madame is so pleased with your progress that I felt you deserved a reward.'

Hettie laughed. 'You have rewarded me enough already in giving me the part of Princess Mimi,' she assured him. When they were talking about work she felt on safer ground.

'Princess Mimi is only the beginning,' Jay told her. 'You just wait and see. I am taking you to Paris for Easter, Hettie. We shall go to the opera whilst we are there and we shall see all the popular shows as well. We shall go to Chanel and I shall buy you one of Madame Coco's stylish gowns, and then I shall take you somewhere equally stylish for dinner. Now, what do you have to say to that?'

He both looked and sounded as excited as a schoolboy, but Hettie's heart had grown heavier with each word he had spoken. 'I . . . I cannot go with you,' she told him.

'What? Don't be silly! What nonsense is this, Hettie? Of course you will go with me. That is not negotiable. As to whether or nor you will share my bed whilst we are there, however . . . If that is what is worrying you, I have already booked a separate suite for you, so you need not fear that I am trying to trick you into . . .'

'It isn't that.' Hettie stopped him unhappily.

The truth was that ordinarily she would have loved to spend Easter with him, and to do so in Paris of all places would have been sheer heaven. In Paris there would not be any knowing friends watching and warning her. In Paris, that most daring of all cities, or so she had heard, all manner of things could and did happen. In Paris, she suspected she could easily be tempted to forget that Jay was married and to remember only how her heart sang when he kissed her. In Paris . . . But she would not be in Paris, nor would she be with Jay. She would be in Preston, with her family, and she looked forward to that with much more longing.

'No? Then what exactly *is* it?' Jay demanded angrily.

'I have already promised to spend Easter with my family,' she told him quietly.

'Your *family*? But surely both your parents are dead and . . .'

'My adoptive family,' Hettie corrected herself. 'My . . . my step-mother hasn't been well, and . . .'

Jay shook his head, silencing her as he took her hands in his and gave her a small shake. 'Hettie, Hettie, your loyalty to her does you credit, but what about your loyalty to yourself? To your singing? To me? Be honest, sweet little Hettie, be honest and admit that you would much rather come to Paris with me?'

'Yes, I think I would,' Hettie agreed immediately. But when Jay's hold on her hands tightened and he would have drawn her towards him to celebrate the triumph she could see in his eyes with another kiss, she drew back from him. 'I would *rather* do so, Jay, but I cannot. I have already written to say that I will go home.'

She didn't feel she could explain even to Jay just how dreadfully unhappy her estrangement from her family had made her feel, nor how something inside her she didn't even fully understand herself was urging her to respond to the loving letter Ellie had sent to her, even though a part of her was still afraid that she might be rejected a second time.

'Then write again and say that you have changed your mind,' Jay told her promptly. 'Or if you wish, write and tell them that your slave driver of an employer has insisted that you must work throughout Easter.'

'Lie to them, you mean?' Hettie's mouth trembled, and she suddenly saw with heart-wrenching clarity that, were she to allow herself to fall in love with Jay, there would be many lies and deceits to be both told and endured.

'And do you not think that I, too, will have to practise some deceit in order to be with you?' Jay demanded, oblivious to her recognition of what their future together would be and her place in his life with it. 'But unlike you, Hettie, I consider what we could have together to be worth it. Oh, Hettie . . . Don't make up your mind now,' he begged her. 'Think about what I have said. Please?'

Jay was humbling himself to beg her to reconsider. A huge lump of emotion ached in Hettie's throat, preventing her from speaking. Tears weren't very far away and she longed to be able to tell Jay that she would do what he wanted and go to Paris with him. After all, wasn't it really what she wanted as well?

She was a different person now from the girl she had been. She was living in a different world, with different rules to those from the world she had grown up in.

There was Eddie with his doomed passion for Ivan, and Mary who was so in love with her lord and so convinced that he would marry her. And there were others, whose names were whispered openly in theatre dressing rooms, famous stars adored by their public and fêted everywhere they went, but who were most definitely not married to the powerful men who shared their beds. Hettie could think of any number of such liaisons. There was indeed one very famous singer whose devoted lover was a prominent married politician. He openly visited the elegant Cheyne Walk house where she lived with the two children she claimed publicly to have adopted but who everyone knew were her children by her lover. His wife had retired to the country and it was his lover who accompanied him to balls and house parties and to whom he give his time and his love.

Why should it not be the same for her with Jay? Why should she abide by the petty rules of a way of a life that no longer fitted her? Sometimes she felt so torn between her new life and Jay, and her old life and her family, that just worrying about what she should do made her head ache almost as much as her heart, Hettie admitted.

She wanted to go home and yet at the same time she was afraid of doing so. She wanted to go to Paris with Jay too, but she was also a little afraid of what it would lead to if she did.

Just thinking about going back to Preston aroused all sorts of uncomfortable thoughts and feelings inside her.

Yes, Ellie had written her the kindest and most loving letter in which she had been the mother Hettie had always known and loved. But what if she should change again? What if, when she saw Hettie, Ellie decided that she didn't want to be close to her after all? Perhaps she shouldn't go to Preston. Perhaps she should write to Gideon and say that she had changed her mind. That way at least she wouldn't be hurt again.

PART THREE

TWENTY-THREE

''Ere, guess wot I've just 'eard,' Mary said as she burst into the dressing room. 'We're only going to be running for another six months, that's all!'

As she listened to the mixed chorus of groans and sighs of relief that greeted Mary's announcement, Hettie tried to pretend to be as astonished by Mary's news as everyone else. But the truth was that Jay had told her earlier in the week that the continued success of *Princess Geisha* meant that its run was to be extended for another six months. He had been waiting for her after she had finished her singing lesson.

'Well, wot I wants to know now is how come if we're such a bloomin' success we ain't being paid a bit more,' Aggie complained in an aggrieved voice as she rubbed at the bruise on her ankle where a fellow chorus girl had accidentally kicked her.

'They ain't putting up the price of the seats, are they, so 'ow can they pay us any more?' Jenny argued.

'Is Sukey all right?' Hettie asked Aggie. 'Only she wasn't at rehearsals yesterday.'

'Huh, I'm surprised as 'ow you've noticed, 'Ettie,' Babs broke in a little bitterly. 'Seeing' as 'ow you never seem to have time for us any more, wot wiv them singing lessons and hob-nobbin' with the management and all.'

Hettie felt her face starting to burn. Babs's angry criticism hurt her, but there was no real defence she could make and she knew it. Babs did not approve of the intimacy that was developing between her and Jay, Hettie acknowledged, and had been very quick to say so, and to suggest that Hettie was getting preferential treatment because of it.

'I've told her straight that she ought to stop tekkin them pills,' Aggie answered Hettie, 'but she won't listen. She's not the girl she was,' Aggie continued critically. 'A person can't so much as say a word to 'er now wi'out 'er flying right off the handle and getting in a real temper. Screaming and yelling all sorts at me the other night she was, and just because I told her she'd bin out of step! Going bit queer in the 'ead she is, if you ask me,' Aggie added darkly.

'At least some of us are getting some time off for Easter,' Jenny chipped in. 'Me and Jess was thinking of going down to Brighton, if anyone fancies coming with us?'

Babs shook her head vigorously. 'I'm going 'ome,' she announced. 'To see me family.'

'To see your *family*, Babs, not to see Stan? Or is he going *to be* family soon?' someone asked cheekily.

'And wot if he is, Fanny Holland?' Babs retorted sharply. 'That's no one's business but his and mine.'

''Ere, Babs, there's no need to be so sharp,' Fanny objected huffily. 'I was only 'aving a bit of a joke.'

'Oh, I see! You think that me and Stan is a bit of a joke, do you? Well, I'll thank you to remember that at least me and Stan is decent and respectable, not like some people whose names I won't mention.'

'She means you, Mary,' Fanny announced, nudging Mary in the ribs. 'You and that fancy lord of yours . . .'

Hettie bowed her head, knowing that it wasn't just Mary that Babs had been referring to.

'What about you, Hettie?' Mary asked. 'Wot will you be doing?'

'Sommat as she shouldn't be,' Hettie heard Babs mutter disapprovingly.

'I'm going home, to Preston, to see my family,' she announced sharply, looking determinedly at Babs.

What had she said? A horrible sinking feeling was invading her tummy, making her feel as uncomfortable as though she had swallowed a suet pudding whole.

Only last night, lying awake in bed, she had

admitted to herself how very much she wanted to go to Paris with Jay. She had even daringly wondered if she could afford to buy that silk camisole and French knickers set with the lace trimming that one of the other girls had brought in to show them, assuring them that they were an exact copy of a set being sold in Fenwicks for five times the price.

Only yesterday Jay had whispered to her that Paris was the city for lovers, and how much he wanted to take her there and make her his. And she wanted that too, Hettie admitted. She was a woman now, with a woman's needs and longings. And Jay aroused those needs and longings more strongly every time he touched and kissed her.

She had even mentally written the apologetic letter she intended to send to Gideon and Ellie, explaining that she could not after all come home because of her work. Now she had stupidly said that she was spending Easter in Preston.

But who would know if she did not? a small inner voice whispered to her. She would know, Hettie admitted, and besides . . . Despite the fact that she wanted desperately to go to Paris with Jay, there was still a small part of her that also wanted to go to Preston, a small part of her that wanted to draw back into childhood and the comfort of the family life she had once known. A small part of her that was insisting that it was her duty to go and see Ellie. And that small part of her was somehow a part that had come to her from Ellie, Hettie herself recognised.

'So you mean to go, then? You mean to deny us and go to Preston instead of coming to Paris with me?'

'Jay, please try to understand. Ellie hasn't been well. I owe them so much . . .'

'What about what you owe me, or doesn't that count?' Jay demanded angrily, repeating his earlier argument.

'Jay,' Hettie protested unhappily. 'Please, listen to me.'

'Damn you, Hettie, no! I will not listen and I shall not understand. No.'

Jay had taken Hettie to Fortnum & Mason's for afternoon tea, but now abruptly he stood up and summoned the waitress, ignoring Hettie's pleas, as he thrust some money towards the girl and then stormed off, leaving Hettie to sit white faced and dismayed whilst the waitress started to clear away their unfinished tea things.

Jay was so very cross with her and she could understand why. But didn't he understand that she was disappointed too? She swallowed back her tears, and stood up.

Now tomorrow, instead of travelling with Jay to Paris, she would be taking the train to Preston. She had so hoped that Jay would understand and sympathise with her plight. But instead he had been furiously angry with her.

As she started to made her way towards the exit, Hettie saw a couple being shown to an empty table. The young man was too engrossed in his companion to notice or recognise Hettie, but she recognised him. He was Mary's 'lord'.

Hettie frowned. Hadn't Mary said that he had told her he would not be able to see her over Easter because an elderly relative had died? Maybe the pretty young girl he was escorting was another member of his family, Hettie wondered, as she waited for her coat.

'Hettie! Over here!'

Hettie looked along the platform to where three eagerly waving males were calling her name, the anxiety and unhappiness that had been her companion during the long train journey from Euston disappearing as she recognised Ellie's two sons, along with a tall and very handsome young man who she realised with a jolt was Philip.

'I say, Hettie, have you got any picture post-cards of yourself you can sign for me to take to school?'

'Hettie, is it true that you are a famous singer now?'

'Stop pestering her you two brats. Remember what your parents said. You were only allowed to come and meet her if you promised not to make a nuisance of yourselves. Take no notice of these two young ruffians, Hettie.' Philip grinned, taking hold of his nephews and pretending to bang their heads together.

'Goodness, Philip, I hardly recognised you.' Hettie laughed.

'And what about us? Did you recognise us, Hettie?' Ellie's younger son demanded.

Philip was blushing slightly, and it suddenly struck Hettie how very much like John he looked, although Philip was ten years younger than his brother.

'We're all jolly excited about you coming home, Hettie,' Philip told her enthusiastically. 'Our Ellie has been boasting to everyone about you, and she's got all your reviews . . .'

The unexpectedness of being met off the train by the three boys lifted Hettie's spirits and eased her apprehension.

'Tell me about Mam . . . Ellie,' she begged Philip when he had sent the two younger boys on ahead with her case. 'How is she?'

'Much recovered,' Philip reassured her immediately. 'And much more our old dear Ellie again, as you will soon see for yourself. You may not know, Hettie, that I am now working for Gideon,' Philip went on to tell her.

'No, I did not,' Hettie admitted.

'Unlike John I had no idea of what I wanted to do with my life after I left school. I certainly did not want to enter the church as my aunt and uncle originally planned. I like working with my hands rather than my head, and so Gideon has put me

373

in charge of making sure that the properties he owns and lets out are properly maintained. Hey, you two, be careful with Hettie's case,' Philip called out as the two boys started to tussle with one another.

'They are grown so,' Hettie marvelled. 'The last time I saw them they were shorter than me.'

'They are a handful.' Philip chuckled.

'Ellie wanted a daughter so very much.' Hettie sighed.

She could see Philip frowning at her. 'But Hettie, Ellie has a daughter,' he told her fondly. 'She has you. And I should warn you that she has several treats lined up for your visit already. I believe a visit to the pot fair is being spoken of, plus Ellie is determined to show us all her famous egg rolling skills on Easter Monday.'

Hettie couldn't help but laugh. They had all grown up hearing about how, as a young girl, Ellie had challenged Gideon to an egg rolling contest, and how she had won.

'We wanted to bring Binky with us to welcome you home as well,' Richard called out earnestly as they waited for Hettie and Philip to catch up with them. 'But Dad wouldn't let us.'

'Binky, but that's John's dog surely?' Hettie questioned.

'Yes,' Philip agreed. 'Gideon asked John if he might keep Binky when John moved away. Ellie had taken a shine to him and I think Gideon felt he gave her some comfort.'

'Is she truly better, Philip,' Hettie asked anxiously.

'Very much so,' he assured her. 'As you shall soon see for yourself.'

They were outside the house now, and the front door was opening. Hettie's heart thudded apprehensively as she saw Gideon and Ellie standing there together, and then suddenly she was running through the gate and up the path and into Ellie's arms, as though she were still a little girl and not a grown up young woman.

'Oh Hettie. *Hettie.* Oh, how grand and grown up you are looking,' Ellie praised as she wiped away her own and Hettie's tears, whilst Gideon shepherded his little flock of tearful women and boisterous young men inside the house.

'Boys, go and tell Cook please that Hettie is here and that we should like some tea. Ellie, my love, why do not you take Hettie into the sitting room.'

'Oh, Hettie, let me look at you properly,' Ellie demanded as she sank down into a chair and Hettie dropped to her knees on the floor in front of her, just as though she were a small child again.

'Oh, you are so very very pretty,' Ellie announced fondly.

'Hettie, love, would you mind pouring for me?' Ellie begged after Gideon had brought in the tea things, pausing to look up at Gideon who returned her smile with one of his own. 'Only, Gideon fusses so and will not let me do anything.'

'You know perfectly well that is not true, and that I am only following Iris's instructions,' Gideon told her calmly.

'Hettie, I can't wait to hear all your news,' Ellie told Hettie. 'We are both so very proud of you, aren't we, Gideon? And so excited. I have put your reviews in an album, along with some photographs, and your father has promised me that he will take me to London so that we may see you in *Princess Geisha* . . .

'You know that we are hoping to have John home this Easter as well?' Ellie asked cheerfully.

Hettie stared red faced at the tea she had, out of shock, slopped into one of the saucers.

'Never mind, love,' Ellie comforted her, passing her a napkin to mop up the spillage. 'I imagine you must be tired after that long journey and here I am being selfish and keeping you with me instead of letting you rest. Oh but Hettie, there is so much I want to say to you, so much I want to *tell* you . . .'

Again Ellie exchanged a long look with Gideon.

'Connie is to come over on Monday and if the weather keeps fine we are all to go to Aveham Park so that her little ones can roll their eggs just as she and I and John used to do. Do you remember when we used to take you to roll yours?'

Hettie nodded, emotional tears coming from nowhere to fill her eyes.

'So many happy memories, Hettie,' Ellie said quietly, reaching for her hand. 'I have missed you so much, love, and I am so glad you have come home to us, even if it is only for a short visit. Now,' Ellie continued briskly, 'we want to hear all about your life in London, Hettie, and what you are doing.'

'Well, I am having singing lessons, and Archie, that is the composer, is going to write a new musical with the main female part to be sung by a soprano lyric – that is the correct term for my voice, you see . . .' Hettie began earnestly.

TWENTY-FOUR

It amazed Hettie how easy she was finding it to slip back into her old life. After Easter Friday's traditional fish only meals, and Saturday's walk to Preston's busy market with its pot fair bargains, she had attended church with Ellie, Gideon and the rest of the of the household on Easter Sunday, wearing the new 'Easter Sunday' hat she had found waiting for her in her bedrdoom. It was a gift from Ellie and Gideon that had brought emotional tears to her eyes, even if the hat was rather less fashionable than what she now wore; the kind of hat the girl she had been would have delighted in, rather than one she might have chosen for herself these days.

Now they were all standing outside the church in the bright spring sunshine, having been cornered by Ellie's formidable neighbour and aunt, along with her doctor husband, their elder daughter Cecily, plus Cecily's husband and their children.

'It is such a pity, Ellie dear, that you have not

had daughters,' Hettie overheard Cecily saying gently to Ellie. 'Especially since you have inherited the best of our family's famed good looks. My own girls look more like their father than they do me, unfortunately.'

Not wanting to hear any more or to have any shadows thrown over the brightness of the day, Hettie immediately moved away to go and tuck her hand through Gideon's arm as he smiled down at her.

'We have all missed you, puss,' he told her lightly. 'But most especially your mother. She has informed me now that she will not rest until I have promised to take her to London so that she may see you singing.'

Hettie bit her lip and looked away, all too aware of the complications a visit from Ellie and Gideon could cause, especially if she were obliged to introduce them to Jay.

'I wouldn't want you to do anything that might make Mam poorly again,' she told Gideon.

She could see that he was beginning to frown as though he were about to question her comment, but to her relief, before he could do so, Ellie herself came hurrying over to them, immediately putting her hand on his arm and saying urgently, 'Gideon, Cecily has been asking me some very particular questions . . .'

'Are you saying that you think she has guessed?' Gideon demanded, their exchange completely baffling Hettie who couldn't understand what they were discussing. But, sensing that it must be private, she started to move away.

Immediately Ellie stopped her, placing her hand on Hettie's arm and saying softly, 'Hettie, love, don't go. There is something we want to tell you . . .' She looked up at Gideon and then back at Hettie. 'We had meant to wait a little while longer yet, but since Cecily seems to have guessed . . .' She looked imploringly at Gideon and then back at Hettie. 'Love, I am to have another child.'

Hettie stared at her in shock. How could Ellie stand there and smile so happily after what had happened? Hettie looked up at Gideon, but he was looking just as happy as Ellie.

'But surely,' Hettie began anxiously and then stopped, unwilling to remind Ellie of how ill she had been. 'I know what you must be thinking,' Ellie acknowledged, smiling gently at her. 'But Iris has assured us that there is no cause for any concern. And indeed she has said that she thinks it a very good thing indeed. To be truthful I *was* worried at first, Hettie, but I feel different this time. I don't seem to have the concerns I had with that poor lost baby. I do so hope, though, that this new little one will be a girl.'

'Yes, I am sure that you must,' Hettie agreed, her forced smile twisting painfully at her own heart. Of course Ellie desperately wanted to have a daughter. And her happiness was not, as Hettie had so foolishly let herself think, because Hettie had come home but because of the child she was now carrying.

Suddenly she couldn't wait for the holiday to be over so that she could return to her own life.

As he watched the countryside speed by through the railway carriage window, John noticed not just how the landscape was changing as he travelled north but also how spring itself came later to Lancashire than it did to Oxfordshire.

Here the daffodils were only just opening, and the blackthorn hedges had only the beginnings of unfurling new green leaves, whereas the hedges along the country lanes around the airfield were already densely green and the daffodils were in full flower.

There was, though, something invigorating about the sharpness of northern air, a certain refreshing sharpness that he was already anticipating. And, of course, he would be seeing his family.

He had only decided to make the journey at the last minute, previously having felt, conscientiously, that he should not take any time off, despite what he had told Polly. Because he was afraid that a selfish action on his part could lead to yet another tragedy? He looked out of the window. Would he have either the time or the courage to visit the abandoned airfield whilst he was here? Could he bear to do so?

Why must life contain so much pain? He started

to think about Polly, compassion darkening his eyes. She had been very cross with him when he had continued to refuse to join the party she had organised, but John had remained steadfast in his determination not to go to France. He sensed, too, that Polly regretted having confided in him such very shocking and intimate details of her unhappiness. There was certainly a new coolness in her manner towards him, which in many ways caused him to feel relieved. On the other hand, though, he genuinely liked Polly and felt concerned for her.

So much excitement. Hettie had nobly volunteered to keep Connie's children occupied prior to the whole family setting off for Aveham Park and the fun of rolling the specially prepared hard-boiled eggs down the hill in Preston's famous Easter Monday egg rolling ceremony.

Afterwards there would be the fair itself to look forward to, plus, if there was time, a trip in a pleasure boat on the River Ribble. With the sun shining, and the large basket of eggs waiting, it was no wonder that Connie's young children were impatient and getting over excited.

In order to keep them entertained, Hettie had been reading them a story, complete with an imitation of all the necessary animal noises, so that when John walked into Ellie's drawing room all he could hear was childish giggles and one determined little voice begging, 'Do the piggie again, Hettie!'

Throwing herself into the spirit of things, Hettie obliged, producing a convincing snuffling sound that sent the children into gales of giddy laughter before she delivered a hearty, 'Oink oink!'

'Oink oink to you, too.' John laughed, unable to resist the tempation to join in.

Immediately the children ran to him, leaving Hettie kneeling on the floor, her face bright red with embarrassment.

No one had confirmed that John was definitely coming home, and the last thing she wanted was to have him find her sitting on the floor like a schoolgirl, pretending to be a pig.

'Oh John, you are here after all,' Ellie cried as she spotted him and, to Hettie's relief, within seconds he was surrounded by his sisters and their husbands, leaving her to recover her dignity as best she could.

He looked the same and yet somehow different, Hettie acknowledged, surreptitiously studying him as she dusted down her skirt.

He looked broader somehow, and . . . and bigger, very much a man now, rather than a boy, Hettie recognised with the benefit of her own growing worldly wisdom. And a very handsome man, too, with good strong features and a firmly chiselled jaw line. The flash of white teeth she caught as he smiled at something someone had said sent a small unexpected quiver of sensation dancing down her spine.

Give over, do, she warned herself sternly. You're

grown up now, and any road, Jay is just as handsome.

'Hettie, come and say hello to John,' Ellie urged.

'Hello, John,' Hettie responded coolly, firmly keeping her distance.

'Oh ho, so you can speak, then.' John laughed, teasing her. 'I wasn't sure if you were going to give me a moo moo or a baa baa.' He was forcing himself to be as light and jovial in spirit as he could, for Ellie's sake mostly, but it was taking an effort on his part.

Everyone was laughing, and Hettie forced herself to join in although she deliberately kept as much distance as she could between herself and John as they all set out for the park.

'Now, Connie,' Gideon teased his sister-in-law as Ellie linked her arm through her husband's, and Connie linked hers with Ellie's. 'No going off to the fairground!'

Connie laughed heartily and shook her head.

'Ooh, Gideon, do you remember how strict our mother used to be about not letting us do anything that was fun because "she was a Barclay sister"!' Ellie and Connie said together before dissolving into giggles.

'I can certainly remember the first time I saw Ellie,' Gideon responded. 'It was . . .'

'Preston Guild, 1902,' Ellie announced promptly. 'Do you remember how John had run off, despite being told he was not to do so, and I went after him and would have been crushed to death by the crowd if you had not rescued me, Gideon?'

'Aye, but Gideon had seen you before that, hadn't you, Gideon?' John laughed, joining in the happy reminiscing.

'You mean when I walked down Friargate and the three of you were standing in the window over your pa's shop?'

'Yes. You were doing some tricks,' John remembered.

'Showing off,' Ellie put in severely, but Hettie could see the happiness in her eyes.

'And when you called round to see if I was all right, Gideon, Mam was so disapproving because you were working with Da's brother, droving sheep.'

'She certainly made it clear that she didn't think I was good enough for her daughter,' Gideon agreed ruefully.

'If she had but known it, the truth was that, in the eyes of the world, I was the one who wasn't good enough for you, Gideon.' Ellie sighed, and then added quietly, 'It's a Guild year this year, of course, and Gideon was asked to join the main committee, but my ill health prevented him from accepting.'

'Prevented nothing,' Gideon contradicted dismissively. 'We shall be able to enjoy the Guild fun all the better for me not having had 'owt to do with organising it, if you ask me.'

'That's enough reminiscing, you two,' Harry

joined in! 'Let's go and see if Ellie really is as good at egg rolling as she claims.'

John shook his head and warned his brother-in-law, 'You won't win, Harry. Do you remember how she beat you, Gideon?'

Hettie saw the private look that Ellie and Gideon exchanged and wondered what had caused it, not knowing that it had been the tussle that had followed Ellie's determination to have her egg win the race that had led to hers and Gideon's first kiss.

They had reached the park and had to make their way through the crowd to get to the top of the hill to join the queue waiting there to roll their eggs.

'Come on, Hettie,' Connie's eldest cried, 'otherwise you won't be able to join in.'

Hettie could see John's mouth twitching with amusement at this innocent inclusion of her in the children's party, but rather than pout and sulk as the old Hettie would have done Hettie simply tossed her head and ignored his amusement, calling out, 'I'm coming, but remember the pink egg is mine . . .'

'I think I'd better go with you,' John told her firmly. 'Remember, I know how you like to cheat at this . . .'

The words were delivered with a straight face but Hettie could see the laughter in his eyes.

'Just because I picked up the wrong egg once,' she protested.

John was laughing openly now. 'Ah ha, so you do remember? And it was my egg you picked up.'

'And you let me do it and didn't give me away,' Hettie recalled softly, starting to laugh herself.

'Oh Hettie, I'd forgotten what fun you are,' John told her impulsively, reaching for her hand and then stopping abruptly as he realised where his own emotions were taking him.

All he had heard all day from Gideon had been a proud father's boasting about the successful future that now lay ahead of Hettie. There was no room for him in her life now, John acknowledged. He had lost the opportunity he might once have had to pay court to her; the entrancing young woman she had become would quite obviously have any number of eligible young men falling in love with her. She may even be courting someone now for all he knew. He looked away from her, overwhelmed by his own despair, and so missed the anguished look of appeal she was giving him.

The daylight was giving way to dusk when the last eggs rolled. Eyes and tummies contentedly full from the excitement and treats of the afternoon, the whole party made their way back to Winckley Square, the younger members of the family carried there on the shoulders of their fathers and uncles whilst Hettie took her place with the women.

Connie and Harry and their children were spending a few days in Preston with Ellie and Gideon, and with the younger children to be fed and made ready for bed, John excused himself. He had also promised, he told them, to go and see his old friend and mentor, the Preston photographer for whom he had once worked, and with whom he had arranged to stay, prior to returning to Oxfordshire in the morning.

'Oh John, love, I do so wish you could stay longer,' Ellie told her younger brother as she kissed him fondly.

'Yes, John, you haven't told us anything about Lady Polly,' Connie twitted him teasingly. 'And yet you've bin full of her in your letters.'

John felt acutely uncomfortable. He knew that Connie meant no harm and was only ribbing him, but the truth was that he had hardly mentioned Polly to her at all, other than to comment on how sad it was that she had lost her fiancé.

So that was why John had dropped her hand so quickly, Hettie realised miserably. She ought to have guessed. After all, she had heard enough about Lady Polly from Connie at Christmas.

No wonder John wasn't interested in her – a mere singer – if he was mixing with posh titled folk.

'Bye, John love.' Connie smiled, going over to kiss him.

'Hettie,' Ellie urged, 'come and say goodbye to John before he leaves.'

'Goodbye, John,' Hettie responded stiffly, staying exactly where she was and flashing a too bright and totally false smile in the general direction of where John was standing before returning her attention to Philip.

'Hettie, love, I have missed you so much and it is lovely to have you here,' Ellie announced lovingly, reaching for Hettie's hand as they and Connie sat together in Ellie's pretty sitting room, waiting for the men to return from an evening stroll to the local public house.

'I am determined to persuade Gideon to make arrangements for us to come to London and see you in your operetta, though.'

'Ellie, is that wise?' Connie objected. 'With this baby due in less than four months. Not that you are showing much yet, I must say.'

'No, I'm not, am I? I was exactly the same with Richard, the merest bump and then at six months suddenly I was huge. And Connie, for heaven's sake stop fussing,' Ellie told her sister firmly.

'With a railway system that is the envy of the world, Gideon and I can go to London, see Hettie, and be back again without the baby even noticing.'

'Oh, Ellie, it is so good to see you returned to your old self,' Connie said emotionally. 'I do so hope that this baby will be a little girl for you, a daughter, don't you, Hettie?'

'Yes. I too hope you will have a daughter of your own,' Hettie agreed quietly.

'Boy or girl, he or she will be very welcome,' Ellie told them both serenely.

'I am rather tired,' Hettie fibbed, getting up. 'If neither of you mind, I think I will go up to bed. My train leaves early in the morning and I do not want to oversleep and miss it.'

She had so many mixed feelings, both happy and painful, Hettie acknowledged as she sat up in her childhood bed, her knees drawn up under her chin and her arms wrapped around her knees.

It *had*, as Connie had said, been wonderful to see Ellie restored to her old self, and she had had such fun this afternoon with Connie's children and her step-brothers.

But seeing John had also brought back memories – and aroused not so old emotions. And that had been painful.

In London, busy with her own life, it had been easy to convince herself that her feelings for John didn't matter. In London, after all, there was Jay and all the heady excitement of everything he wanted to give her. Jay made her feel grown up and desirable, whereas John made her feel like an awkward young girl again.

But there was one thing both men had in common, which was that a relationship with either of them would bring her pain – Jay because he was a married man, and John because he loved another woman. Not, of course, that there was any suggestion that John *wanted* to have a relationship with her.

There was a soft knock on her bedroom door

followed immediately by Ellie's voice as she opened the door and came in, gently closing it behind her.

'I was hoping you would still be awake,' she said tenderly as she came and sat down on the bed. 'It's been so lovely having you here, Hettie.' Ellie smiled as she took hold of one of Hettie's hands, clasping it within the warmth of her own. 'I know how difficult and unhappy I made life for everyone during that time when . . . when I wasn't well.'

'That wasn't your fault,' Hettie assured her immediately. 'Iris explained how it was.'

'You have all been very patient with me, Hettie, expecially my dearest Gideon.'

'It must, you must, I'm glad that you're glad about . . . about this new baby, Mam,' Hettie managed to say awkwardly at last.

'I *am* glad. And I am happy as well because I know that this time I feel as I should do, as I felt with both the boys. You will understand more what I mean when your own time comes, Hettie. Right from the start I was worried about that other poor baby. It was as though part of me knew . . .'

'Mam, don't,' Hettie begged her, distressed. 'I know how much you wanted a little girl, a daughter.'

Ellie had started to frown. 'Another girl would have been nice,' she allowed, stressing the word 'another', 'but Hettie I already have my daughter.'

Hettie looked at her. 'But I am not, you are not . . .' she blurted out.

391

'I am not what?' Ellie demanded. 'I am not your mother? Is that what you think, Hettie? It is certainly not what I think, for I *know* you are my child, my *daughter*, just as much as I know that the boys are my sons. You are my daughter, Hettie, and you became mine from the minute you first looked at me and held out your little arms to me.' Tears had blurred both Ellie's eyes and her voice.

'You touched my heart then, Hettie, in such a way I can't explain it to you, only to say that it was as though I immediately loved you. It was for you that I took your mother in . . . for you, because I loved you. You were my baby, my beloved little daughter.

'And it was of you that I thought as I trudged those wretched streets looking for somewhere for us all to stay. My little Hettie of Hope Street, for it was on Hope Street that I finally found somewhere for us all.

'Of course I was sorry about your mother's death, and I grieved for her and for you, but you were already mine before she died, Hettie, even though you yourself cannot remember that.

'Should this new baby be a little girl, she will be my second daughter and she will be the sister I longed so much to give you when you were growing up so that you might love her as I loved Connie. But you are my eldest child, my beloved first child, my first daughter, and because of that you will always be extra special to me.'

Hettie discovered that she was both shaking and

crying at the same time as she sobbed, 'Oh Mam, I didn't know.' And allowed Ellie to draw her into her eager arms.

'Hettie, Hettie . . . So much of you is of me . . . The way you smile, the way you walk and talk . . . Gideon has often remarked on it and others too, and I am so very, very proud of you. A mother's pride, like my mother's love. Girl or boy this new baby will be loved, but never more than you, Hettie . . .'

TWENTY-FIVE

'So it looks as though Sukey ain't going to be coming back. Turned 'er orf there and then 'e did, and told 'er never to audition for one of his shows again. A right state she were in an' all. Mind you, I can't say as 'ow she weren't asking for it, like, as you might say. Screaming all sorts at the director she was, and the language, it would 'ave made a docker blush it would, it were that ripe. It were a right old temper Sukey had on her and no mistake, and then when she threw them pots at 'im . . .'

Aggie started to shake her head. 'Orf her head she were and no mistake. So it was no wonder Ivan went and sent for Jay Dalhousie.'

Tiredly Hettie tried to keep her eyes open and listen to Aggie. It was only an hour since she had got off the London train, and although her body was here in London her thoughts – and heart – were still in Preston with Ellie.

''Ettie, you aren't listening to me,' Aggie complained.

Aggie had been deprived of an audience for her juicy piece of gossip all of Easter weekend and now that Hettie had returned she was quite naturally making it plain that she felt aggrieved that Hettie was not responding to her dramatic revelations about Sukey's dismissal with the shocked disbelief she had expected.

''Ere, 'e didn't tell you he were going to give her the old 'eav' o, did he?' she questioned Hettie suspiciously. 'Only all of us knows how close you and 'im have got, like.'

'No, of course not,' Hettie denied immediately. 'I would have told you all.'

'Well, I should have 'oped you would an' all,' Aggie said, slightly mollified. 'Us girls 'ave got to stick together and don't you go forgetting that, 'Ettie. It's all very well when these posh fellas come sniffing round wi' their soft talk, promising a girl everything, but it seems to me that there's not many girls like us as ends up wi' a ring and respectably married to 'em,' Aggie warned her.

'Was it because of those pills she's been taking that Sukey got in such a state, do you think?' Hettie asked worriedly, deliberately ignoring Aggie's final comment.

''Oo knows.' Aggie shrugged. 'All as I know is that she's bin told to go, and that she has. Took the first train back to Liverpool yesterday and said she was glad to be going an all. So wot about you, 'Ettie, did you 'ave a good time with your family?'

'It was very nice,' Hettie told her lamely, adding,

'Me mam and dad are going to try to come down to London to see the show.'

'Well I never . . .' Aggie declared, momentarily distracted. 'Now *that* would be sommat, wouldn't it? Me Mam has never so much as set foot outside of Lancashire in her life. Not that she would want to, mind. She wouldn't have no truck with southerners, wouldn't me Mam. She allus says as 'ow you can't trust 'em, and I'm beginning to think she's right.'

Aggie had said that Jay had given Sukey the sack from the show – did that mean that he hadn't gone to Paris, or had he simply sacked Sukey and then gone? Hettie didn't want to ask Aggie too many questions, because she didn't want the other girl demanding to know why she was so interested in Jay's whereabouts.

Would he forgive her for not going with him? Did she want him to? Hettie wondered uncertainly. Going home and being with Ellie and Gideon had reminded her of the values they had instilled in her. There was no doubt in her mind about how they would feel about the kind of relationship Jay wanted to have with her.

But it seemed that when it came to John and his fancy lady friend things were different. What was she like, this Lady Polly who John didn't want to discuss but who nevertheless seemed to be playing such a large part in his new life?

Why was she thinking about John and his life and feeling so unhappy when her own life was so exciting? Hettie wondered crossly. Just because as a silly girl she had thought of John as such a hero, and been falling in love with him, that didn't mean anything now, did it? She was going to be a famous singer, she reminded herself stoutly as the door opened and the twins hurried in, almost immediately followed by Mary and then Babs.

It was Jenny who noticed Babs's ring first, squealing out excitedly, "Ere, Babs, you've never gorn and got engaged, 'ave you?'

'And what if I 'ave?' Babs responded, tossing her head and both laughing and blushing as they all rushed forward to study the ring on her left hand – a small ruby surrounded by equally small diamonds.

'And there you was, Mary, telling us all as how you would be the first to get a diamond ring on your finger,' Aggie reminded Mary bluntly.

'Well, as it so happens, I 'ave got a diamond ring, so there,' Mary boasted sharply.

'Oh you 'ave, 'ave you? Well, let's see it then,' Aggie demanded, plainly not believing her.

'You can an' all, then,' Mary told her, drawing off her gloves and displaying the large solitaire diamond that was flashing on her right hand.

"Ere, Mary, that's never real, is it?' Jess breathed in awe.

'O' course it's real,' Mary told her contemptuously.

'Mebbe so, but it ain't some family heirloom

like wot all them toff fiancées wear. After all, you ain't no Edwina Ashley, 'er as has just got engaged to that Lord Louis Mountbatten, are you?' Aggie scoffed. 'And you ain't wearing it on your left hand either, are you?'

Mary tossed her head and asserted fiercely 'I wanted me own ring not sommat someone else 'as worn. And as for me left hand, well, we're wanting to keep it to ourselves for now.'

'So why are you telling us, then?' Aggie asked pithily. ''Ere, Babs,' she continued, turning her back on Mary. 'When are you and Stan going to get married, then?'

'Probably next year,' Babs told her. 'Stan's already been booked to work the summer season in Blackpool again – in fact, he were wanting me to audition for a summer show there on the pier so as we could be together, and I would 'ave done an' all if'n *Princess Geisha* had finished.'

''Ere, Mary, 'ave you and his Lordship set a date yet? H'i expects as 'ow you will be getting married in Westminster Abbey, and wearing a tiara, will yer? That's if you really are engaged,' Aggie finished challengingly, her accusation almost drowned out by the noise made by Mary slamming the door as she stormed out.

'Huh, I don't know what she's getting so 'ot under the collar about,' Aggie complained. ''Is sort never marries our sort, and Mary's daft if she thinks any different.'

* * *

'That's very good, Hettie. It is too late for you to sing in one of the great operas.' Madame Bertrice gave a small dismissive shrug. 'For that you would have had to have had proper lessons as a child, but you are a hard working pupil and the audience can hear now that you are a good soprano lyric, and you have a voice strong enough to sing the lead part.'

They were wonderful, wonderful words, and the best compliment she could possibly hear, Hettie acknowledged joyously as she thanked her teacher. Not so long ago, the very first thing she would have done after hearing such good news would have been to rush and find Babs, but Babs didn't seem to have very much time for her any more, and had even made several sharp comments about the fact that Hettie was having private singing lessons at all.

All in all, her spirits were lower than they should have been, Hettie admitted as she left her singing teacher's house and stepped out into the bright spring sunshine.

'Hettie!'

'Oh, Jay,' Hettie exclaimed, putting her hand to her chest as she heard Jay calling out her name. 'You almost made me jump out of me skin.'

Jay looked at her sombrely as he fell into step beside her. 'I would have sent Hudson to collect you in the motor, but I didn't want to wait that long to see you. Have you missed me, sweet Hettie? I should not feed your vanity, I know, especially after you refused to come with me, but I have certainly missed you. Paris just wasn't the same without you.'

'Oh Jay.' Hettie was torn between confusion and delight.

He had missed her Jay admitted, although his time in Paris had been far from solitary. But not even the obliging beauties of the Follies had been enough to totally banish Hettie from his thoughts.

'So how was Preston?' he asked her mockingly. 'Worth missing Paris for?'

He *was* still angry with her, Hettie recognised, even if he was concealing it with a smile.

'I was glad that I went,' she told him truthfully. 'Me mam is ever so much better. She and me da are hoping to come down to London to see *Princess Geisha*. They wanted to know all about everything I was doing.'

'But you didn't tell them "everything", I hope, pretty Hettie?' Jay asked her.

Hettie looked away from him. Somehow Jay's warning made her feel both unhappy and ashamed.

'I told them all about my singing lessons and that you had been very good to me.' She ducked her head and refused to look at him.

Jay sighed and took hold of her hand, holding it tightly. 'You are angry with me, Hettie, why?'

'I am not angry with you,' she denied. 'But I think you are still angry with me, because I didn't go to Paris with you.'

She heard him sigh again as he held her hand

tighter and pulled her around gently so that they were facing one another.

'Enough of this. I am not angry, only disappointed because you weren't there with me.' As he spoke Jay knew that it was the truth. 'Just tell me that you missed me as I missed you, Hettie. That is all I want to hear you say.'

'I missed you,' Hettie told him solemnly. It was, after all, true. She had missed him.

'That is better. And look, here is Hudson with the car. He will take us back to the Ritz, and we shall indulge ourselves with afternoon tea.'

Hettie hung back. 'But Jay, there is a rehearsal this afternoon and even if there wasn't . . .'

'Even if there wasn't, what?' Jay challenged her.

'I don't feel comfortable about going to the Ritz with you, Jay. That friend of yours . . .'

'You mean Harvey?'

'Yes.'

'You don't like him?'

'No.' Hettie admitted. 'He made me feel . . . He frightened me,' she told him simply. 'And . . .' she ducked her head again. 'And everyone must know that you are married, and even though I haven't done anything wrong I feel . . .'

'Hettie, Hettie. How many times must I tell you that my marriage has nothing to do with us, and that it need not and must not come between us?'

When she didn't anwer he pressed her determinedly. 'When a marriage is a matter of religion and practicality, and is not and never has been of the heart, surely it cannot be wrong for a man to want to be with the woman to whom he *does* want to give his heart? In France such a liaison is perfectly acceptable. And it happens here too in your country more than you perhaps realise. Especially in our business, Hettie.

'Were you to accept my love and give yours to me in return, to give yourself to me,' Jay emphasised, his voice suddenly thickening, 'I promise you that you will never regret it. You will be the wife of my heart, little Hettie, and you will be treated as though you were a queen.

'Think, Hettie, think of all we share together. When you bring the audiences of Broadway to their feet as they give you a standing ovation, I want to be the one at your side. I want to present you to my country as the woman I love, Hettie, instead of merely a gifted singer I have found.'

The images he was conjuring for her were so very, very tempting. 'But your wife?' Hettie protested.

Jay leaned forward, cupped her face in his hands, and then looked down into her eyes, so deeply and intently that Hettie felt as though he were looking right into her heart itself.

'She does not matter. You and I are what matters, Hettie,' he told her fiercely.

John heard the latest gossip about Polly as soon as he walked onto the flying club's premises. The party of young people that had eventually spent the Easter holiday together had included some of the younger members of the club, and they had now returned, and were relating what they had witnessed, in the flying club's bar.

'Lady Polly was in the very best of good spirits, wasn't she, Bosie?' John heard one of them asking of another.

'I'll say. Never seen her look better,' the other confirmed. 'M'sister said she could tell how it was with them the moment she saw them together. And, of course, there is a family connection with young Ralph being Oliver's cousin.'

'Well, good luck to them, I say,' someone else joined in. 'Bloody bad show Oliver being killed like that, just when we thought it was all over.'

'Bloody bad show,' the first speaker agreed.

'Isn't young Ralph only just up at Magdalene, though?'

'He was. From what I've heard, Lady Polly is urging him to leave. Can't bear the thought of being without him, I heard. Pity if he does.'

'Why? My bet is that Lady Polly will be able to teach him everything he needs to know – and then some, if what I've heard about her is true.' Someone laughed coarsely.

Instinctively John's hands clenched into two hard fists and he started to step forward, only to check and fall back as he recognised his own foolishness. He had no right to protect either Polly or her reputation. He was simply an employee working for her brother.

'M'sister says that Lady Polly is very dashing,' another speaker agreed.

'I wonder what the Lascelles family think about the liaison,' the man who had spoken so coarsely earlier asked pointedly.

John frowned as he made his way past the group of young men. Virtually all the members and pupils of the flying club were either members of or closely connected with the aristocracy, and there had been other occasions when their arrogance jarred against John's working class beliefs, but their gossip about Polly touched him far more personally.

He wasn't in love with her – he had realised that this Easter in Preston when he had looked at Hettie and been struck with the sensation of a giant fist squeezing his heart – but her vulnerability aroused his protective instincts, and he liked her. She had spirit and panache. She had been angry with him because he had refused to spend Easter with her, he knew that, and he certainly wasn't the kind of blockhead who assumed that her new relationship had come about because she wanted to prove something to him. But he was concerned about it. Even whilst he hoped profoundly that she had at last found happiness, and someone who could fill the empty place Oliver had left.

TWENTY-SIX

Spring had well and truly arrived, and the aristocratic London season was in full swing, the newspapers and society magazines filled with photographs of expectant debutantes, and of course the newly engaged Edwina Ashley and her fiancé Lord Louis Mountbatten.

Young men sporting the newly fashionable wide Oxford bags were photographed with pretty girls wearing tennis dresses and looking very sporting. Whilst the temperatures rose, Madame Coco Channel pronounced that no fashionable young lady should be without the latest accessory of a 'suntan'.

Hettie and the other girls had taken to spending as much of their free time as they could sunning themselves in Hyde Park, where Hettie, to everyone else's envy, quickly turned the prettiest and most enviable shade of golden brown.

'Ooh, ouch,' Aggie complained late one afternoon as she, Mary and Hettie walked back to their lodging house. 'I 'aven't half gorn and burned meself. Me face looks as red as fire. It's all right for you, 'Ettie,' she protested as Hettie giggled. 'Just look at you, you lucky thing.'

Hettie was wearing a pretty sundress with a matching short-sleeved bolero that showed off her toasted arms. She had removed the bolero in the park the better to 'tan' her skin, and she couldn't help preening a little as a group of young men whistled cheekily as the three girls walked past them.

'Look, I'm going to get meself some calamine lotion,' Aggie told the other two. 'I'll catch up with you in a minute.'

'Are you seeing His Lordship tonight, Mary?' Hettie asked conversationally, once Aggie had gone.

Mary shook her head. 'No, 'e's away at the moment. E's gorn to H'Inchfield, that's 'is family seat,' she explained proudly. 'His mam and dad wanted to see him about sommat.'

'Is it very grand, the family seat, I mean?' Hettie asked her.

'Oh yes, ever so,' Mary confirmed brightly. 'It's got over a hundred rooms, you know.'

Although Mary was smiling, it seemed to Hettie that her smile was strained, and she certainly looked thinner, Hettie decided,

'Mary, you aren't taking those pills that Sukey was taking, are you?' she asked her urgently.

'Course not,' Mary denied, but then to Hettie's surprise her eyes suddenly filled with tears.

'Oh Mary,' Hettie soothed. 'Whatever is it, what's wrong?'

'Nuffink,' Mary denied vehemently, sniffing and wiping the back of her hand over her eyes. 'And don't you go saying anything about this to the others, 'Ettie,' she ordered fiercely.

Hettie had been due to spend the day with Jay, who had promised to drive her to Brighton, but he had had to cancel their outing at the last minute because of some urgent business. However, he was waiting for Hettie when she left the theatre after the evening performance.

'Hettie, I have received the best of news from Archie. He has already written two songs for you for the new musical, and he intends to post copies to me.'

'Two songs? But I thought you had still to decide upon a story for the musical?' Hettie protested as Jay hurried her into the waiting motor – a new Rolls Royce, Hettie noticed admiringly as she sank into its cream leather seating.

'Yes, that is so, but Archie and I are both agreed that no time must be lost in taking advantage of the success we have had with *Princess Geisha*, and so if necessary we can open on Broadway with that if we can't get the new musical ready in time.

'And I have another surprise for you as well, Hettie,' Jay announced.

He was obviously in very high good humour,

Hettie recognised as he laughed at her bewilderment and caught hold of her hands.

'Hettie, you and I are going to go to New York!'

'New York!' Hettie could only stare at him.

'Ah ha, *now* I have silenced you, my little song bird.' Jay grinned. 'Yes, Hettie, New York. It is all arranged. I have already instructed my agents to book us a passage to New York. And that is not all.' He glanced towards Hudson's rigid back and whispered to her, 'I have listened to what you have said to me, Hettie, and I have also instructed my agents to find you an apartment.'

'An apartment?' Hettie was still trying to come to terms with the news that she was to go to New York. It seemed like another planet.

'Yes. As the star of my new show it is unthinkable, of course, that you should lodge with chorus girls as you do here in London. New York does not care for cheapskates, and besides, an apartment will give us privacy, Hettie, and I shall be able to visit you . . . frequently.'

They had reached the Ritz, and the doorman was opening the car door for her.

'In fact,' Jay told her, placing his hand over her own beneath the cover of her coat and squeezing her fingers gently, 'I have also arranged for us to look at a pretty little house in Chelsea tomorrow. It has its own small music room where you can practise, and a delightful bedroom where *we* can be alone. But we'll speak more of this later,' he told her, releasing her hand so that she could get out of the car.

Hettie's head was spinning. New York. An apartment. A house in Chelsea.

She had known, of course, what Jay's intentions towards her were. She knew too that she found him very attractive. Jay created an atmosphere of excitement around him that she suspected few women would be immune to, and they had a shared interest in their work. With Jay she could achieve her dreams. And prior to returning home to Preston to see her family, she would have said that there was nothing she wanted more than that.

But now . . . Ellie and Gideon would hate the thought of her becoming Jay's mistress. Ellie would be shocked and hurt. Gideon would be shocked and angry. They would want to protect her from what they would see as a shameful liaison, and she would not be able to make them understand that things were different in the theatrical world and that, whilst her relationship with Jay could never be acceptable in their world it was in hers.

But what if she were able to keep her relationship with Jay a secret from her family? In London that might not have been possible, but surely in New York it would be? Her heart started to beat faster. Jay excited her in a way that she only half understood. His touch made her flesh tingle and her whole body feel as though it were holding its breath waiting for something, some pleasure she did not as yet know.

Impulsively Hettie turned towards him, wanting to express what she was feeling, but as she did so, Jay stared at her, and then stepped back from her, his whole body rigid with anger.

'Jay, what is it? What's wrong?' Hettie demanded as he hurried her down the now familiar corridor and into the lift which would take them to his suite. But instead of answering her, he gave a tight-lipped shake of his head, and then didn't speak to her again until they were inside the suite.

Then he demanded savagely, 'What the hell have you done to yourself?'

'What do you mean?' Hettie asked him worriedly. 'I haven't done anything.'

'Yes you have.' He grabbed hold of her and turned her round so that she could see her own reflection in the mirror behind them.

'Look at yourself,' he instructed her. 'Look at your skin,' he persisted when Hettie gave him a puzzled look.

'My skin? Jay, I don't understand.'

'It's dark . . . *brown*. Like a . . .' His mouth compressed and he shook his head as though unable to trust himself to say any more. Then he released her and walked away, only to turn round and tell her bitterly, 'Don't you know what you look like with your skin that colour?'

'It's the fashion,' Hettie protested. 'Coco Chanel says . . .'

'I don't give a damn what some bloody French

dressmaker might say. Where I come from a woman's white skin is more important – of more *value* – than her virtue.'

'Her white skin?' Hettie repeated as she struggled to understand why Jay should get in such a state of fury simply because she had been sunbathing.

'Come with me,' Jay ordered, taking hold of her arm and almost dragging her into the salon where he picked up a copy of the *New York Times*, and turned over a few pages before thrusting it beneath her nose. 'Read this,' he told her furiously.

Apprehensively Hettie began to read the article he was showing her which reported that a 'black' boy had been tortured and then burned at the stake for allegedly raping a white woman.

By the time she got to the end of the article, Hettie was crying and shaking with shocked, numbing anguish. It was one of the most awful things she had ever heard.

'Do you know why they did that to him, Hettie?' Jay demanded. Without waiting for her to answer he told her, 'They did it because he was "black" and she was white. Do you think they would have done the same thing to a white man who had been accused of raping a black woman?'

'Jay, it's horrible . . . awful. That such a dreadful thing should have happened, I agree it's terrible. But what has this to do with us and my . . . me?' she asked him.

'I've told you about my family history, Hettie. Where I come from, a woman with brown skin is deemed to come from slave stock. The richest men in New Orleans want to be seen with only the palest skinned women.' He paused and then looked away from her before saying in low voice, 'I loved the pale milk whiteness of your skin.'

Hettie could feel the hot tears burning her eyes. 'It's only a suntan,' she told him, trying to smile as she added, 'It isn't for ever and if I don't sunbathe any more then it will go away.'

But something inside her was hurting very badly. If Jay was not married would he still only want her as his mistress because of the colour of her skin? Because of her mixed race heritage? Suddenly Hettie was seeing the superficiality of Jay, of his world, and she didn't like it, not one bit.

'Ralphie, darling, do please let me introduce John to you. John is the wicked unkind person who refused to give me flying lessons,' Polly announced as the tall young man standing at her side inclined his head a little awkwardly in John's direction.

He was, John admitted, a strikingly handsome boy and it was obvious from the way he was looking at her that he adored Polly. But it worried John to see the almost desperate determination in Polly's eyes as she smiled back at him and then turned to John to say, 'Ralphie has proposed to me, John, and I have accepted his proposal, so even if I cannot lay claim to being a lady, I shall at least become a countess. John, do you think I shall make a good one?'

It was plain to John that Polly's comments were embarrassing her companion, but etiquette prevented him from doing anything other than remaining where he was, and inclining his own head slightly as he said formally, 'May I offer my congratulations, Your Grace.'

Immediately Polly gave a peal of laughter. 'Oh John, how absurd you sound, and besides, Ralphie is not a "Your Grace" as yet since his grandfather is still alive. But see, he has given me the most beautiful ring.'

Still smiling she displayed the huge emerald surrounded by sparkling diamonds which flashed on her wedding ring finger.

'I say, Polly,' John could hear her new fiancé protesting awkwardly.

'Oh, it's all right, Ralphie, John isn't merely employed by my brother. He is one of Alfie's friends as well.'

She was fitting a cigarette into an elegant holder, and immediately Ralph Lascelles leaped up to light it for her, his movements as eager and awkward as those of a young untrained puppy.

'Now come along, darling, you've spent enough time here talking with your chums,' Polly chided him. 'And I'm taking you to that new roadhouse tonight. Remember?'

They had almost reached the door to the

clubhouse when it opened to admit one of John's least favourite pupils.

Sir Percival Montford was a heavily built middle-aged man with cold, too pale blue eyes and a ruddy complexion. He treated all those he considered lower down the social scale than himself so unpleasantly that he never managed to keep any staff for more than a year. He was both a heavy drinker and a heavy gambler, and some very unpleasant rumours about him had begun to circulate, suggesting that he was not always honourable in both his dealings at the card table and his treatment of women.

Although not married himself, it seemed that he preferred the company of married women to that of single young ladies, and, like any other man, John had drawn his own conclusions from the gossip he had heard about him. Alfie had mentioned to him that he would have liked to have barred Sir Percival from joining the flying club, but had felt it was not politic to do so.

'Dashed difficult to prove anything against him, what!' had been his rueful comment.

Now as Sir Percival walked into the club, he looked immediately at Polly and seemed about to step in front of her until she moved quickly to her new fiancé's side, tucking her hand through his arm whilst giving Sir Percival a defiant look. But John, who was standing to one side of them, saw that beneath her defiance she was afraid.

He was probably worrying unnecessarily about

Polly, John tried to reassure himself, but she was still in his thoughts later in the day when the oppressive heat had driven him out of his small office in an attempt to find somewhere cooler.

The sky was a brassy shade of intense blue. He had a free afternoon and suddenly more than anything else he wanted to be up there where there were no limits and complications, just the never-ending magic of the thrill of flight.

'Gawd but it's 'ot.' Aggie puffed. 'Anyone fancy coming to Hyde Park with me?'

Jenny and Jess shook their heads, giggling as they looked at one another and then explained that they were spending the afternoon with two admirers.

'What about you, Ettie?'

Hettie also shook her head. Ever since Jay's outburst about her tan earlier in the week she had been doing her best to keep out of the sun and to return her skin to its previous pearly translucence. She had even gone to trouble of rubbing handfuls of salt into her skin until it glowed red and stung in an effort to rub the tan away. But deep down inside herself, Hettie knew that Jay's horrified reaction to her suntan had left her feeling upset and very unhappy.

She had been brought up in a home where it was the kind of person you were inside that mattered, not the way you looked on the outside. She wanted to please Jay, of course she did, but somehow what she was now doing was rubbing a little sore place inside her heart.

They were saying in the papers that the country was having the highest May temperatures for fifty years, and the air in the small room Hettie was sharing with Babs was stifling, even with the window opened to its widest extent.

Outside in the street she could hear an ice-cream man crying his wares, and her mouth watered.

She was half way down the stairs when the front door opened and Mary came rushing in, her head bent, oblivious to Hettie's presence until Hettie spoke to her.

'What are you doing here? I thought you'd all be in the park,' Mary exclaimed.

'It's too hot for me,' Hettie fibbed. 'I was just going to get myself an ice. Do you fancy one? Mary, what is it, what's wrong?' she demanded urgently when she saw that Mary was crying.

'Nothing . . . Nothing's wrong,' Mary told her fiercely, but Hettie could tell she was lying.

Mary had pushed past her and continued to hurry up the stairs, though, before Hettie could challenge her. Hettie hesitated in the hallway, wanting to go after her, but longing for the cooling freshness of an ice-cream.

Opening the front door she hurried to the end of the street where the ice-cream cart was stopped, and asked the smiling Italian man who was watching her to put two helpings of ice-cream, instead of one, into the bowl she was holding out to him.

'Want to share it with me?' he asked her with a wink.

'No thanks, my friend is waiting for me to get back,' Hettie told him firmly, handing over her money and taking the bowl from him.

Mary's room was on the floor above her own and Hettie hesitated outside the door before knocking on it and then turning the handle as she announced, 'It's only me, Mary. I've got us some ice-cream, but you'll need your own spoon. Oh Mary, whatever's to do?' she asked anxiously as she walked into the room and found Mary lying on her bed, crying her eyes out.

'Go away, will yer?' Mary told her, but Hettie ignored her and instead sat down on the side of the bed.

'Mary, whatever's to do?' she repeated gently. And don't tell me nothing,' she added firmly. 'Because it's as plain as plain that there is something and I'm not leaving here until you tell me what it is.'

Mary sat up, still crying. 'It's 'im, His bleedin' Lordship,' she revealed bitterly. 'He's only gorn and got himself engaged to some toff's daughter, that's all. I've seen it in the papers.'

'What? But . . . What do you mean, Mary? He's engaged to you,' Hettie protested. 'There must be a mistake.'

'Oh, there's no mistake. Went round to his rooms meself, I did. 'E weren't for letting me in at first, but I told him I'd scream the place down

417

unless 'e did. Seems that the others were right all along, 'Ettie,' Mary told her in between her tears. 'And all 'e wanted from me were a bit of fun. Told me I were a fool if I'd ever thought someone like 'im, would marry someone like me. Said that it had been arranged when they was kids that he and this Lady Arabella would be getting married. Oh, 'Ettie. Wot am I going to do? The others will laugh themselves sick when they 'ere about it, especially Aggie.'

'No they won't, Mary.' Hettie tried to comfort her, but she could see that Mary didn't believe her.

'Broken me 'eart, he has,' she told Hettie forlornly. 'Not that 'e bleedin' well cares.' She had flung herself full length on the bed and started crying again.

'Well, if you asks me it were obvious from the start what were going to 'appen, and Mary were daft for thinking he would marry her,' Aggie pronounced.

They were all at the theatre – apart from Mary herself, who had said she had a bad headache and felt too sick to go to rehearsal.

'Well, she might have brung it on herself, but that doesn't stop me from feeling sorry for her,' Jess put in.

'Me neither,' her twin agreed.

'Well,' appen you're right,' Aggie agreed, softening. 'But let this be a warning to you, 'Ettie,' Aggie urged. 'They're all the same, these toffs, and just because Jay Dalhousie is an American that don't mean that he's any different. And what's more, he's married already.'

'Oh, there's no point in talking to 'Ettie, Aggie,' Babs chipped in, tossing her head. 'She thinks she's a cut above the rest of us now.'

'Babs, that isn't true,' Hettie protested unhappily.

'Yes it is,' Babs snapped back immediately. "As she told the rest of you yet that she's movin' in to her own place?' she asked whilst Hettie's skin coloured up, betraying her instantly.

'Singing lessons. Dinner at the Ritz nearly every bloody night. Now your own lodgings. We wasn't born yesterday, you know, 'Ettie,' Babs told her sharply.

'Your own house? And you never said so much as a word about it to us, 'Ettie,' Jessie reproached her.

'It isn't definite . . . about the house,' Hettie protested guiltily. 'Jay only mentioned it the other day . . .'

'Oh, it's "Jay" now, is it?' Babs mocked her unkindly.

Why was Babs treating her like this? Hettie wondered miserably.

'Not that I cares wot you do because I'm going back to Liverpool,' Babs announced with a toss of her head. 'Given in me notice, I have, and I'm leavin' at the end of the week.' She looked down at her left hand and twisted her small engagement ring.

'You're missing your Stan, that's what it is, isn't it?' Aggie guessed immediately.

'So what if I am? We don't all want to be bloody famous singers, you know . . .'

''Ere, Babs. There's no call to go flying orf the handle wi' me,' Aggie objected.

'Mebbe not,' Babs agreed grudgingly, giving Hettie a cold and pointed look.

Hettie had to wait until bedtime to speak privately with Babs. Her friend's sharp words to her had hurt, but where previously she had been reluctant to raise the subject Hettie now felt that she didn't want them to part without at least making an attempt to find out what had gone wrong between them.

Babs had undressed in silence, blocking all Hettie's attempts to talk to her, and now that they were both in bed Hettie took a deep breath and begged her anxiously, 'Babs, I thought you and me were friends, but . . .'

'So did I, 'Ettie. But you've changed,' Babs told her sharply. 'You aren't the girl you was in Liverpool, and if you ask me it's all on account of you gettin' a bit above yourself, and thinking you're too good for the rest of us now.'

'Babs, I don't think that,' Hettie insisted humbly. 'Honest . . .'

'Yes you do. You don't want to be bothered with us any more. You wouldn't even come to 'Yde Park with us yesterday.'

'But that was because . . .' Hettie began eagerly and then stopped. Things *had* changed, she admitted sadly, because now she felt reluctant to expose herself by telling Babs what Jay had said to her, whereas once Babs would have been the first person she would have taken her fears to. But how could she now when Babs had made it so obvious that she disapproved of Hettie's relationship with Jay?

'I know what it was "because" of, 'Ettie,' Babs told her. 'I've seen it 'appen before. Me own cousin were just like you. Started orf in the chorus together, we did, and then the next thing was she didn't want anythin' more to do wi' me because she'd been given a solo spot. That full of herself, she was, she couldn't get 'er head through the door it had got that swelled.'

'I didn't know you cousin was on the stage. Where is she now, Babs?' Hettie asked her.

Babs gave a bitter laugh. 'I don't know. Last I 'eard of her, she'd run off wi' some chap from Manchester. Good riddance an' all, if you ask me. I saw the way you was lookin' down your nose at my Stan, 'Ettie.'

'Babs, no. I didn't . . .'

'Yes you did. At Christmas when he asked if you wanted ter sit on his knee. Turned yer back on 'im, you did, and walked orf with yer nose in the air.'

Hettie stared at her. 'But that was because . . .' She broke off, recognising that she could not tell this new Babs who had taken the place of her friend that she had refused Stan's offer of his knee as a seat because she hadn't wanted her friend to think she was flirting with her man.

An aching sense of loss filled Hettie. Was *this* the price she was going to have to pay for success? The loss of her friends? Her family? Her identity? She gave a small shiver of apprehension.

Reluctantly John acknowledged that with the light already fading it was time for him to return to the flying club. The sky was a miraculous colour of deep dense blue fading away to palest lemon against the horizon where the sun was setting. It had been a perfect afternoon for flying, and he had ached to have his camera and a co-pilot so that he could have captured the beauty of it all.

He missed the life he had lived in Preston, he acknowledged as he brought the small plane down safely and taxied her to a standstill. The more gentle pace of his old life there may have brought him less money but it had also allowed him time for his photography; time to be with his family and his friends.

The harsh, agonising pain and guilt of Jim's death had eased to a more bearable sense of sadness and loss, which was ironic, he admitted, because the feelings of sadness and loss he felt with regard to Hettie had actually intensified.

The ground staff had all gone home for the day, and the airfield was deserted. John did not normally mind the solitude of his own company, but tonight the warmth of the balmy air, the sense of summer coming, and life flowering all around him made him sharply aware of his loneliness.

There was a small pub on the other side of the village, which somehow reminded him of The Lamb and Shepherd, an ancient drovers pub on the outskirts of Preston and a favourite haunt of his late father and uncle.

The Pride children's Uncle Will had been a real character – a sheep drover who had kept two families, one in Preston and another close to Lancaster.

John grinned to himself as he got into his motor and started the engine. Their mother had thoroughly disapproved of her disreputable brother-in-law, but John had loved him. It had been through Uncle Will that Gideon had brought John his first and much longed for collie pup.

Boys and pups, they were meant to be together, John reflected ruefully as he drove down the now darkening country lanes. He still missed Rex, the collie pup Gideon had given him when he was ten, even though the dog had gone to his rest over four years ago now.

Overhead the full moon was illuminating the landscape with soft silver blue light, the sky a vast bowl of darker blue broken up by the various stars and their constellations.

John had been keenly interested in astronomy as a boy. Will Pride had had every countryman's knowledge of the stars and their movements, which he had passed on to his nephew, and later John had spent many happy hours studying them through the telescope owned by the photographer for whom he had worked. As a little girl Hettie had loved looking up at the sky and listening to him whilst he taught her the names of the great constellations. Hettie . . . Would she never leave his thoughts?

The public house was only a couple of miles outside the village, and as John stopped his car he saw Polly and Sir Percival Montford standing several yards away from him beside their own motors, so engrossed in the argument they were obviously having that neither of them had seen him.

Polly with Sir Percival? What were they arguing about and why were they meeting here at this remote country public house?

Sir Percival had started to walk away and John watched as Polly ran after him, obviously still arguing with him. But Sir Percival pushed past her. She then turned round and started to walk towards her roadster, getting into it and immediately starting the engine and driving off in her normal dashing way, leaving Sir Percival to stare after her before getting into his Daimler and driving off in the opposite direction.

What was going on? Why should Polly, who John had seen making her dislike of Sir Percival all too plain, be meeting him here?

It was none of his business, John said to himself.

Polly had a fiancé now to protect her and look after her. But somehow worrying about her and feeling protective towards her had become a habit he couldn't break, John acknowledged ruefully half an hour later as he tucked into the steak and ale pie the landlady had brought him.

TWENTY-SEVEN

Even though they had not parted as the close friends they had once been, Hettie still missed Babs. The small room they had shared felt empty without her, and Hettie – to her own chagrin – had even found that at bedtime she was chattering out loud about the events of her day, just as though Babs were still there.

Her skin had almost returned to its normal colour, and although nothing had been said between them about how angry he had been with her, Jay had been hinting to her about wanting to buy her 'something pretty', and he was also pressing her to agree to move into the house down by the river in Chelsea, which he had described as 'small and simple' but which to Hettie had seemed far too luxurious. So much so in fact that the second time Jay had insisted on taking her to view it she had actually felt uncomfortable being there.

'What is it about it you don't like?' Jay had

pressed her when she had shaken her head and cut their inspection short.

'I don't know,' she had told him honestly. 'It just feels so . . .' She had shrugged, giving up her struggle to find the words to express to him how uncomfortable the house, with its heavily flounced curtains and furnishings, its too thick rugs and its too delicate furniture, had made her feel. In the same way Hettie felt unable to explain to Jay that the rooms, with their heavy, still over-perfumed air, made her feel as though she were trapped in some kind of cage.

In Preston, in Winckley Square, the house, the home in which she had grown up, had had rooms that smelled of male tobacco and leather, rooms delicately scented with Ellie's favourite rose water, a kitchen rich with the delicious smell of cooking food, and a nursery that smelled of baby powder. All those different scents had made the Winckley Square house a home, whereas the Chelsea house felt more like a prison.

She had told Jay that she wanted to stay where she was.

'Ah, you are still angry with me, aren't you?' he had commented.

Was she? Hettie didn't really know sometimes how she felt about him now. Part of her felt dizzyingly excited and grown up, knowing that he desired her. Part of her felt thrilled and shocked because of the eager curiosity he made her feel to break the rules she had been brought up with and give herself to him. But part of her, too, shrank from that, especially now after what had happened to Mary. And yet another part of her, perhaps the most important one of all, couldn't stop thinking of John and the stolen kiss.

'No, I'm not angry,' she had told him. 'But . . .'

'But what?' he had challenged her.

'But maybe we should wait until we go to New York to live together,' she had answered him.

'Do you realise how cruel that would be?' he had asked her softly. 'I don't know if I can wait that long for you, my little Hettie. My body is so hungry for your sweetness,' he had told her, and then shockingly he had taken hold of her hand and placed it firmly against his body.

The great throb of that most male part of him beneath her nervous fingers had sent a burn of colour up over her skin that had remained even after Jay had allowed her to snatch her hand away.

So much was changing so very fast, Hettie acknowledged uneasily as she crossed Trafalgar Square, making her way past a brewery dray pulled up outside a public house. The landlady, plump arms akimbo, was standing over a thin skivvy, watching her scrub the stone step. Hettie gave a small sigh, thinking of Liverpool where its house-proud women not only scrubbed their front steps but donkey-stoned their edges as well to make them look white.

Shaftesbury Avenue and Drury Lane were

always busy at this time of the morning – not with theatre goers, of course, but with delivery boys on their bicycles, theatre workers yawning their way to early rehearsals, landlords and restaurateurs setting their premises to rights for the day and evening's trade, and, of course, the area's night-shift workers making their way home. Hettie quickly averted her gaze from the sight of a still drunken prostitute lurching along the pavement. The girl, although only around Hettie's own age, had open running sores around her mouth and bruises on her too thin arms. She also had a small baby in her arms, and on a sudden impulse Hettie stopped and opened her purse, turning back to give the girl a few pennies.

The blank eyes widened and the girl stared at Hettie in disbelief.

'For the baby. Buy it some milk,' Hettie told her quickly before hurrying away.

She had no idea what had prompted her action. Many of the area's prostitutes were loud mouthed and sometimes violent, and often hurled not just insults but sometimes even missiles at the girls when they left the theatre at night.

With two of the understudies now taking the place of Sukey and Babs, two new girls had joined the troop, Londoners with sharp cockney accents who made it clear that they thought themselves a cut above the show's northerners.

Already there was a different and sometimes hostile atmosphere in the dressing room, with barbed comments being made, and antagonism crackling on the cheap-scent laden air.

Everyone was beginning to say they wanted the run to end, and since audiences were now beginning to dwindle Jay had told Hettie that he did not intend to keep the show going until the end of September, which was when the lease ran out.

If Babs had only waited another few weeks she might have been returning to Liverpool and her Stan anyway, Hettie reflected as she crossed the road and headed for the theatre and the busy dressing room where she still looked instinctively for Babs before remembering she was now hundreds of miles away.

Mary was standing several feet away from her, her whole body bristling with defensive anger as one of the other chorus girls taunted her, 'So, His Lordship is going to mek someone else Her Ladyship then, eh Mary, and not you!'

'Shut your mouth, Dinah. And keep that long ugly nose of yours out of my business, otherwise I'll be pushing it out of it for you,' Mary warned her viciously.

Dinah tossed her head and refused to be cowed, saying sneeringly, 'So much for that bloody ring you've been flashing in front of us. I'll bet it ain't even real.'

'Yes it is,' Mary told her, red faced.

'Huh. That's what you say. Here, girls, come and look at this,' Dinah called out, rummaging in her bag and producing a newspaper. 'It's all in 'ere.

An announcement of the engagement and a picture as well.'

Ignoring Mary, several of the girls pushed forward to look at the page Dinah was brandishing with such glee, whilst Hettie's heart ached for Mary. She went over to her and stood protectively at her side.

''E did love me, 'Ettie,' Mary told her quietly. ''E swore he did and he swore he were going ter marry me an' all, else I would never . . . It's that bloody mother of his wot made 'im change 'is mind. If'n I could just talk to 'im, 'Ettie. But he's refusing to see me.' Tears filled her eyes.

The hot weather seemed to have put everyone's tempers on edge, Hettie decided later when the director had called a halt to the rehearsal.

'This isn't the correct piece of scenery,' he complained angrily. 'I gave orders that it was to be changed. Where is the new piece?'

The stage manager was sent for, and whilst they were waiting for him Hettie could not help noticing how immediately and intimately Ivan had gone to talk to the young male dancer who was his constant companion. He even continued to stand with him when the stage manager arrived, ignoring the other man for several minutes before finally turning towards him.

'I gave instructions that this piece of scenery was to be repainted,' Ivan announced.

The stage manager mopped his face with a large

spotted red handkerchief. 'Yes, Ivan, I know,' he agreed. 'And I passed on your instructions.'

'So why have they not been carried out?'

The stage manager mopped his forehead again. 'Unfortunately, our set designer isn't very well at the moment.'

Hettie tensed as she listened, anxiety gripping her stomach. Eddie had been at the theatre earlier in the week because she had seen him, although not to talk to.

'Not well? You mean he is sick?'

Someone behind Hettie sniggered and muttered, 'Aye, sick from drink. He spends more time in the Flag and Drum than he does in here.'

To Hettie's relief the director was too far away to have overheard.

The young dancer tugged on the director's sleeve. Ivan bent his head towards him and the boy whispered something in his ear.

'It seems that the set designer is not so sick that he cannot leave his sick bed to carouse in every filthy drinking den between the theatre and Piccadilly Circus,' the director spat out acidly.

Eddie was well liked by those who worked with him, unlike the director, and Hettie saw how anxious and uncomfortable the stage manager looked. 'I'll send someone round to his lodgings and tell him to get here,' he offered.

'That won't be necessary,' the director told him coldly. 'But you can tell him that I intend to talk to Mr Dalhousie about his inability to do as he is told.'

The director was going to tell Jay about Eddie? Hettie exhaled slowly. Well, she too could talk to Jay about Eddie and she would make sure that Jay knew how Ivan had tormented and persecuted his former lover, flaunting his new partner in front of him and treating him so cruelly that Hettie was not surprised poor Eddie was drinking more and more.

In addition to her normal singing lesson Hettie was now also practising singing the new songs Archie had sent from America, with both Hettie and Madame sworn to secrecy because Jay did not want anyone to know what he was planning to do.

With so much to learn it was no wonder that she was feeling tired, Hettie acknowledged as she left Madame's rooms and stepped out into the sunshine.

She was meeting Jay for lunch, having persuaded him that instead of eating in a restaurant they should picnic in Hyde Park.

'Picnic? Why on earth would we want to do that?' he had complained.

'Because its fun,' Hettie had told him determinedly, even though a part of her had recognised that Jay in his elegant town clothes would not be comfortable sprawling on Hyde Park's dusty grass in the same way that John would have been. So she was not entirely surprised when Jay ushered her past the entrance to the park and towards an elegant café instead.

'I'm sorry I was a bit late meeting up with you,' he told her as he summoned a waiter. 'Ivan wanted to see me.'

Hettie put down her menu. 'Not about Eddie?' she asked him anxiously.

Immediately Jay started to frown. 'It was connected with him, yes,' he agreed curtly. 'But such matters need not concern you, Hettie.'

'But they do concern me,' Hettie told him fiercely.

Jay put down his menu and waved away the hovering waiter. 'I'm not sure that I understand you. How can the fact that my set designer is too drunk to perform his duties in a proper manner concern you?'

There was a warning note in Jay's voice but Hettie chose to ignore it. 'It concerns me because Eddie is my friend,' she told him. 'And . . . And I happen to know that Ivan has been very unkind to him. Oh, Jay,' Hettie implored emotionally. 'I am sure that it is because of the way Ivan has been treating him that poor Eddie has been drinking so much.'

'I don't think . . .'

'Jay, please please listen to me. Poor Eddie, can you not understand that he loves Ivan so much and Ivan has been horribly cruel to him? Eddie told me that they were together in Paris, and that Ivan swore to him that he loved him and . . . Jay!' Hettie protested in bewilderment as Jay pushed back his chair and stood up, his face dark with revulsion as he threw down his napkin.

'How can you speak of such filth?' he asked her angrily. 'It is an abhorrence . . . a loathsome disgusting perversion, and those who steep themselves in its filth should not be allowed to contaminate others with their presence.'

'But Eddie loves Ivan.'

'What is this you are saying?' Jay demanded savagely.

'Eddie loves Ivan, and now Ivan has taken one of the dancers to his bed and poor Eddie is inconsolable,' Hettie repeated stubbornly.

'He has dared to tell you that? For that alone in Orleans he would be horsewhipped. You will never, ever mention such a subject again. You do realise that these unnatural practices are forbidden by law, I trust?'

Hettie was bewildered by Jay's reaction. He was making her feel as though *she* had done something wrong, but everyone in the theatre knew that the law he spoke of was constantly being broken.

'You are speaking as though you didn't know about, about men like Ivan and Eddie, but you must have done,' Hettie defended herself spiritedly. 'Everyone who works in the theatre knows of such men.'

'Everyone may know of them, Hettie, but that does not mean that their vile way of life should be condoned. I certainly do not condone it. If I had my way they would have their wretched perversion beaten out of them,' Jay told her in disgust.

435

Hettie didn't know what to say. She had never imagined that Jay would be so cruelly unkind. John, she knew instinctively, would have shown far more compassion. Shockingly her eyes suddenly misted with tears.

'Now let us have an end to this matter,' she heard Jay saying forcefully as he re-summoned the waiter.

Hettie shook her head, refusing to take a menu. 'I'm not hungry,' she told him stiffly.

'John, I want you to do me a favour.'

John frowned as he looked at Polly. She had burst into his office minutes earlier, insisting that she must see him.

'What kind of favour?' he asked her.

'I want you to give this to Sir Percival Montford for me,' she told him curtly, pulling off her gloves and then opening her handbag to produce a brown paper parcel tied with string.

'I'd give it to him myself only I've got to drive over to Oxford to pick up my darling Ralphie. His mother wants to see me and he wants to come with me to protect me because she is such a dragon. Too sweet of him.' She laughed but John could tell that her laughter was strained.

He looked at the parcel she had placed on his desk and then at her. 'Polly,' he began uneasily. 'I know it is none of my business but this . . . friendship that has developed between you and Sir Percival . . .'

'Friendship?' What . . . what do you mean?' she demanded.

John looked down at his desk and then at her.

Had she not approached him like this he would probably not have said anything about what he had seen, but since she had . . .

'I saw you and Sir Percival Montford together at the public house outside the village.'

'No, you couldn't have done,' she denied immediately. Then she shook her head and began to laugh wildly. 'Dear God, John.' She broke off and sank down into the chair next to his desk, covering her face with her hands as she wept. 'Oh John, I am in the most dreadful fix . . .'

'What kind of fix?' John asked her.

'I have done the most dreadful thing, but I cannot tell you about it. I cannot tell anyone.'

'Not even Lord Ralph?' John questioned gently.

'Especially not him. He must *never* know about any of this. John, you haven't said anything to anyone about about seeing me with . . . with *him*, have you? Please tell me you have not.'

'Polly, what . . .'

'No, you are not to ask me any questions. I forbid you to do so. I cannot bear it. I cannot . . . Especially not about *him*.' Polly shuddered and then said in a low tortured voice, 'Now I cannot even bear to say his name and yet . . .'

'Polly, I hate to see you so distressed. If you cannot tell Lord Ralph what is upsetting you, then surely there must be someone who can help you? Your brother?'

'Alfie? No, never.' She made a small violent movement and the brown paper parcel slid from the desk on to the floor.

Automatically John bent to retrieve it, but the string had become dislodged and as he picked it up he saw to his shock that the parcel contained bank notes.

He looked up at Polly, unable to conceal his feelings, and saw that she was looking back at him. 'Polly . . .'

'I have to give him the money, John,' she whispered. 'He told me that if I do not he will tell . . .'

Her lips were trembling so much she could barely speak.

'He is *blackmailing* you?' John guessed, appalled.

Polly nodded her head.

'But . . . Why? How?' John demanded and then frowned as he wondered if perhaps Polly had confided to Sir Percival in an unguarded moment the same private secret she had told him. If so . . .

'John, please, don't be shocked or turn away from me,' she begged him, white faced. 'I have been so very silly but I was so lonely, and he seemed kind at first. And fun. And then Alfie went all stuffy and told me that he was not considered the thing and was a "bit of a bad egg".' She mimicked her brother. 'Well, you know that I can't resist a challenge, John, and how I hate being told what to do.' She lifted her chin defiantly. 'So I thought . . .'

She paused and bit her lip as she looked away from him. 'He invited me to have dinner with him, and I agreed. We arranged that I would go up to London and foolishly I imagined . . .' She looked down at her lap and then twisted her hands together agitatedly before suddenly touching her engagement ring as though it were some kind of talisman.

'He met me from the station and he was driving the most beautiful roadster, John. I begged him to let me drive it, and he said that he would, but that first he wanted to show me something.

'I thought he was just taking me to see some famous sight or other, but he took me to this house . . .' She gave a small shudder. 'I should never have gone inside. I wasn't going to but then he asked me if Alfie had warned me against him and of course after that I *had* to prove to him that I could do as I pleased.

'He took me into the house, a dreadfully small shabby little place in Chelsea, of all places. Everyone knows that that is where men house their mistresses,' she added disparagingly. 'He made us both drinks. I can't remember how many we had. And then he said that he would have to get changed before we went out for dinner. And then . . .' She looked at him and John knew without her having to tell him what had happened.

'He didn't force me, John,' she told him unsteadily. 'I *could* have left. I *should* have left. But I had had so much to drink and . . . It was horrid. Awful. And I felt so . . . I couldn't bear to look at my darling Ollie's photograph afterwards. I felt so ashamed of myself, John.' Tears were rolling down her cheeks. 'I told him that it must never happen again but he just laughed at me and he kept on . . . And that was when I decided that the only way I could save myself was by marrying Ralphie.

'But now Sir Percival is threatening to tell Ralphie's family everything unless I pay him five hundred pounds.' She paused. 'He told me to take the money to our old rendezvous at the road house tomorrow evening, but I just can't. I don't want to. I'm so afraid of him now, John, and of what he might try to make me do. Please say that you will give him the money for me? I know he comes here most days, and you are the only person I can ask. I know what you must be thinking about me, but please don't judge me too harshly.'

'Oh, Polly.' John reached for her and took her in his arms, holding her as carefully as though she were made of glass. He ached with compassion for her and with savage anger against the man who was trying to destroy her.

'I must go. Ralphie will be waiting. He telephoned this morning to say that he wanted to see me urgently before we go to see his mother. The poor darling probably wants to remind me not to smoke in front of her. She's frightfully strait-laced, John, and I don't think she aproves of him marrying me at all. But he is so sweet, isn't he? And so very like my darling Ollie.'

This was not the time to question the wisdom of her marriage, John acknowledged. She already had more than enough to bear.

'You will see Sir Percival and give him the money for me, John, won't you?' She begged him again as she pulled on her gloves.

'Yes,' he assured her.

'And you will never, ever mentioned what . . . what we have talked about again, to anyone, not even to me?'

'Never,' he told her.

'Oh, John.' There were fresh tears in her eyes as she leaned forward and brushed her lips against his chin, and then she was gone in a flurry of silk and scent, the tiny veil of her hat pulled down to shield her face as she stepped out into the sunshine and hurried back to her roadster.

Such happy news we have had from Iris, love. Not that I had any concerns, for I am feeling so very well. Mind you, your father was delighted when she assured us that everything is just as it should be and that we can expect your new brother or sister to be born on the due date.

We had planned to come down this month to see you in your show, but your father felt that this excessive heat we have been having might be too much for me. He is writing to John today with some good news for him as well. Someone from the government has been in touch with Gideon making enquiries about John's airfield. It seems that the Royal Air Force are interested in buying the land from them.

Oh Hettie, love. I am so very happy – the only thing missing to make life perfect here in Winckley Square is you. I miss you so much and would love to have you here with me now. But I must not be selfish. You have your singing and I know now how much it means to you.

If we can't get down to London to see you before the baby arrives, could you perhaps come home to see us? I miss you so much, Hettie.'

Your Loving Mother.

Hettie had read the letter Ellie had sent her over and over again, and as she wiped the tears from her eyes she told herself stoutly that they were tears of happiness and relief and not tears of misery or despair.

She missed her family and especially Ellie more than she wanted to admit – even to herself. She was, Hettie acknowledged, beginning to under-stand why Babs had given up her place in the chorus to return to Liverpool and Stan.

She had begun to long for Ellie's next letter as soon as she had received the previous one, and she had taken to telephoning home twice a week instead of once.

Gideon and Ellie had both assured her that Ellie was perfectly well and that there were no fears for either her safety of that of her baby, but it wasn't just her anxiety that made her long to see her, Hettie admitted. She missed Ellie in so many different ways, and she hadn't even told her family yet about Jay's decision, and that she was going to be leaving England in a few weeks' time to travel to America and New York. She had been planning to tell them about it when they came to see her, but she could well understand why Gideon had not wanted to risk bringing Ellie to London whilst it had been so very hot.

Ellie's baby was due early in July, and would be born whilst she was in New York. Fresh tears filled Hettie's eyes. Suddenly more than anything else she wanted to be in Winckley Square. So much so that her longing for Ellie was a physical pain.

Ellie and Gideon would be so shocked if they knew of the future Jay was planning for her. She could always refuse him, of course, but did she really want to? She was being offered a once-in-a-lifetime opportunity. And it wasn't as though she was going to New York for ever, Hettie comforted herself. Jay was already talking about bringing the new show over to England once it had achieved success on Broadway.

'But Jay, what if it isn't a success?' Hettie had asked him worriedly. 'What if no one in America likes me?'

'America won't *like* you, Hettie,' Jay had answered her steadily, and her heart had lurched against her ribs as she wondered if he had been having second thoughts about her. And then he had given her a wide smile and had laughed as he told her, 'Hettie, America will *love* you. Just as I already do,' he had added softly, leaning forward in the privacy of his suite to kiss the vulnerable spot just beneath her ear, where his touch made her long to throw herself into his arms and beg him to do whatever he wished with her, despite her misgivings about him.

'I have booked us adjoining suites for our Atlantic crossing, little Hettie,' he had whispered to her, and Hettie had known that if at that moment he had swept her up into his arms and carried her through to his bedroom she would not have made one single word of protest. Or denial.

But he had not done so, and later, tucked up in her narrow single bed, she had admitted to herself that as much as she had been disappointed then in the heat of her excitement, now she was relieved.

Part of her problem was that without Babs she had no one to whom she could talk, or in whom she could confide; no one from the world she now inhabited who might have helped her with its unfamiliar rules and mores.

Very carefully Hettie folded Ellie's letter. She had neither a rehearsal nor a music lesson this morning for the very important reason that Jay had cancelled both on her behalf because he was taking her for lunch and then, or so he had said, he was going to take her to Bond Street so that he could buy her a gown grand enough for the dinner party he was giving at the Ritz after their final show, and to which he had invited all manner of important theatrical people.

'You will be my hostess that evening, Hettie,' he had told her firmly. 'My hostess, my leading lady, and my love.'

Tucking Ellie's latest letter inside the box where she kept the others, Hettie opened her bedroom door. Mary was coming up the stairs in a terrible state of distress, clinging to the bannister rail as though she didn't have the strength to walk. She was as white as a sheet, and tears were pouring down her face.

'Mary, what is it?' Hettie demanded anxiously, immediately rushing to her aid, putting her arm around Mary's waist as she helped her.

'Oh gawd, 'Ettie,' Mary gulped as Hettie helped her into her own room. 'I dunno what's to become of me.'

'You'll find someone else to love you, Mary.' Hettie tried to comfort her but Mary shook her head and laughed wildly.

'It's not that, 'Ettie,' she said fiercely. 'I'm carrying . . .'

'Carrying?' Blankly Hettie looked at her, but her hand had slipped from Mary's waist to the tell-tale small bulge.

'I'm up the spout, 'Ettie,' Mary elaborated. 'Dun for, and no mistake. And there 'im as wot's responsible for it won't even let me tell 'im that I'm 'aving his brat, never mind . . . Oh gawd, gawd, 'Ettie. I'm showing already and I've bin that sick.'

The two girls looked at one another.

'But surely His Lordship will do *something* for you, Mary?' Hettie whispered, both shocked and horrified.

'Not 'im. No, there's only one thing for it, 'Ettie, I'm going to have to get rid of it, and the sooner the better.'

'Get rid of it?' Hettie looked at her. 'You mean, you will give your baby to a foundling hospital for adoption, Mary?'

'No! If'n I have me way there won't be no baby,' Mary told her bluntly, and then added shakily, 'Poor little bastard 'ud be better off not being born anyway. Me Mam won't have me back 'ome, no way. Married again after me Da died, she did, and him as she's married . . .' Mary's face closed up. 'Seems like he thought his marriage licence gave him the right to 'ave me as well as 'er. Well, I soon let him know where 'e could get off, but me Mam went spare, called me a liar and a slut, she did.' Fresh tears filled Mary's eyes. 'Said as 'ow I were mekkin' it up and threw me out, she did. Fourteen, I were.'

'Oh, Mary.' Hettie's own eyes were full of tears now as well.

Emotionally the two girls hugged one another.

'I wish that Babs was here,' Hettie told Mary.

'Why? There's nuffink she could do. There's this doctor as I've heard about, 'Ettie. From one of the other girls.'

Releasing Hettie, Mary stepped back from her and started to twist the diamond ring on her right hand. 'Expensive he is an' all, but 'e's supposed to be good. Doesn't mek any mistakes, and doesn't leave yer butchered and bleedin' to death like some of 'em do, if you knows what I mean.'

Hettie didn't, at least not entirely, although she was beginning to guess what Mary meant.

'Mary, you can't mean . . . you aren't thinking,' she began, horrified.

But Mary didn't let her get any further. 'I've got no choice, 'ave I?' she demanded bitterly. 'Who's going to give a part to a chorus girl with a nine-month belly on her? No one, that's who! And I ain't goin' back 'ome to end up in the bleedin' factory and 'avin' everyone knowing. He would 'ave married me, 'Ettie, I know 'e he would. It's his family as won't let him. And if he had married me then this in 'ere would be going to be born a little lord or lady,' she told Hettie savagely. 'But he ain't married me and this what he's put in here, ain't going to be born.'

'Oh Mary, surely he will do something to help you?' Hettie protested.

'Not 'im. Not now. Too scared of his family, he is. Gorn away to stay with his fiancée's family, he has. It's in all the papers.

'No, 'Ettie, me mind's made up. Bin thinkin' about it all week, I have. I reckon if I pawn his ring then I should 'ave more than enough to pay this doctor to get rid of his brat for me.' Mary tossed her head defiantly. 'Going to see the pawn-broker this afternoon, I am, and then . . .' Mary shrugged. 'At least this doctor as I've heard about knows his stuff. Lots of theatre girls 'ave been to 'im and none the worse for it. If you ask me it certainly beats drinking a bottle of gin and jump-ing off the top of the stairs,' she added grimly.

'Maybe there's another way,' Hettie wondered shakily. She hadn't forgotten how the loss of her baby had affected Ellie – how could she ever forget it? And yet here was Mary talking about her coming baby as though she hated it, and talking about doing something that Hettie knew would be a terrible risk legally and physically.

Mary laughed bitterly. 'Like what? I don't want to be loaded down with a bastard brat anyway. Bloody nuisance it would be. No. I've made up me mind, 'Ettie. I just think 'Is bloody Lordship should be the one as has to pay for it and not me, that's all.'

'Mary, please don't do it. When are you going to see this doctor?' Hettie asked, thinking swiftly that maybe she could offer to go with Mary and try to dissuade her.

Mary hesitated and then told her dismissively, 'I don't know yet. And as for not doing it, like I just told ycr I 'avcn't got any choice, and see 'ere, 'Ettie, don't you go blabbing about this to anyone else. Especially not yer own chap. I've got enough to worry about wi'out losing me job as well. And mind as how the same thing don't 'appen to you an' all, 'Ettie,' she added grimly.

The same thing happen to her? A shudder of terrified dread seized Hettie. Although she had been worrying about the disgrace and shame that would face her if she did become Jay's mistress, until now she had naively not even thought of the kind of consequences Mary was facing. And she did not want to think about them now, Hettie admitted. It was too frightening.

'But Mary, don't you think you should tell the other girls?' she suggested hesitantly.

Immediately Mary grabbed hold of Hettie's arm, her fingernails biting deeply into Hettie's flesh.

''Ere, 'Ettie, don't you go saying nothing to them. I've got enough on me plate without 'aving to listen to them sayin' as 'ow they knew all along sommat like this would 'appen. And besides . . .' She frowned and looked at Hettie. 'I shouldn't 'ave said anything to you about any of this, 'Ettie, and if I was you I'd forget that I 'ad. If you tek me meaning.'

'You mean about . . . about the baby?' Hettie asked her unhappily.

'Wot baby? I ain't 'aving no baby, and mek sure you remember that, 'Ettie,' Mary warned her fiercely.

By rights she ought to be enjoying her afternoon with Jay, Hettie reflected as Jay touched her arm and drew her attention to the gown displayed in the window of the Bond Street salon they were approaching, saying jovially, 'That would suit you, Hettie. Come along, let's go inside . . .'

Hettie held back and shook her head. Jay might be in high spirits, the sun might be shining, but instead of the elegant outfit in the window all she could see was Mary's tear-streaked face.

John looked at his watch. It was 9.00 p.m. and the last of the growing number of more experienced pilots who owned their own flying machines, which they kept at the airfield, had just left. Sir Percival Montford certainly wouldn't be coming into the club now, since officially it closed to non-experienced pilots at 6.00 p.m. The money Polly had left with him was safely locked away in his desk drawer.

Bitterly John acknowledged that, whilst Sir Percival might in terms of protocol be able to claim the title of gentleman, he would never be able to call himself a true gentleman. The man was an utter cad, 'a bounder', to use the term favoured by the young graduates who flocked to the club for flying lessons. And John had one or two things he intended to say to him about the kind of men who bullied and blackmailed vulnerable young women. John would have liked to see him barred immediately from membership of the flying club, but it concerned him that that might lead him to take revenge by blackening Polly's name.

Something as serious as this was really a matter for the police, but John could well understand why Polly preferred to give Sir Percival the money he was demanding. Blackmailing a woman, having forced her into an intimate relationship, must surely be the most sickening of all male crime. But, even though he would be condemned and excluded from his social circle were his behaviour ever to come to light, it would be Polly who would suffer most from the salacious gossip that would inevitably result. Even so, John hated the thought of Sir Percival getting away with what he was doing. It offended not just his friendship with Polly but his sense of justice as well.

The June evenings were light and warm, and he had a sudden nostalgic yearning to be back in Lancashire, standing atop one of its hills and looking down the length of the Ribble valley. He missed the north and its people; the easy life of indulgence he was living here in the lush richness of Oxfordshire didn't suit his northern temperament.

He missed his family, too, and his friends; what he wanted, John admitted to himself for the first time, was to go home.

The morning's post had brought him a letter

from Gideon alerting him to two offers for the airfield. One from the Royal Air Force, and the other from English Electric, who owned Dick Kerr's, Preston's tram-making business, and more famous some people liked to think for its all girls football team than for its trams.

English Electric wanted the airfield for their new flying machine construction business, and Dick Kerr's second cousin, Harold, had written to say that if John did feel like moving back up north they would be very keen to make use of his expertise.

The light was fading fast now and if he didn't make a move he would be going to bed supperless, John warned himself as he stood up and stretched.

Did Hettie, like him, miss Preston and her family? The thought caught him unawares, jarring his whole body mid-stretch.

Hettie was gone from his life and should be gone from his thoughts, too, he told himself grimly as he started to lock up. His life and his future was here, now, in Oxfordshire, where he himself had chosen it to be. He had even begun to make new friends in the nearby village. Only the previous Sunday the wife of one of the church wardens had left her bashfully blushing daughter to step up to him and invite him to have his dinner with them next week after church.

TWENTY-EIGHT

The shrill, sharp ring of the telephone that Alfred had insisted on having installed in John's quarters woke John up immediately, although it was several seconds before he realised just what had disturbed his sleep.

Getting out of bed, he hurriedly made his way to the living room, the telephone's unexpected summons far too urgent for him to waste time switching on any lights.

The minute he picked up the receiver he recognised the voice of Ethel, one of the local exchange's small team of telephone operators, telling him in relief, 'Oh, thank heavens you've answered, Mr Pride, only they want to speak to you urgent, like, up at Moreton Place.'

John could tell from Ethel's voice that she had been crying, and his stomach muscles tightened as a presentiment of bad news gripped him.

'It's His Lordship's batman who wants you,' she told him. 'I'll put him through now . . .'

There were a few faint crackles and then John heard Bates saying emotionally, 'Is that you, Mr Pride?'

All at once the fog of sleep that that been clogging his mind cleared, leaving in its place an icy cold certainly of fear and dread. Something had happened to Alfred . . .

'Yes. It's John Pride, Bates,' he confirmed. 'What's happened? His Lordship?'

'Oh Mr John.' John barely had time to register the old retainer's use of his name in a fashion that virtually included him as member of the family before Bates's broken voice continued, 'The police are here, wanting to ask some questions, and . . . and Lord Alfred's . . .' John heard him blowing his nose. 'I'm sorry to bother you, Mr John, but you was the only one we could think of and . . . None of us can . . . And . . . I was just wondering if you would mind coming up to the house?'

'Of course I will, Bates,' John assured him. 'I'll leave immediately.'

It was only as he pulled on his clothes that John realised he hadn't even asked Bates what had actually happened.

Twenty minutes later, as he pulled his small Austin to a halt outside Moreton Place, he saw that the forecourt was filled with two police cars plus a large Bentley he didn't recognise at all.

He had expected Bates to open the door to him, but instead he discovered that the front door was being guarded by a stern-faced and very large policeman, who enquired brusquely, 'And who might you be, Sir?'

The front door had opened and another, obviously more high-ranking policeman, had stepped out.

'John Pride,' John introduced himself. 'I'm an employee of Lord Alfred's. Bates, his butler, telephoned me and asked me to come over.'

'It's all right, constable,' the more senior officer announced. 'Come in, Mr Pride. Sorry about that,' he apologised as John stepped into the hallway. 'But I'm sure you understand that in a situation like this the last thing anyone wants is Fleet Street's press hounds descending on the family. Shocking business,' he added with a shake of his head. 'I'm Inspector Philpot, by the way.'

'I'm sorry, but could you tell me what exactly?' John began as he shook the hand the Inspector had extended, and then broke off as Bates came hurrying towards him. The older man had plainly been crying and looked somehow smaller and shrunken.

'His Grace is in the library, Mr John. The doctor's with him but . . .'

'If I could have have a minute of your time first, Sir?' The Inspector asked him quietly, drawing John to one side.

'It's a matter of someone having to identify the body, you see, Sir,' he explained heavily. 'According to the local doctor, His Grace is in too much of a state of distress to do it, but the staff here told us that you were well acquainted with Lady Polly. And I have to warn you that on account of the severity of the accident . . .

This couldn't be happening, John decided. He could not be standing here in Moreton Place listening to this inspector talking about Polly as 'the body'. And it couldn't be happening because if it was that meant that Polly, laughing, lively, fun-loving Polly, was dead. And surely that was impossible. She couldn't be. He had only seen her this morning. His thoughts went round and round in slow disjointed eddies.

'What . . . What do you mean?' he heard himself asking the Inspector hollowly. 'Lady Polly can't be dead.'

The Inspector had started to frown. 'Walters, bring a chair here and be quick about it,' he ordered. 'Sit down here, Sir,' he instructed John when the chair was duly produced. 'Didn't anyone explain to you what has happened?'

'No,' John told him. 'That is, Bates . . . He looked up at the Inspector. 'I only saw Polly, Lady Polly, that is, this morning and I thought . . . I'd assumed . . . I thought it was His Grace who must . . .'

'Very distressed is His Grace, Sir,' the Inspector told John. 'And quite naturally.'

'You mean it's true, then? Polly is dead?' John asked him numbly.

'I'm afraid so, Sir.'

456

What happened?' John asked.

'Motor accident, Sir.'

'A car accident,' John echoed.

'Yes, Sir. Seems like Lady Polly must have been on her way back here when it happened.'

'Back here. But she was going to Oxford to pick up her fiancé and then they were going to his home,' John protested, remembering what Polly had told him.

'Yes, Sir, I believe that was what was planned,' the Inspector agreed with a solemn expression.

Bates was hurrying towards them. 'His Grace is asking for Mr John,' he informed them.

'Excuse me, Inspector.'

As he hurried to the library John could scarcely take in what he had been told. How could Polly possibly be dead? It couldn't be true.

Alfred was seated behind his desk but he stood up the moment he saw John, exclaiming with relief, 'John, my dear chap. Thank you for coming.'

'It isn't true, is it?' John asked him. 'Polly isn't . . .'

Immediately Alfred's eyes filled with tears, and he bowed his head. 'Yes. She's gone. Dead. That bloody roadster. I always did tell her she drove too fast. I . . .'

'Steady on, old chap.' John tried to comfort him, taking hold of his arm and guiding him to one of the chairs by the fire.

'I've told the police I want her brought back here,' Alfred told him brusquely, lifting his hand to wipe the tears from his face. 'But they want me to identify the . . . her first. Damned bureaucracy. Want you to come with me, if you would, John. Can't face going by myself, don't you know. Shameful, what! Bloody coward.'

John could feel his heart slamming painfully into his chest wall. He wanted to refuse, but he knew that he couldn't. Inside his head he could see Polly as she had looked earlier in the day. He bowed his head. 'You aren't a coward, Alfred,' John assured him, his throat raw with pain.

Dawn was paling the sky to the clearest and freshest of perfect blue, the sun just starting to rise on a day filled with the promise of warmth and sunshine, when John and Alfred left the hospital. But not for Polly, John reflected bleakly. There would be no more days of sunshine and warmth for Polly, whose body they had left behind in the cold of the hospital morgue.

She had still been been wearing the dress John had seen her in that morning, her face turned towards them, one cheek upon the pillow, her eyes closed so that she might almost have simply been asleep.

Her neck had been broken by the impact of her car hitting a tree, the doctor had explained.

Alfred had been totally overcome, sobbing brokenly, as he looked at her. John had been too numb to cry at first. He had reached out for her hand, pale and so cold, and he had kissed it. It had only been when he had leaned forward to kiss her cheek, and felt the warmth of his tears on her skin, lending its deathly pallor a false life, that he had realised he too was weeping.

All Jay could talk about was New York, and Hettie was beginning to get caught up in his excitement. She had not said anything to the other girls as yet about Jay's plans, but they themselves were in high spirits following Jay's unexpected announcement that, due to a recent surge of renewed interest in *Princess Geisha*, he intended to continue the run for a further three months from the end of June.

'I thought you were going to close the show down at the end of June?' Hettie commented.

'I was,' Jay agreed. 'But like all gambling men I am superstitious,' he told her ruefully. As he signalled to the wine waiter in the Ritz's beautiful dining room, he commented, 'The Lyceum Theatre has been lucky for me, Hettie, and I want that good luck to continue, so I have decided to extend my lease on the theatre so that it will be here waiting for us when we return in triumph from Broadway. And since I am doing so, I may as well extend *Princess Geisha*'s run, although I do not expect to make as much money from it in the coming three months as I have done in the past five,' he said with a laugh.

'*Princess Geisha* has repaid my initial investment more than a hundredfold,' he told her expansively. 'And it, and you, are the best invest-ments I have ever made, Hettie. Your understudy will have to take over your part, of course. She is nowhere near as good in the role as you are, Hettie, and no doubt the audiences will be disappointed not to see you, but that will not concern us, my little love, because we shall be in New York, where we will have a success even bigger than *Princess Geisha.*'

He broke off and turned towards the waiter, who was standing waiting patiently at a discreet distance, and instructed him, 'A bottle of Moët champagne, please.'

'Tonight, Hettie, you and I are celebrating,' Jay told her, reaching across the table to take hold of her hand and squeeze it tenderly within his own, for all the world as though he were free to make such intimate gestures to her, Hettie noted.

'You and I have already brought one another good luck, Hettie. It is my belief that in New York we will create more of it.'

The champagne had been poured and was sparkling palely in their glasses.

'To us, Hettie!' Jay toasted, lifting his glass. He was holding it in the palm of his hand, caressing it almost, and when Hettie glanced at his glass he laughed softly and told her, 'Didn't you know, Hettie, that the champagne glass was originally modelled on a woman's breast? And, for that reason, whenever a man holds one he is immedi-ately filled with a longing to caress the beautiful breasts of the woman he loves in the same way that he is caressing his glass.'

As he spoke Jay's gaze dropped from her face to her own breasts, causing Hettie's heart to pitter patter frantically fast.

She was wearing a new gown that was rather more daring than anything she had ever worn before. Hettie had spotted it on a market stall close to Covent Garden. And the thin, hard-eyed stall-holder with the shrill Cockney accent had insisted that it was an exact copy of one of Worth's newest designs, and that she could make it up exactly to fit Hettie's slender frame.

All the chorus girls had their own, often jealously guarded secret sources of copied couture clothes, not the discreet 'little dressmakers' favoured by the aristocracy but cockneys, like the girl who had sold Hettie her gown.

In order for the new tube-like gowns to fit properly, young women were discarding the now old-fashioned heavy corsetry favoured by previous generations. Beneath the fine silk of her gown, with its beading and diamanté embroidery, Hettie was wearing a pair of new and very risqué silk satin French knickers, and a matching, equally shocking fine camisole top. Now with Jay looking so hotly and deliberately at her, her face burned with a mixture of confusion and excitement. She could feel her nipples tightening and pushing against the delicate fabric, and a seething molten sensation was filling her lower body.

Jay released her hand and leaned across the table to whisper wickedly to her, 'Hettie, once we are on board the liner and on our way to New York, I promise you that I am not going to be denied the pleasure of seeing your breasts as nature intended me to see them. And I won't just be looking at them, my little Hettie. I fully intend to hold them and to stroke them and to taste the sweet ambrosia of them, whilst I whisper soft kisses against the little buds of your nipples . . .'

'Jay. I . . . I would have liked to go home to see my family before we leave,' Hettie told him, deliberately changing the subject. 'I have written to tell them that I am to visit New York, of course, but . . . My step-mother is to have another child, and I would just like . . .'

Hettie had no idea why she felt so awkward and embarrassed not only discussing Ellie's pregnancy with Jay – especially when in a very few short weeks now she would be sharing the most intimate of physical relationships with him – but also about disclosing to him her feelings of love for her family. Jay never discussed his family with her, and she had never heard him speak about his sons.

'We are only going to be gone two months and you will be able to visit them when we come back, Hettie,' Jay pointed out. 'There is a great deal we need to do together before we leave. Archie has sent two more songs, and I want you to learn them before we go. I have alerted the purser to the fact that we shall be travelling and I have suggested to him that the captain may want to invite you to sing for certain specially chosen guests.'

Hettie stared at him. 'I can't do that,' she protested.

'Of course you can.' Jay laughed. 'They will love you, Hettie, and even before we reach new York they will be wanting to hear you sing. Everything is arranged now for *Princess Geisha* to open there the week after we arrive. You will, of course, be singing, and I have made sure that the press over there have seen your reviews. The whole of New York will be flocking to hear you, and then, when we open with the new musical next year, they will come back.'

Hettie hoped Jay was right. To her, it seemed an extraordinary thing to do, to take her to New York to sing there for a mere six weeks and then come back, instead of waiting to go to New York until the new musical had been fully written.

'And remember,' Jay cautioned her, 'not a word to anyone else of our plans for the new musical.'

Hettie nodded.

So far as anyone else knew she was simply going to New York to sing for six weeks whilst Jay found a suitable American singer to take over the role.

'Eddie!' Hettie smiled in pleasure. 'I haven't seen you in ever such a long time.'

'Well, you wouldn't do, would you? Eddie answered her sourly. 'After all, you're hardly ever here any more, are you?'

Hettie flushed a little at the accusatory tone of his voice.

'I've been having extra singing lessons,' she explained, her expression brightening as she continued, 'But it's good news that the run has been extended, isn't it?'

'Is it?' Eddie demanded bitterly. 'It might be for you, Hettie, but I certainly don't consider the thought of having to endure Ivan's cruelty for another three months as good news.'

'Oh, Eddie.' They had been standing in the shadows but now as someone pushed past them they had moved and a harsh beam of sunlight coming in through one of the skylights suddenly illuminated Eddie's face for Hettie to see properly. He was unshaven, and his skin looked grey, his face thinner and his eyes bloodshot. Despite the warmth of the summer air, he was shivering and Hettie couldn't help but see how much his hands shook as he tried to light a cigarette.

Everyone was talking about how much he was drinking and his frequent outbursts of drunken fury, and there was other more hushed gossip as well about his growing use of drugs.

She reached out and touched his arm, and then sucked in her breath in shock as she discovered how thin it felt beneath the sleeve of his shirt. Immediately he pulled away from her and pushed past her.

''E's going to get hisself in trouble if he doesn't watch it,' one of the girls commented darkly, whilst

Hettie watched him anxiously and then turned to look at Mary who was hurrying down the corridor towards the dressing room. As she pushed open the dressing room door, Hettie saw that she wasn't wearing her ring.

It was three days now since Polly had been laid to rest, but John still could not really believe that she was dead. A part of him was still expecting the door to open and Polly herself to come hurrying in, bringing with her laughter and excitement.

But she was dead, no matter how little he wanted to accept that fact, and he still had a duty to perform on her behalf, even though it was not the duty she had originally given him.

In his pocket was the money she had left with him. He had telephoned Moreton Place and asked Alfred if he might see him, but now as he left his parked car and approached the familiar door he admitted to himself that he was not looking forward to what lay ahead.

Sir Percival Montford had not visited the flying club since Polly's death and John had heard a rumour that he had actually left the country. True or not, he was glad that he would not be forced to endure the presence of the other man, because were he to have to do so John was not sure he could trust himself not to take him outside and quite literally beat him to a pulp.

Bates opened the door to his ring. The house was still dressed in mourning, a black ribbon attached to the door and the curtains closed.

Alfred came into the hall to shake John's hand and show him into the library.

'I wanted to give this to you,' John told him abruptly, removing the semi-wrapped money from his pocket and putting it down on Alfred's desk.

Alfred frowned as he looked at it. 'What is it?'

'It's some money that Lady Polly left with me,' John told him quietly. He took a deep breath and then continued firmly, 'She told me that it would not fit into her handbag and she asked me to keep it for her until she returned from seeing Lord Ralph.'

He had practised the lie every day since the funeral, fiercely determined not to break the confidence Polly had given him but equally determined that her money must be returned to Alfred.

'I cannot for the life of me think what Polly would be doing with so much money,' Alfred told him unsteadily. 'But I thank you for returning it to me, John. I spoke with Lord Ralph yesterday,' he added quietly. 'The poor chap is in the most dreadful state.'

John bowed his head in silence. Alfred had already told him that Lord Ralph had informed the police that he and Polly had had 'a tiff' and that she had announced that, instead of going to visit his mother, she was going to return home.

'At least now she is at peace, and with Oliver,' John told him thickly.

Alfred put his hand on John's shoulder. 'Yes, that is what I am trying to think as well. I confess to you, John, that I was not convinced this engagement of hers to young Lascelles would have worked. But he, poor fellow, blames himself, and says that if they had not quarrelled . . .'

John ached to be able to say that if anyone was to carry the blame that it should not be Lord Ralph Lascelles but Sir Percival Montford, because deep down inside himself John felt bitterly sure that the other man's relentless hounding of Polly had been the cause of her death, if only indirectly.

But for Polly's own sake he could not say so.

Hettie put down the letter she had just been reading and wiped the tears from her eyes. It was from Ellie and it contained the news of Lady Polly's tragic death.

'Her poor young fiancé is heart-broken and poor John is, as you can imagine, most affected by it,' Ellie had written.

Had John secretly loved Lady Polly? Hettie wondered compassionately as she re-read the letter and then folded it carefully and put it back in her pocket, hearing the girls coming up the stairs after their morning's rehearsal.

'Fancy coming out with us for a bite of lunch, 'Ettie?' Jenny asked, adding before Hettie could answer, ''Ere, you'll never guess as what 'as happened, will she girls?'

'What?' Hettie asked her, her mind still on John,

and more to humour Jenny than because she really wanted to know.

'It's Eddie,' Jenny told her. 'Only gone as mad as a hatter he has and . . .'

''Ere, Jenny, you don't half go round the 'ouses to tell a tale,' Aggie interrupted her. 'Let me tell her what's happened . . . There were a real to do with Eddie and Ivan this morning, 'Ettie, and Jay come down and told Eddie he 'ad to collect his things and go.'

'Yes, and that's not all,' Jenny butted in excitedly. 'Eddie only went and 'ad another screaming fit with Ivan, and then he starts throwing pots of paint all over one of the sets. Like a madman he were, weren't he, Jess?'

'Yes,' her twin agreed eagerly. 'And then he threw one at at Ivan, red paint and all, and it were dripping all over him and you know what a dandy he is! Eddie were screaming all sorts of stuff and crying like he were a girl, one minute telling Ivan as how he hated him, and wanted to kill him, and the next saying as 'ow he loved him and couldn't live wi'out him.'

Hettie went cold as she listened to the three of them describing what had happened, and how Jay had been sent for again but how Eddie had fled the theatre before Jay could have him physically ejected.

Hettie knew Jay well enough now to know how furious he would be.

'Hettie, where are you going?' one of the girls

called out as Hettie suddenly started hurrying towards the door.

'I'm going to see Eddie,' she told them.

Since it was a Saturday afternoon the city was busy, the streets filled with people, and it seemed to Hettie that in every street she turned down she was having to fight her way against the flow of people going the other way. Piccadilly Circus was indeed a circus today – a circus of trams disgorging their passengers whilst others waited to get on.

Finally Hettie managed to make her way through the tightly packed mass of people. As she bypassed the theatre she saw that a queue was already beginning to form for the matinee performance, for which she would not be needed since her understudy was now doing the afternoon performances – a fact which had caused some sideways looks to be cast in her direction, as well as several comments about 'some people getting special treatment'.

She half hesitated outside the public house she knew to be one of Eddie's favourite haunts, but as a woman on her own she could hardly enter the main bar area, and she doubted that she would find Eddie in one of the small snugs set aside for women to use. Besides, her instincts were telling her that, with Eddie in the distressed state the girls had so graphically described, he would be turned away from any public house and was more likely to have gone to ground at his lodgings.

As she made her way through the warren of interlinked and increasingly poor streets, the crowds thinned out until there was only the odd solitary beggar standing on a street corner. As always Hettie stopped to give what she could, before hurrying on.

There was no need for her to knock on the heavy door to the lodging house since it was already open, but she did have to squeeze her way past a heavily made-up and extremely odd-looking woman, who was standing in the doorway smoking, her mannerisms more those of a man than a woman, Hettie decided, and her appearance that of a pantomime dame. But despite her observations it still shocked her to hear a passerby call out, 'Wotcha, Frank,' as he walked past.

The stairway and landing were empty and the door to Eddie's room closed. Hettie knocked firmly on it and waited anxiously. Even if Eddie were here and opened the door for her, she had no idea what she was going to say to him or indeed what she could do to help him.

She was just about to knock a second time when she heard him call out, 'Who is it?'

'It's me, Hettie, Eddie,' she answered. 'Please let me in . . .'

She held her breath as she heard sounds of movement, bedsprings squeaking and then the soft shuffle of feet followed by the click of the key turning in the lock.

She turned the door handle herself without

waiting for Eddie to open the door for her and hurried inside the room.

'I take it that you've heard what's happened,' Eddie drawled as he stood back to let her in.

Hettie nodded. He was calmer than she had expected, and actually smiling, even if it was an odd, vacuous sort of smile. 'Are you all right, Eddie?' she asked him anxiously.

He seemed to be having trouble focusing on her, Hettie realised as he frowned and then blinked before telling her slowly, 'Not yet, but I am going to be soon . . . Very soon now, Hettie. You shouldn't have come here.'

'I was worried about you,' Hettie told him. 'You know that you won't be able to come back, don't you, Eddie? I'll talk to Jay but . . .'

'It's too late,' He told her. 'In fact, it's too late now for anything, Hettie.' He looked at her and started to laugh. 'Do you know, when you knocked I actually thought it might be *him* . . . I thought that somehow he might have guessed and that he would come to be with me out of remorse, if not love. Perhaps he will still come.'

He walked away from Hettie and went and sat on the bed. 'I want him to come, Hettie. I want him to be here with me when it happens. I want him to see what he has done to me. I want him to see me take that last breath and to feel my body grow cold beneath his touch. I want him to beg me not to die, to plead with me to live. To weep and tear at his clothes, to . . .'

471

A horrible, unthinkable fear had taken hold of Hettie. 'What do you mean your last breath?' she demanded urgently.

Eddie turned to look at her and gave her a shockingly sweet smile. 'I mean that I have taken steps to bring my life to an end, Hettie. It won't be long, I don't think. Already I can feel how my heart is slowing . . . Don't cry, Hettie.'

'Eddie, *what have you done*? Let me go and find a doctor . . .'

'It's too late,' he told her simply. 'No doctor can reverse what I have put in train, Hettie. The silent mercy of death is already in my veins.'

He was speaking and moving so slowly that Hettie felt her own anguished fear increase. She looked blankly at him, not understanding what he meant.

'I have taken the ultimate panacea for my pains, Hettie, and am going to join the opium eaters amongst the heavenly fields of poppies,' he told her drowsily. 'Opium is such a Machiavellian drug – take just a little and one merely enters paradise temporarily, but once paradise has been entered one longs constantly to return. Now I have ensured that this time I shall stay there for ever . . . You will not mind if I lie down, will you, Hettie? Only . . .' He stopped speaking as they both heard footsteps on the landing outside his room.

Immediately his thin face flushed and a look burned in his eyes that Hettie could hardly bear to see.

'You must go, that will be him, my beloved Ivan. I knew he would come back to me. I knew he would not leave me to die alone! Open the door for him, Hettie . . .'

Hettie had heard the footsteps continuing down the landing but she still got up and opened the door.

'Ivan!' Eddie called out feebly.

'There is no one there, Eddie,' Hettie told him.

'There must be. He must be there, Hettie . . . He must be! Ivan . . . Ivan!' Eddie was struggling to sit up but his strength was fading so rapidly that watching him was like watching water run from a leaking vessel, Hettie acknowledged in despair.

She closed the door and hurried back to the bed but, by the time she got there, Eddie had slipped into unconsciousness.

Cold and sweating at the same time, Hettie didn't know what to do. Her instinct was to run and find a doctor but some deeper awareness told her that there would be no point.

She pulled up a chair and sat down beside the bed, reaching for one of Eddie's cold hands and holding it within her own. As though her touch disturbed him, he shuddered violently and called out something in a language she could not understand, his whole body arching off the bed and then dropping back on to it so quickly that she didn't even have time to register her own horror.

This time he lay there rigidly, breathing harshly whilst Hettie trembled with shocked anxiety. She

473

wanted to leave him and find someone to help but she was afraid that he might die whilst she was gone and she didn't want to leave him to die alone. Instead she stayed where she was, praying that someone would walk past the door and that she would be able to call out to them.

But the landing remained silent, and the minutes became hours, and Eddie's breathing had become such a frail movement of his chest that several times Hettie had to rub her tired eyes to see it.

The afternoon was fading into evening when suddenly Eddie opened his eyes and called out wonderingly in the voice of a young child, 'Mama!' whilst he gripped Hettie's hand.

And then, shockingly, his breathing changed and became a raw gasp that turned to a hideous rattle followed by complete silence.

Hettie could hear men's voices outside the door. Numbly she sat staring into Eddie's still face, willing him to breathe even though she knew that he would not.

Someone was knocking on the door. Very gently she released Eddie's hold on her hand and stood up, leaning over him to gently kiss his forehead before going to open the door.

Two men she didn't recognise were standing there, both of them so femininely handsome that she knew at once what they were.

'I think Eddie is dead,' she told them, and then burst into tears.

*   *   *

It was gone ten o'clock and the streets were dark, but Hettie had refused to accept an escort back to her own lodgings. The doctor who had been sent for had confirmed Eddie's death and then asked her so many questions that her head began to ache. She had been careful, though, not to say anything to him of Eddie's admission to her that he had taken his own life. It was against both the law of the land and the law of the church for anyone to commit suicide, and so Hettie had been as circumspect as she could be, saying only that she had called to see Eddie because he was a friend and she knew he had been poorly.

Now as she stumbled into Piccadilly Circus she realised that she was trembling from head to foot. Suddenly she longed for Jay and the comfort of his presence. The comfort of his arms. On impulse, she found a hackney carriage and instructed the driver to take her to the Ritz, vaguely aware of the look he gave her and the fact that she was not dressed either for the evening or such an elegant venue.

Guessing that Jay would be in his suite, since he had told her the previous evening that he had some work to catch up on, she used the side entrance, hurrying passed the doorman on duty and summoning the lift.

The corridor leading to Jay's suite was empty, but as Hettie hurried towards the suite door, another door suddenly opened and Harvey stepped out into the corridor in front of her. Immediately Hettie froze.

'Well, well, if it isn't Jay's little song bird. And where might you be going, my pretty? he asked mock jovially as he stood in front of her, deliberately blocking her way.

'I'm going to see Jay,' Hettie told him, making to step past him, but as she did so, to her shock he took hold of her, laughing down into her shocked face as she demanded to be set free.

'What for? Jay isn't here. He's gone off to see one of his other love birds, so why don't you and me enjoy ourselves instead, eh?'

As he spoke he was pushing her into the hallway to his suite and back up against the wall, pinning her there with the weight of his body whilst he groped her breasts with his free hand, pinching at her nipples and grinning coarsely as he watched her impotent struggles to break free of him.

'Let me go, let me go.' Hettie wept as she struggled against his constraining hand.

A familiar suffocating sense of fear and loathing was spreading weakeningly through her as she remembered Mr Buchanan.

She could smell the acrid, sickeningly musky odour of Harvey's sweat, his breath a heavy rasp in her ear and the grip of his hand on her breast painful as well as terrifying.

'You can protest all you want, my little dove, but soon you will be singing a different song, and I promise you I shall make you sing it every bit as sweetly as Dalhousie.' Harvey was breathing thickly in her ear. 'Come on, stop pretending you aren't eager for me. Women like you are always eager, and I promise you I won't be ungenerous. These pretty ears of yours will look even prettier wearing a pair of diamond earrings.'

His hand was tearing at her bodice and suddenly the fabric gave way and his hard biting fingers were grabbing painfully at her breast, squeezing and kneading her tender flesh, his mouth a wet red gash of lust in the bloated flesh of his face.

'No . . .' Hettie moaned. 'No . . .'

'What the devil?'

'Jay!'

Hettie sobbed weakly in relief as she was suddenly released, her trembling fingers pulling at the torn fabric of her bodice as she ran to Jay's side.

'Don't listen to her, Jay. It was her idea.' Harvey was gabbling wildly. 'She told me she knew you weren't here and . . .'

Without a word Jay took hold of Hettie and put her to one side and then with a speed that made her blink he grabbed hold of Harvey by the fabric of his shirt and slammed him back against the wall in much the same way as Harvey had done her. Then, whilst Harvey was still standing there, Jay hit him with his bunched fist so hard that Harvey dropped to the floor.

Horrified, Hettie looked at him. There was a thin trickle of blood oozing out of his mouth.

'Jay, you've killed him,' she whispered.

'No I haven't. Are you all right?'

Hettied nodded. 'Yes, but I wouldn't have been if you hadn't saved me . . .' She was shivering and tears were rolling slowly down her face.

'Come on,' Jay encouraged her, guiding her towards his own suite. 'What exactly are you doing here, Hettie? You knew that I was going to be busy. You weren't trying to check up on me by any chance, were you?' he asked her dryly.

As he opened the suite door for her and guided her inside, Hettie shook her head and told him emotionally, 'No, of course not.'

'Then what?'

'Jay, I *had* to see you. The most dreadful thing has happened . . .'

'What dreadful thing?' He was frowning now.

'Eddie is dead.'

'*What?*' As he closed the door Hettie saw how Jay's expression had changed and hardened. 'How do you know about this, Hettie? Who told you?'

He was guiding her into the salon. Hettie stopped him and turned to him, telling him, 'No one told me, Jay. I was there with him. I'd heard about . . . about what had happened at the theatre with . . . with the scenery, and how you'd dismissed him, and I . . . I decided to go and see him. I knew where he was staying because, well, anyway, when I got there he let me in and then he told me . . .' She stopped and gulped. 'He told me that he was going to die and that he taken something . . . opium. Oh *Jay*.'

Tears filled her eyes and spilled down her cheeks as she relived those terrible moments. 'He thought I was Ivan. He wanted me to be and he really believed that Ivan would come to him.'

She started to sob, but instead of comforting her Jay ordered her sharply, 'Stop that, Hettie. Damnation, what the hell were you thinking of, going round there in the first place? A scandal like this could destroy everything I'm working for and us with it. Who else have you spoken to about this?'

'No one,' Hettie told him. 'Some of Eddie's friends came and they got a doctor.'

'And he saw you, this doctor?'

'I said that I was a friend of Eddie's.'

'Did you tell him anything about what had happened at the theatre?' Jay demanded sharply.

'No. But everyone knows what happened there, Jay. All the girls were talking about it.'

'They might have been then, but my guess is they'll keep their mouths closed now they know he's dead. It won't pay any of us to have a scandal on our hands. It's a pity the damned fool didn't wait until we'd left for New York,' Jay remarked with a brutal lack of compassion that jarred Hettie.

She had come to Jay expecting to find comfort and reassurance. Instead she had almost been raped by Harvey and now here was Jay himself talking about Eddie so callously that Hettie could hardly believe this was the same man who had whispered such tender words of love to her.

'Has he any family, do you know?' Jay asked Hettie curtly.

'Yes,' she confirmed. 'But he told me that they had disowned him.'

'They're not likely to want any awkward questions being asked, then. Thank the Lord for that. If I had my way, he and all his kind would be . . .'

'Jay, please don't,' Hettie begged him.

But Jay didn't seem to have heard her as he paced the floor and then announced, 'You'd better go back to your lodgings. No doubt the authorities will be informing me of his death and it wouldn't look good if they found you here. Especially since you were with him when he died.'

TWENTY-NINE

John unfolded the letter he had only just refolded and smoothed out the single sheet of paper, re-reading it although he had only just finished reading it, and indeed had read it a hundred and more times since he had first received it earlier in the week.

It was from Hettie, the writing shaky, and the words smudged from what he knew must have been her tears.

She had begun by offering him her sympathy on the death of 'your dear friend Lady Polly', but then she had gone on to tell him that she too had 'lost a very dear friend in the most unhappy of circumstances'. The words 'unhappy' and 'circumstances' were wobbly and very badly smudged, and John smoothed his thumb over them now, desperately trying to visualise Hettie writing them, although he had no idea of where her lodgings were or what they looked like and instead had to picture her seated at the small desk in his sister Ellie's sitting room.

'I cannot say any more, John, and have already said too much. I don't want to burden you when you have your own grief to carry. Eddie is to be buried tomorrow but we are none of us from the theatre to go to the funeral. His family have come and taken him and he is to be buried with his mother.

'I did say my prayers for him on Sunday when I went to church, though, and for Lady Polly as well.

'I hope and pray that you may find some comfort and peace in your own grief, John, and that God will keep you safe. Jay, Mr Dalhousie, says that I will feel better once we leave England for New York, where I am to spend six weeks singing the part of Princess Mimi as well as learning the songs for Jay's new musical. Jay says that I am to put what has happened behind me, but I confess that I am not finding it easy to do so.'

John folded the letter again. From the first moment he had read it he had had the strongest of urges to go to London to see Hettie. But for what purpose? Ellie had already mentioned in *her* letters to him that she suspected that a romance was developing between Hettie and the American she mentioned so frequently in her letters home. The same American who was taking Hettie away from them to New York. And besides . . . he had nothing he could offer Hettie. Or at least nothing she would want. They lived in a different worlds now.

*   *   *

Eddie's death had cast a sombre shadow over the whole theatre and everyone who worked in it, or so it seemed to Hettie. And the director, whose temper had always been short, was now savagely unmerciful with anyone who made any kind of mistake.

'Anyone would think that I was responsible for his death,' Jay had complained angrily to Hettie about the sullen silence that greeted him whenever he left his office to come down to the stage.

Hettie had not been able to make any response. Although people had sometimes mocked Eddie behind his back, they had nevertheless been fond of him. As Aggie had put it, 'He may have been one of them but he were one of us as well.' And they felt that Jay had not treated Eddie either kindly or fairly.

'But surely if anyone should be blamed it should be Ivan and not Jay?' Hettie had tried to defend Jay, but Aggie had shaken her head uncompromisingly.

'It were Jay as give 'im the sack,' she said.

Hettie had repeated this comment to Jay, without telling him from whom it had originated, her voice faltering as she saw the anger in his eyes.

'Goddammit,' he had cursed. 'What was I *supposed* to do?'

But as everyone said, in true theatre tradition, the show still had to go on, and Jay had elevated Eddie's assistant Bryn Davies to take his place. Bryn was a small, sturdy Welshman with twinkling eyes who claimed that he was the 'only Welshman on earth who could not sing'.

'Mary's in bed this morning,' Aggie announced as the girls clattered downstairs to the dingy back parlour where their landlady grudgingly provided them with their breakfast.

As soon as they hurried into the room, the grubby tweeny maid appeared and plonked a heavy tea urn down on the stained sideboard announcing, 'Toast's off this morning on account of cook forgettin' to send out for bread, but she said I wuz to say she's mekkin' porridge instead.'

Jenny and Jess both groaned, and pulled a face.

'Aggie, what's wrong with Mary?' Hettie asked worriedly as she poured herself a mug of tea.

Mary hadn't said another word to Hettie about her unwanted pregnancy or about her plans to have it terminated, but Hettie had already seen that Mary wasn't wearing her diamond ring and wondered if she'd already visited the doctor.

'Nothing much,' Aggie told her. 'She's just very bad with her monthlies. Kept me awake all night almost she did wot with 'er wailing and moaning.'

If Mary was having her monthlies then that must mean that everything was all right, Hettie decided with naive relief. 'I'm not going for my singing lesson until later on this morning, so I could pop up later and take her a cup of tea,' she told Aggie.

'Aye, you do that. I told her last night that she ought ter get herself down to the kitchen and mek herself up a hot water bottle. Works a treat on belly cramps, it does.'

Holding the cup of tea she had just persuaded 'cook' to let her make for Mary in one hand and the hot water bottle she had filled for her in the other, Hettie climbed the stairs carefully, not wanting to spill any of the tea.

The door to the room Mary shared with Aggie was already open, and the curtains were still pulled across the window, blocking out the summer light. Mary was lying in bed with her back to Hettie, but it was obvious from the way she was moaning that she was not asleep.

'Mary, I've brought you a cup of tea,' Hettie called out as she walked into the room. 'And I've made you up a hot water bottle. Aggie said that it would help your cramps.'

'Wot?'

Reluctantly Mary turned over and struggled to sit up. Her face was puffy and pale and Hettie could see how she was shivering as she pulled the thin bed covers round her body.

'Aggie said this morning that you were bad with your monthlies,' Hettie told her sympathetically as she sat down on Aggie's bed and put the cup of tea on the small table between the two beds before holding out the hot water bottle to Mary. 'I've got some aspirin if you want some?'

As Mary moved she winced and shuddered, and then told Hettie, 'Oh gawd, 'Ettie, it feels like I'm bloody well bleedin' to death. And if'n he knew he'd want me to an all. Tek my advice, Hettie, don't you ever believe it if'n some posh fella tells you 'e loves you, because he'll be lyin'.'

She reached out to pick up the mug of tea and then cried out sharply.

'Mary, what is it?' Hettie asked in alarm.

'It's me insides, 'Ettie. Gawd knows what that bloody doctor's done to them. 'E told me that I'd bleed a little bit, but 'e never said as how it were going to be like this. You should 'ave seen what he done to me.' Tears filled her eyes. ''Ad ter hold me down they did whilst he put this thing right up inside me, the pain were that bad. Eee, 'Ettie, I thought it were never going to be over, and then . . .' Her whole body heaved with her sobs.

'And it's today as His bleedin' Lordship gets married to 'er,' Mary added, still crying. 'Lady Arabella . . . Oh gawd, 'Ettie, but I 'ate him so much now. And I wish as I'd never met him never mind let him get me in the family way.' She started to shiver. 'I'm that cold 'Ettie.'

'I'll go and get you one of the blankets off my bed,' Hettie told her. 'Here's the hot water bottle. Aggie said you were to put it on your belly.' Without thinking Hettie stood up and lifted back the bedclothes intending to place the hot water bottle beneath them, but when she saw the bright red stain on the bed, and smelled the hot salty scent of Mary's blood, she couldn't move.

Some deep-seated instinct she hadn't previously known she possessed warned her that something was seriously wrong. It couldn't be right, surely, that Mary should be bleeding like this? Quickly she let the bedclothes drop back over Mary, who looked at her and said fiercely, 'Don't you go saying nothing about this to anyone, 'Ettie. Do you 'ear me? If Ma Jenkins knew I was like this she'd have me out of here and on the street.'

'Mary, shouldn't we get a doctor?'

Mary started to laugh bitterly. 'A doctor. No thanks. That were how I got in this state in the first place. It'll be all right, 'Ettie, I just need to get some sleep that's all.'

'How's Mary?' Hettie asked anxiously. She hadn't been able to concentrate on her singing lesson because she was so worried about her and now, instead of meeting Jay as she was supposed to be doing, she had come hurrying back to the boarding house.

But as she looked into Aggie's set face her stomach lurched and a sick premonition gripped her. 'Aggie . . .'

'She's in hospital,' Aggie told her grimly. 'And bloody lucky to be alive to go there an' all, by all accounts. If'n I hadn't come back on account of forgetting me purse this morning, she'd more than likely have bin a gonner. Found her in the lavvy,

I did, bleeding like she was . . .' Aggie's mouth compressed. 'She tried to tell me as how it were her monthlies, but I could see straight off what was up. Me Mam used to do a bit of midwifing, aye and a bit of the other stuff as well, and I knows what it means when a woman bleeds like that.

'I told Mary to tell the doctor as how she'd lost it natural, like, and to keep her mouth shut about anything else, no matter what they said to her.'

Hettie sat down on the stairs. 'She is going to be all right, isn't she?' she asked Aggie fearfully.

''Oo knows? From wot I could get out of her, the doctor as she went to see is supposed to be a good 'un, not like some of 'em who just butcher yer and leave yer to die. But she'd left it a bit late, like. She said as how everywhere were clean and how he'd told her to wash herself with salt and water. That were what she were trying to do when I found her. Silly cow didn't know as how she were supposed to let the bleedin' stop first. Not that she should have been bleedin' that much,' Aggie added darkly.

'If she dies it will be my fault,' Hettie said bleakly. 'I should have stayed with her this morning. I should have . . .'

Aggie's expression softened. 'There's no call for you to go blaming yerself, 'Ettie. Mary's no one but herself to blame for the mess she's in and she knows that 'erself. If she hadn't got too clever and above 'erself, this would never 'ave happened. We warned her as how no lord would ever marry the likes of her, but she wouldn't 'ave it. Daft she was for thinking he would. Stands to reason that, like any other man, he wants to marry with 'is own kind.'

Aggie looked at Hettie and said briskly, 'And let this be a lesson to you an' all, 'Ettie. Don't think cos we don't say nuffink about it that we don't know what's going on.'

THIRTY

'Hettie, what's *wrong* with you? You used to be such fun to be with' Jay objected irritably.

Obediently Hettie forced herself to smile, but the thought crossed her mind that, increasingly when she was with Jay, she was having to pretend she felt differently than she actually did in order to please and placate him.

'This time next week we shall be embarking at Southampton and on our way to New York.'

Hettie's smile was genuine now. She was as eager as Jay to leave London behind and start their new shared life together.

It seemed that every day more of the new clothes Jay had ordered for her were being delivered to his Ritz apartment, where the new trunks he had also bought for her were waiting ready to receive them.

Jay had planned a big farewell dinner the night before they left for Southampton, to which he had invited everyone involved with *Princess Geisha*, and, although she knew she should be looking forward to the dinner, Hettie was dreading it.

For one thing Eddie would not be there, and there would be other absent faces she would miss as well: Babs, who had been such a good friend to her but who had turned against her; and Mary, who, although she was now recovering from her illegal abortion, was still too weak to return to work and had instead gone to stay with a cousin who kept a guest house in Blackpool.

The same fate that had befallen Mary must not befall her, Hettie warned herself. But what if it did? What would she do? What *could* she do? Jay had said that he loved her, but he was a married man after all.

Somehow Jay's reaction to Eddie's death had planted a small seed of doubt inside Hettie's heart about him. Sometimes he could display a ruthlessness that shocked her. But he *had* rescued her from Harvey Meyerbrock, she reminded herself, and when they were out together he always treated her like a lady and was wonderfully protective, even if she had seen from the looks in other people's eyes that they recognised she was not due the respect they would have accorded a married woman.

In America it would be different, Hettie assured herself. After all, Jay had told her that it would be. Only yesterday she had made some purchases of her own for her forthcoming trip, whisper-fine silk camisoles and delicately pleated French knickers in palest peaches and creams, lavishly trimmed with Chantilly lace. Brassieres and silk stockings, a bed jacket in ecru trimmed with swansdown, and a breathtakingly beautiful satin nightgown with a matching peignoir.

Jay had told her that when they got to New York he would buy her sables for New York's cold winters, and then he had shocked and delighted her when he had whispered to her that he would lie her naked upon a sable robe and make love to her.

'You blush so delightfully, little Hettie,' he had whispered to her as he kissed her. 'For sure those blushes will light our whole cabin the first night we are together. And you need not fear that I will be unkind when I take your maidenhead, Hettie. Your only cries will be those of sweet pleasure.'

Even now, remembering his thick impassioned words, her blood sang hotly and wantonly through her veins and her breath came a little faster. But even when she was wanting Jay with such reckless and urgent excitement a small part of her hung back in anxious fear and shame, as she thought about how Ellie and Gideon would feel if they knew what she was doing. And what John would think.

John, who had sent her the kindest and most compassionate of letters in response to her own to him. So kind, in fact, that it brought tears to her eyes now just to think of it.

'I have some business to attend to,' she heard Jay telling her. 'But we can meet later for tea at

Fortnum & Mason's, Hettie. I haven't forgotten that there was a very pretty hat there that suited you particularly well,' he added indulgently.

Hettie shook her head and told him firmly, 'I have enough hats already, Jay.'

''Ettie, there's bin a telephone call for you and you are to ring back immediately,' Jenny announced importantly the moment Hettie walked into the dressing room.

'Yes,' Jess chimed in. 'It were from your dad and . . .'

Gideon? A huge, sharp-nailed fist seized her stomach in a cramping grip. Hettie could think of only one reason why Gideon would telephone her and leave such a message. Ellie was still a month off her due time and, although Ellie had written the happiest and most reassuring of letters to her, Hettie had been secretly worrying that something might go amiss with this baby as it had done with the poor little one Ellie had lost.

Now it seemed her dreadful fears might be confirmed.

'What did he say?' she demanded. 'Did he leave a message? Did he . . .'

''E said as how you was to ring home ugently,' Jenny repeated. But as Hettie whirled round and headed for the dressing room door, Jenny insisted, ''Ere 'Ettie, you can't do it now. We're about to go on for rehearsal.'

But Hettie wasn't listening. Jay wasn't in his

office which meant that it would be locked so she could not use the telephone in there, and she certainly wasn't going to ask Ivan if she could use the telephone in his office. But there was a public telephone box in Piccadilly Circus, and Hettie ran out of the theatre, dodging in and out of the press of people thronging the streets, her heart pounding with sick despair.

To her relief the telephone box was empty. She hurried inside and picked up the receiver, asking the telephonist who answered her to put her through to Preston's telephone exchange. Her hands were trembling so much that she dropped the pennies she needed to pay for the call. As she bent down to pick them up she heard the telephone whirring and clicking and then a voice with the familiar Preston accent asking her what number she required. Anxiously Hettie told her.

'I'm sorry but the line is busy,' the operator informed her.

'But I must speak to my father. My mother. I *have* to speak to them,' Hettie told her tearfully.

''Old on a minute, dearie, I'll see what I can do.'

There were more clicks and silences and then suddenly Hettie heard Gideon's tired and strained voice.

'Oh Da, it's me, Hettie. I've just got your message. What's happened? Mam . . . Is she . . .'

'Ellie's very weak, Hettie, and she's asking for you. The baby came early, a little girl. Ellie has been through a right bad time of it and she's afraid that the baby won't thrive on account of her being early and so small.'

Hettie could hear the exhaustion and the tears in Gideon's voice. 'She wants you to come home, Hettie. We need you. Ellie needs you, and so too does the new baby.'

'Hettie, are you still there?'

'I'm here, Da,' Hettie assured him shakily as she struggled to take in what she was hearing.

Ellie. Her mother was asking for her. Ellie and the new baby needed her.

But in five days' time she was due to leave England for New York, and the exciting new life waiting for her there. A life where she would be able to show the world how well she could sing. A life she had spent the last six months working towards. A life that included Jay and Jay's love. Tears filled her eyes and rolled down her face to splash unregarded on the black bakelite telephone.

'You don't mean that.' Jay's voice harsh with shock filled the tense space of the trunk-filled room.

Hettie hung her head, her own voice low and trembling. 'Yes, Jay, I do mean it,' she told him. 'I have to go home to be with my mother.'

'I'm not going you let you go,' Jay told her angrily. 'For Chrissake, Hettie, use some sense. Sure right now your mother isn't too well. But you wait and see, a couple of months from now she'll be fine. Hell, if it helps I'll even pay for a nurse to make sure that she is.' He gave a dismissive shrug. 'But what I am *not* prepared to do is to rearrange my plans so that you can go and hang around her sick bed taking care of some mewling brat.'

When Hettie recoiled he looked at her angrily.

'Aw come on, Hettie. Don't try to bamboozle me that this kid really matters to you. It isn't even a blood relation. And besides, you've got more important things to worry about than an ailing step-mother.'

Hettie stared at him, unable to comprehend how he could be so unfeeling. Couldn't he understand that nothing could be more important to her right now than being with Ellie? She had expected him to be irritated by her decision not to travel to New York when they had planned, but she had assumed that once he had calmed down he would reorganise their sailing dates, thus giving her time to be with Ellie when she most needed her.

But Jay wasn't merely irritated. He was furiously and implacably angry, more angry in fact than Hettie had ever seen him. Tears filled her eyes and, seeing them, Jay cursed beneath his breath and came over to her.

'Hettie, honey, I can see that you're upset, but listen to me and trust me. I promise you I know what I'm doing. Sure, if we weren't due to leave next week you could take some time off to be with your ma, but right now that just isn't possible. We've got more important things to do. New York is waiting for us. I've arranged meetings, made plans . . .

'This is your big chance, Hettie, our big chance, and if you turn it down there won't ever be another one. You once told me that singing was as important to you as breathing.'

How was it possible for words to hurt as much as though they were sharp stones, Hettie wondered miserably. 'But . . . but Ellie needs me. She's been asking for me. Surely you can understand how I feel?' she appealed to him.

'No, I'm not sure that I can,' Jay told her shockingly. 'You see, Hettie, I thought that you and I, we were two of a kind. I thought we shared the same outlook on life, the same kind of ambition, the same kind of hunger for success. But now seemingly you're telling me that you're prepared to throw all that away for the sake of a woman who isn't even your real mother.'

'But she needs me.' Hettie wept.

Jay shrugged coldly, 'Sometimes in life we have to make hard choices, Hettie, and let me tell you that if your career means as much to you as I thought it did you wouldn't even think twice. Sure you're upset and worried, but you can be just as upset and worried in New York.'

'I owe Ellie and Gideon so much . . .'

'And what about what you owe me?' Jay demanded savagely. 'Or haven't you thought about that? I've put one hell of a lot on the line for you, Hettie. I've called in favours and swung deals, taken risks to get you top billing in a show like no other that New York has ever seen. And that costs.'

'Is *that* why you want me to go to bed with you?' Hettie suddenly heard herself asking him in an unfamiliar, tight, cold little voice she hardly recognised as her own.

A small ugly silence followed her words and then Jay drawled unpleasantly, 'Well, I sure as hell wouldn't be laying out the money for gowns from Worth and Chanel for you if I wasn't looking to having the pleasure of taking them off you, Hettie. No investment is ever interest free, and I guess you could say that you are my little bonus payment to myself.'

Hettie stared at him in shock as the meaning of his words dripped into her heart like icy poison.

'So you didn't . . . You don't *really* love me at all,' she managed to say, white faced.

'Do you love me?' Jay shot back. 'Because it seems to me that if you did, it would be our future together you'd put first, Hettie.'

'Jay, all I'm asking is that you delay our sailing for a month,' Hettie pleaded with him. She couldn't believe she was actually hearing what he was saying to her. She didn't want to believe it, Hettie admitted to herself.

Although she had been apprehensive about telling Jay that she wanted to go home for a week or so to be with Ellie, she had never imagined that he would react like this. Yes, it was true that she had recognised he was not always a compassionate man, but she had believed that their own relationship was special and that he genuinely cared for her.

'And I'm telling you that either we sail next week together or I sail back to New York without you. There are plenty of singers who'll jump at the chance you're being given, Hettie,' he warned her.

Hettie lifted her head and looked at him. 'Yes, I'm sure they are,' she agreed quietly.

The harshness started to leave Jay's face. 'That's a sensible girl,' he approved, patting her arm. 'I knew you would see sense in the end. Why don't we go out and have another look at that pretty diamond necklace we were looking at the other day?' he added softly as he bent his head to kiss her.

Tears burned at the back of Hettie's throat and eyes. She longed to throw herself into his arms and to feel him cover her mouth with his own; to feel him sweep away all her doubts and fears and to take her and burn them away from her in the fierce heat of his possession. Her body ached and hungered for that so desperately that it hurt.

Closing her eyes Hettie clung to Jay and kissed him back as fiercely as he was kissing her. She could feel the heavy, uneven thud of his heart as though it were trying to beat within her own body as well as his. She could feel too the shallow excited counter pattern of her own heart racing.

'I knew you'd see sense,' Jay whispered exultantly against her mouth.

Hettie kept her eyes closed, wanting to steal just a few seconds more happiness. And then she opened them and stepped back from him, her voice brave but her heart bleak with pain as she told him, 'I won't be going to New York with you, Jay. I've already booked my train ticket and I'm leaving for home tomorrow morning . . .'

THIRTY-ONE

The train journey seemed to take for ever, and the fact that she had had to pack everything and bring it home with her meant that she had to wait for a hackney carriage instead of being able to run straight home. But now at last she was here.

The door opened and Gideon was standing there, looking thinner and worried but his arms still opened to hold her as Hettie hurled herself into them, sobbing, 'Da. Oh Da . . .'

'Hettie, lass. I'm right glad you've come back,' Gideon, told her gruffly as he held her tightly. 'Ellie has never stopped asking for you.'

'How is she?' Hettie asked urgently.

'She scared us all half to death,' Gideon replied without answering her question. 'She kept on saying that the cheese she'd eaten for supper must have given her indigestion and then, two o'clock in the morning it was, she woke me up and said that she thought the baby was coming.'

'Da, how *is* she?' Hettie interrupted him fiercely.

Gideon shook his head. 'She's very poorly, Hettie. Very poorly. I didn't want to tell you how bad she is over the telephone, lass, because I didn't want you to be worried. We've feared the worst. The doctor says it's a miracle that the baby was born at all. And the midwife thought the same as well, I could see it in her eyes. The baby was turned the wrong way you see, and couldn't be born, no matter how hard the midwife tried to turn her back.'

Gideon's voice thickened with tears. 'I thought I was going to lose them both, Hettie. We had to get the doctor out, and what with Ellie getting weaker with every breath, and the pain she was in, all day and then into the night again as well. But then seemingly like a miracle the midwife managed to get the baby turned so she could be born.'

'But Mam will be all right, won't she?' Hettie asked anxiously. 'They'll both be all right? Mam and the baby?'

Gideon hesitated and his eyes filled with fresh tears. 'I don't know, Hettie. The baby's that small and Ellie can't feed her, and now Ellie's got a fever, burning up with it, she is. Your uncle's sent a nurse to be with her, but he says there's nothing we can do now other than wait and pray. Eee, lass, I'm that glad you're here,' Gideon told her again emotionally.

'Connie's wanted to come over, but her youngest's gone down with scarlet fever and even though he's on the mend now he isn't well enough yet for Connie to be able to leave him.'

'Can I go up and see Mam?' Hettie asked him. Gideon nodded.

Pausing only to remove her hat and light summer coat, Hettie ran up the stairs to her parents' room, followed more slowly by Gideon.

As she opened the door the first thing she noticed was the familiar smell of Ellie's scent, light and delicate and sweetly fresh on the soft air filling the room through the open windows.

A nurse in a stiffly starched uniform was seated in the shadows watching over Ellie, but Hettie barely noticed her, hurrying instead to the bed itself where Ellie was lying propped up against the pillows, her eyes huge in her thin and worn face, her gaze fixed on Hettie as she ran to the bed and kneeled down beside it, putting her hand over Ellie's.

'Mama,' she whispered brokenly. 'Oh Mam.'

'Hettie, love, there's no need for you to tek on like this.'

Hettie could see what an effort it was for Ellie even to speak and how much doing so was draining her fragile strength, and the fear that had been growing in her ever since she had received Gideon's first telephone call exploded inside her like shrapnel tearing into her flesh. Her eyes stung with tears and her body shook. She wanted to cling to Ellie like a child and beg her not to be ill. She felt desperately afraid, and filled with panic.

'Hettie . . . The baby . . . My little Hannah. I want you to look after her for me, and no one else. Promise me that, will you . . .'

The thin words, spaced out between painful breaths, tore at Hettie's heart. Unable to speak she bit down hard on her bottom lip and nodded her head.

'You are a good girl, Hettie.' Ellie smiled. 'A good daughter.'

Hettie could see the rapid jump of her pulse in the thin pale flesh of her throat.

The nurse had got to her feet warningly. 'That's enough for now, if you don't mind, miss,' she told Hettie firmly, coming over to the bed.

As Ellie's eyes closed Hettie begged the nurse as she had already begged Gideon, 'She will get better, won't she?'

'That's for God to know, miss, and for us to pray for,' the nurse told her quietly as she straightened Ellie's bedclothes.

Gideon was waiting for Hettie outside on the landing.

'Mam has asked me to look after the baby,' she told him emotionally. 'Where is she? Where is Hannah?'

'Upstairs in the nursery,' Gideon answered her tiredly. 'As I say, Ellie couldn't feed her on account of the baby being early and Ellie herself being so weak. So we've been having to give her formula milk, but she cries that much whenever she's near Ellie that the nurse has said she should be kept in the nursery so that Ellie can get some rest. I've got a nurse for her, but what with worrying about Ellie . . .'

'Can I go up and see her?' Hettie asked.

Gideon nodded his head.

To Hettie's surprise the nursery looked much as it had always done, with no special decoration having been done for the new baby.

'Ellie wanted to wait until the baby was born before she had it decorated,' Gideon explained as though he had guessed what Hettie was thinking. 'She said she was afraid it would be bad luck.'

A stern-looking nanny was sitting beside the fire whilst the baby's crib stood under the half open window, the curtains and crib drapes flapping in the cool evening breeze.

'Babies need fresh air.' The nanny sniffed sharply when Hettie shivered as she hurried over to the crib.

Immediately the nanny spoke, the baby started to cry, a thin, sharp, high-pitched sound that tore at Hettie's heart so fiercely that she had reached into the crib and lifted out the tightly swaddled little body before she could stop herself.

The baby was tiny and thin, its limbs too brittle and delicate beneath the tightly wrapped swaddling cloths that held her arms to her body. A small cap covered her head, and the tiny red face was screwed up tightly as wail after wail filled the nursery.

'I don't approve of babies being picked up every

time they cry,' the nanny commented sharply, getting up and walking over to Hettie, plainly intending to take the baby from her.

'Perhaps she's crying because she's hungry,' Hettie suggested uncertainly.

'If she's hungry it's her own fault. She refused her bottle at dinner time and babies, like everyone else, have to learn that if they don't eat when they should then they have to go hungry until the next meal time.'

'She's very wet,' Hettie worried.

'I'll thank you to give her to me please, miss. It isn't time for a change yet. It helps them to understand what's what if they aren't changed every time they wet themselves.'

The nanny was having to raise her voice to make herself heard above the baby's anguished screams. On the point of handing her over to her, Hettie suddenly hesitated. Ellie had asked *her* to look after the baby. But she didn't know anything about babies . . .

'If you please, miss,' the nanny was insisting impatiently, her mouth thinning as she glared at the baby. 'You've got a real temper on you, haven't you, missie. Well, we'll soon teach you to curb that. Babies as wot screams in temper has to learn to mind their manners. Don't you worry, Mr Walker,' she added, her face softening as she looked almost maternally at Gideon. 'I won't let this little madam cause you any trouble. And there's no need for you to worry yourself keep coming up these stairs neither. I'm sure you've got enough on your plate what with your poor wife at death's door, and folks as wot should know better descending on you and making a nuisance of themselves.'

Warning bells started to ring inside Hettie's head. The nanny seemed to be more interested in 'mothering' Gideon than she was in mothering the poor little baby who was still screaming in Hettie's arms. And as for her comment about Ellie being close to death's door . . . Hettie hadn't missed the anguished look in Gideon's eyes as he listened to her. Despite her bossy manner the nanny was probably not all that much older than she was herself, Hettie decided as she studied her thin mouth and too pale, watery blue eyes.

She took a deep breath. 'I'm sure we're very grateful for everything you've done for the baby, but I'm here to look after her now. My father will pay you for the full month, of course, as is customary.'

And with that Hettie swept past her and sat herself down in the chair she had vacated, cradling the baby against her shoulder as she whispered softly to her whilst determinedly ignoring both the furiously outraged look on the face of the nurse and the appalling stench emanating from the baby's wrappings.

'Hettie,' Gideon protested worriedly.

'It's all right, Da,' Hettie assured him with a confidence she was far from feeling. 'Mam wants *me* to look after little Hannah.'

'You! You don't know the first thing about looking after a baby,' the nanny snorted, tossing her head.

'I know enough not to leave her lying hungry and cold in dirty wet things,' Hettie retorted spiritedly before appealing directly to Gideon, saying fiercely, 'Da, I can do it, I know I can, and it's what Mam wants . . .'

'Oh, don't you bother about me, Mr Walker.' The nanny sniffed. 'I wouldn't stay here now – not if'n you was to pay me a hundred pounds. I feels that sorry for you, I really do,' she added spitefully as she glared at Hettie. 'Aye, and sorry for the baby as well. Like as not *she'll* be the death of it . . .'

Hettie watched, forcing herself to remain outwardly impassive, whilst the other woman gathered together her belongings and pushed them into a carpet bag. It was the sight of that carpet bag – worn and shabby – that almost changed Hettie's mind. The woman wasn't much older than she was herself, after all, and no doubt she needed the work.

The work, Hettie acknowledged, hardening her heart. But not Gideon. And it was obvious to Hettie that that was what the other woman was after. A well-to-do widower with a small baby to bring up and his wife only recently dead. Who should he turn to but the nurse who was already caring for his child?

Well, Ellie wasn't going to die and the baby

didn't need a nanny, because she had family to look after her. And she *would* look after her, Hettie decided fiercely, telling the scowling nanny, 'I'll ring for someone to take your bags down for you. Da, why don't you take the nanny downstairs and pay her what's owing to her?'

She had never imagined she would ever see Gideon looking like this, Hettie acknowledged. Her tall, handsome adopted father looked stooped and dazed, older and weaker. A broken man.

The nursery door opened and Tom Wood, the ex-soldier who Gideon had taken on out of charity to help out around the house, came in.

'Nanny is leaving, Tom,' Hettie told him. 'Oh, and could you bring some kindling up for the nursery fire when you've got time, and tell Mrs Jennings that I'll be coming down to the kitchen to have a word with her about little Hannah's milk and formula.'

Gideon, Tom and the nanny had barely gone, their feet still clattering on the stairs, when unexpectedly the baby opened her eyes and looked right into Hettie's own – or at least so it seemed to Hettie.

A fierce pang that seemed to physically wrench at her own womb gripped Hettie as she looked back into the baby's dark blue eyes, oblivious to anyone and anything else, and fell immediately in love.

Falling in love was one thing but dealing with the practicalities of caring for a very new and four-week early baby, plus gently picking up the reigns of a household shocked into despair by what had happened, was quite another, Hettie recognised. Her heart started to thump unevenly at the thought of what she was taking on.

But Mam had faith in her to do it, she reminded herself stoutly, and it wasn't going to be for very long after all. Connie, with her experience of running her own nursery come orphanage – where Hettie herself had helped out during her school holidays – would surely be able to help Gideon to find a more suitable nurse for the baby than the one Hettie had just so determinedly turned out?

And Ellie and Gideon's housekeeper, Mrs Jennings, normally a well-organised, phlegmatic woman, would surely be able to run the household until Ellie herself was well enough to do so once again. Once she too had recovered from the distress.

She heard slow, tired footsteps on the stairs. The door opened and Gideon came in, going straight to one of the nursery's comfortable chairs and slumping into it. His eyes were red rimmed with lack of sleep and emotion.

'Has she gone?' Hettie asked him.

'Aye, lass, but she weren't very pleased about it.' He paused and rubbed his eyes tiredly. 'Hettie, love, I know you meant it for the best, but that nanny . . .'

'Mam wouldn't have wanted her taking care of little Hannah, Da,' Hettie told him fiercely, with all the conviction she truly felt in her voice. 'And you do not need to worry about anything, Da,' she told him more gently. 'I can manage. I'm a woman now, Da, and besides I promised Mam,' she repeated, trying to sound more confident than she was actually feeling. 'I'm going to change Hannah now, and then I'm going to go downstairs and have a word with cook. It might be a good idea with so many people coming and going if she boiled up a pan of nourishing soup. Oh, and some chicken soup for Mam as well. Remember how she always said when we were little as how it was good for us . . .'

'Eh, Hettie, lass. I'm that glad to have you here.' Gideon got to his feet and wiped the emotional tears from his eyes.

Half an hour later, as she stripped the swaddling bands off the baby, Hettie wrinkled her nose at the smell, immediately dropping the soiled things into the bucket of boiling hot water she had asked cook to send to the nursery via the tweeny maid.

In order to wash the baby she had found an old-fashioned ewer and basin set and, carefully holding Hannah she held her in the basin and gently started to wash her, talking soothingly to her when the unfamiliar feeling of the water on her skin made the baby cry.

'There you are,' she told her tenderly when she had finished. 'All nice and clean. Now I'm going to dry you and put some nice clean things on you.'

Hettie had already found clean swaddling bands and nightgowns for Hannah. But she was going to need more clothes, she decided, as she patted her dry. Then on some impulse she couldn't name she leaned forward and kissed her little hands.

She must have learned more at Connie's nursery during her enforced school holiday work there than she had realised, Hettie acknowledged when she had finished securing a fresh band over the baby's navel, and then fastened her nappy.

Now instead of smelling so unappealing, Hannah smelled sweetly of talcum powder and soap. Nanny might have chosen to wrap her from neck to toes in constraining swaddling bands in the old-fashioned way, but at Connie's nursery even the smallest babies were allowed to have their arms and legs free to wave about.

'Cook's heated up the bottles like you asked for miss. One just wiv milk and one wiv formula. And I've brought them up for you like you wanted.'

'Oh thank you, Molly,' Hettie smiled at the tweeny.

'Could you put them there on the table next to that chair for me, please?'

As she did so the maid added, 'And cook said to tell you that she's mekkin' some of your favourite biscuits and that there'll be a nice chop for you when you're ready. Oh, and she's told Tom he's to go out first thing in the morning and get some chickens from the poultry shop in Friargate.'

'Please thank Mrs Jennings for me when you

go back to the kitchen, Molly, and tell her that I said I shall be looking to her to help me keep house as Mam would want. Whilst I'm here standing in for her,' Hettie added diplomatically.

Once Molly had gone Hettie settled herself in the comfortable rocking chair beside the fire, and, holding Hannah in the crook of her arm reached for the bottle of warm milk.

'I don't suppose either of us are going to be very good at this, Hannah,' she told her softly as she sprinkled a few drops of the warm milk on her own arm to test its temperature, as she had seen the nurses do at Connie's, and then offered Hannah the rubber teat.

The baby gave a thin wail, her small face screwing up. Hettie's heart thudded with anxiety. What if the nurse had been right and she out of ignorance did cause Ellie's new baby to die?

And Hannah would die if she didn't have her bottle. Hettie had seen how very thin she was when she had bathed her.

'Hannah you must have your milk, sweetheart,' she told her as she tried again, this time squeezing a few drops of milk from the teat into Hannah' mouth when she opened it to cry.

'Mmm, isn't that good?' Hettie whispered. 'Want some more?'

It took her ten minutes of patient coaxing to get Hannah to suck properly on the teat, by which time Hettie herself was stiff with anxious tension.

She had read the instructions on the side of the

tin of formula very carefully before mixing it, and, according to what she had read, Hannah was to drink the whole bottle. But already her eyes were closing and she was drifting off to sleep, and the bottle was only just over two thirds empty.

Suddenly the teat sliped out of Hannah' mouth and her whole body stiffened as she screamed in pain, her face bright red. Terrified, Hettie stared at her. What had she done?

'That sounds like wind to me,' she heard Gideon's voice saying gently from the doorway.

Wind . . . Of course!

'Give her to me. I'all do it for you. Ellie always has said that I was better at winding babies than she is.'

'How is Mam?' Hettie asked him as she handed Hannah to him. 'Sleeping, thank the Lord,' Gideon answered as he deftly laid the small baby against his shoulder and patted her back, both of them laughing when she suddenly produced a loud burp.

'Hettie, I can't tell you how grateful I am to you, or how proud of you I am for what you're doing,' Gideon told her emotionally as she took the baby back from him.

'Mam asked me to do it,' Hettie repeated. 'And . . . and I want to. After all,' she told him, looking up at him with tears in her own eyes. 'It's no more than what she did for me.'

Inwardly Hettie contrasted her present life here at home to the life she had been living in London. In London she had had admiring crowds clapping her singing every night; singing lessons, the offer of her own little house, pretty clothes and jewellery, and of course Jay and all that he wanted to give her. Fame of the kind her parents could never really understand.

Here, she suspected she would barely have time to leave the nursery, and she certainly would not be wearing exensive fashionable clothes; a sturdy cotton frock with a pinny over it would be more like it. Her hands would be in and out of hot water all day long, and like as not, when she wasn't looking after Hannah she would be worrying about Ellie.

And yet, ridiculously, being here, holding Hannah, in her arms, witnessing Gideon's joy and relief because she was there, was filling her with a sense of wonderfully happy purposefulness and satisfaction.

As Gideon's arms enfolded her, Hettie leaned her head on her adopted father's chest and gave way to her tears, the baby held safely between them.

And that was how John saw her when he pushed open the nursery door, having been told by Tom that that was where he would find Gideon.

'John!' Gideon exclaimed with pleasure, releasing Hettie.

She stepped back from him, returning to the rocking chair, so that she could coax Hannah to finish her bottle.

'I came as soon as I could. How is Ellie? How is the baby?'

'Ellie is very weak,' Hettie heard Gideon telling him soberly. 'But little Hannah seems to be thriving now that she has Hettie here to take care of her.'

Gideon's praise was as premature as Hannah herself had been, Hettie acknowledged, and she could see from the look on John's face that he probably thought so as well.

But his arrival reminded her of her newly assumed duties and so she turned to Gideon and said calmly, 'I'd better go down and tell Mrs Jennings that there will be one more for dinner, and then I'll make sure that a bed's made up for John. Mrs Jennings is going to make some chicken soup for Mam tomorrow. It will help to nourish her.'

John couldn't stop looking at Hettie. He had thought he had stored mental images of every mood he had ever seen her exhibit, but he admitted they did not include an image of her like this, a serene madonna determined to protect the child she was holding and those in her care.

Where and when had the girl he remembered become the woman he saw now?

A yearning ache seized his heart, and closed his throat so that he could not even trust himself to speak.

Hettie, misunderstanding his silence, thought it came from his dislike of the fact that she should be there.

*　　*　　*

Hettie tiptoed into the nursery, gently pushing open the door. It was hard to believe she had been here for three days already, they had passed so quickly. Hannah was still asleep. Hettie smiled tiredly at the sleeping baby. At least she was thriving, unlike Ellie who had been so poorly the previous evening that the nurse had urged Gideon to send for the doctor.

Childbed fever was notoriously hard to treat, Dr Barnes had told them sombrely, and there was nothing they could do but wait.

Tiredly Hettie lifted her hand and rubbed her eyes, then frowned as she felt the crackle of paper in her apron pocket. Reaching into the pocket she removed the letter. It had arrived this morning and she had recognised Jay's handwriting the minute Gideon handed it to her.

She waited until she was alone in the nursery before opening and reading it. He was, Jay had written, prepared to give her one more chance. She was to meet him in Southampton and he had enclosed a rail ticket for her.

'Think of what you are throwing away, Hettie,' he had written. 'Think of what you are denying us both, and for what?'

Hannah gave a sleepy murmur. She was not due to have a feed for another two hours, and Hettie was hoping that she would continue to sleep so that she could go and sit with Ellie and thus relieve the nurse.

She heard someone opening the bedroom door

and immediately swung round, a warning finger to her lips, expecting to see Gideon but instead it was John who stood there.

'I have come to say goodbye. I am returning to Oxfordshire this morning,' he told her distantly.

Hettie nodded, unaware that she had dropped her letter until John bent down and picked it up.

'It can't be long before you leave for New York,' he commented.

Hettie looked away from him. 'I was, but I'm not going now. I've changed my mind.'

John looked at her. 'Hettie . . .'

'I can't go,' she told him passionately. 'I can't leave Mam and the baby. Not when they need me . . . You must see that?'

'*Hettie . . .*'

She had no time to be either shocked or surprised – one minute John was standing in front of her the next he was holding her fiercely in his arms, and he was kissing her.

John was kissing her.

Hettie closed her eyes and clung tightly to him, returning his kiss with all the passion locked in her heart.

'I'm sorry, Hettie, I shouldn't have done that.'

Hettie forced herself to smile but inwardly she felt more like crying. These last few days had shown her so clearly just how very deep her true feelings for John actually were. 'That is twice now that you have apologised to me for kissing me, John,' she reminded him unevenly. 'But truly there is no need. After all, it is not as though . . .'

'Not as though what, Hettie?' John asked her with a frown.

Hettie sighed and moved away from him. 'I just wish that I did not always make you so cross.'

'You make me cross?' John repeated, looking bewildered. 'Hettie, I could never be cross with you.'

Hettie couldn't help but laugh. 'John, that is such a fib,' she teased him. 'Remember how cross with me you were when I first went to Liverpool to sing at the Adelphi?'

'Aye, I was a right fool then,' John acknowledged gruffly.

'You disapproved of my singing and you disapproved of my new dress and I was so upset about that, John, because I'd been looking forward to showing off my dress to you.'

'You looked a fair treat in it, Hettie, but I were that jealous knowing that other men 'ud be seeing you in it that I couldn't stop meself from saying what I did. I didn't mean to hurt you, lass, and I'm right sorry that I did.'

I was hurt, Hettie admitted softly to herself. 'You were my best friend, John, my very best friend,' she emphasised. 'I loved you so much.'

'I loved you an' all, Hettie,' John admitted. 'But it were not as a friend that I loved you,' he told her meaningfully.

The colour came and went in Hettie's face, but she managed a small emotional smile. She had given up hope that she would ever be able to talk to John like this – as openly and as honestly as she had done as a child. And yet here they were doing just that, and all because of a kiss.

'I felt so grown up in that dress and I desperately wanted you to tell me that I looked grown up,' she admitted. 'I felt that hurt and upset when you didn't, but John what hurt me even more was when you didn't come to hear me sing.'

Even now the memory of those feelings filled her eyes with tears.

'Oh, Hettie,' John groaned, reaching for her hand and giving it an apologetic squeeze before releasing it again.

'You didn't even write to me to say that you were sorry or to explain why you weren't there, not even though I had written to you. And all Mam and Da would say when I got upset was that you must have been too busy.'

Now the tears were rolling slowly down her face as she relived her pain.

'Hettie,' John repeated pleadingly in the kind of deep gruff voice she had heard leading male actors use to convey intense emotion, but somehow that particular note in John's voice affected her in a way that theirs had not. 'I didn't mean to hurt you,' he told her thickly. 'In fact,' Hettie watched as he took a deep breath. 'Hettie let's go for a walk. I . . . I need to talk to you and . . .'

There was so much emotion and urgency in his voice that Hettie felt her heart beat extra fast in response to it.

She looked hesitantly towards the crib where Hannah was fast asleep and, as though John had sensed her reluctance to leave the baby, he pressed fiercely, 'Hannah will not even know you have been gone, I promise. We could just walk through the park and then down to the river, just for half an hour, Hettie. Please?'

'I was going to go and sit with Mam.'

'Gideon will do that. Unless, of course, I am pressing you to do something you do not want to do, Hettie, and if that is the case then . . .'

'No,' she assured him quickly. 'No. I would like to go with you for a walk, John.'

Try as she might she could not stop a delicate pink blush from warming her face, Everyone in Preston knew that when a lad asked you to walk in the park with him of an evening it was as good as saying he wanted to walk with you permanently.

'I'll just have to warn Mrs Jennings that I'm going out and ask her to keep an eye on Hannah. I wouldn't want her to wake up on her own,' she warned John, but she could see from the way he was smiling at her that he knew he had won her over.

The summer evening was light and warm, but Hettie still enjoyed the way John fussed over her, asking if she would need a coat in case she might feel cold. The sun had dropped low enough in the sky to throw long golden shadows across the square as they walked side by side towards the park as they had done so many times in years gone by. Then, though, she would probably have hopped or skipped at John's side, or even tucked her arm through his, Hettie recognised as they entered the park.

As though he had actually been thinking the same thoughts, John announced, 'You had best take my arm now, Hettie, for it is a steep walk from here down to the river and I would not want you to fall.'

'I often think of our park here in Preston when I am in Hyde Park in London,' Hettie told him as she slipped her arm through his. 'And I have to say that I prefer our own dear Aveham Park.'

'Aye, it's a fine park indeed,' John agreed before saying abruptly, 'Hettie, there was a reason why I did not – could not – attend your first singing performance at the Adelphi Hotel. But I asked Ellie and Gideon not to speak of it to you.'

They were walking downhill and Hettie was tempted to stop and demand to know what he meant, but she sensed that John felt more comfortable talking to her as they walked and so she waited as patiently as she could.

'I didn't want you to be upset, you see, Hettie, and that was why – well, to tell the truth I was in such a state myself at the time that . . .'

'What happened? What was it?' Hettie asked him.

'A most dreadful thing, Hettie,' John answered her sombrely. 'A terrible, terrible accident. One of my pupils at the flying school ignored my instructions and took up a flying machine even though he was not experienced enough to do so. He had three other young men with him . . . I was on my way to . . . to come to Liverpool when I saw . . .'

Sensing his distress as he brushed his free hand across his eyes Hettie automatically squeezed his arm comfortingly but kept silent.

'The flying machine crashed into the buildings at the airfield. Jim was inside them.'

'Jim?' Hettie's voice betrayed her shocked distress.

'They were all killed, all of them, the four young men and Jim.'

'Oh John.'

'I didn't want you to know because I didn't want to cast a shadow over your excitement or your memory of something I knew was so special to you, Hettie. I'm sorry if I did the wrong thing, and caused you pain.'

'Oh John,' Hettie repeated even more emotionally. 'How generous of you to want to spare me. I was such a silly, selfish child then.'

'You have never been selfish, Hettie.'

'Yes I have,' she corrected him ruefully. 'But I hope I have learned to become wiser now, John. Poor you, I know how close you were to Jim. And poor Jim and those boys, too.'

They had reached the river and although they were now on level ground John still kept her arm tucked through his, and Hettie didn't make any move to remove it.

It felt so right to be here with John like this. So very, very right, as though it and he were something she had been travelling towards all her life, she recognised emotionally.

'There is so much I want to tell you, Hettie.'

'And I you, John.'

'Can you forgive me?'

'For kissing me?' She couldn't resist teasing him.

There was a very purposeful male glint in his eyes when he looked back at her.

'If you do,' he warned her, 'then I may very well be tempted to do so again.'

'Well, in that case I may very well be tempted to forgive you,' Hettie said softly.

THIRTY-TWO

'Here you are, Mam.'

Deftly and expertly Hettie transferred three-month-old Hannah from her own arms and into Ellie's, pausing to smooth down the baby's thick dark curls and smile at her before moving to plump up Ellie's pillows.

'Oh Hettie, what would we do without you?' Elle smiled appreciatively as she cradled Hannah in the crook of her arm and reached out to squeeze Hettie's hand lovingly. 'Oh look.' She laughed. 'See how Hannah looks to *you*.'

'She will start to look to you now that you are well enough to take care of her, Mam,' Hettie said gently.

They had come so close to losing Ellie that even now Hettie hardly dared to so much as think about those first two weeks after her return home. She had been so afraid that Ellie might slip away from them and equally determined to stop her that she had taken to spending most of her time sitting in a chair in Ellie and Gideon's room, watching her step-mother and willing her not to die, Hannah in her crib beside her so that she could tend to the new baby as well as watch over Ellie.

Gideon, and John too during his increasingly frequent visits home, had gently chided Hettie and urged her to remember how much the whole household was depending on her and how important it was that she keep up her own strength. But Hettie had ignored them.

Some deep instinct she could feel but not explain had driven her to keep up her bedside vigil, and to keep telling Ellie how much they all needed her.

The night Ellie's fever had been at its height, and Dr Barnes had been and told them gravely that there was nothing more he could do, Hettie had laid Hannah in Ellie's unrecognisng arms and whispered fiercely to her to remember that she had a baby who needed her.

'You didn't leave me, Mam, and you mustn't leave this little one either. She needs you and I need you too. We all need you . . .'

In the morning, when Ellie's fever had broken, Dr Barnes had declared that it was a miracle.

And now, although she was still a little weak, Ellie was out of danger and well on the way to full recovery.

'Hannah doesn't look like either of the boys,' Hettie commented, 'and she doesn't really look like you or Gideon either.'

Ellie smiled tenderly as she stroked her new daughter's curls.

'She has my father's hair, Hettie, and his eyes, and in that way looks very much as John did as a baby. But this pretty olive tinted skin is, I think, a gift from Gideon's father, Richard. I am so blessed in having two very beautiful daughters. But Hannah is most blessed of all in having such a loving sister.'

Hettie felt emotional tears pricking at her eyes. 'I had been so afraid that I would be jealous of her because she was yours and I was not, but Mam the moment I looked at her, I felt . . . I *knew* here inside, I just loved her so much.'

'That was exactly how I felt with you, Hettie,' Ellie told her. 'This is such a very special gift that we have, Hettie, this love between us, mother to daughter and sister to sister. Hannah would have died without you to love and cherish her, and so would I . . .'

'Just as I would have died without you to love and cherish me,' Hettie reminded Ellie.

'You are the daughter of my heart, Hettie. I can't bear to think of you leaving us and going back to London.'

Hettie pulled her hand free of Ellie's and stood up. 'I have decided not to return to London but to stay here in Preston.'

Joy flooded Ellie's expression quickly followed by concern.

'But Hettie, love, your singing? I know how

much that means to you now, even if I did not do so before.'

'Things change, Mam. Or maybe it is me who has changed. My singing, the stage, those things that once seemed so exciting and important . . .' Hettie shook her head whilst images formed inside it. Babs turning her back on the stage because she wanted to be with Stan. Mary, white faced with despair when she told Hettie what had befallen her. Eddie's hand cold in her own.

'I can sing anywhere, Mam, but I cannot be with my family anywhere . . .'

Ellie looked at her. 'Hettie, I don't mean to pry, or cause you pain, but you wrote so often of a certain someone that I had felt . . .'

'I did think I had fallen in love with Jay, Mam,' Hettie agreed quietly. 'But he already had a wife.' She sighed and then smiled. 'He wanted to make me a big star and for a while I thought that that was what I wanted too. But even if he had not been married, even if he had wanted to marry me.' She paused and shook her head before continuing earnestly, 'He couldn't understand why I had to come home to be with you.'

Hettie and Ellie looked at one another over Hannah's head. Two women sharing knowledge and a love that did not need words or explanations.

'I . . . I have been thinking about what I shall do,' Hettie said quietly. 'I have been speaking with Miss Brown and since she does not want to teach

528

any more she has suggested I might want to take over her pupils.'

'And you would want to do that?'

'I have learned so much that I could teach them, Mam,' Hettie replied eagerly. 'It isn't just the singing they need to learn, there's the dancing as well, and so much more if they wish to become professionals. And there is opera too. I can't teach it myself, but I could find a teacher who could.'

Ellie shook her head and laughed fondly. 'Such ambitious plans, Hettie,' she teased her. 'You are so much Gideon's daughter.'

Hettie laughed too. 'I *have* told Da what I would like to do,' she admitted, 'and he says he will look out for some premises for me.'

'Oh Hettie . . . Hettie. This is just such wonderful news. First John is to come back to Preston and now you are to stay here as well.'

Hettie leaned forward to tickle Hannah's chin, not wanting Ellie to see her betraying blush.

It wasn't because of John that she had conceived her plan for starting up a school for singers and dancers, she assured herself, even if her heart had given a fierce thrilling thud of excitement the day John had told her that he had decided to come home.

Their shared concern over Ellie's illness had brought a closeness between them that Hettie could never have imagined them sharing six months ago. Those long bleak hours of watching and waiting that John had insisted on sharing with her whenever he had been home had led to them exchanging the kind of confidence Hettie would once have thought impossible.

They were equals now, and John had recognised that fact. They had talked about so much that once might have been impossible, and with an openness that had delighted Hettie.

John had told her of his feelings at his friend's death, and Hettie had wept as she talked of Eddie and his death.

'I know many would condemn him for his . . . his way of life, but his love was as true as any other person's, John, and I cannot help but ask myself if it is wrong that he should not have the right to have those feelings honoured. You do not agree with me, I can tell,' she had whispered to him when he had looked at her in silence.

He had reached for her hand then and said simply, 'I have no right to sit in judgement of any other human being, Hettie. If I was silent it was simply because I felt humbled by your own compassion and wisdom.'

They had gone on to talk of Mary, and of Lady Polly.

'Did you love her?' Hettie had forced herself to ask.

'As a friend, yes. I felt for her, Hettie. She had such passion and so much to give. Do you love Jay Dalhousie?' he had asked her in turn.

'I thought I did. I wanted to. He made everything seem to be possible and so exciting, but there was nothing there underneath that excitement,' she had told John sadly. 'Jay couldn't understand why I had to come home. And I could never love a man who did not understand that.'

'You have grown so much in such a short time, Hettie,' John had told her, 'and it seems to me that in doing so you have fulfilled my worst fears.'

'What do you mean?' Hettie had asked him uncertainly.

'As a young man I waited impatiently for you to grow up, Hettie, so that I could tell you of my love for you. But once you did begin to grow up I became fearful that you would grow beyond me. That was why I didn't want you to sing. And now you *have* grown beyond me . . .'

'No, you must not say that,' Hettie had told him emotionally. 'I have always loved you, John. I have always loved you,' she had repeated, her eyes widening as she realised the truth of her own words.

And now, like her, John was choosing to make his life in Preston. *She* had known that before anyone else.

John exhaled contentedly as Tom let him in. Gideon and Ellie's house had always been a second home to him. Six months ago he would have rejected the very idea of Hettie being able to take over the running of this house from Ellie so expertly that everything was just as his sister would have wanted. But she had done so, and with a

531

mature serenity that had seemed like an oasis of heavenly calm to him after the intensity and trauma of Polly's death and Ellie's illness.

The hallway smelled of beeswax polish and fresh flowers and sunshine.

Whilst Ellie gave Hannah her bottle, the baby fixed her gaze unwaveringly on Hettie.

But Hannah was not her child, no matter how much she loved the baby, Hettie reminded herself. Determinedly she stood up.

'I'd better go down to the kitchen. Mrs Jennings wants to see me about something.'

As she opened the door she heard Hannah crying for her and her small cry wrenched at Hettie's whole body.

But Hannah was Ellie's and now that Ellie was so much better it was time for Hannah to be reunited with her true mother.

Even so, Hettie had to blink the tears from her eyes as she hurried down the stairs, so intent on her own thoughts that she didn't see John until she had almost reached the hallway.

When she did, she had to stop and place her hand over her heart because it was beating so fast.

'John, we were just talking about you . . .'

'Good things, I hope?' He paused and then began urgently, 'Hettie, there is something I want . . .'

The front door suddenly opened and Ellie and Gideon's two sons, along with John and Ellie's younger brother Philip, burst into the hall.

'Hettie, they're putting notices up about the Bank Holiday fair. We're going to shoot at the firing range, and win some prizes. Hettie, will you come with us? Hettie, can we . . .'

'Goodness, what a noise.' Hettie laughed. 'And as for the fair and the firing range, you will have to ask your father. He is out at the moment.'

'Then we will go up and ask Mam.'

'If you go down to the kitchen now I dare say you might be able to persuade Mrs Jennings to give you a piece of the fresh gingerbread she has just made, and then you can ask your father about the fair when he comes back.'

'Clever,' John remarked once they had gone.

Hettie laughed. 'I love them so, but Mam still needs to rest.'

John reached out and took hold of her hands. 'Hettie, this is probably neither the time nor the place but I cannot wait to ask you any longer. Dearest girl, do you think if I am very patient you could one day come to return the love I have for you?'

'Oh John, I told you, I love you already,' she said softly, adding simply, 'In fact, I do truly believe I have always loved you, only I was too silly to know it.' Hettie paused and looked up at him. 'I cannot regret what I have done, though, or what I have learned.'

'Nor would I want you to,' John told her. 'Life is changing, Hettie. Our lives are so very different from the lives of our parents. And you and I

. . . We have known and seen things beyond the experience of even those closest to us. We have left the world of our childhood and gone out into a newer, different world. But now we have come back with all that we have learned.

'I love you, Hettie,' he told her thickly.

'And I you, John.'

'And you will be my wife?'

'I will.'

She was as eager to be in his arms as he was to have her there, and it was only the sound of Richard's voice as he exclaimed, 'Philip, John and Hettie are kissing!' that finally drew them apart.